ANDREA DARIF

A KISS OF SPICE

POCKET BOOKS

New York   London   Toronto   Sydney

An *Original* Publication of POCKET BOOKS

POCKET BOOKS, a division of Simon & Schuster, Inc.
1230 Avenue of the Americas, New York, NY 10020

ISBN: 0-7434-6349-8

First Pocket Books printing November 2004

10 9 8 7 6 5 4 3 2 1

POCKET and colophon are registered trademarks of Simon & Schuster, Inc.

Front cover illustration by Franco Accornero

For information regarding special discounts for bulk purchases, please contact Simon & Schuster Special Sales at 1-800-456-6798 or business@simonandschuster.com

The candles caught the highlights of gold in his
lean face—amber eyes, tawny locks, jaw ablaze
with pinpoints of stubbled fire—and Olivia was
suddenly aware of a tingling heat spreading out
to her most intimate places. . . .

"Max! Thank God you have finally arrived," cried Cara.
Belatedly recalling her manners, she looked around with
an apologetic smile. "It seems I shall have the pleasure of
introducing you to my brother sooner rather than later."

"I'll be damned." A growl, low but distinctly disturbed, sounded from the gentleman by her side. "What
in the blazes are *you* doing here?"

*So much for imagining the man might feel a spark of
pleasure in finding their paths had crossed once again.*

"Good evening, Lord Davenport." Eyes crinkling in critical appraisal, Olivia fixed the viscount with a cool stare.
She had learned long ago how to hide disappointment.
"Your wound appears greatly improved since our last meeting. Would that I could say the same for your manners."

PRAISE FOR THE FIRST NOVEL IN
ANDREA DARIF'S SPARKLING NEW SERIES

THE TIGER'S MISTRESS

"DaRif makes a big splash. . . . Don't miss it!"
—*Romance Reviews Today*

"An enjoyable tale."
—*Romantic Times*

The Tiger's Mistress is also available as an eBook

For Kevan, with love
I could not ask for a better critique partner

A KISS OF
SPICE

Prologue

"Its power comes from love."

The small statue glittered in the firelight, its ruby eyes bright as burning coals. "So the legend goes." The man raised his palm to the flames, then slowly curled his fingers closed. "It is said that the very first pasha of our tribe carved this lion, the king of beasts, to watch over his family and keep it safe from all threats."

"Fascinating," murmured the Englishman. "Might I have a closer look?"

There was a flicker of hesitation. Several of the tribal elders shifted nervously, stirring a faint whispering of silk. Shadowed by the folds of his headdress, the Persian chieftain's features took on a certain tautness. However, as custom dictated a hospitality to strangers, he gave a courteous bow.

"Over the years it has been handed down with great ceremony from father to son," he continued softly, passing the statue over to his guest. "For you see, it comes with both a blessing . . . and a curse."

"A curse?" The Englishman's brows arched, expressing an equal measure of surprise and skepticism as he inspected the delicate workmanship. With its gilt mane and ebony body, highlighted by tiny gold claws, it was a fetching little piece. Though in truth he had seen many more impressive talismans during his recent travels through the region. Barely three inches long and half as high, the beast was hardly something to inspire fear and awe. But as a diplomat with the English legation visiting Syria, he would never be so rude as to say so aloud.

"Yes, a curse." The chieftain nodded gravely. "Tradition has it that a powerful curse will fall upon the pasha—and all his heirs—if ever the Ruby Lion is taken from its rightful realm. Misfortune. Grief. Untimely death," he intoned. "And the thief and his family shall suffer the same. Until such time as the talisman finds its way home."

"A powerful curse, indeed." Turning the statue in his fingers, the Englishman gave a small chuckle. "Surely in this day and age, you don't believe in such things as curses or spells anymore, sir. We, too, have such stories in England—they are called fairy-tales."

His words were met with an unblinking stare.

"They are told to frighten children," he continued. A gust of wind swirled at the tent flaps, drawing a sharp hiss from one of the elders. Clearing his throat, the Englishman lowered his voice. "While educated men like you and I know better than to give credence to ancient superstitions."

"I employ one of your countrymen as a tutor to my sons because I believe it important to understand modern ways, Mr. Bingham. That does not mean I have abandoned the faith of my ancestors." With a flourish of his white robes, the chieftain reached for the Ruby Lion. "A wise man respects the past, as well as the present and the future."

The Englishman nodded politely, but to himself, William Bingham could not help but scoff at such nonsense. Curses? The word conjured up fanciful notions of clanging chains, headless specters, and haunted castles.

It was the stuff of fiction—and rather lurid fiction at that.

With a sudden clap of his hands, the chieftain summoned a procession of servants, who began offering thick Arabic coffee and sugared sweetmeats to those seated around the fire. Rather than resume his place on the pillows, however, he turned and slipped silently into the shadows.

Curious, Bingham kept an eye on the other man's movements as he nibbled at a date. It was quite dark beyond the ring of firelight, but a pair of hanging lanterns cast just enough illumination for him to see the ghostly blur of white approach a large cabinet at the back of the cavernous tent. Reaching inside, the chieftain removed what looked to be a small box. In no more than a wink of brass, he opened the lid, slipped something inside and returned it to its place.

A moment later, as if carried on the wings of a desert sirocco, the chieftain was back in front of the flickering flames. "We shall leave you to your rest now. You have a long journey ahead of you." Another soft clap prompted the other guests to rise and withdraw. "The caravan will leave at dawn, and after a stop in Ar-Ruhaybah, it will escort you on to Damascus to meet up with the rest of your party."

"And from there, to Tyre and back to England," murmured Bingham.

"May you have a safe journey home." The chieftain touched his fingertips to his forehead and then to his lips. "I will be gone when you arise, for I take a trading party east, and we must reach the bazaars by nightfall."

"Thank you for your hospitality. You have been more than generous."

"It is the tradition of my people. I trust you will pass the night comfortably here in my own private quarters. However, if there is anything you desire, you have only to ask."

Whether it was the richness of the lamb stew, the effect of the strong coffee, or the prospect of sailing for home after spending so many months in foreign lands, Bingham felt much too restless for sleep. Circling the fire, he spent some time admiring the items that lay ready for transport to Damascus—richly patterned carpets, heavy silver bracelets, and razored daggers curved like crescent moons.

He wandered past the bales of silk and suddenly found himself facing the mysterious cabinet. In the flickering light, he studied the latticework doors, intrigued by the intricate geometric patterns—and by the fact that one of them was slightly ajar. Unable to contain his curiosity, he reached for the silver knob. There was no harm in looking, he decided, seeing as it was unlocked.

The door swung open to reveal the brass box he had spied earlier.

Bingham brought it out into the light and slowly

opened the lid. Sitting atop a bed of wine-dark velvet was the Ruby Lion. Once again he took the small statue in his hand.

"Ha, you do not look so very dangerous," he whispered, stroking a thumb over its paws.

Nor, for that matter, did it look all that very valuable. Just a bit of gold and two small gemstones. But it was rather exotic, and he could not help thinking how well it would look on his brother's curio table. Charles was an avid collector of fanciful animals. The crouching ebony form would make a perfect mate for the ivory elephant their cousin had brought back from India.

He stared for a moment longer. That it came with such a devilishly entertaining story made for an opportunity that was too good to pass up.

And if there was one thing William Bingham couldn't resist, it was a cracking good story. . . .

Chapter One

❦

Blue-deviled.

With a muzzy shake of his head, the gentleman twitched at the damp greatcoat draped over his shoulders. No, he decided, that was not quite an apt description of his current mood. At the moment, it was more of a viscous black. Blacker than the squalling night that had forced him to put up at the ramshackle inn for the night. And likely to bleed into a deep, brooding claret after he polished off the two bottles of wine that had just been set down before him.

At the heavy thump of pewter tankards upon a nearby table, the throbbing at his temples grew more pronounced. His surroundings, hazed with the fumes of cheap ale, raw tobacco and labored sweat, only served to further darken his spirits.

It had been nearly a year since that very painful period in his life when disappointment and disfigurement had him seeking solace in the oblivion of alcohol. Since then, he had managed enough of a recovery from old wounds to keep his personal demons at bay. But the letter tucked away in his pocket had reawakened a whole regiment of devils in his head. Given its contents, he supposed he might be forgiven for turning back to the strategy of trying to drown the enemy in a surfeit of spirits.

He shifted his bleary gaze, somehow knocking his empty glass to the floor as he squinted through the swirls of smoke. Had that been his fourth brandy? Or fifth? He had lost count.

One thing seemed certain enough—the red-headed barmaid, who mouthed an airy kiss as their gazes met, seemed quite willing to overlook his jugbitten condition. On delivering his latest round of drinks, she had rubbed up against his thigh, then brushed her hand across the front of his breeches while apologizing for an errant spill.

The parted lips, ripe with hints of promised pleasures, had been inviting. He had not objected when, on shifting her tray, she contrived to tumble into his lap.

"It'll be another hour 'til I get off work, luv," she murmured, ignoring the jeers of the neighboring patrons. "The old goat kicks up a dust if we ain't running ragged right up to closing. But have no fear, I'll have plenty o' legs left ta please a fine gentleman like yerself." Her gaze slid from the creased collar of his coat to the tips of his muddy Hessians, and her smile broadened. Despite the travel-worn state of his dress, its quality was unmistakable. "By the by, what shall I call ye?"

"Just . . . Max," answered Viscount Davenport, seeing no need to mention his title, or his full name—Maxwell James Prescott Bingham.

"Now that's a right 'andsome name fer a right 'andsome feller." She traced a finger along his cheek. "A jealous husband?"

"A French dragoon. And as you can see, one who was a good deal more skilled at trying to put a period to my existence than any Town cuckold."

It was said with a sardonic drawl, but Davenport stiffened at the barmaid's touch. A special salve had worked miracles in reducing the once ugly gash near his eye to naught but a faint scar. Still, he was self-conscious of its existence. In truth, he felt flawed enough inside without being reminded of his other imperfections.

Sensing her flirtations had struck a raw nerve, the barmaid moved quickly to assuage the damage. "Well, it makes ye appear real rakish. An' a little bit danger-ous." Her hand wove a sensuous trail through his tawny locks. "An' very, very sexy." Tilting his head back, she ran her tongue over his lower lip.

"Janey!" A bellow came from behind the taps. "The gennulmun may be paying ye te lift yer skirts, but I ain't! There's other customers wot need te be serviced."

A chorus of ribald comments rang out in agree-ment.

"Hold yer water," she shouted in reply.

"I will if ye hold me pego," called one wag.

Amid shouts of laughter, she gave a coy flounce of her curls, then one last caress to the viscount's chin. "I can't linger any longer, Max. But I'll come back soon."

Davenport grimaced as she sauntered off to mock applause. Lud, it had been an age since he had been with a woman! Perhaps he should consider the offer. He was not, by nature, a man of ungoverned passions. He prided himself on keeping his feelings well disci-plined—like the troops he had commanded under

Wellington, they had been drilled to march in orderly ranks, unbending to urge or whim. To surrender even the smallest measure of control had always seemed a dereliction of duty.

But tonight. . . .

Tonight, it was tempting to forget about duty and honor. About past mistakes. And lingering regrets. Staring morosely into the depths of his claret, the viscount rubbed at the thin white scar on his cheek. Perhaps the saucy wench might provide enough of a distraction to keep his mind off a certain other female.

The truth of the matter was, a lady had nearly as much to do with his current state of malaise as the paper crumpled in his waistcoat. No matter how hard he attempted to banish her from his head, she had bedeviled his dreams for nearly a year.

The Lady in Red.

Sizzling beauty. Fiery spirit. Was it any wonder that Olivia Marquand had burned an indelible image in his brain?

And yet . . .

The viscount winced as his nails dug a bit too deeply into the old wound.

And yet, he had allowed her to sail back to India without so much as a simple goodbye.

It had been a wise decision, he assured himself.

Women were naught but trouble—Sirens in silk who lured gentlemen to their doom. Once, in his youthful folly, he had allowed himself to be seduced by a blond beauty's song. Too naive to listen to the warnings of his friends, he had sailed headlong onto the rocks. The temptress had, of course, been quick to jilt him as soon as a more attractive prospect appeared on the horizon. The other fellow had lacked Davenport's pedigree, but possessed a great deal more poise and polish than a reserved young lord with little experience in Town.

Not to speak of a great deal more money.

And so he had been left to founder, his heart battered and bruised among the splintered wreckage. The pain had dulled over time to no more than an intermittent ache, but he had no intention of ever making himself so vulnerable again.

Only a bloody fool made the same mistake twice.

Quickly draining the last drops from the first bottle, the viscount started in on the second.

It was not that Olivia was anything like Arabella, he admitted. Like many Diamonds of the First Water, his former fiancée was spoiled, vain, and manipulative, intent on selling her striking looks to the highest bidder. In all fairness, he supposed she could hardly be blamed for her shallowness. Highborn young ladies were trained to think of aught else but making an advantageous match.

Olivia, on the other hand, coolly refused to submit to the tyranny of the *ton*. Though the daughter of an earl, she had chosen to run away from her domineering father rather than be forced into a marriage of convenience. Through a heady combination of brains and pluck, she had dared to break all the rules and create a new life for herself. One in which she controlled her own destiny—not to speak of a vast spice empire and shipping company.

Davenport forced a frown. The irony was that if she

were a man they would likely be friends. He admired her for such strength of character and gritty courage, no matter that Society did not look at all favorably upon such traits in a female. And she possessed the same sort of loyalty and resilience that he valued in his male comrades. And yet, he reminded himself roughly, it would be foolhardy to allow his feelings to grow into anything other than grudging respect. Their differences were too great—she was rich and supremely self-assured, while he lived on a marginal income and was still battling an army of self-doubts.

Friends? Never. How absurd to imagine he could ever be friends with such a female. Duty would require him to seek a bride at some point, but she would be a quiet, biddable young lady who would never question a command, not an unflinching female who spoke her mind as if she were an equal.

The viscount's mouth thinned to a taut line. To say the least, Olivia's cool self-confidence was damned unnerving! During their short acquaintance—a time when both of them had been involved in helping the Earl of Branford track down a traitor to the Crown— she had not only questioned his authority, but had possessed the audacity to disobey several direct orders—something not one of the seasoned soldiers of the Peninsular campaigns had ever dared.

The last of those occasions had turned out to be the final time he had seen her. He had thought about paying her a visit during the weeks that followed. It would have been the gentlemanly thing to do, considering all the risks they had braved together. But, for some inexplicable reason he had kept putting it off.

And then, suddenly it had been too late. She had left for India on one of her own merchant ships, no doubt to resume the running of her spice empire.

Well, it was all for the good that she had sailed out of his life, he assured himself.

Like her costly blends of rare peppers and piquant curries, Olivia Marquand was much too hot and exotic for his taste. What with her streak of fiery independence, spark of keen intelligence, and flashes of cynical wit, each encounter with the lady had left him feeling rather singed around the edges.

And then, of course, there was her smoldering sensuality. Jet-black hair that looked as shimmeringly soft as the silks she wore. Flawless complexion as lappingly inviting as a mouthful of Devonshire cream. Sinful body with curves . . .

The room suddenly seemed hellishly hot, and the wine like fire on his tongue. Shoving aside his glass, Davenport began to tug at the knot of his cravat, only to find his fingers replaced by a softer touch.

"Warm down here, ain't it, Max?" Having loosened the length of linen, the barmaid started on the fastenings of his shirt. "I promise ye, it will get even hotter if we was te go upstairs te yer room."

Maybe the only way to fight fire was with fire.

Thrusting himself up from his chair, Davenport caught her laughing face between his hands and covered her mouth with his. The touch of her lips, warm and pliant, set off a flare of burning need. He was achingly aware of a desperate craving to hold and be held. To feel flesh against flesh, thigh against thigh, tongues entwined. Two as one—the pure, primal act of coupling would, for a fleeting moment of ecstasy, surely fill the raw void of emptiness.

The tips of his fingers slid down to trace the line of her jaw, the curve of her neck, the swell of her bosom. "Lud," he groaned, his hands closing over her breasts. They felt heavy and ripe beneath the thin muslin.

The barmaid arched eagerly into his embrace, her hips swaying back and forth across the front of his breeches, her nipples pressing hard against his palms. "Max." The word trailed off in a seductive sigh as she teased a lapping kiss along the length of his scar. "Come now, a man like you ain't made to be spending the night alone."

Stumbling slightly, he groped for his coat.

In the haste to turn for the stairs, her hair ribbons came undone. Burying his face in the tumble of tresses, the viscount fisted a handful of curling strands across his stubbled cheeks, breathing in the earthy muskiness. It was nothing like the subtle scent of florals and spice that perfumed his memory. . . .

He forced his eyes open, determined to focus on the present and not the past. But in the guttering light of the candles, the coppery highlights of the barmaid's hair appeared a vivid red.

Damn the color.

In an instant, the fire went out, leaving naught but ashes. Davenport stepped back, the faint crackle of paper a further reminder that duty must always vanquish desire. Gently freeing himself from her grasp, he pressed a coin into her hand and quickly turned away, his boots sounding a staccato tattoo as he climbed the stairs alone.

*   *   *

"This is a delicious blend of tea, my dear Cara," exclaimed the dowager Countess Ranley. Turning from her hostess to the lady seated at her left, she raised the delicate Sevres cup. "Do you not agree?"

Seeing as it was a creation of her own company—and a highly profitable one at that—Lady Olivia Marquand allowed a small twitch of her lips. "Indeed," she murmured. "Quite . . . unique."

"It is the toast of the Town," added Lord Henniger. "And more costly than champagne."

"You don't say?" she replied blandly, wondering just what the gentleman's reaction would be if he knew all those guineas were going straight into her own coffers.

No doubt he would be shocked beyond expression. But then, she had grown well-used to the notion that most people would find her activities quite beyond the pale. Few things were as odious to the *ton* as "engaging in trade." And she had certainly broken that rule—in spades. Or spices, to be more precise. Unbeknownst to all but a handful of people in England, she was sole owner of a trading company, controlling a fleet of merchant ships that commerced in exotic spices, as well as flavored teas. In India, where she had lived for the past seven years, the strictures of society were a good deal more relaxed and she had been accorded more freedom to go about her business as she pleased.

But here in London?

Despite feeling the naughty urge to stir things up a bit, Olivia added nothing but a cool smile as she raised her own cup to her lips. Now that she had returned to

England for good, she must remember to behave like a proper lady, no matter how . . . boring.

Boring. The taste of the tea lost a bit of its spice. It was true that her life had been a trifle flat since she arrived back in London. She still made all the important decisions concerning Grenville and Company, but much of the day-to-day running of the business had, for practical reasons, been delegated to her longtime man of affairs. It was, in many ways, an ideal arrangement, yet even with her frequent visits to the office, her role did not bring quite the same thrum to her blood as being able to play an active role in negotiations. However, the *ton* would quickly ostracize any female who presumed to preside over the arrangement of shipping schedules and bills of lading rather than tea trays and plates of pastries.

A laugh from across the breakfast table recalled her from her reveries. The conversation had shifted to a new topic, though in truth, she didn't expect the day's activities to be any more adventurous than a discussion on tea.

However, Olivia was quick to remind herself that one of the reasons she had accepted the invitation to the country estate was to enjoy just such an interlude of rural peace and quiet. On the surface, life in London was far more placid than in Bombay, and yet, the subtle undercurrents of all its rules and regulations made it rather treacherous to navigate. She had suddenly felt the need to escape from the glittering ballrooms, the crush of curious callers, and the attentions of would-be suitors while she pondered a number of decisions regarding her future.

". . . a crack shot with a bow and arrow? Is that so, my dear Cara?" Lord Haverstock waggled a brow at his cousin, then darted a mischievous glance at the others. "Then perhaps the young ladies of the group would care to match off against the gentlemen in a display of archery?"

"What an excellent suggestion, Richard." Lady Cara, the hostess of the small house party, favored him with her first real smile of the day. "I am sure we would all welcome the chance for a bit of vigorous outdoor activity after being cooped inside for the past few days."

The heavy rains and chill winds were not the only forces to have dampened the spirits of the small gathering. The estate library had been broken into several nights ago, and although Lady Cara had made every effort to appear unperturbed by the incident, it was clear that the intrusion and subsequent visit by the local magistrate had been a trying ordeal. And so, the suggestion of a spirited competition was met with a hearty murmur of agreement from the others at the table. Without delay, Haverstock rose and went off to arrange for the target to be set up beyond the garden wall.

"Allow me to offer an arm, Lady Olivia. The path is a trifle rough." As Lord Henniger jumped up to assist her out of the chair, Olivia could not quite keep a spark of exasperation from flaring in her eyes. He was no doubt a perfectly pleasant gentleman. And with his glossy dark curls, well-cut features and trim height, she imagined most ladies would consider him quite attractive. Yet his fawning attentions and conventional conversation had set her teeth on edge.

She took care to mask her momentary irritation, yet as she followed along behind her hostess, she couldn't repress an inward sigh. Perhaps she was simply not cut from the same cloth as most other young English ladies. She preferred exotic saris to prim muslins. Not to speak of her taste in hues, which ran to bold tones of spicy cinnamon and lush saffron rather than pale shades of peach and cream.

Had it been a glaring mistake to return to a society where females were not expected to have an ounce of color?

Over the years, she had trusted her own instincts in making a great many difficult decisions, but in this question, she was as yet uncertain of the answer.

Chapter Two

As the dowager and her companions took up position as spectators, Cara signalled for Olivia and the other two young ladies of the party to gather around her.

"I suppose I ought to have inquired whether any of you are familiar with the sport before accepting my cousin's proposal." A taut thrum pierced the air as she tested a bowstring. "However, I find it hard to resist a challenge, especially one that implies we ladies are not capable of handling any implement larger than an embroidery needle."

"My brother has taught me the basics," volunteered Miss Enfield.

Miss Chatfield nodded. "I have had some rudimentary instruction as well. If the distance is not too great, I should be able to manage a hit."

"Excellent. Then perhaps we shall not disgrace ourselves." Olivia did not miss the slight hesitation as Cara turned to her. "And you, Lady Olivia? Of course you needn't feel obliged to participate. The three of us are country misses, well-used to the rough and tumble outdoors, but perhaps . . ."

"I should be delighted to join you." Olivia picked

up one of the bows and gave a flex to the length of yew. "I am a bit out of practice, but like you, Lady Cara, I am not quite willing to concede defeat to the gentlemen without any show of opposition."

Haverstock returned, followed by a pair of grooms lugging a large wooden easel and a bull's-eye target painted upon a sack of straw. After the rules had been agreed upon and the distance paced off, the quivers and bows were laid out in readiness.

It was decided that the two younger ladies would shoot first, followed by Cara. Olivia, who had asked to go last, chose to step back and wait for her turn in the shade of an apple tree, a vantage point that afforded the chance to observe both the contestants and the path to the target.

She had long ago learned that paying careful attention to the small details could make the difference between success and failure. Gauging the drift of the breeze, noting the spin of each arrow, judging the spring in each bow—all were nuances that might be used to gain a winning edge.

"A game try, Miss Abigail," called Henniger as the young lady's arrow barely nicked the outermost circle. "But according to the rules of the competition, you, too, are eliminated." He grinned at Haverstock. "Ashton is out as well, but so is Miss Marianne. The gentlemen are up by one."

"Don't start your crowing just yet." Cara nocked an arrow, drew it back past her ear and let fly with an angled shot.

"Blue!" called one of the grooms as he pulled the tip out from the middle circle.

"Well done." Cara's cousin fingered at his chin. "Can you match that, Henniger?"

He did, but just barely.

Haverstock then stepped to the line and promptly scored a hit just inside the yellow circle.

Everyone applauded.

"I'm afraid you will have to strike the bull's-eye to tie the score and send it into a second round," he murmured as he offered Olivia the bow.

"Thank you, but I think I prefer this one."

As she picked up the shortest of the lot and plucked at the string, Haverstock's smile stretched a bit wider. His amusement, however, quickly took wing, along with the spinning blur of wood and feathers.

Twock!

"Dead center!"

"What skill," cried Cara, with a clap of her hands.

"What luck," riposted her cousin.

What fun. Olivia stilled the quivering bowstring with her thumb but it was not quite so easy to control the twitch of her lips. She ought to be acting like a proper lady, not some primitive savage—even if, at heart, a part of her remained untamed. But by nature, her spirit was rebellious. It always had been.

As a result, life was not always easy for her. In the eyes of most people, to be different was to be dangerous. She already saw that the two younger misses were looking at her not only with awe, but a bit of trepidation. But at times, she simply could not help allowing herself a bit of freedom to be . . . who she was.

And be damned with the opinion of others.

It was hardly an attitude designed to curry favor in

Polite Society. She gave silent thanks that unlike most young ladies, she was not on the hunt for a husband. She could afford the luxury of ignoring the rules.

"Step aside, Lord Harold." Cara marched to the line and surveyed the target, which had been set back another ten yards. "Fred is signalling a miss, so you are out," she announced. "Seeing as Mr. Gavin-Smith failed to hit aught but air, that leaves just three of us." As her mouth took on a determined little tilt, she examined the end feathers on several of the arrows before making a final choice. "Be forewarned, Richard. I mean to make you work for a win."

He smiled. "With you, cuz, I have long ago learned to expect a good fight."

Olivia watched her hostess draw back the bow with a firm hand. A young lady with fight—now, that was interesting. Haverstock's teasing only corroborated what she herself had begun to sense. Over the last few days, she had observed that Cara possessed a more forthright manner than most gently reared females. She had opinions of her own and was unafraid to voice them in the presence of the gentlemen—even going so far as to contradict her cousin on a matter of the corn laws. That had earned her a lecture from the dowager on proper feminine deportment, once the ladies had withdrawn from supper.

Though she had refrained from retort, Cara's momentary scowl had indicated how little in agreement she was with the notion that a female should be seen and not heard.

A kindred soul? Olivia wondered. It was still a bit

soon for a final tally, but the young lady had certainly scored some points in her favor.

Cara's shot flew true, striking once again well within the yellow circle. "Hah!" She turned to her cousin with a gleam in her eye. "If Lady Olivia hits the target—which I fully expect she will—you will have to score a bull's-eye in order to tie us."

Haverstock took a goodly amount of time setting his feet and taking deliberate aim.

There was a faint whoosh of air, and a moment later, the groom's hand shot up. "Bang on the mark!"

"It looks as if you ladies are going to have to go it another round. Unless, of course, Lady Olivia matches her earlier feat." Haverstock winked at the other gentlemen before inclining a polite bow. "I do hope your arm is not growing too fatigued."

"How kind of you to be concerned, but actually, I feel as though I am just getting warmed up." In one smooth motion, Olivia drew an arrow from the quiver, spun around and let it fly.

With a sharp crack, it split the other arrow in two.

"Da—" Haverstock cleared his throat. "Er, deucedly remarkable shot."

Henniger's surprise was a trifle less muted. "Where on earth did you learn to shoot like that?"

"Hunting tigers in Jaipur," she replied. Her lashes fluttered. "It is great sport, and very educational, as it does tend to teach you excellent aim."

The gentleman looked as if he wasn't sure whether to be impressed or insulted.

Biting her lip, Cara ducked down to collect the other bows.

"Hmmph! Sounds rather outlandish, if you ask me," grumbled the dowager countess. "Females have no business roaming the wilds." She gave a sharp rap of her cane to her seat. "Be warned, gels—nothing to be gained but damp feet and a freckled nose by straying too far from the civilized comforts of a proper house."

In answer to the preemptory summons, the two gentlemen went to offer their escort, while the rest of the party gathered the shawls and overcoats shed during the heat of competition.

"As if anyone asked for your opinion," muttered Cara. She looked up. "I, for one, would love to hear more about such fascinating adventures—"

"Lady Cara!" Lady Ranley's stick was now jabbing heavenward, indicating the dark clouds scudding down from the moors. "Come, gel. Do not forget your duties as a proper hostess. There is a chill in the air and rain is threatening. Hurry along and see that the servants have tea set out for us."

"Perhaps later," murmured Olivia, noting that the sky was not the only thing looking rather stormy.

"Please excuse me. As you can see, I am expected to exercise naught but feminine skills. Like arranging platters of strawberry tarts." Adding a distinctly unladylike word under her breath, Cara gathered her skirts and headed for the manor house.

Cursing roundly at everything in his path, Davenport was in a truly foul temper by the time the wheelwright fixed the broken spoke. Nursing an aching head and numerous flea bites from the previous night, he was already chilled to the bone from the spitting rains. As he resumed his perch and gave a snap of his whip, the journey north did not look to be taking a turn for the better.

Despite the mud and ruts churned up by the storm, the roads turned out to be passable enough. After he had made it over several steep stretches without mishap it seemed likely he might cover the final miles by nightfall. Not that the thought was of much consolation, he decided, as his phaeton veered onto the main coaching route for York. Judging by his sister's letter, he was only heading into a more treacherous swirling of thunder and lightning.

Urging the horses into a steady trot, the viscount once again mulled over the scribbled plea begging him to travel to Saybrook Manor without delay. Cara was a solid, sensible young lady, not given to flightiness. So her rather disjointed narrative took on an even more disturbing tone. It was bad enough that she hinted at dark trouble threatening their younger brother. But to toss in mention of an exotic heirloom, an ancient curse, and odd specters stalking the night? If he didn't know better, he would think she had been seduced from her usual sound judgment by reading too many of Mrs. Radcliffe's novels.

His lips could not help but give an involuntary twitch at the notion. That was not very likely, for when his sister's nose was buried in a book, the subject was bound to be on crop rotation or the latest advances in plow designs. . . .

But people change.

Davenport's hands tightened on the reins. As he had

spent so little time with his family over the past few years, it might very well be, for all practical purposes, a total stranger who came out to greet him.

The unsettling realization caused another pinch of guilt. In all truth, he could hardly lay claim to being the same older brother who had taught Cara how to ride astride, bait a fishing hook, and help birth a mare. He had certainly gone out of his way to avoid her—and Kip. He had treated both of them as if they were mere ghosts from the past whose existence was a haunting reminder of a more carefree life.

His whip flicked out to knock away a low-hanging branch. Perhaps it was just as well he was being forced to confront the reasons why he had turned away from those he loved most.

He did not care to think of himself as a coward. . . . Oh, to be sure, no one had ever questioned his physical courage. On the battlefields, he earned a fistful of medals for valor. Yet the brutal truth was that he had not faced his own inner doubts with the same un-flinching resolve he had shown in the face of flashing sabers and whizzing bullets.

Just because it was a good deal easier to confront an enemy he could identify was no excuse for turning tail and running from a more shadowy opponent.

Davenport's brow furrowed as a gloved finger traced along the length of his scar. The thought of strange shadows brought him back to puzzling over the mysterious incidents spelled out by his sister. Her words concerning a rash of local thefts and the odd behavior of their younger brother made little enough sense, but even more puzzling were her strange references to the Ruby Lion.

He vaguely recalled the family heirloom—a small statue brought back from Persia by his uncle William. Carved out of ebony, with rubies for eyes and a gilt gold mane, the curio was a valuable item to be sure. Yet the fact that it had been the cause of a nasty quarrel between Kip and their father shortly before the Earl of Saybrook had left for his hunting box in Scotland hardly seemed to warrant her tone of near hysteria. Not to speak of her giving credence to the ridiculous stories they had been told in their youth—something about an ancient curse that would bring terrible misfortune to the family should the dratted thing ever fall into the wrong hands.

The dull throbbing in the viscount's skull suddenly became more pronounced. As if family troubles were not enough to cope with, a postscript to Cara's letter mentioned that a cousin was visiting from London, along with a group of his friends. The party was apparently a small one, but even so, the presence of strangers could only make the meeting with his siblings more awkward.

There was, however, one note of consolation to the whole affair. On learning of the gathering, he had dashed off a note to Spencer Sprague, an erstwhile army comrade whom he had ignored for far too long, asking the former major to join him at Saybrook Manor. So, in between calming Cara and lecturing Kip, he could at least look forward to catching up with an old friend. Even under less trying circumstances, long rides over the moors and relaxing evenings lingering over port and cigars were infinitely preferable to being a part of any frivolous group festivities.

* * *

"Why, Lady Olivia . . . that is a most unusual design. I don't believe I have seen anything like it in the pages of the *Fashion Gazette*."

Olivia turned from her perusal of a lovely little landscape painting in the alcove of the study, an expression of faint amusement on her lips as she watched her hostess draw the door closed. "I do not doubt it, Lady Cara, seeing as I drew it up myself."

"How very . . . original."

"The fabric is also rather unique. It can only be found in a small village high in the foothills of Darjeeling." She fingered the soft folds that were gathered at one shoulder and watched as a subtle shimmering of iridescence rippled across the finely woven silk. "And as the sort of stitching required to achieve the right drape would likely send a French *modiste* into a fit of vapors, I don't imagine it will ever become a popular style."

"No," agreed the other young lady with a pensive nod. "It is much too interesting for that." Having recovered from her initial surprise at finding someone else in the room, she, too, seemed mesmerized by how the play of the candlelight upon the cloth caught every nuance in the jewel tones of mulberry. "I did not have a chance earlier to say how much I admire your creativity—in all endeavors."

"Are you interested in fashion?"

"Not at all." Cara gave a self-deprecating laugh. "Indeed, my brothers have often teased me about being more comfortable in their cast-off breeches and outgrown boots than a fancy ball gown and slippers.

And I fear they have the right of it." She gave a small shrug and gestured at the painting hanging above the mantel. "Just as well, I suppose, that my interests lie more in learning the latest methods of shearing wool than in capering across a ballroom floor. As you can see, it is my brothers who inherited my mother's celebrated looks along with my father's towering height, while I was endowed with naught but the Bingham propensity for growing as tall and skinny as a stalk of wheat."

Like her laugh, Cara's words were shaded by sharp ironic humor rather than any self-pity or resentment. Olivia found her curiosity even more piqued than before. Her hostess was looking more and more as if she did not fit the usual pattern card for a wellborn Society miss—and not just on account of her willowy form and angular features.

"Indeed, they look to be very handsome fellows," she murmured after a moment of studying the portrait. The artist had depicted the pair of lithe, long-limbed young men leaning up against a paddock fence, their chiseled features flush from a rousing gallop and, by the look of their boyish grins, some shared private joke. "I imagine they cut quite a dash in Town," she added, her gaze lingering on the taller of the two. The flickering shadows obscured much of the detail, and yet there was something vaguely familiar about the set of the broad shoulders and the angle of the jaw.

"Actually, my older brother chooses not mingle much in society. He is quite reserved. Perhaps too much so."

Shifting her attention from the painting back to her hostess, Olivia thought she detected a tautness to the other lady's tone.

"But of late, Kipling seems hell-bent on stirring up enough trouble for two." It was said lightly, but the earlier note of good humor now sounded terribly strained. As she stepped rather abruptly toward the desk at the far wall, a small key slipped from her fingers.

Olivia moved to help find it, using the opportunity to make a surreptitious study of the other young lady's visage.

While it was true that Cara was no Diamond of the First Water, her features had a strength to them that transcended mere prettiness. Her wide cheekbones accentuated slightly slanted hazel eyes, and her nose was perhaps a tad too long, drawing attention to lips that were lushly full, though firm as those of a man. At the moment, however, they were pinched into a thin line and the color had leached from her unfashionably tanned face.

"Forgive me for straying uninvited into your private study," said Olivia quietly as she held out the key. "Given the recent robbery, I am sure that you would prefer some time alone, rather than being obliged to entertain a stranger."

"Oh, please—it is I who should apologize. I fear I have been a less than hospitable hostess." Cara brushed an errant lock of hair from her cheek, then quickly tucked it into her sash. "In truth, I have been rather distracted . . ."

"With good reason, it would appear," observed

Olivia dryly. "Have the authorities made any headway in discovering the identity of the thief?"

"No." Cara's gaze remained glued on the Oriental carpet, her lashes obscuring her expression. "But it is really a minor matter," she said softly. "S-something must have frightened off whoever it was before he could take anything of value."

"Still, it is unsettling to think of some unknown intruder prowling through your home." Olivia was not fooled by the show of unconcern. She had enough experience in observing people to sense that the other lady was not nearly as composed as she wished to appear. "Speaking of which, I apologize again for intruding on your privacy. I shall return to the drawing room."

"Don't go. That is, I would be grateful if you would stay a bit. I have enjoyed your company very much. Indeed, it has been immensely refreshing to be able to converse with another lady on less frivolous topics than usual." Cara forced a smile. "And I meant it when I said I should like to hear about India."

Olivia flashed an answering smile. After a small pause, she asked, "Do you find other young ladies frivolous?"

"I confess that I do."

"You need not say it as if you feel guilty as a burglar."

This time, Cara's show of humor was unfeigned. "I can't help it. I know that I break a good many of Society's strictures, for a gently reared young lady is supposed to care for aught but fancy finery, dancing until dawn, and snaring a proper husband. Things which I find a crashing bore." Her hand flew up to cover her mouth. "I-I hope I am not shocking you. Among my many bad habits is the tendency to say exactly what I am thinking."

"I assure you, Lady Cara, there is very little you could say or do that would shock me."

"I had a feeling you might not be . . ."

"A proper lady?" Olivia's brow arched in amusement.

Cara's face turned nearly the same hue as the heated red embers in the hearth. "Oh, I-I didn't mean—"

"Actually, I take it as a great compliment." Her eyes strayed to the portrait of the two young men. "It is not always easy for a young lady of highborn family to speak her mind."

Cara was quick to follow her meaning. "Actually, my brothers have always encouraged me to explore the subjects that truly interested me, rather than wasting my time on embroidery and watercolors. Just as they have always encouraged me to voice my opinion. Papa didn't always agree, but with their support, I always managed to bring him around."

"Good looks and good sense—they sound like paragons of perfection," replied Olivia, not without a slight trace of irony to her tone.

"Ha!" The candlelight caught the wry grimace. "Do not think I am so blinded by sisterly affection to think them without fault. They most definitely are not."

"Flawed angels? Why, you make them sound even more intriguing." Olivia rather doubted she would find the two handsome young gentlemen any more interesting than the other young blades she had met in town. Yet something about their sister's praise had her giving the painting a second look. "Perhaps at some point I might make their acquaintance. I seem to recall your cousin mentioning that he expected Kipling to be part of the party. Will he be joining us?"

Cara looked away, her expression becoming more shadowed. "I am not sure of Kip's plans. But you will no doubt have a chance to meet my older brother. I expect him to arrive on the morrow." With that, she quickly changed the subject. "But enough of life here in Yorkshire, which aside from the recent spate of robberies, is usually quite tame. But India . . ." She sighed. "India must be wildly different."

"It is," agreed Olivia.

"If ladies are permitted to take part in tiger hunts, it sounds not only very exotic, but very exciting." It was not merely the flicker of the flames that sparked a flash of light in the other lady's eyes. "What other sorts of interesting activities were allowed?"

Olivia hesitated. Her business affairs were not something she revealed to many people, and for good reason. An errant word, however innocently dropped, could be ruinous to her reputation. And yet, on seeing Cara's look of longing, she sensed she could trust in the young lady's discretion. "I am afraid I cannot tell you too much about social gatherings, save to say that things are a good deal more informal than they are here in England. There are ladies who play polo, or who think nothing of venturing into the bazaars without escort. However, my time was spent mostly around the docks, overseeing my shipping company."

Cara's eyes widened. "Ladies may own and run their own businesses without censure?"

"I would not go quite that far," she replied dryly. "Even in India, I had to be extremely discreet about it. And here in England . . ." Olivia gave a rueful smile. "Suffice it to say there would be hell to pay if the secret ever became known."

"Oh, you may count on me never to breathe a word of it." The young lady's expression of surprise turned to one of undisguised admiration. "But how did you manage it? As I, too, am the daughter of an earl, I know how hard it must have been to bend all the rules that govern our behavior."

"I did not simply bend the rules, Lady Cara, I left them broken in so many pieces you would need a quizzing glass to find them all. Not that I ever looked back. Or regretted my actions, however shocking they may have appeared. I could not bear the life my father had planned for me, so I ran away, trusting that my knack for numbers and solving practical problems would allow me to live on my own." Olivia's lips crooked at the memory of those long-ago days. "I was fortunate to meet with a kindly merchant who took me under his wing, despite his failing profits. We started with one leaky brig and an equally risky idea, but it all paid off. Mr. Grenville is no longer alive, but the company I inherited now owns a fleet of swift ships."

"How very enterprising of you!" Cara did not appear in the least shocked. Indeed, she quickly voiced an eagerness to hear more. "What sort of merchandise do you trade in?"

"Grenville and Company imports high quality teas,

including the blend you tasted at breakfast. We also supply a good deal of the exotic spices that make their way to England."

"I should love the chance to—" Before Cara could go on, a brusque knock interrupted her words.

"Cara?" The door opened a crack.

The young lady turned and rushed toward the tall, travel-worn figure who had just stepped into the room, flinging her arms around his neck despite the mud spattering his carriage coat and the drops of rain clinging to his wide-brimmed hat.

A clap of thunder suddenly rattled the window-panes, followed by a bright flash that momentarily lit up the heavens.

Could lightning strike twice in the same place?

As a bolt of fire sizzled straight to her very core, Olivia blinked, wondering if she had been blinded by the afterglow.

But no, standing tall in solitary splendor, the breadth of his shoulders accentuated by the fluttering capes of his coat, the gentleman was still there, looking severe, serious, solemn. And supremely sensuous.

The candles caught the highlights of gold in his lean face—amber eyes, tawny locks, jaw ablaze with pinpoints of stubbled fire—and Olivia was suddenly aware of a tingling heat spreading out to her most intimate places. . . .

"Max! Thank God you have finally arrived." Belatedly recalling her manners, Cara looked around with an apologetic smile. "It seems I shall have the pleasure of introducing you to the eldest Bingham sooner rather than later."

"Ol—I'll be damned." A growl, low but distinctly disturbed, sounded from the gentleman. "What in the blazes are you doing here?"

So much for imagining the man might feel a spark of pleasure in finding their paths had crossed once again.

"Good evening, Lord Davenport." Eyes crinkling in critical appraisal, Olivia fixed the viscount with a cool stare. She had learned long ago how to hide disappointment. "Your wound appears greatly improved since our last meeting. Would that I could say the same for your manners."

Chapter Three

❦

Cara could not contain her astonishment. "Do you mean to say the two of you are acquainted?"

The slap of wet felt hit the side table, followed by the thud of sodden wool. The sight of Olivia Marquand, looking stunningly voluptuous in an unusual gown of shimmering silk, had quite literally taken his breath away. But in the few moments it took to remove his outer garments, Davenport recovered enough from his initial surprise to manage a gruff reply.

"Yes." Peeling off his gloves, he inclined a stiff bow to his sister's companion. "Good evening, Lady Olivia. Accept my apologies. I was taken by surprise at the unexpected . . . pleasure of your company."

"Unexpected, yes," she murmured, just loud enough for him to hear. "But somehow it does not appear as if you take the least bit of pleasure in it."

The hardness of her voice matched the steel of her eyes. Clearly she had no intention of forgiving his unintended rudeness—present or past. He was almost relieved that the battle lines were so plainly drawn and she appeared hostile. It made it easier to treat her as an adversary.

"Appearances, as we both know, can be deceiving,"

he shot back, making a pointed reference to their first meeting. At the time, she had been masquerading as a wealthy widow.

A faint tinge of red stole to Olivia's cheeks, the only outward sign that his barb had drawn blood.

Fighting the urge to reach out and brush away the faint trace of hurt, Davenport turned abruptly for the decanter on the bookshelf and poured himself a drink.

"I—I don't quite understand." The exchange had taken place too quickly for Cara to catch the words, but she was far too observant to miss the tension thrumming through the air. "How on earth did you come to meet? Lady Olivia has only recently arrived in England. And you, Max . . . you rarely choose to go out in Society."

Davenport took a long swallow of sherry, hoping that a strategy of silence might discourage further questions along those lines.

It was Olivia who answered. "I was here for a brief time last year. Your brother and I had cause to meet through Lord Branford."

"Why, I did not realize you were a friend of Alex!" exclaimed Cara.

"The acquaintance is not a longstanding one, yet I hope that the earl considers me as such," replied Olivia. "Unfortunately, I have not seen him since my return to England. Apparently he and his wife are away on another adventure with Baron Hadley." A ghost of a smile flitted across her lips. "I trust it will not prove quite so confusingly treacherous as the last one."

Touché. So she, too, was capable of wielding the past

as a weapon. "There is no need for concern. I doubt any experience they might encounter could prove half so terrible as that."

"The Hadleys?" repeated Cara, quick to pounce on the name.

Davenport turned to refill his glass, silently cursing the fact that Olivia Marquand was not the only lady in the room who could put two and two together.

Just as he feared, his sister took only a moment to form her next question. "Why, does that mean you were involved with Max and Alex in their special mission for Whitehall? Max has been most obstinate in refusing to reveal the details, but I do know it had something to do with the Hadley family, and the theft of a mysterious document that was critical to England's alliance with Russia."

"In a manner of speaking." An angling of her face threw Olivia's profile into shadow. "For a time I was their main suspect."

"Good Lord, are you telling me you were the elusive 'Lady in Red' whom they suspected of being the villain?"

"I am afraid so."

"Surely my brother and Alex could not have been so bacon-brained as to think a lady like you would ever betray your country?"

"We had damn good reason," answered Davenport through gritted teeth. "The evidence was overwhelming."

"It was," agreed Olivia.

Eyes narrowing, Cara suddenly took on the look of a terrier who had just got hold of a particularly pungent bone. Davenport recognized that stubborn expression all too well. Reluctant though he was to discuss the matter, he decided an explanation was his only hope of putting it behind them once and for all.

"As you already know, Anthony Taft, an old army comrade and senior minister at Whitehall, asked Alex for help in tracking down a stolen document vital to our alliance with Russia. It had to be handled unofficially, as our government did not wish the Tsar to know it had gone missing, which made the task even more difficult." Drawing a deep breath, he sought to keep his words as succinct as possible. "In the course of his investigation, Alex came up with two likely suspects—the daughter of Baron Hadley, a noted antiquities scholar who had suddenly disappeared from town, and a mysterious widow by the name of Mrs. Grenville, who—"

"Who was me," interrupted Olivia. "I believe the earl also referred to me as the Lady in Red, as I dressed in that color to distract attention from my face. My masquerade was forced by a personal family matter which had nothing to do with Lord Branford's quest." Again, she smiled faintly. "But naturally, when the earl—with the help of your brother—discovered my ruse, and the fact that I secretly owned a fleet of swift ships, they suspected the worst."

Davenport stared into his drink as he thought back to the tempestuous events of a year ago. With consummate skill, Olivia Marquand had presented a number of different faces during the search for the enemy. And it was only fitting, given the complexity of her character. She was one of the rare individuals, male or female, who possessed the sharp intelligence and steely nerve necessary to be the mastermind of such a nefarious plot.

However, in no mood to dwell on the lady or the past, he placed his glass down upon the shelf. "Let us try not to spend all evening recounting the tedious details. Alex was also following Portia Hadley, whom he had observed purloining papers from a London townhouse. We soon learned the ladies were innocent of any wrongdoing. In fact, the baron had been kidnapped by the real enemy in hopes that he could be forced into deciphering the stolen document for the French." Shrugging in impatience, he finished in a rush. "Suffice it to say, once the misunderstandings were ironed out, Miss Hadley and Lady Olivia were instrumental in laying a trap that led to the capture of the dastard and the recovery of the papers."

Olivia gave a small cough. "Your brother has left out the part about rescuing me from a brute who had a knife at my throat."

"Hmmph," he growled. "And Lady Olivia has omitted mention of firing a pistol at a man taking aim at my head."

Cara slowly let out the breath she had been holding. "I imagine there are a great many other parts I would find interesting. Tell me, did not Alex marry Miss Hadley?"

The viscount's jaw set. Yes, Branford had been smart enough to marry Miss Hadley. While he . . .

"For God's sake, Cara! Enough of ancient history!" he snapped. "I haven't driven hell for leather to Yorkshire in order to revisit the past. According to your letter, we have much more important things to discuss."

Cara looked embarrassed by his outburst. "Max, you must—"

"Must be anxious to be done with the duty of making polite conversation." Her elegant skirts swishing softly about her ankles, Olivia glided past him without so much as a sideways glance. "I shall leave the two of you with some much needed privacy."

As the door clicked shut, Davenport turned away from his sister's reproachful gaze and poured another measure of spirits.

"Max, that was unspeakably rude," she chided. "Lady Olivia will think you a savage—"

His mouth thinned in a cynical smile. "I assure you, the lady cannot form a worse opinion of me than she already has." Before Cara could respond, he picked up the poker and stirred the embers of the dying fire. "Curses be damned! You have a good deal of explaining to do."

The damnable attraction was hard to explain, even to herself. Repressing a sigh, Olivia found herself wondering whether she ought to catch the first ship back to Bombay. Perhaps if her body were transported halfway around the world, it would not be reacting in such an intensely physical way to the viscount.

She swallowed hard, trying to loosen the tightness in her throat. In India, she had been free to feast on all sorts of exotic treats, but her hunger for something more elusive had brought her back to England. What was it she craved? A taste of Davenport's mouth crushed to hers in a passionate kiss?

Her lips crooked. If so, she would likely die of starvation. . . .

Lord Ashton gave a discreet cough. "Er, it is your turn to discard, Lady Olivia," he said in a low murmur.

"Yes, of course." Forcing her thoughts back to the game, she stared blankly at her cards. "Let me think for a moment longer."

He patted her arm. "Don't tax yourself. We gentlemen know it is deucedly hard for you ladies to keep such a complicated count." A laugh punctuated his words. "Lose track myself sometimes."

Biting back an acid reply concerning profit projections and cost-base analysis, Olivia promptly slapped down the jack of spades to win the trick, then fanned the rest of her cards on the table. "I may be in error, but I believe that the rest of them are mine as well."

Ashton's face lost a bit of its smugness as he surveyed the winking of red diamonds. "No, er, that appears to add up right," he mumbled. After scratching down the score, he quickly gathered the deck and shuffled for a fresh hand.

"Will my cousin be joining us?" inquired Lord Haverstock as a footman set up the tea tray on the sideboard.

"Lady Cara begs you excuse her from the rest of the evening," she replied. "Her brother has just arrived and she wishes to give him a full accounting of the recent trouble."

"Ah. So Kipling has finally seen fit to grace us with his presence?"

"No, sir. It is the viscount who has come up from London."

"Max?" Haverstock's brows rose in skepticism. He waited for the servant to quit the room before adding, "I am surprised to hear he has stirred from his self-imposed solitude."

Lady Ranley, who had already shown herself to relish a bit of good gossip, nodded in agreement. "One of the most eligible men in Town, and yet he turns down every invitation that comes his way." She chose an iced pastry from the platter of cakes and took a bite. "Much to the chagrin of every mama with a daughter of marriageable age."

"I daresay he is still smarting over the scandal of his broken engagement," suggested Henniger as he dealt out a new round. "Though it's been well over a year."

Loath though she was to give any attention to idle chatter, Olivia could not help but look up sharply. "Scandal?"

"A very public jilting. It was the talk of the Town for months," explained Lady Ranley, with rather more enthusiasm than was seemly. "The chit led him on a merry dance, flirting shamelessly with every buck of the *ton* before accepting his suit. Then she left him at the altar in favor of a mere Mister—and one whose mother was a Cit at that."

"But a very wealthy Cit," drawled Henniger. "The fellow was rich as a nabob."

"Not to speak of possessing a great deal of polish and charm." The dowager dusted a few crumbs from her fingers. "While Davenport makes no effort to curry favor of those around him."

Olivia's lips gave a rueful purse. No doubt she was the only one of the group who saw such unyielding disdain for toadeaters as a mark in his favor.

"Soon after that, he returned to his regiment in Portugal, where misfortune struck again." Her finger exaggerated a slash through the air above her powdered cheek. "Nearly beheaded by a French dragoon. They say he's never quite recovered."

"Melancholy Max." His cousin sighed. "Believe it or not, he was not always so brooding. Indeed, he can be excellent company when he so chooses, for he has a keen intelligence and finely honed sense of humor."

"Well, he certainly seems to have lost any such admirable qualities somewhere along the way," said Henniger. He leaned across the table and lowered his voice to a confidential whisper. "According to rumors about Town, Lord Davenport is afraid to face Society on account of a hideous scar. Furthermore, word has it he drinks to excess and even partakes of . . . opium."

"Afraid?" Olivia's eyes took on the color of tempered steel as she fixed the gentleman with her most cutting look. Though the viscount's rudeness could be extremely irritating, it angered her to hear his character criticized by some fribble who had never squared off against anything more perilous than a round at Gentleman Jackson's boxing saloon. "How odd—I was under the impression that Lord Davenport is a highly decorated war hero, who risked life and limb for his country countless times over during the brutal Peninsular campaign."

Two spots of color came to Henniger's cheeks. "Er, yes, well, I didn't mean to imply—that is to say . . ."

"You are quite right, Lady Olivia. Max is certainly no coward. " Haverstock interrupted the other man's stuttering. "As for being disfigured, I confess I have not seen him since his return from the Peninsula, where he nearly lost an eye to a French saber, so perhaps that part of the rumor is true enough."

"Having met the viscount only an hour ago in Lady Cara's study, I can assure you his visage is perfectly pleasant." That was true enough, she added to herself. Save for when it was puckered in a scowl directed at her. Picking up her cards, Olivia snapped them into order. "The scar is still there, but it is only a faint white line."

"I am sure a good many young ladies will be vastly relieved to hear it," said Lady Ranley with a fluttery sigh. "Such a mark will only serve to make him more dashingly romantic in their eyes."

"All because of that idiot Byron and his dreadful poems." Haverstock shook his head and shrugged. "But enough talk of rogues and recluses. Shall we play?"

"Disappeared?" Davenport frowned as his fingers traced over his cheekbone.

"Both Kip and the Ruby Lion." Cara resumed her pacing before the hearth. "And that's not the worst of it. Mary Gooding appears to have gone missing as well."

It took a moment for him to realize that his sister was referring to the daughter of a neighboring farmer who, despite their differences in rank and gender, had been Kip's closest childhood friend. He vaguely recalled a skinny little sprite, whose dress had appeared to be in a perpetual state of disarray. "Little Maizy with the gap teeth? The chit who always seemed to have mud on her cheeks and ink on the end of her braids?" His expression deepened to disbelief. "Why, she's naught but a child. In any case, surely you are not suggesting she is in any way connected to Kip and the other problems at hand?"

"It's been nearly five years since you've laid eyes on Mary," reminded Cara. "She is no longer a gawky schoolgirl, but has grown into the belle of the village." Seeing the skepticism writ plain on his face, she added firmly, "Just as Kip is no longer a grubby schoolboy. They have been good friends since childhood. It seems a rather odd coincidence that they both are nowhere to be found."

"Look, just because the two of them were thick as thieves—"

"Max, this is nothing to joke about!"

"Forgive me, Cara, I know you are upset. And rightly so. But when you start speaking of ancient curses, exotic talismans, and spectral strangers, I find it difficult to view the matter in a serious light."

A very unladylike word sounded under her breath before she removed the key from the folds of her sash and stalked to her desk to unlock the top drawer. "Here, read this." She withdrew a folded sheet of paper and thrust it into his hand. "Perhaps it will help cast a different sort of illumination on recent occurances."

Davenport quickly skimmed over a neatly penned list, then lifted his eyes. "Where did you find this?"

"Hidden in the schoolroom, beneath the marble bust of Homer. It was where Kip was wont to keep the naughty penny prints and other secrets he didn't wish Papa or Mr. Tristan to find."

"Bloody hell."

"My sentiments exactly. It matches to the letter the list of items that Squire Tweeding told me were stolen from local estates over the last several weeks. Including the last entry—the Ruby Lion." Her fingers drummed the leather blotter. "And it is definitely Kip's handwriting, in case you were about to ask."

"No, I recognize it as well." After another perusal of the paper, he pursed his lips in thought, his military training in intelligence matters taking charge over emotion. "Hmmm. All of the pieces appear to have several things in common. They are quite small, making them easy to hide, and quite valuable, making them easy to turn into ready coin." There was a slight pause. "But even more interesting is the fact that they all seem to be Eastern in origin—from Persia or Belutshistan, by the sound of it." Davenport refolded the paper. "Have you any idea as to why?"

Cara shook her head. "Not a clue."

"Damn."

Her look of dismay deepened. "Max, I—I may have done a great wrong, but I did not tell the magistrate that the Ruby Lion had been stolen from Papa's study. I said that nothing was missing, save for a small ormolu clock and a silver inkwell." She swallowed hard. "And I certainly did not mention the list you are holding."

His fingers tightened, causing the paper to crackle in his grip.

"I know I should not lie, but—"

"You did the right thing, Cara. Until we can know more, it is best to keep such incriminating evidence to ourselves."

"Yet I fear that may not be possible. I am not the only one who has noticed Kip's odd behavior of late. He has been spotted at the Bull and Bear in the company of some unsavory strangers, and the stablehands have admitted that on most nights in the last month he has been out until dawn, his horse all muddied and lathered from being ridden hard." Davenport saw that her own hands were now clenched together. "Unless Squire Tweeding is a complete numbskull, he is bound to stumble upon such talk and begin asking some awfully uncomfortable questions."

"I, too, have some very uncomfortable questions to ask of our brother when I get my hands on him," muttered the viscount. "I don't know what sort of devilish pranks the young pup is up to, but I shall take a birch to his backside to thrash some sense into him—"

"This goes far beyond mere boyish pranks!" Cara bit at her lip. "I am at my wit's end, Max. I know in my heart that there is not an ounce of evil in Kip, but of late something terrible has come over him. The curse of the Ruby Lion—"

"Hell's teeth, Cara, that was a tale Uncle William told to frighten us children."

"He certainly succeeded. In spades." Hugging her arms around her chest, Cara gave a small shudder. "I have always disliked the dratted thing, staring out with those blood-red, unblinking eyes."

"And here I have written to my friend Sprague that you are a rational female."

At that, her look of dismay turned to one of defiance. "Well, look at Uncle William—he died shortly after returning from that trip to the East."

Davenport gave a snort of derision. "Uncle William suffered from a bad heart—exacerbated by a propensity to overindulge in spirits and . . . certain other strenuous activities."

Ignoring his sardonic humor, she went on, "Then there were your troubles."

"My troubles had naught to do with some ornamental lion," he growled.

"Whether caused by a curse or not, I am confused by what has happened, Max. And frightened."

"Why didn't you tell me of this sooner?"

"I did." Averting her eyes from his, she stared at the portrait of the two smiling young men. "But mayhap my earlier letters went astray."

There was an awkward silence. Davenport moved to the sidetable and poured himself a glass of brandy, though he knew the spirits would do little to douse his feelings of guilt. "I was in Ireland for some weeks, and then I—" Closing his eyes, he took a long swallow, letting the amber liquid burn a trail down his throat before going on. "Lud, Cara, I am sorry. I know I deserve to be raked over the coals for my neglect."

"And skewered with a red-hot pitchfork," she added with a faint glimmer of her usual forthright frankness. But as she turned and tried to smile, he saw her lips were trembling.

"What else can you tell me about Kip's behavior of late?"

"Only that he and Father had a terrible row on the eve before Father left for Scotland." She looked a bit guilty. "I—I couldn't help but overhear some of it. Kip asked for money, but Father refused to hand over so much as a farthing, accusing him of spending it on foolish pursuits, such as painting, not to speak of wasting his time with artists and other people beneath his station in life."

Davenport could well imagine the earl's unbending ire. Their father, a hard man in many ways, had always held very firm notions concerning family honor.

"Kip was told he should join the army—like you," continued Cara. "Or engage in manly risks like Uncle William, adventuring with a diplomatic mission to faraway places. Father told him those were the sorts of things that reflected well on the Bingham name, rather than putting a brush to canvas, or mooning about with lowborn females like Mary Gooding. As you can imagine, Kip did not react well. He stormed out, and when I tried to ask him why he needed the money, he refused to tell me." Though she tried to maintain a stoic face, her eyes were wet with tears. "Have you any idea what to make of it all?"

"Not yet." His hands came up to massage his temples. "Look, let me think it over. There has to be some reasonable explanation for all that has happened, and I shall find it." He did not add that the most obvious one seemed to be that their younger brother, for whatever the reason, had sunk into a life of crime.

"Thank you, Max. Although the facts looks grim as

of now, I know you will come up with a way to prove his innocence." She hesitated, then brushed a light kiss across his cheek. "But let it wait until morning. You've had a long and tiring journey."

Up close, he could make out the fine lines of worry and fatigue etched around his sister's eyes, and the sight caused another twinge of conscience. "You go on, Cara. I shall follow along shortly."

Yet as soon as he was alone, Davenport refilled his glass and slumped into the armchair by the hearth, rather than seeking his bed. Despite the numbing weariness in his bones, he had no illusions that sleep would come any time soon.

He had come home expecting to face one battle, not two. Cara's disquieting tale would test every ounce of his mettle. But at least it was a war worth winning. As for the sudden reappearance of Olivia Marquand into his life? That was a far more difficult conflict, for the real enemy was himself.

His hand clenched the glass, seeking to keep his defenses from crumbling. There was, he assured himself, no choice but to dig in and fight the attraction. Even if he wished to make peace, what terms could he offer? He was a scarred ex-soldier, with manners as rusty and jagged as an old cavalry saber. His only tangible assets were a modest title and an even more modest purse, for despite all of Cara's valiant efforts with the estate, the lands had yet to recover from years of neglect. And it would hardly help his cause that she had known him at the very lowest point in his life. He had changed a great deal since then, his self-confidence healing along with his face. But perhaps she would see only his former self. Or worse, a fortune hunter crawling around her skirts.

No, it was far better to remain as two opposing forces, rather than risk rejection yet again at the hands of a lady. Pressing the cold crystal to his brow, he stared into the fire. Even though a simmering desire was leaving him achingly aware that his body was at odds with his will.

Olivia.

It was a mellifluous sound, rolling off his tongue with a sinuous elegance, rather like the way the silk of her gowns rippled across the curve of her hips.

"Olivia," he whispered, the word hardly audible above the cracking of the logs. Then, as the heat of the spirits slowly spread from his throat to the rest of his limbs, he growled out an oath.

In that moment, he was more than ready to believe the Ruby Lion was carrying a damnable curse.

The last card fluttered down upon the pile.

"Well done, Lady Olivia. We have won yet another rubber," chortled Haverstock. "Ha, Ashton, it appears by my count that you and Lady Ranley owe us the grand sum of five shillings, tuppence."

Still looking rather dazed, the gentleman reached into his pocket and counted out the coins.

"We can switch to piquét, if you wish a chance to win back your blunt," suggested Haverstock with a sly smile.

"Only if we can switch partners as well. Forgive me for saying so, but I would rather find myself pitted against Captain Sharpe himself than play opposite you for another hand, Lady Olivia." Ashton dabbed a handkerchief to his forehead. "Luck has certainly been on your side tonight."

Feeling that Fate—in the form of an aloof aristocrat—was actually aligned against her, Olivia shook her head and pushed back from the table. "It is well known that Fortune is notoriously fickle, so if you will excuse me, I think I shall retire for the night."

It was, however, not any feeling of fatigue that had her seeking the refuge of her bedchamber. Assuring her maid with a few quiet words of Hindi that she preferred to disrobe in solitude, Olivia sent her off to the servant quarters for the night. There was no argument from the Punjabi woman, who was well-accustomed to her employer's habits, only a low bow and the whisper of her bare feet on the carpet.

Once alone, Olivia took a moment to light a stick of incense in front of the small bronze statute of Buddha that sat on the dressing table. God forbid that the local curate would ever get wind of such heresy, but the ritual of spending a brief interlude in quiet contemplation had a calming effect on her senses. Over the years, she had come to have a high regard for Eastern philosophy, and its teachings regarding the harmony of mind and spirit.

At the moment, however, her own head and heart were in distinct discord. Unpinning her hair, she took up the ivory-handled brush and tried to relax into the rhythm of the strokes. But after several snagged attempts, she found herself too restless to sit still. Gathering the tresses back into a simple coil, she plucked up a shawl from the back of her chair and stole quietly down the back stairs.

From the pantry hallway, it was only a short distance to the set of glass doors leading out to the gardens. Muffling the click of the latch with her wrap, she slipped outdoors, welcoming the cool breeze on her face. She had yet to readjust to English homes, with their stifling heat by the roaring fires and damp chill pervading the rest of the rambling spaces. Indeed, it had been uncomfortably warm in the drawing room. Still feeling flushed, she brought her hands to her cheeks. One of the footmen must have been a bit too zealous in stirring the flames.

But as heat slowly suffused her fingertips, coursing up her arms and down her legs, Olivia once again found herself consumed by thoughts of Lord Davenport.

Damn her maddening body!

And his.

The hardening of his handsome features had been eloquent enough in expressing his displeasure, even without the gruff growl.

Despite their differences, she had thought that a camaraderie of sorts had been forged between them during the last, desperate moments when they had foiled the plot of a diabolical traitor. A bond based on mutual respect, for they both possessed an unbending strength of character that set them apart from the crowd. Obviously, she was mistaken, and it had been no more substantial than the wisp of fog now drifting in and out of the boxwood hedge.

In retrospect, she should not be surprised. Why, he

had not even bothered to pay a courtesy call on her in Town, once the enemy had been apprehended and the danger had passed. Not a note, not a casual word conveyed through their mutual friends.

Not a bloody thing.

She, of all people, ought to be pragmatic enough to know what that meant—like the vast majority of men, the viscount preferred bidability in a lady, rather than any show of spirit or intelligence. Which most certainly did not auger well for them ever getting along with each other.

Drawing her shawl a bit tighter around her shoulders, Olivia quickened her pace, leaving the house behind. It was not quite so easy to distance herself from disappointment. It held fast, cold and clammy, like the drops of moisture clinging to her lashes.

With an angry sweep of her sleeve, she brushed them away and marched on.

Thank Buddha—along with Shiva, Vishnu, and all the deities on high—that she did not need the approval of any male to go on as she pleased. More than enough of her youth had been spent in conflict with a domineering father. She had finally escaped from under his thumb, taking enormous risks to achieve the money and freedom to control her own destiny. She would much rather be alone than consider subjecting herself to such male tyranny again. . . .

"I would not advise continuing along this way, memsahib. It leads to the forest."

Olivia's head came up with a jerk.

"Better to take the fork to the right." Her longtime

servant materialized from out of the mist and fell in step beside her.

"We are in England, not Utan, Vavek. It is quite safe for me to take an evening stroll without a body-guard." She smiled. "There are no tigers or cobras lurking on the lawns of Yorkshire."

"No, memsahib," he agreed. His bejeweled fingers stroked through his beard, then settled on the hilt of the dagger hidden beneath his tunic. "But wild beasts are not the only creatures that prowl the night."

Her steps slowed. "You have seen something out here?"

"Shadows." His eyes darted toward the row of pear trees. "Strange shadows."

"In a foreign land, many things may appear strange. That does not mean they are dangerous."

He gave a slight lift of his shoulders but made no move to leave her side.

Olivia frowned yet could not help feeling a sudden prickling at the back of her neck. On more than one occasion, her servant's uncanny ability to sense trouble had saved her from dire consequences.

"Oh, very well, if you insist," she sighed, turning back the way he had indicated. As nothing seemed to be going her way that evening, the best course of action seemed a prudent retreat.

Chapter Four

❧❧❧

"You are bamming me."

"Unfortunately, I am in deadly earnest," said Davenport.

The morning had not shed any new light on the facts, but at least it had brought with it the arrival of his old army comrade, Spencer Sprague. A number of fellow officers found Sprague's blunt speech and barracks humor too caustic for comfort, but over the course of the grueling Peninsular campaigns, the viscount had come to have a high opinion of the other man's down-to-earth common sense when faced with a challenge. So much so that he had barely allowed his friend to kick the dust from his boots and unpack his valise before suggesting a ride out over the moors.

"Hmmph." Sprague took some time to adjust his stirrup before turning in his saddle and quirking a brow. "You know, there are rumors flying around Town about the Valiant Viscount," he drawled. "Dark whispers concerning the demons of drink and the perils of the poppy."

"Sod the rumors. I am neither soused in spirits or addicted to opium." Davenport reined his stallion to a halt. "Though I admit, the story I've just told you sounds like the ravings of an utter lunatic."

His friend grinned. "It does appear you have a vivid imagination. Perhaps you should consider a career as an author, now that your soldiering days are over. I am told by my cousin that gothic tales of melodrama are all the crack these days."

"Stubble the jokes," growled the viscount. "And leave off calling me by that ridiculous nickname if you don't want your deadlights darkened."

"Very well, enough banter for the nonce." Sprague's expression slowly sobered. "Let us go over the facts once more. You say this Ruby Lion was brought back from Persia by your uncle?"

"When we were naught but sprats, the old fellow took great delight in frightening us with some story about an ancient curse attached to the damned thing. Such silly tales had long ago slipped from my mind, but apparently Cara never quite forgot the lurid details. And when she found it had been stolen, her fears took on a greater urgency."

"Is that why she wrote to you?"

"It was one of the reasons. She had already begun to suspect that something shady was going on."

"Ah, yes. The specters." Davenport could see that his friend was trying very hard to maintain a neutral expression. "She claims to have them prowling in the woods?"

"No," he replied somewhat defensively. "She was merely repeating what Kip told her."

"Hmmph." The grunt was eloquent in its skepticism.

"I know, I know. It seems absurd. And yet, the other objects that have gone missing are of foreign origin. . . ." Even to his own ears, the observation sounded rather lame. After all, the vast majority of the objets d'art decorating English manors had been brought back from abroad. His friend's silence seemed to confirm that such a theory was naught but a wild goose chase. "So," he demanded. "What are you thinking?"

"Probably much the same as you are." Sprague shrugged. "I assume you didn't invite me out here to listen to a string of toadeating platitudes, so I'll be frank. The most likely explanation is that your brother fell in with a bad set in Town. Like a good many other young cubs, he was probably drawn into running up debts he couldn't pay off. He quarreled with your father over money, and when the earl refused to bail him out of the River Tick, he became desperate."

"It fits together logically," admitted Davenport. "Indeed, it's a rather clever plan that he and Mary Gooding came up with. The girl must have a friend working as a maid or tweenie in nearly every estate in the area, so it would be easy to learn where the valuables were kept and what part of the house would afford an undetected entrance."

"And on top of all that, your brother would be one of the last people the authorities would suspect of committing such a crime," pointed out Sprague. "He could count on them chasing after shadows, or, with any real luck, stumbling onto some other petty thief and charging him with the misdeeds."

The viscount gave a bleak nod.

"I'm sorry, Max. If I could think of any other plausible alternative, I should be quick to voice it."

"My family travails are hardly your fault."

There was a short silence as Sprague watched a lone hawk soaring above the heathered hills. "So, what are you going to tell your sister?"

"The truth."

His friend winced. "I consider myself a loyal friend, and a stalwart soldier, but it would take a regiment of bayonets at my arse to get me to accompany you on that mission. Take care to bring along a very large bottle of vinaigrette and plenty of fresh hankies."

"No, no—Cara is not the sort of female to fall into a fit of vapors," protested Davenport. "I have given you the wrong impression. She's a solid, sensible young lady, with a very practical head on her shoulders. If truth be told, since my father has little interest in the day to day affairs of the estate, she has been handling things in my absence for several years now. And with great skill, I might add."

"Hmmph." The other man made a scoffing sound. "Don't care for managing females. In my experience, they are more trouble than they are worth."

Reminded of a certain other lady, the viscount could not refrain from making a face. "I heartily agree," he muttered. "Though Cara is . . . different."

"Sisters don't count," replied Sprague with a faint grin. Shading his eyes to the sun, he gave one last look around the craggy moors. "Come, we had best be heading back, seeing as you promised her we would join the guests for supper and the evening's entertainment."

"Aye, I suppose you are right."

"I'm surprised you agreed to the request. Thought

you had sworn off any interest in the petticoat line."
Sprague's expression turned slyly speculative. "But
mayhap you have changed your mind?"

Davenport shook his head. "You can be damn sure I
have not."

"Well, I am not loath to admit I wouldn't mind a
closer acquaintance with Miss Hanford. With that
tumble of auburn curls and saucy smile, she looks to
have a bit of a spark about her. And then there is the
raven-haired beauty. There seems to be an intriguing
air of mystery about her. . . ."

The viscount's hands tightened on the reins. There
was no mystery surrounding his own feelings. He
would gladly have paid a king's ransom to avoid the
coming encounter with Cara. Or, for that matter, with
any of the ladies present at Saybrook Manor.

Most particularly a certain raven-haired beauty

Speak of the devil.

Davenport forced his eyes up from the plunging
neckline. "I should have thought that you would want
to assume a more muted color," he said gruffly.

"You don't approve of saffron?" Olivia regarded him
coolly from over the rim of her champagne glass. "As I
recall, you didn't appear to care for red either."

He stared down at the drink in his hand. Not that
it helped distract him from thoughts of her stunning
décolletage. He seemed to recall having read that the
rounded curves of the cóupe were based on the exact
shape of Diane de Poitier's breast.

His hand tightened around the stem. "All I meant
was that it might be prudent to consider wearing less

vibrant hues in order to keep from stirring up old gossip."

"I assure you, my scarlet past is all but forgotten. New scandals always spring up to take the place of the old." She gave a cynical shrug. "In the minds of the *ton,* the Lady in Red has already faded away to a very dull shade of pink."

"Hmmph." The viscount took a moment to study her reflection in the mullioned glass. Lud, she was even more beautiful than he had remembered. Throughout the meal, it had been a fight to keep his eyes off of her.

He had meant to avoid her in the drawing room, too, but they had somehow ended up alone by the bowfront window, while the rest of the party had drifted off to view a portfolio of landscape etchings brought down from the library. Caught in the swirl of a light breeze, the scent of her perfume stirred an unsettling awareness of her closeness. Jasmine. Spiced with hints of clove and a sweetness he could not name. . . .

With a brusque cough, he cleared his throat. "And have you given up your involvement in trade, along with your penchant for red? It may be that your current choice of fashion raises no embarrassing questions, but I rather doubt the *ton* will be quite so tolerant of your business interests, should they become public knowledge."

"I don't need you to lecture me on how to go about in Polite Society, Lord Davenport. Regardless of what you seem to think, I am well aware of the rules governing a lady's behavior," she replied tartly. "I still own Grenville and Company, and oversee the major decisions. However, I have entrusted the day-to-day operations to my business manager. It is all very discreet."

"I did not mean to sound . . . critical, Lady Olivia."

His words brought a glint of ironic amusement to her eyes. "No?"

The effervescence of the wine suddenly felt like a regiment of tiny sabers pricking into his tongue. Even to his own ears, he had come off sounding like a pompous prig. And yet, he didn't dare allow himself to be seduced into letting his guard down. No matter that he found himself wishing that, just for once, they might sheath their swords. . . .

The approach of his sister saved him from having to make an actual reply.

"Lady Olivia, I've not yet had the chance to say how pleased I was to discover that you and Max are friends."

"I am not really sure you could call us that," murmured Olivia, lowering her lashes. "Perhaps . . . passing acquaintances would be a more precise way to put it, seeing as our contact was purely . . . professional." Although her expression remained neutral, her voice had a faint mocking edge. "Wouldn't you agree, sir?"

So it was back to cutting remarks. Davenport finished off his champagne in one swallow. "Just so, Lady Olivia," he drawled, exaggerating the curl of his lip. "Quite fleeting—like ships sailing by in the night."

He thought he detected a slight flush, but other

than that, she appeared unruffled by the thinly veiled reference to her mercantile fleet. The same could not be said for Cara, who looked clearly taken aback by his deliberate curtness.

"Why, Max," she chided, fixing him with a quizzical frown. "Lady Olivia is going to think you unconscionably rude—"

"Not at all," interrupted Olivia. "You needn't apologize for your brother's manner." She still had not looked his way. "Passing though the acquaintance might be, I have come to expect blunt speaking from Lord Davenport."

His glass clinked down on one of the sidetables. "Excellent. Then you will take no offense if I excuse myself. I promised Sprague that once our duty was done with the guests, we could spend the rest of the evening at billiards." Without waiting for a response from either lady, he stalked off.

"I have no idea what is prompting Max to behave so badly," apologized Cara, her face still scrunched in embarrassment. "He is not usually so lacking in manners."

Out of the corner of her eye, Olivia could see that the viscount's spine was still stiff as steel as he moved across the room. She had no trouble guessing the reason for his surly mood, but she did not see fit to mention it was due to her presence. "No doubt your brother has a number of more pressing concerns on his mind than playing host to a houseful of strangers."

"That does not excuse his actions. Especially as you are most definitely not a stranger," insisted his sister.

"Even a rakehell rogue like Lord Branford can comport himself like a perfect gentleman. Max should manage it as well." Cara plucked at her sash as she crooked a rueful smile. "I suppose it is a distinct advantage to be sinfully handsome and have a certain aura of intrigue."

"It makes for a potent combination—what woman wouldn't be tempted to swoon at such a man's feet," murmured Olivia. "And yes, you are quite right. There is no question that the Earl of Branford can be devilishly charming when he wants to be."

"Unlike my bear of a brother, who insists on snapping and snarling as if a thorn were stuck up his . . . paw."

Olivia managed not to burst into outright laughter. "With that tawny mane and amber eyes, I would more liken the viscount to a grumpy lion."

"Whatever the animal, his behavior has been beastly."

"Actually, he has good reason to be acting annoyed at my reappearance into his life. As you heard, I caused him a good deal of trouble last time we were together."

Cara made a face. "I am of the opinion that Max ought to consider himself the most fortunate of men to have made your acquaintance."

"I doubt he would agree," she said softly.

The young lady looked unconvinced. "I can't help but imagine how frightfully exciting it must have been for you and Lady Branford! To think of matching wits against a cunning adversary . . ." Cara's mouth screwed into a self-mocking grimace. "While my biggest enemy is the load of manure that must be shifted from the stables to the fields."

"It was not quite so glamorous as you think," assured Olivia. "We made a number of foolish mistakes and were lucky to escape any real harm. Thanks in no small measure to the courage and resourcefulness of Branford and your brother."

"I have yet to meet Alex's wife. She must be a remarkable lady to have reformed such a notorious rogue."

"You would like her very much. The two of you have much in common."

"Ha! No more than chalk and cheese." Cara's expression turned even more wry. "Max says she is both brilliant and beautiful. As you see, I am not overly endowed with either such sterling quality." A small sigh slipped out. "Indeed, if I had any brains at all, I might not have needed to worry Max about . . ." The rest of the words trailed off as she lifted her glass to her lips. "Forgive me. I am beginning to sound not only like a peagoose, but a shrew."

"I am quite sure you are neither," said Olivia quietly, taking note of how tightly the other lady's fingers were clenched around her glass. "I would venture to guess that the trouble is more serious than a minor burglary."

"You are right," admitted the viscount's sister. "Ours is not the only estate that has been broken into over the last few months, and a number of valuable artifacts have gone missing." She bit at her lip, seeming to debate the prudence of offering further explanation. But after a flicker of hesitation, she added, "I have reason to suspect that our younger brother may know more about the matter than he should."

"Hmmm." Olivia studied the random swirl of bubbles in her champagne. "What does Kipling have to say in regard to your concerns?"

"That is part of the problem." Cara blinked. "You see, he has disappeared as well."

"That certainly adds a very disquieting note of intrigue."

"Oh, I assure you, the story gets even more lurid than a horrid novel. I have yet to make mention of the Ruby Lion and its ancient curse, or the strange shadows said to be stalking the area."

"Strange shadows?" Olivia's head jerked up.

"Yes, on top of everything else, Kip claimed to have seen . . . something prowling in the woods." Despite the attempt at self-deprecating humor, it was clear that that young lady was deadly serious about all she had recounted. "Though he is being rather diplomatic, I have a feeling Max thinks I've taken leave of my senses."

Olivia could not repress a quirk of a smile. "As your tale is no more bizarre than the one he heard from Alex and the Hadley clan, I trust he will not be quick to dismiss it."

"But I have no proof. Only . . . intuition."

"I would also hope that the experience of last year has given him a healthy respect for feminine logic." That was, perhaps, a slight exaggeration, but Cara looked as though she could use some encouragement. "From what I have seen, Lord Davenport may not have the most polished manners, but he possesses a keen analytical mind and a knack for sorting through difficult conundrums. I am sure you can count on him to figure out what is going on."

"Yes, no doubt you are right." Cara lifted her chin. "You have been more than kind to lend a sympathetic ear."

"I should be happy to do more than that. If there is anything I might do to help in—" She left off with a discreet cough as Lord Haverstock came up behind his cousin.

"Come, you ladies have spent enough time discussing the latest fashions and furbelows." He moved around to offer them each an arm. "Can I tempt you into sitting down to a hand of whist?"

"You two go on." Olivia stepped aside. "If you don't mind, Lady Cara, there is a copy of *La Belle Assemblee* in your study that I have been wishing to examine more closely."

"By all means. I am sure you are anxious to study the latest style of bows for bonnets."

"Indeed, I am simply knotted in anticipation."

The subtle teasing went right over the gentleman's head. He gave an indulgent smile, then pursed his lips. "And I was so looking forward to relieving Henniger of another hefty sum."

"Luck is no substitute for experience," replied Olivia with an enigmatic smile. "Enjoy your game."

Swearing under his breath, Davenport reached for the decanter of red wine, hoping to wash away the sour taste in his mouth. He hadn't meant to imply he disapproved of her choice of colors. Quite the opposite. To his eyes, a bold palette—rich ruby, spicy saffron, iridescent indigo—suited her perfectly, accentuating her creamy complexion and jet-dark hair. In comparison, the other young ladies looked rather washed out in their demure pastels, the shades too pale to create any hint of individuality.

"You have every gentleman in the room looking daggers at you." Sprague came up to join him at the sideboard.

And at least one lady. The viscount took a long sip of the claret.

"Stealing a march on the rest of us, eh?" continued his friend. "Can't say I blame you for having a change of heart concerning females." He slanted an appreciative glance at Olivia, then grinned. "The lady is a stunner."

"Neither my heart nor my intentions have shifted a whit," snapped Davenport. "She's merely an . . . acquaintance, and as such, manners dictated that I pay her a civil greeting."

"Ah." Sprague also helped himself to a measure of claret. "So no interest in pursuing the lovely Lady Olivia?"

"None at all," he replied through gritted teeth. "I told you. I'm not looking for any involvement with a lady, especially one who possesses such a stubborn streak of independence. And I assure you, none is more so than . . ." He cut off abruptly, swallowing any further explanation along with the rest of his wine.

"Sounds rather intriguing."

"Lud, you don't know the half of it," muttered Davenport.

"Well, now that you have piqued my curiosity, I am certainly not going to let you leave it at that." His friend refilled both of their glasses. "Just how did you meet her?"

There was a slight hesitation before he replied. "Through Alex. If you recall, I told you about the investigation he undertook for Anthony Taft—"

"The bare bones of it," said his friend, darting another look at the lady. "But apparently you neglected to flesh it out with all the juicy details."

Davenport was irritated to find a flush of heat stealing to his face. "As it involved certain delicate matters of state, Tony has sworn us to secrecy concerning much that happened. Suffice it to say Lady Olivia joined forces with the former Miss Hadley—now Alex's wife—and both ladies proved helpful in seeing that a traitor to the Crown was apprehended."

"If Lady Olivia is anything like Lady Branford, it will take a very brave man to face up to such a challenge." Sprague chuckled. "Brains and beauty—it is a daunting combination in a female. Though I must say, Alex does not seem to be having any regrets."

Indeed he does not, thought Davenport glumly.

"And I can well imagine that a fiery spirit affords a number of, er, interesting diversions," added Sprague with a roguish grin.

His temper already dangerously frayed, the viscount caught himself on the verge of snapping altogether. "Put a damn cork in it, Spencer," he warned. "Branford would no doubt darken your deadlights if he heard you speculating about his relationship with his wife—in or out of bed." Setting aside his empty wine glass, he turned for the door. "So let us drop the subject, shall we, and move on to billiards. The growl became more pronounced. "Or I just might do it for him."

The look on the viscount's face was enough to assure Sprague that, unlike his own words, the threat was no jest. "Very well." Assuming a more sober mien, he made to follow along. There was, however, a lingering twitch at the corners of his mouth. "If anything is to be thumped, I prefer it be a clutch of ivory balls rather than my peepers."

Leaving Howland and Cara to join the rest of the party, Olivia hurried down the hallway and slipped into the deserted study, grateful that the solitude afforded a chance to collect her thoughts. She usually had no trouble at all maintaining a cool composure, no matter what the situation. But for some reason, the viscount, for all his brooding scowls, continued to kindle an odd spark of . . .

Of what?

Turning her face to the fire, she watched the flames licking up from the logs and felt the same quixotic heat flare inside her. After a moment, she pressed her palms to her burning cheeks and swore softly in Hindi. She had long ago sworn to steer clear of emotional attachments. It had been a bruising struggle to break free from the fetters of her bullying father. In daring to make her own way in the world, she had come to rely on reason and logic. Over the years, she had managed to build a very comfortable life for herself through the exercise of an iron will and an uncanny knack for numbers and logistics.

This strange stirring of desire was definitely not part of the equation.

Being far more skilled with sums than words, she

was having difficulty articulating the attraction, even to herself. It was definitely not on account of any practiced charm on Davenport's part—he had none to speak of! Yet despite his outward show of rudeness and rigidity, he had a depth of character she had never encountered before. Indeed, he was perhaps the most honorable man she had ever met.

During the war he had been dubbed the Valiant Viscount by the London newspapers on account of his exploits in battle. In their hunt for the traitor, she had seen firsthand a display of his admirable qualities. *Loyalty. Courage. Integrity.* A sigh squeezed from her lips. Lud, she of all people knew how rare it was to meet a flesh-and-blood hero. Over the years of building her business, she had met so many scoundrels and liars, she had come to believe such a person could exist only as a dribble of ink on the pages of a novel.

But Davenport? Davenport made her forget such cynicism. Like the naive schoolgirl she had never been, she found herself yearning to win his respect, his regard, his . . . Olivia gave herself a shake. As one who prided herself on having her feet planted firmly on the ground, she was in danger of letting her head drift up into the clouds.

Perhaps, she thought with grim humor, the attraction was merely physical—a passing ailment, like a fever or cartagh. It was impossible to deny that Davenport had a powerful animal magnetism. Lean and lithe, he moved with the sort of whipcord grace that brought to mind a stalking lion. The thick mane of dark blond hair, worn unfashionably long, only reinforced the image. As did his eyes, which were an unusual shade of intense amber. In her experience, most men who possessed such good looks showed a certain self-absorbed awareness of their appeal. Davenport's sensuality was all the more alluring for the fact that he seemed unconscious of his effect on women.

Her mouth crooked in a rueful twist. On second thought, he seemed not only unaware of her interest, but quite consciously determined to convey how little he cared for her regard. It was usually she who had to discourage unwanted admirers. To find the position reversed was rather unnerving. Stepping back from the hearth, she began to pace along the length of the carpet, her expression taking on an even more cynical bent. Was that, perchance, part of the allure?

There was no denying that she had always been attracted to a challenge. But she knew in her heart it was not a game that had her longing to break through his stiff reserve. She had seen hints of a much different man beneath the shell of grim aloofness. His exchanges with his friend Branford had revealed a quick wit and a finely honed sense of humor. And, on the rare occasions when he had actually allowed his lips to bend upward, a sinfully sexy smile.

Damn. A liquid shiver tingled at her core. Mayhap the only way to get over the maddening distraction was to sleep with the dratted man! A night of passionate lovemaking might serve to quench the strange current of desire thrumming through her veins. And then she could turn her thoughts back to business.

Crossing her arms across her chest, Olivia felt her fingers dig into bare flesh. She was no stranger to physical pleasure. In India, the languorous climate and mixing of cultures had created an atmosphere where the strictures of Society were a good deal looser than in England. A more adventurous attitude was permitted—assuming, of course, that one was discreet about it. She had taken a lover, and although the affair had been temporary, she had enjoyed the intimate interludes, the feeling of senses aroused and limbs entwined.

She choked back a throaty laugh. Just how would the viscount react if she were to enter his chamber, naked beneath a thin shift of silk, and slide between his sheets?

With a roar of disgust, most likely.

Heaving a harried sigh, she turned for the door, deciding it was time to seek out her own bed. Despite the fact that it was going to be cold and empty.

❧❧❧

Chapter Five

"The curse of the Ruby Lion!"

"Damnation, Cara! I wish you would stop saying that." Davenport balled the sheet of paper and flung it into the fire. "I know you to be an intelligent person, but if you keep jabbering on about such nonsense, I will be forced to revise my opinion on the female capacity for rational thought."

"You may hurl all the insults you want." Her chin rose defiantly. "But that does not change the truth. Nor, for that matter, does simply tossing the evidence onto the coals because it does not agree with your own opinion."

"Sorry." He watched the last of the letter turn to ash. "Forgive me for snapping at you. We are both overset at the moment, but let us try to maintain a modicum of common sense in considering what has happened. Accidents do occur, unrelated to ancient curses. Or black magic, or wiccan spells, or—"

A glare from his sister caused him to let the rest of his sarcasm trail off.

The letter had been delivered just after dawn. A groom had ridden through the night from Scotland, arriving muddied and exhausted with the grim news that their father lay hovering near death, the victim of a snapped girth while hunting on the moors. Davenport turned toward the window, not wishing for Cara to see the deepening of his dismay. It was, he assured himself, an unfortunate coincidence. That such an accident should take so soon after the dratted artifact had disappeared was due to mere chance, and not anything more ominous.

Yet his jaw slowly tightened. He most certainly did not believe in occult powers, but, loath though he was to admit it, neither did he believe in coincidence. It was all too convenient an explanation for a string of suspicious events that had suddenly befallen the Bingham family, and his experience in military intelligence had taught him to be very skeptical of easy explanations.

"Accidents do happen," muttered Cara. "But doesn't it bother you just a little that so many of them have occurred in such a short span of time? It said in the letter that one of the other riders saw something in the mists that appeared to spook Father's horse." She drew in a deep breath. "There is something at work here that goes beyond mere happenstance."

Davenport started at hearing his own uncertainties voiced aloud.

"Something evil," she intoned.

"Cara—"

Her hands set on her hips. "And don't tell me I am waxing melodramatic, or I swear, I—I shall plant you a facer!"

He flashed a rueful grin in spite of the seriousness of the situation. "Seeing as it was I who taught you the fundamentals of pugilism, I am well aware that you throw a very credible punch. But you should also try to remember that if you mean to hit someone, it is not a good idea to give fair warning."

"I shall keep that in mind." The attempt at a smile ended in an uncertain quivering of her lips. "Oh, Max. I am not ashamed to admit that I am very frightened. Kip is no thief. But he's in deep trouble—I just know it in my heart. And Lady Olivia says we females should trust—"

"Lady Olivia!" Davenport's head jerked around. "What the devil does she have to do with this?"

"Nothing, really," replied Cara. "Save for that she has made me feel at ease in talking about things more important than the state of the weather or the shape of a bonnet. I find her to be a lady of shrewd intelligence and insight. And she offered sage advice—"

"Bloody hell, Cara! You hardly know the lady. You should not be confiding family problems to a near stranger."

"You and Alex appeared to have every confidence in her abilities," countered his sister.

"That was different," he growled.

"Well, I trust her, too. Even on short acquaintance, it's clear she is a very sensible and pragmatic lady. What's more, I like her." She paused in her pacing. "Don't you?"

"That has nothing to do with the matter." Consternation caused his voice to grow even rougher.

Cara cocked her head. "She's right. You do tend to sound like a lion with a thorn in his backside when—"

His fist came down upon the desk. "I don't give a fig for what Lady Olivia thinks of me." Realizing he was perilously close to shouting, Davenport paused to inspect the book that lay by his hand. Finding it naught but a volume on wildflowers, he shoved it aside. "And let us not stray from the subject," he said in a more moderate tone. "Believe me, I have been trying to make sense of all you have told me, and I can see no explanation—save for the obvious one."

"Then you must look harder!" Her pacing became more agitated. "I am leaving for Scotland as soon as my cases are packed, but we cannot abandon Kip to whatever horrible fate he is facing. Not without a fight."

Davenport's teeth clenched so tightly his molars were in danger of cracking. "You cannot think I would turn my back on my own family?"

Her face had gone very pale. "In truth, we have seen so little of you, I'm not quite sure what to think. I am not sure I know you anymore."

The weight of guilt caused him to slump into the chair. "Christ Almighty. I . . ." He wasn't sure how to go on.

"Just as you cannot know what sort of man Kip has grown into. He is a good one, I swear. Sensitive, gentle, and artistic—more so than Father would like. As I told you, it had become quite a bone of contention between them over the last several years. Father was constantly admonishing him to leave off his painting and his friendship with the artistic set in Town, and . . . show the steel of a true English gentleman. Like his older brother."

Davenport's eyes squeezed shut, not that he could blind himself to the fact that she should not have to be explaining this to him.

"Father kept railing at him for lacking the spunk and grit of a real Bingham. Mayhap this is about Kip rebelling against such high expectations. I don't know," she sighed. "But one thing I am certain of is that the Max of old would fight like a lion to protect his brother and sister."

"And I shall do so now. Down to the last tooth and nail."

Cara came up beside him and brushed a lock of hair from his scarred cheek. "You have been like a lion. But one who has spent too long holed up in his den, licking his wounds. It's time to come out from the shadows."

"And what would you know of shadows?" he whispered bleakly.

"Enough to understand they can engulf you in blackness. But only if you let them."

He watched the play of the early morning sun upon the patterned carpet, then turned away from the mullioned windows.

"Promise me you will find Kip. And the Ruby Lion, for somehow I have a feeling it will prove a key to solving the mystery."

"I give you my word on it, Cara. I will not fail to unearth the truth, whatever it is," he answered. His eyes closed for an instant. "But I cannot promise that you will like what comes to light."

"Sorry to hear the news about Uncle Charles. Terrible shock." Haverstock adjusted his coat collar. "Er, figured I could be of most help at the moment by arranging for all of us to leave you in peace."

Davenport acknowledged the words with a slight nod as a traveling barouche lumbered up the front drive. "I regret that your party has been asked to make such a hasty departure."

His cousin waved off the apology. "Hardly appropriate for the gathering to continue under the circumstances." There was a slight scuffing sound as he shifted his weight. "This is deucedly awkward to bring up, but as I haven't had a chance to speak to you in private, I feel I would be remiss if I left without bringing a certain matter to your attention." A sidelong glance seemed to seek permission to go on.

Clasping his hands more tightly behind his back, Davenport nodded for him to continue.

"Thought you might care to know that Kip has been keeping company with a reckless crowd in London. A set that seeks its pleasures in the more, er, disreputable parts of Town. There have been rumors of gaming hells and brothels, the sorts of places where one runs up debts that take a great deal more than a modest quarterly allowance to pay off." He coughed. "Didn't care to upset Cara with such news, but it was clear she was concerned about his absence. And, well, servants do talk. So I gather Kip took a rather abrupt—and heated—leave-taking from home."

The viscount muttered a low oath. Though it had been ages since he had left off wearing an eyepatch for his wound, it appeared he had been even more blind than he realized to the trouble stirring right under his nose.

"I'm sorry, Max. Forgive me if I have overstepped—"

"No." He heaved a harried sigh, deciding Cara's mild tongue-lashing had not been nearly so cutting as he deserved. "On the contrary, I appreciate your frankness, Richard. I—I should have been keeping a closer watch on the scamp."

"I daresay you had your hands full . . . what with the war and all."

His cousin might offer him excuses for such shameful neglect, but Davenport was well aware of his guilt. "Well, apparently it is time to turn my attention to a battle raging closer to home."

The arrival of Haverstock's valet put an end to the conversation. Directing the man to place the last portmanteau atop the trunks in the boot, Haverstock climbed inside his carriage and signaled the driver to be off. "Do let me know if I can be of any assistance," he said, his voice trailing off in the crunch of the wheels on the gravel.

The viscount watched the lumbering vehicle roll down the drive, then slowly returned to the entrance hall. There was just one more guest to see off. Not that he was looking forward to the duty, but at least it would make for one less distraction. As it was, he had quite enough problems to face without worrying whether his manners were causing offense.

A low sound rumbled in his throat. A lion with a thorn in his arse? He had a good mind to take a birch to his sister's backside for discussing him with Lady Olivia. . . . Although there was no sound, Davenport suddenly sensed a presence on the curved staircase. Looking up, he saw a flutter of cinnabar silk.

An instant later, a turbaned figure appeared, his

bare feet light as feathers upon the treads despite the heavy trunk on his shoulder. A thick beard and moustache, highlighted by a sheen of scented oil, hid the man's expression, but there was a slight stirring in his coffee-colored eyes as he met the viscount's gaze.

Davenport gave a curt nod of acknowledgment. He had met Vavek on several previous occasions, and had heard enough concerning the Indian's lethal skills with his bare hands to know the man was no ordinary servant.

There was a whisper of cloth, but Vavek remained silent as he padded by, merely inclining a fraction of a nod in return.

"Please convey my concern to your sister." Olivia's approach was nearly as noiseless. She had been waiting in the side parlor, and was now drawing on her gloves in preparation for the coming journey. "I am sorry I did not have the chance to bid her farewell before she left."

Davenport couldn't help but note how her hands moved with a sinuous grace, the fingers long and slender. Just as he couldn't help wondering what they might feel like touching his cheek. . . .

His jaw clenched. "She was anxious to be on the road as soon as possible," he replied, rather more harshly than he had intended.

"Understandably so." Olivia calmly shook out the folds of her cloak. "Still, I regret that I did not have the opportunity to pass on my regards. She is a very interesting—and intelligent—young lady."

The viscount's lip took on a sardonic curl. "You sound as if that surprises you."

"It does." In the subdued light of the hall, her gray eyes looked dark as rainswept slate.

There was a sliver of silence as he searched for some sufficiently caustic reply, but she went on before he had a chance to speak.

"But not for the reason you seem to think." Her tone was further evidence that he had set her back up. "Must you interpret everything I say as an insult? My words were not intended as any negative reflection on you, Lord Davenport. It is just that I find it rare to meet a lady whose spirit and imagination have not been put under tight rein. I should have been pleased to get to know her better."

"I have always encouraged Cara to think freely. However, she has enough unorthodox ideas in her head without you spurring her on."

"I shall certainly try not to be a bad influence on your sister if we should meet again." Olivia's face maintained its icy composure. "It is quite understandable for you to be worried—after all, you are one of the few people who are aware of my dirty little secrets."

Davenport drew in a deep breath. "I didn't mean—that is, I . . . respect what you have done with your life, Lady Olivia. I should not like for you to think otherwise."

She gave a chilly smile. "But naturally you do not approve of it." Before he could answer, she turned up her collar and moved toward the door. On reaching the threshold, she hesitated, then turned back to meet his lidded gaze. "Lady Cara left me with the impression that your father's accident is not the only family crisis you may be facing. Loath though you may be to accept it, I should be happy to offer any assistance I can."

"Thank you," he said with rigid politeness. "It is a magnanimous offer. Yet in all truth, I cannot imagine how you might be of help."

Steel striking flint. Davenport's jaw hardened as he watched her walk toward her carriage. Seeing as they seemed to throw off nothing but sparks when they rubbed together, it was just as well they were about to part ways. And yet, there had been a slight glimmering in all the heated words, an intriguing hint that she did not loath him. He felt a stab of regret that he could not pursue it.

But his family was his paramount duty, and he was an experienced enough officer to know how impossible it was to wage two campaigns at once.

"So, what do you intend to do first?"

"Damnation, Spencer, I haven't a clue. But I promised I would dig until I get to the bottom of it," answered Davenport. "And I will." He blew out a perfect smoke ring, then stared at the tip of his glowing cheroot. "No matter that I fear Cara will be terribly disappointed with what I uncover."

His friend nodded. "Likely to be a messy business. But I can't see as you have any choice."

"No." Looking upward, the viscount watched as the smoke pulled apart in the breeze and then disappeared, leaving no trace of its fleeting existence.

Surprised by the note of despondency, Sprague slanted a sideways look at his friend. "Perhaps I can be of some help in poking around."

"I can hardly ask you to get involved in such a sordid affair."

"I'm not in the habit of abandoning an old comrade, just because the going may get a trifle rough." He made a wry face. "Besides, it promises to be a good deal more interesting than dealing with straying sheep or leaky roofs back home." Grinding the butt of his cigar beneath his heel, Sprague stood up. "The devil take, Max, I'm bored with the life of a country squire. You would be doing me a great favor if you let me lend a hand."

"I would be grateful to have you along," acknowledged Davenport. "If only for the good company."

"Then come, scrape the mud from your boots and that hangdog expression from your face. I am not joining forces with you only to admit defeat before we begin. We may yet come upon fresh facts that will help clear your brother's name."

Davenport found his spirits buoyed by his friend's enthusiasm. Squaring his shoulders, he got to his feet. "You are quite right. One can never predict what will happen once the battle heats up. We both have seen how victory can often be snatched from the jaws of defeat."

The viscount was not feeling nearly so sanguine by the end of the following day. An interview with the local magistrate had elicited naught but the facts he already knew, and he had dared not press harder, for fear of raising suspicions that were best left unstirred. Nor did subsequent visits to several of the other burglared estates unearth any useful information. The owners had simply complained—loudly and at great length—over the scandalous state of society and the incompetence of the authorities.

The sun was dipping near the tops of the distant moors by the time Davenport and his friend came to the last of their rounds, a meeting with the father of Mary Gooding as he was returning from his fields. It did not begin as the most cordial of conversations, for though the farmer dared not show any overt hostility, it was clear he held Kipling Bingham responsible for the disappearance of his daughter.

The first bit of questioning yielded only muttered assurances that his daughter was a good girl, whose recent behavior had given no hint that any trouble was preying on her mind. But when pressed, Gooding admitted he had noticed young Mr. Bingham taking a queer turn of late. He then suggested that the viscount might want to make some inquiries at the local tavern, where Kipling had been spotted meeting with some strange company.

Davenport shifted in his saddle, finally feeling they had a real lead to pursue. "I'll have a talk with Hutchins and see if he overheard anything that might prove useful." A touch to the brim of his hat signaled to Sprague that he was ready to take his leave. "Just one last question. If Mary were in any sort of trouble, is there a close friend with whom she might seek shelter?"

Gooding's weathered face puckered in thought. "Well, she might have looked te Lizzie Stokes. Except fer Lizzie has been gone now fer nigh on six months. Got some fancy job in Lunnon."

"I see." The viscount gathered up his reins. "Thank you for your help. If you think of anything else, however small, send word to the Manor. In the meantime, I shall keeping looking. They cannot have vanished into thin air."

"Aye." The farmer gave a grudging nod. "Godspeed, then. I'm trusting in the Almighty that you will find a way to put things right, milord."

As he and his friend spurred their mounts toward the tavern, Davenport prayed that he was finally moving in the right direction. But despite having his goodwill lubricated by several tankards of his own ale and a discreet exchange of coins, Hutchins was of no help. The vague descriptions of Kip's companions could have fit any number of the travelers who passed through the area. And much to the barkeeper's chagrin, he had to admit that Kip had chosen a table tucked away in a far nook, so that eavesdropping had been impossible. All he could say for sure was that he had never seen the men before, and they did not look like the sort of company that young Mr. Bingham was accustomed to entertaining.

It did not make for a particularly pleasant ride back to the Manor, especially as a light but chilling drizzle started to fall soon after they left the tavern.

"Damn the devil to hell," swore Davenport as he stomped into the entrance hall and shook the rain from his coat.

"Not much to go on," admitted Sprague, who had remained tactfully silent throughout the journey home.

"Not much? There's not one single, bloody thing to

go on!" His dripping beaver hat skidded across the top of the sidetable, sending a shower of spray over a small bust of Aristotle. Glaring at the placid stone countenance, Davenport felt his own face twist in a more pronounced grimace. "And don't wax philosophic on patience and fortitude. Not when I am all too aware of the futility of trying to discover that which doesn't exist."

His friend drew him toward the study, where a large fire was burning in the hearth, then poured a measure of strong Scottish whiskey for both of them. "Very well, I shall foreswear spouting any such platitudes." Eying the viscount from over his glass, he gave a mock salute, then tossed back the spirits in one gulp. "Indeed, I don't plan on saying much of anything. It's been a long day and I mean to take off these wet clothes and get some sleep. I suggest you do the same."

"I shall."

Sprague's footsteps echoed down the darkened hallway, but rather than follow along, Davenport stayed with his boots propped up on the fireguard, staring down at the tiny trails of vapor rising from his sodden breeches. His hopes of helping Kip were also doomed to go up in smoke unless he could find some sort of clue as to where to start looking.

If such a clue even existed.

It had not been mere pique or fatigue that had prompted his outburst. Even Aristotle could not argue that black was white. And so far, the discouraging truth was that all the facts indicated that his brother was guilty. Pursuing some proof of innocence would likely be not only futile, but foolish.

Setting his glass aside untasted, Davenport moved to the desk. He had been a bigger fool for allowing his own personal problems to blind him to the trouble brewing at home. So until he had looked at the matter from every possible angle, he wasn't yet willing to concede the task was hopeless. Kip as a criminal? A part of him still could not believe it to be true. His hand went to the drawer. The one solid bit of evidence was the list Cara had found. Perhaps a more careful scrutiny would reveal something he had missed.

Smoothing out the paper, he fell to examining each entry, going so far as to try rearranging the letters to see if they might form an anagram. But after an hour spent, head in hands, hoping for some flash of inspiration, Davenport was forced to admit that his usual skill with such conundrums seemed to have temporarily deserted him.

Conceding defeat, he refolded the sheet and started to slide it under the blotter. Perhaps in the morning, a fresh perspective—

His eyes suddenly fell on a faint pencil scribble on the back of the page. Blinking, he bent low and slid the candle over to the edge of the paper. The spill of light revealed the cryptic notation of "Grshm. & Bl." followed by a circle with several markings inside it. A closer look showed it to be the face of a clock, the two hands sketched to indicate the hour of seven.

Puzzled, the viscount leaned back. The time of a meeting? But when? And perhaps even more importantly, where? The initial flare of excitement faded as he realized the discovery might prove too vague to be of any help.

As if in concert with his own dimming hopes, the case clock began its slow, doleful chiming. Annoyed by the interruption of his concentration, he directed a black look its way. As he waited for the sounds to die away, his gaze lingered on the ornate scrolled hands, the graceful numerals, the shifting moon, the enameled dial. . . .

Dial!

Seven. Dial. Seven Dials. It was an awfully long shot, but the symbol might possibly indicate one of the more notorious stews of London, a place well known for all manner of vice. He rose quickly and resumed his spot by the fire. Females weren't the only ones who trusted in intuition.

They were getting nowhere in Yorkshire. . . .

The more he thought about it, the more determined he became to set out for London at first light.

Chapter Six

❧❦❧

Olivia put down her pen. "It's quite unusual. Have you any idea as to its origins, Winslow?"

"Late seventeenth-century Ottoman," came the immediate reply. "By the color of the turquoise, I would guess it was made in Damascus." The man seated at the other desk then flicked a mote of dust from his cuff. "But I may be wrong on that—I've seen shades of a similar depth from as far east as Baghdad."

"What is it worth?"

Flashing a smile that bordered on a smirk, the man picked up the small, filigreed box and held it at arm's length. "A good deal more than I paid for it." Tucking it away in the pocket of his canary-yellow waistcoat, he heaved a long-suffering sigh. "It is fortunate I have been blessed with a gift for bargaining, as well as impeccable taste, seeing as I earn such a small pittance for my sweat and labors."

"You also have a gift for lying through your teeth," she remarked, her eyes dropping back to her ledgers.

His smile became more brilliant. "Ah, but such lovely teeth they are, don't you think? Pearly as the Gates of Saint Peter."

"And no doubt they are as close to Heaven as you shall ever get."

A peal of laughter rang out in answer. "Sad but true."

"Dare I ask where you found such a treasure?"

He gave an airy wave. "Oh, one of my usual sources. Though I must say, he doesn't often have such, er, fine merchandise in his possession."

Repressing what would have been a most unladylike chortle, Olivia tallied up the last of the columns on the page, then snapped the heavy leather covers shut. "Speaking of merchandise, Hevey and Tweeter wish to buy the entire shipment of cinnamon, but only if it arrives by the end of the month. And the American, Lockwood, is interested in discussing a joint venture for distributing tea in New York."

Her companion's face underwent a remarkable transformation. The look of languid ennui disappeared as his features sharpened and his mouth took on a firmer set. There was a change in his eyes as well, the soft, pastel blue deepening to azure and the gaze focusing into a hard-edged squint. "I have already sent Jervis around to the East India docks, to inquire of the newly arrived ships what weather conditions they encountered." He consulted a sheaf of papers. "Based on the prevailing winds at this time of year, and the fact that Bessemer is one of our best captains, there should be no problem with that date, barring any unforeseen storms. However, if we turn up any reason to think there may be a delay looming on the horizon, we have time to negotiate a compromise—say, perhaps, offering an added bonus of Ceylonese cloves to accept a late delivery."

Olivia nodded. "That sounds reasonable. I'll leave it to you to work out the details." Indeed, she entrusted a great many decisions to Devlin Winslow. Since hiring him as her general manger several years ago in Bombay, she had come not only to enjoy his sense of ironic humor, but to respect his business acumen. Not only that, he had shown himself to be unafraid to use his imagination—perhaps to a fault!

Her lips twitched. Winslow had been working a highly profitable gaming venture in one of the more shady establishments on the waterfront when he had first come to her attention. After several lengthy conversations, she managed to convince him that his creative talents could be better channeled into a legitimate business—one that offered the prospects of greater long-term profits, as well as actual survival. As she had expected from someone who was highly flexible and eminently practical, he didn't take long to accept her unconventional offer. The match had been a fortuitous one. Together, they made an odd but highly effective team.

Winslow looked up after a quick review of his notes. "As for Lockwood, I have made a number of inquiries about his reliability and his record of payments to other suppliers. On the whole, I think it is a connection we should consider pursuing, but you may want to take a look at this information from Charleston and Boston." Rising quickly, he moved to her desk and laid out the papers in a precise order. "See here." His finger traced down the suspect columns. "And here."

Employing clipped tones vastly different from the

earlier banter, they spent a good three quarters of an hour reviewing the pertinent documents. In that time, Olivia decided upon a course of action, and after Winslow had respectfully voiced disagreement on several minor points, they agreed on a final strategy.

"I shall try to be halfway as persuasive as you in the final negotiations," he murmured.

"You have a silver tongue, Winslow, as I have ample reason to know."

He fluttered his long lashes. "But I have not your silver eyes, Lady O. Nor, for that matter, certain of your other assets."

"You have your own charms," she replied dryly.

"Ah yes, but unfortunately I don't often get a chance to display them in this business."

"A good thing, too, else some outraged merchant might slice off your . . ." She gave a discreet cough. ". . . your *Trone d'Amour*."

Winslow thumped a hand to the exquisite embroidery of his waistcoat, his palm coming to rest over the general proximity of his heart. "You question my constancy, or the depth of my feelings. Marry me, dear lady and—"

"Put a cork in it, Windy." Olivia capped the crystal inkwell and arranged her pens in a neat row upon her blotter. "You have no more intention of riveting on a legshackle than I do."

A mournful sigh sounded. "If I thought I had a snowball's chance in hell of changing your mind . . ."

"Well you don't." After straightening a stack of documents, Olivia stood up and gathered her reticule from the top of a lacquered tea chest finished in a stunning shade of vermilion. Yet on this occasion its cheery color failed to brighten her mood. It was, she sighed, no doubt a reaction to having to miss out on the actual negotiations. Instead of orchestrating a complex business deal, she was going to sit through a recital of off-key music on the pianoforte. "I shall expect a written report on the first meeting with Lockwood sometime tomorrow."

His manner was back to business. "It will be on your desk first thing in the morning. As will the preliminary assessment of whether to expand our interest in nutmeg. I have done a rough analysis of domestic demand, along with a breakdown of shipping costs."

"Excellent." She glanced at the clock on the storage cabinet, then draped a shawl of Kashmir wool around her shoulders. "Perhaps I should consider giving you a raise."

Winslow inclined a deep bow. "I ask no more than to serve as your humble servant, ma'am."

"Ha!" Her attempt at a dismissive snort dissolved in a chuckle. "There is nothing remotely humble about you," she remarked, turning for the back door of the offices. Or remotely boring, she added to herself. He might be a rather unconventional choice for a man of affairs, but his savvy intelligence and droll wit—not to speak of his complete acceptance of having a female in charge—certainly made their daily meetings a refreshing change from the rest of her engagements.

"By the way," he added with an approving nod. "That is an absolutely luscious shade of persimmon. It picks up the stripe of your gown, and sets off your ivory skin and ebony hair to perfection." Head tilting slightly, he tapped at his chin. "You know, Kettering has a lovely set of ear bobs that would be a stunning complement to the ensemble. The combination of diamond and topaz is quite unusual. And I could get them for a song."

"The trouble is, I wouldn't dare wear the dratted things in Polite Society, for fear some lady might recognize them."

His lips gave a rueful purse. "I suppose you have a point." He accompanied her down the narrow hallway, and, as he did each day, insisted on unbolting the locks and checking the alleyway, though he had no fear that the nondescript carriage would be late for the appointed rendezvous.

"I shall be leaving a trifle earlier than usual tomorrow."

"Ah?" Winslow's brow arched in expectation. "Have you an interesting engagement for the evening?"

"No, nothing out of the ordinary. The ball promises to be rather boring, but as the Marquess of Granton is a relation, I must do my duty and attend both the private supper and the following festivities."

He looked mildly disappointed. "Surely somewhere among the *ton* is a gentleman worthy of your steel."

"Don't count on it." Olivia could not quite keep the note of resignation from her voice, which drew an odd look from her companion. "But since I will be called upon to dance, not duel, it hardly matters."

The lettering on the sign was so small as to be nearly unreadable from across the narrow alleyway.

Sprague squinted as tendrils of fog swirled about his unshaven face. "Does that say Grisham and Blake?"

A scuff of a boot sounded in answer. After a quick glance in both directions, Davenport pulled his tattered hat a bit lower over his brow and picked his way through the mud and mounds of rotting cabbage. "Grisham & Blake," he confirmed a few moments later, ducking back into the recessed nook below the dripping eaves. His mouth thinned in grim satisfaction—it appeared their informant was more reliable than he looked. "But the doors are heavily locked and the windows are shuttered too tightly for a glimpse inside. We shall have to come up with another way of discovering what sort of business takes place inside."

Sprague nodded. "Aye, but for now, let us not draw attention to our interest by lingering here any longer."

Keeping to the shadows, they backtracked through the rookeries to a narrow lane just wide enough for a carriage to squeeze through. It led to a small square, where the shouts of raucous laughter announced the presence of a gin house. Ignoring the saucy offers from a pair of lightskirts plying their trade, Davenport and Sprague entered the dimly lit place and shouldered their way to a spot in the far corner.

Aside from their height, which they took care to disguise, the two gentlemen were unremarkable from the rest of the shabby crowd, for their garments were of coarse homespun, their nails grimy, and their faces untouched by a razor for several days.

"He's late," muttered Sprague. "Damn, we might miss—" A sharp elbow to his ribs cut off any further words.

"I doubt the fellow carries a timepiece," murmured Davenport, once the barmaid had thumped down their pints of porter and flounced away. "Unless he has lifted one from the pocket of some gentleman."

No more than a few minutes passed before a slight figure sidled around a group of drunken stevedores and sat down beside them. "If yer looking fer dos that traffic in stolen swag, dere's a bunch of udder morts ye awt te turn yer peepers on," he whispered.

"Hand over the list," said Sprague.

The man's lips curled back, revealing broken teeth that had darkened to a shade of tobacco brown. "Wot yer think I am—a bloody gennulman to know me letters?" He leaned in closer. "Ye'll have to listen real good." He quickly rattled off a half dozen names before taking a slurp of the porter.

"Your information has proved accurate so far." Davenport removed a small purse from his pocket and slid it across the table. "There's more to come if you learn anything else of interest about Grisham and Blake."

The man's sleight of hand was so deft that the viscount never saw just how the payment disappeared from the pocked wood. "Not me patch." His fingers gave a slight tug to his greasy locks. "But iffen I hear summat of interest, I knows how te send word te ye." Without further comment, he slipped from his seat and melted away in the crowd.

"Your friend Taft appears to have access to a number of well-informed sources," observed Sprague in a low voice.

Swallowing the last of his brew, Davenport wiped at his mouth. "It is not his usual turf, but he called in a few favors," he replied, the frayed sleeve effectively muffling his words. "Ready to go?"

"Quite."

It took another quarter of an hour to navigate the warren of alleyways and reach the spot where their hired hackney was waiting. Once inside, they lost no time in signaling for the driver to be off.

"Hell, once we are done with this next meeting, I am looking forward to a bath and shave," grumbled Sprague as he ran a hand over his stubbled chin. "You may choose to deprive yourself of Polite Company, but I have no intention of holing up like a monk for the entire time I am in Town. Robert Moreton has sent me an invitation to his mother's ball tomorrow night and I plan to attend."

The announcement elicited a low grunt from the viscount, who was tracking their slow progress through the narrow streets with ill-contained impatience.

"Why don't you come along, Max? It will do you good."

The second rumbling sound was a good deal louder and a good deal ruder than the first one.

"The stews aren't the only places where one may learn something useful," pointed out his friend. "There is always the possibility of turning up a gem of information among the glittering crowd."

Davenport made a face, but after reluctant consideration, admitted the suggestion had some merit. "Oh, very well," he growled.

Turning his attention back to the window, he peered through the streaked glass. The neighborhood appeared only marginally more respectable than the one they had just left, and with only the occasional spill of light from an unshuttered window, it was difficult to make out many details. Holding a scrap of paper up to the carriage lamp, Davenport consulted his directions, then rapped on the trap for the driver to come to a halt.

"There." He pointed to a nondescript facade of sooty limestone. "That looks to be the place."

The marble steps leading up to the front entrance were actually well-swept, and the brass railings recently polished. So, too, was the heavy knocker, which was shaped in the form of a snarling canine.

Davenport let it fall several times before the heavy door swung open a crack.

"Have you an appointment?"

The interior was so dark that the viscount could not make out the face. "We are here to see the Wolfhound," he answered.

"Come with me."

He and Sprague entered a small foyer, bare of any decoration save for a set of heavy velvet drapes hanging opposite the door. They parted with a soft whispering, and a hand beckoned the viscount and his friend to follow. The paneled hallway was lit by several oil lamps set in sconces along the wall. Though the wicks were turned low, the soft illumination showed a rather expensive Oriental runner on the floor and a number of ornately framed paintings hung at eye level. Davenport noted with a cursory glance that all of them were extremely lewd in nature.

Their guide, a man who sported the bullish girth

and misshapen nose of a former pugilist, led them past a staircase. Sprague's expression twitched into a smirk at the sound of female laughter drifting down from the second floor and he gave the viscount a knowing wink.

Davenport, in no frame of mind to be distracted from the task at hand, ignored the look, concentrating instead on how to handle the upcoming meeting. His friend Anthony Taft did indeed seem to know a great deal about the seedier sections of London. As well as setting up contact with several informants within the stews, he had, to the viscount's great surprise, also passed on the name of a former army comrade, suggesting it might be worthwhile to arrange a meeting. Connor Linsley—the Earl of Killingworth—had not been a close acquaintance. He had kept to his own circle of friends, and along with earning a reputation for unquestioned valor in battle, he had garnered a great deal of notoriety as a hardened gamester and practiced rake.

The earl was also said to possess a hair-trigger temper. Davenport imagined he would have to choose his words carefully if he wished to learn anything of import from a gentleman who clearly guarded his secrets closely.

Intent on devising a strategy, he nearly collided with their guide when the man stopped abruptly before a closed door and hammered out three sharp raps.

"In there." In response to a muffled growl, the man's meaty fist hit the latch.

Six men were gathered around a circular table, the green baize of its surface giving their faces a sickly cast. The copious amounts of brandy present no doubt added to the effect—a number of empty bottles littered the floor, with at least a half dozen more standing unopened on the sideboard.

Davenport had no trouble picking out Killingworth. Ever since his university days, the earl's thick black hair had grown liberally streaked with gray, and the distinctive, silvery tone had earned him the moniker of the Irish Wolfhound. And there was, decided Davenport, no doubt that the gentleman had the look of a dangerous predator about him. His features, too hard and angular to be called handsome, were dominated by a prominent aquiline nose and pale gray eyes, whose light color did not disguise their intensity.

The piercing gaze was now locked on the viscount and his friend. "Well, well, what brings the two of you here?" he drawled, taking in their ragged appearance. Cutting to the chase, he added, "If you are down on your luck, you have come to the wrong place."

"Our looks are a matter of choice," replied Davenport.

"Indeed? Finding civilian life so deucedly dull that you need to go looking for a bit of risk in the rookeries?"

"Actually, as I am a rather dull dog, a peaceful existence suits me just fine."

"Then why come to me?" Killingworth's eyes appeared to linger for an instant on the viscount's scar before he allowed a sardonic smile. "I confess I was rather surprised to get your note requesting a meeting."

Davenport watched as the earl removed a card from those fanned in his hand and, with a casual flick of his wrist, dropped it faceup on the table. A low oath sounded from one of the other players, followed by groans all around as the pile of banknotes slid toward Killingworth.

"I was hoping you might be able to offer me some . . . advice."

"You want some advice?" slurred one of the earl's companions, a foppishly dressed gentleman whose intricately embroidered waistcoat bore a splash of claret down its front. "Get too close to the Wolfhound and he'll sink his bloody teeth into you. Tear you apart limb for limb."

The other players stirred uneasily in their chairs, but Killingworth reacted with naught but a growl of laughter. "You lambs go ahead and play a hand without me," he said as he pushed back from the table. "While I see what my old comrades want."

The earl led the way into an adjoining room and dropped his lanky frame into one of the leather chairs set before the fire. "So, Davenport, exactly what sort of advice is it you are looking to get from me?"

The viscount decided to match the other man's bluntness. "I need some information. Anthony Taft thought you might prove a likely source."

"Taft?" Killingworth's eyes narrowed. Reaching over to the sidetable, he selected a cheroot from a cedarwood box and proceeded to light it up. "I don't like the idea of Taft, or any of his damned flunkies at Whitehall for that matter, turning their scrutiny on my activities—"

"They aren't." Davenport spoke quickly, uncomfortably aware of the fact that the earl had not offered them a seat or a smoke. "My problem has to do with a personal matter. Tony is a friend, and his suggestion was quite . . . unofficial."

"Indeed?" The earl exhaled a puff of smoke and watched it drift up toward the ceiling. "I, too, have personal problems. Beginning with a marginal title that brought with it painfully empty coffers. My position in Society is precarious enough without having any speculation stirred up as to how I keep from sinking into the River Tick." The tip of his cheroot glowed a hot orange in the dim light. "I know you to be an intelligent fellow, given your former duties. Surely you realize that while a gentleman is permitted to squander his fortune in places like this, any hint that he may have a . . . business interest in vice would cast him beyond the pale."

"I think you also know me to be a fellow who is not prone to wagging his tongue," replied Davenport. "No word will ever fall from my lips—or Sprague's—concerning your ownership of a gaming hell and brothel." Seeing the assurance met with naught but a hard stare, he decided there was little point in prolonging the conversation. "Look, I should not have come here if I weren't rather desperate. But forgive me for trespassing on an old acquaintance. We'll leave you to your games, then. I certainly understand your reluctance to risk your own hide."

As he turned for the door, Killingworth gave a sardonic laugh. "Am I supposed to feel guilty?"

The viscount's own lip curled. "No, Connor. That sentiment is left to fall squarely on my own shoulders."

The other man's brows drew together, just for an instant. "What trouble are you in, Max?"

"Not me, my younger brother. For longer than I care to admit, I have been shirking my family duties. Now he may be headed for the gallows, unless I can find a way to prove him innocent of some unsavory crimes."

Killingworth appeared to be studying his nails. "And why do you think I may be able to help you?"

"You brought up business—let us just say that Tony thought you might be knowledgeable about those who do business in certain parts of Town."

"Anyone in particular?"

"As a matter of fact, yes." From his pocket, Davenport drew out the scrap of paper on which he had scribbled the names whispered by the informant.

The earl hesitated, then reached out to take it.

"I'm also interested in what you know of a Grisham and Blake, located in Seven Dials."

"Hmmph." The other man's eyes were still on the list. "What are you looking for?"

"A hint of who I might look to if I were seeking someone trafficking in a certain sort of stolen merchandise."

Killingworth crumpled the paper and tossed it into the fire. "Not my line of work."

"Damn it, Connor, I am not suggesting it is!" A nudge from Sprague warned him to keep his temper in check, but the other man's negligent attitude was trying his already frayed patience. "I thought perhaps that you might have enough compassion to—oh, bloody hell, never mind."

Fully expecting an explosion from the earl, Davenport was surprised by the softness of the reply. "I can't afford to have compassion. Not with empty pockets and the pack of wolves out there, all too ready to turn on a lone hound and tear him to pieces if given half a chance."

"Fine, then. Spencer and I will track down the curs on our own."

This time, his hand was on the door handle before Killingworth spoke. "Grisham and Blake own a small fleet of ships."

Davenport frowned. "Seven Dials is a rather odd place for such an establishment. I mean, it is not the sort of location where a clientele would be in need of transporting merchandise."

Killingworth gave a curt laugh. "Oh come now, think on it. There are always people who wish to move merchandise quietly, and without attracting notice, so the out-of-the-way location suits them just fine." He drew in another mouthful of smoke. "I have used their services myself on occasion, to slip untaxed brandy and claret past the revenue cutters."

The viscount started to speak.

"One last thing—if I were on the hunt, I would add Fleming and Rundle to my list."

"Thank you, Connor."

"Now do me a favor, Max," came the snappish reply. "Don't come back here unless you wish to drop some blunt on the table, or your breeches in the upstairs boudoirs. I'm running a business here, not a bleeding charity."

*   *   *

The night had grown a good deal chillier and the mist drifting up from the river had thickened, muffling the sound of their steps on the rough cobblestones.

"Lud, I thought you were about to goad the Wolfhound into going for your throat," muttered Sprague, speaking for the first time in a while.

"I remember Alex telling me his bark is a good deal worse than his bite." Davenport gave a low chuckle as he looked back over his shoulder. "I suppose that if you are going to be in business, a bawdy house is not a bad—damn!"

"What?" Sprague spun around, his hand going for the knife he kept hidden in his boot.

"Over there." Davenport pointed to a sliver of passageway between the earl's establishment and the building next to it. "Did you see that?"

"See what?"

"Something moved." He squinted. "A strange flutter of white."

"Bloody hell. It's naught but a swirl of fog." His friend relaxed somewhat, then gave a tug to the viscount's sleeve. "It's late, and you're tired. So am I, so let's go home."

"You are probably right." But as he made to climb into the waiting hackney, he could not keep from taking a last look at the muddled shadows.

Chapter Seven

"Was dinner that dreadful?" The gentleman spoke in a discreet murmur as he offered his arm. "You looked as if your thoughts had drifted away to the other side of the world."

"Would that my body could have followed them back in Bombay, Thomas," sighed Olivia. "Lord Hartshorn is a kindly old fellow, but there is a limit to how much one cares to know about the pruning of roses."

"Well, selfish though it may be, I am exceedingly happy you have returned to London. And so is Elizabeth." Her brother paused, allowing the rest of the guests to file out of the dining room. "Boring, was it?"

She gave him a wry smile. "At least he left off describing his special mix of fertilizer when the fish soup was served."

He shook his head. "Sorry. I know it is a sore trial for you to sit through such a meal."

"I am happy to do it for you and Elizabeth. And I have not forgotten that your father-in-law used his influence to help squash the rumors that would have made my return to Polite Society awkward at best." Her mouth quirked. "Though I admit, at times like these I wonder whether I should have stayed in India."

Her brother slanted her a curious look. "Tell me, is there no gentleman in Town capable of capturing your interest?"

Olivia averted her eyes, surprised to feel a tinge of color stealing to her face. "I have yet to meet him." That, she assured herself, was the literal truth. Lord Davenport was in Yorkshire. . . .

"The Earl of Branford is certainly an interesting fellow."

"Yes. I consider him—and his bride—to be friends."

"Married, is he?" She nearly laughed aloud at seeing his face fall. "Oh, right. Well, then, his comrade—"

Olivia patted his arm. "You may be in alt over the state of wedded bliss, my dear Thomas. But I assure you, I am quite content with my life as it is."

"All business and no pleasure," began her brother, only to be cut off by an unladylike elbow to the ribs. "Oh, very well. I shall hold my tongue."

Grimacing into the looking glass, Davenport gave one last twitch to the starched linen and stepped back. His valet, a veteran soldier who had returned from the wars with several fingers missing, was not overly adept at knotting a neckcloth, but the viscount supposed the simple folds of his cravat would do. A glance down showed that his coat was freshly brushed and his boots had a decent shine to them, so his appearance, though hardly that of a Tulip of the *ton,* should not be cause for embarrassment.

With a resigned nod, Davenport dismissed the man

for the evening. He did not require any assistance in undressing. Indeed, he much preferred solitude in the late hours, especially given the magnitude of the challenge he was now facing.

The glass caught his deepening frown. It was not as if he was making any meaningful headway, despite spending nearly every waking minute trying to piece together the bits of information he and Sprague had managed to ferret out.

Which were damnably few.

The intriguing tip tossed out by the Irish Wolfhound had so far proved naught but a bare bone. Taft had managed to arrange access to detailed shipping records, and though the viscount had spent an entire day digging diligently through them, he had not been able to unearth a shred of evidence that Fleming and Rundle was anything other than a highly respectable exporter of expensive Staffordshire pottery. Such findings were backed up by the bits of gossip Sprague had picked up while making his rounds of the clubs.

Still, the viscount could not shake the feeling that the neatly penned columns of accounting did not quite tally up. It was nothing he could put a finger on, just a certain sense he had developed from countless hours spent poring over army intelligence reports. He rubbed absently at his freshly shaven jaw. Ink and paper told one story, but it would be useful to flesh out the numbers with a source of inside information. Unfortunately, that was easier said than done, seeing as he had no contacts within the world of London commerce.

There was, of course, one individual of his acquaintance who might be in the position to help. . . .

No, he told himself. Absolutely out of the question.

Shaking his head, Davenport picked up one of his brushes and made a cursory swipe through his locks. The unfortunate truth of the matter was that he and Sprague were likely barking up the wrong tree to begin with. Only the verriest of slowtops could deny that the pieces of the puzzle they had gathered so far formed naught but a very damning picture, no matter how they were shuffled and rearranged.

Dropping the brush, Davenport ran a hand through his hair, undoing what little order he had managed to achieve. Face it, he warned himself, though he could not quite meet the reflection of his own eyes. It was becoming harder and harder to deny that Kip had turned from lighthearted lad to a blackened . . .

A wink of movement in the mirrored glass caused him to spin around toward the window. Seeing no more than a flutter of the draperies in the breeze, he blew his breath out in disgust. For the second time in twenty-four hours, he had thought he had seen something in the shadows. Cara's exaggerated fears must be rubbing off on him if he was beginning to imagine specters stalking through the night.

Clamping his hat firmly upon his head, the viscount grabbed his walking stick and marched for the door. Females might succumb to flights of fancy, but he would be damned if a seasoned soldier was going to fall victim to such nonsense.

Olivia lingered in the shadow of the fluted column, savoring a glass of champagne along with a brief respite from the florid compliments and overbright smiles of her last dance partner. She was beginning to have some sympathy for a fox, as the feeling of being doggedly pursued at every turn was exhausting.

It was, of course, no surprise that her wealth drew a pack of fortune hunters to the chase. The scent of money would always overpower a whiff of scandal. Her mouth thinned to a cynical smile. Perhaps one or two of the gentlemen seeking a turn on the parquet actually saw her as aught but a commodity. Lord Dalwhinnie appeared to have a genuine interest in the flora and fauna of tropical India, while Mr. Lattimer displayed a commendable willingness to discuss the mathematics of latitude and longitude with a female. But for the most part, the males staring at her cleavage were tallying up the profits of ownership with the same cold calculation they would apply to a crop of corn.

As she watched the couples twirl across the floor, Olivia had to admit that ladies were no less mercenary. Indeed, for the *ton,* marriage was more about assets and power than it was about love and romance. She, of all people, understood the basic principles of economics, and yet . . .

The entrance of more guests at the far end of the ballroom drew her attention from abstract theory back to solid reality.

Was it merely a quirk of her imagination or had her gaze caught a fleeting glimpse of squared shoulders and a curling mane of tawny hair?

She turned quickly to scrutinize the new arrivals, searching among the polished smiles and winking jewels for a familiar scowl. It took only a few moments to see that her eyes were not playing tricks on her.

Davenport was there, grim-faced as usual, accompanied by his friend, Mr. Sprague. The two of them had edged away from the crowd to take up position among the towering arrangement of potted palms. A flicker of a smile played on her lips as she noted how the fronds served as a measure of camouflage for the viscount. No doubt the instincts of a soldier never quite faded away.

Shifting slightly, Olivia took another sip of champagne. The gentleman's affairs were none of her concern, and yet she could not help feeling a prickling curiosity as to why he was in London. She had thought that circumstances would detain him in Yorkshire for some time.

Her lips compressed. It was pointless to speculate—

"Ah, there you are, Lady Olivia. I trust you have not forgotten we are engaged for the next set." Lord Bentham, a gentleman whom she vaguely recalled meeting during an outing to Vauxhall Gardens, approached and offered his arm. But as her face turned, and the light of the wall sconce glanced off her expression, his smile faded to a tentative quirk. "Er, however, if you have had enough of dancing, I would, of course, quite understand."

Olivia hesitated, but only for an instant. "On the contrary, sir. I am happy to step out with you."

The first strains of a waltz were already wafting through the air by the time they made their way to an open spot on the floor. With a deft flourish, Bentham drew her close and glided into a lilting turn. She was surprised to discover that he was an excellent dancer. They moved well together, spinning through a series of intricate figures with effortless grace.

Indeed, she found herself enjoying the experience much more than she expected, for he proved to be witty as well as agile, offering a number of pithy observations that brought a glint of amusement to her eyes and a soft laugh to her lips. As they conversed, she became aware that a number of people were staring with undisguised interest. The figures of the dance had brought them close to the oasis of greenery, and though she kept her eyes averted from the leafy palms, a sidelong glance revealed that Davenport and his companion were among the spectators.

Not that the viscount could be described as interested. His gaze seemed riveted on the rim of his wineglass.

Determined to put all thoughts of the man out of her mind, Olivia kept her own eyes firmly focused on the crisp folds of Bentham's cravat and hoped that their steps might take them across the room. However, after a capering crescendo by the violins, the music came to a resounding end, leaving them standing directly in front of the terra-cotta planters.

"Lady Olivia."

Olivia looked around slowly. "Mr. Sprague." She allowed a slight nod, then added, "I had not thought to see you in Town so soon."

"A sudden change in plans," he explained.

Her hand was still resting on Lord Bentham's sleeve. "I see." It was only then that she acknowledged the viscount's presence. "I hope that does not mean your father's condition has taken a turn for the worse, Lord Davenport."

"No."

When it became clear he did not intend to elaborate, she replied with equal coolness. "I am glad to hear it. Please convey my best wishes to your sister."

To her ear, his muttered thanks were barely civil.

Her expression took on a self-mocking twist as she accepted Lord Bentham's offer of an escort to the punch bowl. As someone who possessed a shrewd sense of business, she usually knew when to cut her losses. So why, she wondered, did some small, irrational part of her brain insist on whispering suggestions of a partnership with the viscount when it was quite apparent that he had no interest in pursuing any sort of dealings with her.

Most especially a merger of assets.

She gave an inward sigh. Perhaps it was because it was not her brain that was speaking. . . .

"—or ratafia punch, Lady Olivia?" Lord Bentham's voice trailed off in polite question.

Her gaze angled up. "I believe I prefer a glass of champagne."

Yet despite her resolve to forget about a certain scowling gentleman, the taste of it was rather flat on her tongue. The conversation also seemed to have lost some of its sparkle, and though Bentham continued on with an interesting commentary on his collection of musical snuffboxes, Olivia felt her smile growing more forced. When her next partner stepped forward from the crowd, she excused herself from the set, claiming the need to visit the retiring room and repair the hem of her gown.

The hallway was deserted, and after a flurry of hurried steps took her some distance from the crowded cacophony of the ballroom, she regained a measure of her usual dispassionate control. It was, she told herself, ridiculous to allow the viscount and his glowering visage—no matter how attractive a face it was—to upset her equilibrium.

Her chin came back to a more level cant. More likely, the unsettled state of her feelings was due to the frustration of being shut out from the coming business negotiations, rather than any disappointments of a personal nature. She simply missed the challenge of having her intellect and imagination put to the test.

Swearing softly in Hindi, Olivia turned abruptly to retrace her steps. As that wasn't likely to happen while capering through a country jig or nibbling on a plateful of lobster patties, she decided to take an early leave. Slipping into a recessed alcove near the card room, she began searching the mill of guests for her brother. She would make her apologies and have him send around for her carriage. . . .

"Are you perchance free for the next set, Lady Olivia?"

Even before she turned, Olivia had no trouble identifying the deep voice. Or the brusque tone. "You wish to dance, Lord Davenport?"

"Not particularly. But I would like to have a word with you. A waltz is next on the program and it affords an opportunity for private conversation without attracting undue attention."

"How very . . . practical, sir," she replied, unable to suppress a quirk of her lips at the less-than-gallant request.

The note of faint cynicism did not miss its mark,

for his jaw tightened slightly. "Forgive me if my manners are a bit rusty." The viscount hesitated. "Unlike those of your previous partner."

Did she detect a note of something other than mere gruffness in his voice? Intrigued, she placed her hand on his arm before he could withdraw it. "I think by now you know I appreciate plain speaking, sir. Besides, I cannot help but be curious as to the need for such discretion."

Davenport waited until the music struck up before answering. "The subject is a matter I would prefer to keep private."

Olivia didn't blink. "I should think you also know I can be counted on to keep a confidence."

That drew a small smile from him. "If I didn't believe you trustworthy, Lady Olivia, I would not be making a cake of myself on the dance floor."

"On the contrary, you waltz very nicely," she observed, noting that he did indeed possess a light step and smooth sense of rhythm.

"I have spent too many years in the Peninsula to have need of Spanish coin." Was she mistaken, or did she detect a twinkle of humor in his eyes? "So, if you don't mind, I shall get right down to business."

"By all means. It is, after all, a topic I know well."

"I am counting on that." With a nimble grace, the viscount led her to a less crowded corner of the room. "Are you, perchance, acquainted with an export firm by the name of Fleming and Rundle?"

Olivia thought for a moment. "Only by name. Grenville and Company deals in an altogether different market."

His face betrayed a spasm of disappointment. "Yes. Of course." His mouth compressed, but not before an oath slipped out.

Seeing he was about to apologize for the lapse in language, she hurried to add, "But it would be quite easy to find out whatever it is you wish to know."

"Indeed?" His brows drew together. "And just how would you manage that?"

She couldn't help but smile. "Lord Davenport, running a company is really no different than running an army. One of the keys to mapping out a successful strategy is having efficient sources of information. That way, one knows the strengths and weaknesses of the competition."

He actually laughed. The sound was only a soft rustle, akin to an ocean breeze stirring through mango leaves, but his lips did indeed curve upward. "I hadn't thought of comparing business to the military," he replied. "But you are quite right." His expression betrayed a further little twitch. "And no doubt you would make an excellent general."

"A compliment from you, Lord Davenport?" Olivia felt the oddest fluttering inside her chest, as if some exotic bird were beating its gossamer wings against her rib cage. However, she somehow managed to keep her expression from altering. "I had not imagined I would ever hear such a thing from your lips. Perhaps I should fetch my vinaigrette."

Her tone was light, but the smile immediately faded from his face. "It was nothing more than an observation."

A stab of disappointment knifed through her, its

cut made sharper by the realization of how much she would have liked to hear an admiring word from him. She drew in a harsh breath, furious with herself for having allowed girlish fantasies to take flight. "For a former military intelligence officer, you appear remarkably blind, sir. Only a cawker would fail to see that it is not a very smart tactic to insult someone you mean to ask a favor of."

"I am not quite certain why my comparing you to a general should cause offense." Under his breath he added, "Especially when it is so clear that you must always be in command of a situation."

"Perhaps that is because I take great care not to put myself in the position of having to obey some ignorant oaf who—" Olivia broke off abruptly. The music dictated several spins, during which she managed to recover a bit of her equilibrium. "But why bother to go on, when it seems all we ever do is fight," she said in a low voice. "This conversation will lead to nowhere but a full-blown war of words. And I, for one, have no wish to ruin the remainder of the evening."

With that, Olivia lapsed into a stiff-gaited silence, a posture the viscount matched with equal rigidity. As soon as propriety allowed it, she disengaged herself from his hold and hurried away.

Davenport watched as the flicker of flame-colored silk was swallowed up in the crowd. Would that he could bite back some of his previous words, yet in truth he was not quite sure how his strategy had blown up in his face. Intent on avoiding a repeat of their earlier hostilities, he had meant to strike a friendly note, but somehow his attempt had hit wide of the mark.

Curse his clumsy tongue. And her thin skin. Why was she so defensive, so ready to take umbrage at whatever he said? She seemed more than willing to let her guard down with her other dance partner. They had been laughing together, and exchanging intimate looks as they moved effortlessly across the parquet floor.

Damn. Irritation flared into outright anger. He would not—he could not—allow her to dismiss his request without a fight. His pride might call for an orderly retreat, but Kip's life was at stake. . . .

Turning on his heel, Davenport marched for the set of glass doors opening out onto the gardens.

A row of torches cast a soft illumination over the terrace. Looking around, he saw several couples lingering along the length of the stone balustrades, but no telltale flash of red. She must have continued on down the stairs, he decided. Several walkways led off into the darkened shrubbery, and choosing one at random, he set out in pursuit.

Ducking under a bower of climbing roses, he spotted her standing by a small fountain. Her back was turned to him and as the gentle splash of the water drowned out his approach, she was not aware of his presence until only a stride or two was between them.

Olivia spun around, her face pale as marble in the wash of moonlight. Losing her footing on the wet stones, she would have fallen had he not reached out to catch her.

The viscount heard her gasp as she fell against his chest. "Are you not content with mere verbal assault, sir?" she said in a ragged whisper. "Must you follow me to launch a physical attack as well?"

The tips of her breasts, points of fire against his linen shirt, ignited an equally hot response. "Must you insist on misinterpreting every move I make, Lady Olivia?" He did not release his grip. "Trust me, I would not be pursuing you if duty did not demand that I ignore personal feelings—both yours and mine."

"Whatever your sentiments, sir, I don't see how they have anything to do with me."

"I may only be grasping at straws . . ." Davenport drew her closer. "But I can't afford to overlook the fact that you may have access to the information I seek. Will you help me?"

Olivia refused to meet his eyes. "I—I shall have to think about it."

"Blast it! This is not some game of words we are playing. This is my brother's life we are talking about!" Suddenly, her unfeeling hesitation and unfair gibes ignited his own simmering frustrations into a heat far beyond expression in speech.

Her eyes flared, her lips parted . . .

In a flash, his mouth captured hers in a hard, demanding kiss. *Hell.* If he were to be unjustly accused of assault, he may as well do something to deserve her scorn. She started to struggle but as his tongue slid over her lower lip, she went very still, the steel of her spine melting into his arms. Though he had intended to release her right away, the spice of the wine and the beguiling sweetness of her mouth drew him in deeper.

It was a sound from Olivia—soft, wordless—that

finally recalled him to his senses. Forcing his head up, he thrust her back against the damp stone. "Please make up your mind quickly, Lady Olivia. And let me know what you decide."

Without waiting for a response, he turned away and retraced his steps to the ballroom.

Chapter Eight

❧❦❧

"Missing?"

Sprague nodded. "Three over the last several weeks, judging by what my valet has managed to learn at the Hanged Man." He took care to step over a puddle of slops. "Servants like to gossip just as much as their betters, and the subject has sparked a great deal of talk among those who live in the area."

Davenport turned up the collar of his greatcoat. "Servants leave their posts all the time."

"Not from the elegant establishments of Mayfair. And not without a damn good reason. Such jobs are coveted." A stirring in one of the recessed doorways caused Sprague to feel for the hilt of his knife. "According to one of Lord Kennerton's underfootmen, the three simply vanished without a word to any of their friends."

"Sounds a bit fishy," admitted the viscount. "What's the connection to our missing items?"

"Haven't the foggiest notion." His friend's voice was muffled by the thick mantle of mist drifting up from the river. "Just thought it was worth a mention. Especially as they all are apparently young, well-favored females."

"There appear to be a great many unexplained disappearances coming to our attention of late." Davenport found his tone turning a bit sharper as he kicked at a shard of glass. "Though in the case of pretty lasses, a number of reasons quickly come to mind."

"Such as a rather embarrassing little bundle at the end of nine months?" His friend shrugged. "It happens, of course, that a girl runs out knowing full well she will be turned out without reference as soon as the condition is noticed. But as I said, positions here in Town are carefully guarded, and females take great precautions so as not to be caught in such a desperate plight." He paused to check around the corner before turning down the alleyway. "Three similar situations in the course of a few months simply seem a curious coincidence."

Coincidence. The notion seemed to be shadowing his steps like a damnable specter. As much as Davenport wished to dismiss it as that, Sprague's latest information cast a shade of doubt as to whether that was possible. "Hmmph," he grunted. "I don't see how the matter relates to our problem, but I suppose it would do no harm to follow up on it." Davenport thought for a moment. "Didn't Gooding mention that a friend of his daughter had come to work in London? I believe I wrote down the name somewhere in my notes. Perhaps Woodley could ask around for her direction and try to arrange for a chat."

"That will not be a problem." Sprague made a face as he touched at the haphazard folds of his cravat. "He is handling the assignment of cozening up to the lasses with a good deal more enthusiasm than he brings to his usual chores of ironing a length of linen or putting a shine to my boots."

"A devil-may-care appearance suits our purpose tonight," Davenport replied grimly.

"Aye. I daresay—" At the rustle of other footsteps among the broken bottles and splintered crates, Sprague fell silent, his hand coming up in warning.

Davenport stopped short. From the opposite end of the alley, three figures materialized out of the gloom, one of them tripping with an unsteady laugh and falling heavily against his companions.

"Seems we have found the spot we are looking for," murmured Sprague as he watched the group stumble down several stairs and hammer out a series of raps on the barred entrance. "Come on."

The door opened a crack, and out oozed the rattle of dice, the clash of bottles and the scent of musky perfume. The porter, a hulking brute with the beady eyes and heavyset jaw of a bull mastiff, stood aside to admit the first party. But as Sprague made to follow along, the man moved to block the way. " 'Ere now, this be a very perticalar establishment. Ye need a proper innnerduction te enter."

Sprague leaned in and whispered a name, while slipping a gold guinea into the man's waiting palm.

"Oye, well, if that's who sent ye along, ye gennulmon are right welcome at the Strutting Cock."

It had taken some cajoling, but after much grimacing, Anthony Taft had consented to hand over the names and locations of the most dissolute gaming hells in Town. This particular one topped the list. Taft had warned that it was the most volatile of the lot, catering to a highborn clientele that liked taking risks. Whispers were rife concerning the high stakes, the violent outbursts of the gamesters, and the perverse tastes of the patrons seeking diversions in the upstairs boudoirs.

Once inside, they were relieved of their coats and shown into a large gaming room, the first in a series of connecting chambers, each of which offered a different activity.

"Wot's yer pleasure, luv?"

As his eyes sought to adjust to the smoky haze, Davenport felt a glass of brandy thrust into his hand and a length of bared thigh pressed up against his leg. "For the moment I shall just . . . watch."

The barmaid gave a saucy laugh, and the jiggling of her heavy breasts caused one of her nipples to slip free of the scanty bodice. "Well, don't take too long te decide wot game ye want te play, sir," she cooed, making a show of tucking the point of rouged flesh back beneath the frill of lace. "After all, a handsome gent like yerself gots te know it's ever so much more fun to partake o' the action rather than standing around jes watching."

"I shall give it careful consideration." And yet, the viscount found his thoughts straying from the ripe morsel at his fingertips to the taste of fiery spice on his lips.

Hell. He had no business thinking of Olivia Marquand. Or that incendiary kiss. Not when his attention should be firmly focused on how he might squeeze some useful information out of the doxy, or the dissolute rakehells who were pressed cheek-to-jowl around the gaming tables. Already he could see out of the corner of his eye that Sprague had sidled up to one of the patrons and had struck up a casual conversation.

Davenport drew in a deep breath, heedless of the stale fumes of brandy and tobacco. Still, the memory of his encounter with Lady Olivia remained uncomfortably hot, like a burning coal pressed on bare flesh. She had favored her other dance partner with a warm smile, yet when he had taken her in his arms . . .

There had been a momentary flicker—an instant when she had regarded him with some undefinable emotion that had softened the planes of her face. But it had disappeared in the blink of an eye, replaced by a sudden explosion of anger.

He had yet to make sense of her reaction. She had chosen to twist a straightforward explanation in a way he had never intended. Oddly enough, it was almost as if she wished to hear a compliment from him.

And Lucifer might be invited to take tea with Saint Peter!

Despite her gibe, he wasn't blind to the fact she was surrounded by a pack of eager suitors, all panting to shower her with flowery words. With so many gentlemen seeking to win her hand, why had he seized her lips? Plundered her mouth . . .

No more of Olivia Marquand!

There were enough conundrums to solve without trying to figure out what strange spark had caused her—and him—to burst into flames.

The viscount wrenched his attention back to the small corner of hell in which he stood. A quick glance around at the shroud of smoke and the flushed faces sheened with sweat did nothing to assuage the feeling of being trapped in some devilish underworld. A fortunate few wore looks of wild exultation, but most of the players at the tables had desperation etched on their features, hope turning to anguish as they watched the slow, skidding roll of the ivory cubes.

"Look there." With a sharp nudge, Sprague jarred Davenport out of his dark reflections and directed his gaze to a tall figure leaning in the arch of an alcove. A slight turn of the gentleman's head sent a glint of silver rippling through the shadows.

"I wonder what brings Killingworth here?" added his friend.

"On the prowl for pleasure, I imagine." A chorus of groans interrupted his words. "Or pain. Like most everyone else here."

"The Wolfhound does not have to leave his own den to seek a taste of pleasure."

"An interesting observation, Spencer." Davenport's eyes did not leave the earl. "You are right—Connor does not have the look of a man who is sniffing around for idle entertainment."

Killingworth suddenly turned to meet his stare. After baring his teeth in what might have been a smile, the earl slowly sauntered over to where they were standing. "For a pair of dull dogs who claim contentment with a quiet life, you keep turning up rather far from home."

"Can't rest in peace yet," said Davenport softly. "We are still hunting for a certain item that's gone missing."

"I thought you were advised to dig around elsewhere."

"I did. Nothing of interest turned up."

"Perhaps you didn't dig deep enough." The earl flicked a bit of ash from the end of his cheroot. "You know, you have not yet mentioned whether this item you are seeking is an inanimate object, or something with a bit more life to it."

It was Sprague who spoke up first. "Are you saying you know something about missing persons? Does it have to do with—"

The Irish Wolfhound cut him off with a warning growl. Stepping back several paces, he made a point of turning his back to the gaming tables. "Never tip your hand. Especially in a place like this," he said, raising his brandy glass to his lips.

Davenport took a sip of his own drink before venturing a question. "Would it matter? I mean, would we still be looking in the same place?"

The earl's expression remained inscrutable. "You never know what skeletons may lie buried beneath a proverbial bed of roses."

Skeletons? A mere turn of phrase? wondered the viscount. Or did it have a more ominous reference?

"Is there a reason you are telling us this?" asked Sprague, with a hint of irony. "Aside from your altruistic nature and benevolent concern?"

That drew a reaction, but not the one Davenport expected. Killingworth actually laughed, then gave a small shrug. "Perhaps I am feeling generous." He withdrew a large purse from his pocket and hefted its weight. "Lady Luck has smiled kindly on me tonight, so it may be I am inclined to return the favor." He paused for a moment before shifting his gaze to the viscount. "You are accorded to be a well-versed expert in the field of intelligence." His murmur dropped another notch. "If I were you, I would be on the lookout for a certain . . . connoisseur."

"Oblique son of a bitch, isn't he," muttered Sprague as the Wolfhound moved off. "Was he merely toying with us, as a dog might worry a bone? Or was the hint . . ."

"Just a coincidence?" finished Davenport. "Hard to know what any of it means. However, one thing is clear—our friend Connor is telling us that he isn't about to risk getting his own paws dirty." His lip curled up. "He's leaving it for the terriers to root out."

His friend frowned. "Root *what* out?"

"That we won't know until we start digging."

"Bloody hell. Just when I had the mud cleaned out from under my nails."

Olivia sealed the thick packet and summoned her servant. Winslow had been quite thorough in his report. The information contained a number of interesting details concerning Fleming and Rundle, including a rundown on their trafficking in stolen artwork, an ingenious little side business that had been going on for at least a year with a well-known dealer in Bruges. And along with mention of a connection to Grisham and Blake, whose ships she knew handled the sort of cargo she refused to touch, there were also some unsettling hints of an even more profitable trade. She didn't know whether the viscount would feel any need to follow that line of inquiry, but she knew it was something she couldn't ignore.

"Please have this delivered right away, Vavek," she said, handing over the packet while placing a set of copies in the drawer of her escritoire.

The servant regarded the bold script without expression. "Of course, memsahib. Shall the messenger wait for a reply?"

"No. That won't be necessary." She was not at all sure what such a response might be. A curt word of thanks, perhaps.

If she was lucky.

Olivia sighed. They both had behaved with appalling rudeness. Perhaps it was for the best that they steer well clear of each other to avoid further fireworks. Picking up her pen, she began to review the quarterly budget for the Bombay office of Grenville and Company.

It was perhaps an hour later when a soft knock sounded on the door of her study.

"Come in," she called. The interruption broke in on naught but a brooding contemplation of the burning logs in the hearth. Even the simplest column of sums had proved perversely difficult to tally up, so she had long ago set aside her ledger.

Vavek extended a silver tray, empty save for a single calling card placed squarely in its center.

Her brow rose in question, but he merely bowed his head, the swathing of his turban and curl of his beard making it impossible to read his expression. Olivia hesitated, then turned her attention to the looping letters of engraved script. She blinked, then examined them more closely, to make sure her eyes were not deceiving her.

"Show him in."

"Yes, memsahib." The soft slap of his sandals retreated back down the hallway.

She had barely enough time to smooth her skirts and brush an errant curl from her cheek when the door reopened. With a flourish of saffron silk, Vavek stood aside and motioned for the visitor to enter.

"Lord Davenport." Olivia rose from her chair.

"Forgive my calling at such an unfashionable hour. But I took the liberty of assuming you might be willing to clarify several points in your report without my waiting until the morrow." Standing stiffly, the viscount gave an awkward little shrug. "Besides, you are well aware of my lack of social graces."

"Of course—" Olivia felt a flush steal to her face. "That is," she corrected, "of course I am willing to help. Not of course . . ." Afraid she was sounding like a cawker, she left off abruptly and moved out from behind her desk. With a brusque wave, she motioned to the sofa facing the hearth. "Please make yourself comfortable, sir."

He looked anything but at ease as he assumed a rigid posture among the striped pillows.

She took a seat in the facing armchair, using the extra few seconds of settling in to get over her initial shock.

"First of all, I wish to apologize for my ungentlemanly conduct—" he began.

"There is no need for apologies," she interrupted, having regained control of her oddly fluttering nerves. "No doubt both of us regret allowing emotion to get the better of us during that unfortunate interlude. Seeing as you have expressed a sense of urgency, let us not dwell on the past."

Davenport nodded, yet shifted slightly in his seat, as if there were something else he wished to say before they got down to business. However, the crackle of the paper in his pocket seemed to change his mind. Withdrawing the set of notes she had sent to him, he shuffled them into order.

"Assuming your source is reliable . . ." he began.

"He is," she assured him. "In fact, I would stake my life on it."

The statement elicited an odd little series of tics at the viscount's jaw. "In that case, might I ask just how he has managed to become privy to such a wealth of details?" He fanned the pages with a decided snap. "This type of information is not easy to come by."

"Winslow has his methods." Olivia could not help but allow a rueful smile. "Many of which I don't care to know about."

Davenport did not look equally amused.

"He has a great many contacts to call upon," she went on. "In a great many walks of life."

"So does Anthony Taft." To her ears, he sounded just a trifle miffed that she had handled the job so easily. "Yet his men have not been able to turn up so much as a fraction of what is written here."

"I trust that is not cause for complaint, sir."

"Well, er, no." Looking slightly abashed, he rubbed at the scar on his cheek. "Though I do have further questions regarding some of the things listed. No matter how detailed, the written word never conveys the full story. In the line of duty, I have learned the

importance of meeting face-to-face with a source."
Noticing the cant of her brow, he added, "You see, a
nuance of expression or inflection of voice can sometimes be as telling as the words themselves."

Olivia nodded thoughtfully. "I know what you
mean. I have found the same is true in business." She
allowed a bit of a pause. "So, you wish to meet with
my source?"

Davenport nodded. "Can it be arranged?"

"Quite easily," she replied. "In fact, I have plans to
dine with him tomorrow evening. Would you care to
come along?"

Olivia saw a flicker of indecision in his eyes before
they took on a martial light. "Very well."

Well aware that her words had conveyed a note of
challenge, she was secretly pleased that he had chosen
to accept it rather than back off. "My coach will come
around to your lodgings at seven."

"I look forward to the meeting, Lady Olivia."

Chapter Nine

❧❀❧

As the barouche rolled to a halt in the narrow side street, Davenport was on the verge of revising his thinking. Peeking through the panes of polished glass, he felt his expression darkening at the sight of the grimy brick facades and deserted walkways. "You don't mean to say you were planning on coming here by yourself?"

"Of course. I do it all the time."

"But this sort of neighborhood is hardly the place for a . . ."

"Really, sir, don't be deceived by the look of things. There is no reason to be concerned." Ignoring the grim set of his features, Olivia stepped down to the dusty cobblestones. "Are you coming?" She marched for the entrance of one of the nondescript buildings, leaving him little choice but to trail after her.

The brisk rap of the knocker had not yet died away when the door flew open. It was only with a conscious effort that Davenport kept his jaw from following suit. He had been prepared for some sort of modest chophouse, dark and smoky, yet respectable enough for a female to enter. Not in his wildest flight of fancy would he ever have expected the sight that now greeted his gaze.

The walls of the entrance hall were glazed in a color of soft peach, the honeyed glow highlighted by the flickering candles of a massive, brass Louis XIV chandelier. A decorative swag topped a large gilt-framed portrait of a Scottish Highlander that hung over a rosewood sidetable, the bold damask stripes of salmon pink and ochre echoing the earthy hues of the painting. Shifting his stance, Davenport noted that the marble floor reflected the same palette, its checkered squares a contrasting pattern of swirled beige and terra-cotta.

As his eyes came up, the viscount saw that the man inclining a graceful bow over Olivia's hand was a matching picture of artfully arranged splendor. Glossy chestnut curls were coiffed in the latest style, not a hair out of place to mar the symmetry of his wide, blue eyes, straight nose, and full mouth. Beneath his dimpled chin was a flowing cravat of gauzy silk the color of fine champagne. Its tails were delicately fringed and spilled over a cream waistcoat embroidered in shades of deep gold. His coat matched the color of his hair, and his breeches were a light fawn, tucked into gleaming Hessians that looked soft as butter.

Who in the name of Lucifer . . .

The fellow brought Olivia's hand to his lips with an exaggerated flourish. "As always, I am delighted to have you grace my humble abode, Lady O." Looking up through a fringe of long lashes, he slanted a glance at the viscount and his smile broadened. "And your exalted escort, of course." He lowered his voice, but not nearly enough to keep from being overheard. "Indeed, I am inclined to say that for once your choice of—"

"Snuff it, Windy." Olivia cut him off by dumping her cloak over his outstretched arm. "Lord Davenport is interested in hearing your observations, but not on that particular subject." Turning back to the viscount, she gave a slight shrug of her shoulders. "Allow me to introduce Mr. Devlin Winslow, who handles the day-to-day operations of Grenville and Company. You will soon learn why he so richly deserves his less-formal sobriquet."

Davenport did his best to hide his surprise as her man of affairs extended a well-manicured hand. Surely this dandified clerk was not the primary source of the dirt that had been dug up?

"Charmed to make your acquaintance, my lord."

"The, er, same," Davenport said gruffly. Though somewhat distracted by the surroundings, he did not fail to notice that the man had a firm grip and his palms were deceptively calloused, giving hint that he did more than push a pen over paper.

But before he could give the matter further thought, Winslow glided across marbled tiles. "Come! Come! Let us move into the drawing room, where we can be more comfortable. Then, if you will excuse me for a moment, I will fetch the *prosecco* and a few *amuse-bouches*."

"Italian sparkling wine and a few special little tidbits of food to stimulate the appetite," translated Olivia in a low murmur as she urged the viscount forward with a nudge of her elbow. "You will find both are quite delicious."

The drawing room was just as striking as the entrance hall, its tasteful furnishings designed in a more formal palette of hunter greens and mahogany. Davenport clasped his hands behind his back as he looked at the collection of Chinese vases arranged on the mantel and the paintings displayed along the far wall. His knowledge of art was not all that discerning, but he knew enough to identify the work of a sixteenth-century Spanish master, along with several more recent Italian landscapes.

"Lovely, aren't they?" While Winslow fussed over plumping the pillows on the sofa, Olivia came to stand by the viscount's side.

"It appears that you pay your employees quite handsomely."

"I believe in paying people what they are worth."

"Then your Mr. Winslow must be . . . invaluable."

Her lips quirked up. "Oh, he most definitely is."

For some reason, Davenport felt a flare of irritation at her tone. It was none of his business if their working arrangement included private meetings in the bedroom. Yet the idea bothered him. A great deal, in fact.

"Would you care to have a seat, milord?" asked Winslow with a light touch to Davenport's sleeve. "We don't tend to stand on ceremony here," he added, giving Olivia a broad wink.

"I prefer to remain on my feet," he replied curtly.

The man of affairs' smile stretched even wider. He murmured something in a language Davenport did not recognize.

What was more than clear, however, was the fact that the man was leaning in a trifle too close to the lady's ear for his taste. His fingers clenched. The meal was likely going to leave a sour taste in his mouth if the fellow kept whispering intimacies all evening.

"I pray you two will excuse me for a moment," continued Winslow, returning smoothly to a mellifluous rendition of the King's English. "I will be back in a trice."

"Discussing . . . business?" growled Davenport as soon as the other man had left the room.

Olivia looked at him oddly, then the corners of her mouth began to twitch. "Actually, what he said was . . ."

He waited for her to go on. However, something appeared to catch in her throat, for all that followed was a series of tiny choking sounds. Somewhat alarmed, he looked around for a decanter of spirits. "Are you all right, Lady Olivia? Shall I fetch you a glass of sherry—"

She waved off his concern. "No, no, really. I am quite fine," she managed to gasp.

He then realized that the only thing she was trying to swallow was laughter. "Would you care to share the joke?" he asked. "Or was it something of a private nature?"

Olivia gave another little choke. "Not exactly. He was merely making mention of the fact that he liked the style of your . . ."

Davenport was still waiting for her to finish when the sound of clinking crockery announced the imminent arrival of the refreshments.

"Sorry! The pancetta took a tad longer to brown that I expected. And I had to fetch up another melon from the cellar—the first one wasn't quite ripe." A large silver tray sailed through the doorway, accompanied by a heady swirl of heavenly aromas. Winslow placed the tray atop the sideboard, then held out an elongated crystal glass filled with sparkling wine the color of pale apricots. "It is not every day that we have a gentleman of such heroic stature cross our threshold. This calls for a celebration."

Davenport accepted the drink without comment, watching as the same beverage was passed on to Olivia.

"Oh, wait just a tick." Winslow slipped out again, reappearing a moment later bearing a blue-and-white-patterned Ming Dynasty vase filled with a striking arrangement of tulips and a number of other blooms the viscount could not identify.

Nor, for that matter, could he put a name to his own mixed reactions to the evening so far. Though his initial surprise still lingered, his usual sense of dispassionate observation had begun to take over. All personal reactions aside, what he saw was certainly piquing his curiosity, for intuition had him wondering whether Winslow's show of silky manners and foppish fashion was a calculated display.

For what reason?

Davenport was not yet ready to hazard a guess. However, unless his skills had sadly eroded, he was sure there was more to the man than met the eye.

"I almost forgot these." Casting an inquiring look at his employer, Winslow placed the vase on a sidetable, centering it precisely between two fanciful jade dragons. "What do you think, Lady O?"

Olivia responded with a critical squint. "No, no, not there. The colors clash and the shape is distracting." After a moment of thought, she indicated a round gilt table flanking one of the armchairs. "What about there."

Winslow pursed his lips. "You don't think it too . . . bold?"

The question was dismissed with a wave. "Oh, I believe the occasion calls for a little drama, don't you think?"

"I defer to your taste, at least for tonight," replied Winslow, with a low chuckle. "Now, speaking of taste, you all must sample these tidbits from the kitchen before they grow cold."

Davenport, who had not missed the sly grin that the man of affairs had directed at Olivia, felt his jaw tighten again. There was something deucedly smoky in the air—aside from the delectable smell of seared bacon wafting up from the tray—but of yet, he was unsure just what it was.

"Mmmmm." Olivia's murmur of approval drew his attention back to the lady herself. "How original, Windy," she remarked after finishing the last morsel. "But then, I have come to expect no less from you."

"I like to think of myself as rather talented with a knife or cleaver," agreed Winslow with a saucy smile. "Along with a number of other implements."

"Yes, I doubt anyone can rival your unique blend of talents." With a low cough, Olivia ceased the playful banter with her friend and turned to the viscount. "Lord Davenport, you have yet to sample one of Windy's specialties." Choosing a plump roll of ham and melon, its middle skewered by a tiny silver sword, she held it out to him.

He eyed it askance before grudgingly allowing it to

be passed over. "Original," he muttered, echoing Olivia's words as he studied it more closely.

"It won't bite back, my lord," said Winslow.

"Pay no attention to Windy—his sense of humor is sometimes most peculiar," said Olivia. "Along with a good many other of his habits."

"Alas, Lady O, you know your servant too well," said Winslow in mock despair.

"Servant! Ha!" she retorted. "If you were my servant I would not be obliged to pay you such usurious wages."

"Putting the pinch on you, am I?" inquired the man of affairs with an air of great innocence.

"I'm not quite squeezed dry."

"I'm immensely relieved to hear it."

That the two of them had such an obvious rapport did nothing to lighten Davenport's mood. Seeking to bite down on something other than his own molars, he reached for one of Winslow's creations and ventured a taste. Somewhat to his amazement, he found it delicious.

"What is this?" he asked, his scowl dissolving as he savored both the seductive smoothness and piquant crunch of the ingredients.

"Prosciutto—a special type of ham that I have shipped from Milano. And the melon is a Persian variety that I grow in my hothouse. It's complemented by a purée of fresh fig and a crumbling of pancetta, which is another specialty of the Lombard region," explained Winslow. "The Milanese are as passionate about food as they are about opera." He paused as the viscount washed down the last bite with a swallow of the effervescent wine and reached for a second roll. "I approve of a man with a strong appetite—don't you agree, Lady O?"

Was it his imagination, wondered Davenport, or did Winslow's teasing elicit a brief flare of emotion that turned Olivia's face as rosy as the rolled prosciutto?

"Do you like opera, sir?" Winslow went on, seemingly oblivious to her momentary discomfort. "Lady O has quite a fondness for a well-performed aria."

"I appreciate *Cosi Fan Tutte* and *Don Giovanni*, though I cannot say the same for *Dido and Aeneas*," he replied slowly, taking care to keep a surreptitious watch on Olivia's reaction. He was gratified to see her eyes widen slightly at his show of familiarity with the works of Mozart and Purcell. She might think of him as devoid of civilized manners, but at least she would have to acknowledge that he was not a total ignoramus to boot.

"What think you of *Ariadne?*" inquired the man of affairs. "Lady O is a great admirer of Monteverdi—"

"I assure you that Lord Davenport doesn't give a fig for my preferences in composers," she said rather sharply. "He did not come here to discuss music—"

"Would you care for another glass of prosecco?" asked Winslow with a great show of solicitousness. "Yours appears to be dry."

She replied with a phrase in Hindi that made him blink.

Winslow had already taken up the bottle and quickly refilled all three glasses. "Nothing wrong with indulging in a little sparkling conversation before getting down to more sobering business."

The effervescence of the wine appeared to produce the desired results. After several sips Olivia was smiling again, her momentary ill-humor swallowed along with the faint taste of fresh peaches. However, after the man of affairs teased yet another laugh from her lips, it was Davenport who found his mood had turned flat.

He set his glass down with a force that rattled the silver tray. "Would it be possible for the two of you to begin dispensing more than just food and wine? Lady Olivia has passed on the information about Fleming and Rundle, and I find there are a number of things I would like to have clarified."

Winslow rearranged the rolls into an orderly row. "I don't suppose you would care to wait until after we dine?" A quick glance at the viscount's darkening expression caused him to heave a martyred sigh. "No, I see that you do not. Then might we at least have the discussion in the kitchen?"

"The kitchen?" Davenport frowned. "Why the devil should we do that?"

"So that we might eat sometime before midnight," explained Winslow patiently. He mimed the motions of chopping and dicing. "A great deal of time and preparation goes into making a decent meal."

"You don't—"

"An excellent suggestion, Windy," Olivia quickly cut in. "Why don't we get started."

Winslow removed his elegant coat with a flourish. "Just give me a few moments to visit the wine cellar and pantries, Lady O, then bring our guest along."

As Winslow glided smoothly into the hallway, Davenport could not keep his simmering irritation from spilling over. "For employer and employee, you seem to be awfully good friends."

For an instant, Olivia looked a trifle wistful before her face assumed a more enigmatic expression. "Yes, we are. You disapprove?"

Rather than respond with a cutting remark, Davenport remained silent.

"Friendship, wherever it is found, is something to be valued," she added softly. "Trust, loyalty, laughter—it seems to me that those are the things that are truly important, rather than some paper title or quirk of birth."

"Loath though you may be to believe it, I am in complete agreement with you. On the field of battle, a man is quickly stripped bare of all pretense." He began to toy with one of the tiny silver swords. "Have you known him a long time?"

Olivia brought the wineglass to her lips. "Long enough to have the utmost confidence in his character."

He shifted his stance. "A friend of your family?"

"No. We met in India."

"Ah." The sharpened point pricked against his palm. "A younger son, in need of making a living?"

Olivia paused to take the last sip of her prosecco. "I have never inquired as to his origins."

Although it was none of his concern, he could not help wondering about Winslow's background. Was he a gentleman? The fellow certainly possessed the cultured speech and refined taste of a man accustomed to moving in the highest circles of Society. And as such, their relationship . . .

What, exactly, was their relationship?

As Davenport watched the tiny bubbles in his wine fizz up, he was aware of a corresponding series of explosions taking place in his own head. It took him a moment to realize the sensation was the stirring of jealousy. He was well enough acquainted with Olivia to know it would not matter to her whether Winslow was a commoner, not if she cared for him. She was not bound by convention, or the prejudices of Society. Indeed, it was that very streak of courage and independence he admired most in her. And it wasn't as if the lady had to marry for money. She was as rich as Croesus. Nor did she seem to care about a title.

So what did she want?

"You appear . . . surprised," she went on.

"Somewhat," he replied slowly. "Given the obvious closeness that you and Mr. Winslow share, I should have thought you would know all of each other's intimate little secrets."

"We all have secrets that we keep to ourselves, Lord Davenport." He thought he detected a tightening of her features. "As for what passes between me and my man of affairs, you may wish to reserve final judgment until you have gathered all the facts."

"My military service has taught me the wisdom of just such a strategy." The viscount met her gaze, wondering whether despite all his hard-won battlefield experience, he would ever manage to penetrate her steely gray defenses. "I try to maintain an open mind about most things."

"Do you?" There seemed to be a tiny flicker in her expression.

"You think me too regimented, too prone to forming a hasty opinion?"

Her eyes broke away from his and seemed to focus on the artful arrangement of flowers. "My opinion regarding you is hardly of any importance."

Davenport edged a step sideways, deliberately blocking her line of vision. Leaning closer, he allowed the small blade to graze her wrist. "On the contrary, Lady Olivia," he said softly. "If we are to work together, I should like not always to be at daggers drawn with you."

The touch of the silver sent a shiver through her. "I—"

The clatter of cutlery cut her off as Winslow poked his head through the doorway. "Do hurry along," he began, then cut off with a sharp cough. "Er, unless I am interrupting a . . . private exchange."

"Nothing of the sort," said Olivia.

Winslow took a moment to shift the clutch of ladles and serving spoons from one hand to the other. "Well, then . . . you know how temperamental chefs can be when it comes to timing."

The viscount was tempted to skewer something other than a slice of melon.

"We had better do as he says." With a flutter of silk as soft as the stirring of rose petals, Olivia slipped past the viscount and moved for the hallway.

Davenport could not help wondering whether the ancient family heirloom had him laboring under some strange curse. Be it a lost Lion, a missing sibling, an enigmatic female, or a chimerical specter, he could not seem to make headway with any of the mysteries he was facing. A great many clues seemed tantalizingly within reach, yet when he reached out, his fingers closed on naught but air.

Poof. Like a swirl of fog, they eluded his efforts with mocking ease.

Jabbing the tiny sword into the remains of the *amuse-bouche,* he turned to follow.

Chapter Ten

"Come in, come in."

A wink of light flashed off the blade of the cleaver as Winslow waved them toward the trestle table. He smiled on seeing Davenport hesitate. "I have always found the sights and smells of cooking to be most conducive to conversation, but perhaps you are not of the same opinion, milord," he remarked, as the viscount's gaze traveled slowly from the pots bubbling atop the cavernous iron stove to the vegetables soaking in granite sinks, to the small army of glass jars arrayed on the shelves of the spice rack.

"It is not a subject to which I have given a great deal of thought."

Olivia had recovered enough of her composure to smile as well. In the face of all the eccentricities of the evening, the viscount's dry sense of humor had not entirely evaporated. "I daresay the kitchens and pantries at Saybrook Manor are far more extensive than these," she murmured.

Tearing his eyes away from the collection of utensils hanging over the table, he gave a wry grimace. "I would likely need a trail of bread crumbs to lead me to their precise location."

Winslow made a low clucking sound as he reached around for a bundle of parsley, a handful of basil, and a bowl of briny black olives. The staccato action of his knife quickly reduced the ingredients to three finely minced mounds.

Taking a tentative step onto the stone floor, Davenport made a quick survey of every nook and cranny. On seeing no one else present, he looked a bit perplexed. "Don't you leave that to the hired help? Surely your chef—"

"Le chef, c'est moi," replied the other man with a grin and a bow.

"You do the cooking?"

"Why, yes," responded Winslow with a waggle of his brows. "Why hire someone to do what is such fun?"

Olivia saw that the viscount's face now betrayed an expression of patent disbelief.

"It's the truth, sir," she assured him.

"In my experience, the task is usually consigned to crotchety old women," he muttered.

Winslow had moved back to the table and was now cutting an onion into matching slices of uniform thickness. "Ah, but what about the army, sir? Surely there was many an occasion on the Peninsula when you officers were forced to live off the land."

"Well, that was not out of choice. Besides," added Davenport with a grudging twitch of humor, "I would hardly call it cooking, as the results would not have been deemed edible by anyone who wasn't in danger of starving."

"That is because, like in other creative endeavors,

you must put some passion into preparing food." The man of affairs directed a broad wink at Olivia before laying out several paring knives. "Here, perhaps you and Lady O would care to help." Turning to the sink, he extracted a colander filled with an odd assortment of crinkled shapes and slid it across the chopping surface. "You could begin by slicing these."

Davenport peered suspiciously at the jumble of earthy browns and beiges. "What in the name of God are they?

"Fungi." Winslow hummed a bit of Verdi. "Or, if you prefer, mushrooms."

"What I prefer is to eat something I can identify." He took a closer look. "But they are all different."

"Yes, cremini, woodcock, and portobello, among others. And these"—he indicated a small earthenware bowl filled with shriveled shards plumping in a bath of hot broth—"these are dried porcinis." He gave a reverential kiss to his fingertips. "From Italy."

Olivia edged a small paring knife toward Davenport, then plucked up a handful of the mushrooms and set to cutting them into thin slices. "I imagine a seasoned cavalry officer won't have any trouble mastering the technique."

"Indeed," chimed in Winslow. He slashed his spoon through the air with an audible whoosh. "I'm sure the Valiant Viscount knows more about the fine points of slicing than any of us."

An awkward silence suddenly descended over the table.

Drawing in a sharp breath, Olivia felt her own blade waver. There was no denying that the evening had been a test of sorts. She had wanted to observe the viscount's reaction to her friend, in part to confirm her suspicions that beneath the shell of stiff-rumped reserve, he was not nearly as rigid as he chose to appear. But never had she meant to embarrass him.

"Lord Davenport, I pray you will forgive Windy's unfortunate slip of the tongue. I—I am quite certain he meant no offense."

"Indeed, sir," A look of contrition had wiped the saucy humor from his features. "I am not usually so cow-handed."

The viscount slowly looked up from the mushrooms. In the angled light of the wall lamps, the thin white scar on his cheek was more pronounced than before. His lips began to twitch in an ominous fashion and Olivia couldn't help but recall his sister's analogy to a wounded lion. She found herself tensing every muscle, fully expecting a fierce roar of outrage.

What came forth instead was a strange sort of purring. It took her a moment to recognize it as a chuckle.

"Having experienced the art of wielding a blade from both ends, I daresay you are right, Mr. Winslow," he said with a faint smile. "A pity you are not serving beefsteak, seeing as I am more accustomed to whacking at flesh than a bit of fungus. However, I shall try not to disgrace myself on the field of battle." He tested the point of the paring knife against his thumb. "At least the damn things won't be poking back at me. Any more cuts to my phiz and I will begin to look like a sampler stitched by some clumsy schoolroom chit."

"I assure you, Lord Davenport, you could never appear anything less than gallant," replied Winslow softly. "As I am sure Lady O would heartily agree. Isn't that—"

The viscount cut him off with a curt laugh. "No need to ask. I'm well aware of Lady Olivia's opinion of me." Gingerly lifting several of the mushrooms out of the colander, he began to slice them with a slow, methodical stroke. "Might we discuss the report you compiled while we work?"

Olivia quickly took another handful of the fungi. *Ha!* she jeered at herself. Lord Davenport had not a clue as to her real thoughts!

Which might be just as well, seeing as the curve of his mouth and the burnished warmth that a touch of humor brought to his eyes were causing all manner of strange little lurchings in her stomach. Ones that had naught to do with hunger for her friend's Italian cuisine.

Seizing the excuse to appear concentrated on the task at hand, she bent over the table, listening with only half an ear as the viscount began to question the other man. As he probed for details on what Winslow had learned about Fleming and Rundle, she was grateful that her own inner feelings were not undergoing the same scrutiny.

They were not so easy to explain, even to herself.

Like the tangled patterns of light and shadow on the table, her interest in Maxwell Prescott Bingham remained far too quixotic to isolate each individual element. Oh, the physical attraction was undeniable. His brief kiss, though fired by anger rather than any real desire, had done nothing to quench her longing to reach beneath those layers of starched linen and stitched wool.

Yet the more she came to know him, the more provocative were his less-obvious attributes. She knew a host of handsome gentlemen, but not one of them possessed a fraction of Davenport's incisive intelligence and taciturn courage in the face of adversity. And one had only to look at his loyal commitment to his family and friends to see he was a man of unyielding principle.

A man capable of love.

Staring down at the tiny nick she had just made to her finger, Olivia warned herself to be on guard. If she wasn't more careful, she was going to be in grave danger of breaking one of her own cardinal rules of business. Allowing herself to become emotionally involved was dangerous.

Her head told her it was too risky, yet her heart . . .

With a ruthless slice, she finished off the last of the mushrooms. She hadn't survived all these years by listening to her heart. It was all very well to feel tempted to experience a physical liaison with the viscount, but she must not allow the attraction to go more than skin deep. That would only be begging for trouble.

And she had sworn to leave tumult and trouble—along with her red gowns and rejected childhood—buried deep in the past.

Seductive smells began to fill the kitchen—cooking tomatoes, freshly chopped basil, baking bread, and the pungent sizzle of garlic frying in olive oil. Winslow paused from his stirring long enough to uncork one of the bottles of wine he had brought up from the cellar. He passed around the glasses, then voiced a short toast.

"*In vino veritas.*"

"Let us hope so," replied Davenport. "The truth has proved damned elusive of late." Raising the wine—a red the color of polished garnets—to his lips, he took a small taste. "Excellent," he murmured. "Speaking of truth, I am not usually fond of the stuff we get from the Frogs."

"Ah, but this is from Tuscany, near Florence, where living well is an art," said Winslow. "The nebbiolo grape has its own unique character."

Davenport took another sip. So, too, did the man who was preparing the food with such zestful enthusiasm. Somewhat to his surprise, he found his initial dislike for Winslow was slowly mellowing into a grudging respect. He was, to be sure, still uncertain as to how he felt about Winslow's relationship with Olivia—whatever it was. However, extensive questioning had revealed that the fellow's odd humor and insouciant manners were underscored by a savvy intelligence and a keen eye for detail. The viscount imagined that a great many people made the same mistake as he had at first, thinking the man of affairs naught but a fluttering fop.

He was now well aware that very little escaped the other man's notice. It would, he reminded himself, be wise to bear that in mind.

"Finished with the fungi, are you?" Winslow examined the slices and gave a nod of approval. "Then would you mind grating the *pecorino* while Lady O shells the peas?"

The viscount accepted the wedge of hard cheese without argument. Perhaps it was the rhythm of the chopping or the heat of the stove or the tantalizing aromas—or the delicious red wine—but somehow he found his own conversation flowing more easily than usual. Not only was it impossible not to be impressed by the keen observations and insights of the other man, but Winslow was entertaining as well. The fellow's clever jokes and witty double-entendres slowly had his own tongue loosening enough to answer tit for tat.

"Pray, see what a dextrous touch His Lordship possesses, Lady O," said Winslow with a flutter of his thick lashes as he watched the viscount work the grater. "It must come from rigorous training in hand-to-hand combat."

"I fear you might be greatly disappointed," drawled Davenport. "I have far less experience in that than some of my former comrades—the Earl of Branford comes to mind."

Out of the corner of his eye, he saw Olivia look up, and though he thought there might have been a glimmer of amusement in her eyes, she ducked away too quickly for him to be sure.

"Oh, I think you are being far too modest, sir." Winslow gave a teasing wag of his finger. "I daresay you would have no difficulty in holding your own, should you choose to engage in the fray. Lady O seems to think you—"

A rather sharp cough from the lady cut off any further observation. "Windy, pray use your breath to cool the broth—it is in danger of boiling away. And mind that you keep stirring the carrots, else they will burn."

Much as Davenport would have liked to hear what her man of affairs was about to say, he was just as happy as she was to change the subject, for mention of his friend Branford had brought to mind another question. "If the Black Cat is no stranger to you, I would venture to guess you also know something of the Irish Wolfhound."

Winslow paused in his peeling of some unrecognizable root. "Ah, now there is an interesting beast. I wouldn't want to wager on whether he is more wild than domesticated. From what I hear in certain parts of Town, he's more of a fierce predator than a tame lapdog. And a solitary one." Dumping the shavings into a bowl of slops, he took up a different blade. "But then again, if I were a peer of the realm, I, too, would go to great lengths to guard my privacy. After all, the *ton* may tolerate a great many peccadilloes, but actually owning a bawdy house and gaming hell in Seven Dials, rather than simply putting one's purse and prick at risk in such an establishment, is likely stretching things a bit too far."

Taken aback at such blunt speaking in the presence of a lady, Davenport nearly choked on his wine. However, Olivia did not appear the least perturbed by the language or the subject matter. His slanted glance showed that the announcement, rather than elicit any maidenly blushes, had roused her from the preoccupation with her own private thoughts.

"Who?" she asked flatly. "And why wasn't I aware that a titled lord was doing business in the stews?"

Her man of affairs cleared his throat. "Lady O, I don't seek to sully your lovely ears with every bit of dirt I dig up—"

"Stubble the long-winded flattery, Windy." She fixed him with a steely stare. "You know I like to keep abreast of what goes on in Town."

Winslow's murmur, no louder than the hiss of steam rising up from the kettle, was inaudible to all but the viscount, who managed to catch only the words 'magnificent' and 'breasts.'

"What did you say?" she demanded.

Raising his eyes to the ceiling, the other man assumed an air of great innocence. *"Moi?"*

"Yes, *toi.*"

"Lady O, as the matter had no bearing on our own area of commerce, I didn't think it important enough to bring to your attention."

"I should hope not," growled Davenport, which earned him a gimlet glare from the lady.

"Who?" she repeated.

"The Earl of Killingworth," replied Winslow. Without further hesitation, he ticked off a few salient facts with clipped efficiency. "Connor Linsley. Irish mother, reputed to be a great beauty, and an even greater flirt. Died in a carriage accident, circumstances rather hushed up, as it appeared her companion was someone other than her husband. Father a feckless wastrel. Left the family coffers sunk deep in the River Tick by the time he shuffled off his mortal coil."

"A friend of yours?" she asked Davenport.

"We are acquainted." Then feeling a twinge of guilt over sounding disloyal to an old comrade, he felt com-

pelled to offer a bit of a defense for the earl. "Killingworth may have a certain reputation for wildness, but
he was also considered a stalwart soldier, unflinching
in the face of adversity. It appears that when passed a
tainted title and ruinous debts, he chose a bold strategy to recoup his losses, rather than throw up his
hands in surrender."

"His establishment is actually one of the more, er,
enlightened places of its kind," offered Winslow. "The
girls are treated well, and receive a generous compen-
sation for their . . . work."

"I suppose the gentleman should be given some
credit for showing enterprise." Her lips gave a small
quirk. "Is he turning a profit?"

"A modest one," replied her man of affairs with a
faint grin. "Though given the traffic, I wonder that it
is not a good deal more."

Davenport took the opportunity to voice his own
question. "Does he do business by foul means or fair?"

"I take it you are asking whether he is an unprinci-
pled cad or a cheat?" The other man thought for a moment. "My sources tell me that the Wolfhound is a
hard man, and a dangerous one to cross, but he plays
fair. His blunt at the tables is earned by virtue of skill
and savvy rather than subterfuge or swindle."

The answer was more welcome than Davenport
cared to admit. Despite the earl's show of sardonic indifference, the viscount did not think Killingworth
was quite as jaded as his snarls would indicate.

The relief must have shown on his face, for Olivia's
eyes narrowed. "If the gentleman is not a friend, why
the interest in his affairs?"

"It was the Wolfhound who tossed me the bone of information concerning Fleming and Rundle. Along with a few other scraps." He slowly dusted the last few cheese shavings from his fingers. "Speaking of which, have you perchance heard of anyone called the Connoisseur?"

Winslow's brow furrowed. "Sounds like someone I would be aware of. However, the name rings no bell. Why do you ask?"

"It was just something he said in passing, but . . ." Davenport shrugged. "In any case, while I have no reason to think the earl would lie, it does no harm to seek an outside assessment of his character."

"He makes few appearances among the *ton*," said Olivia. "But at the next opportunity, I shall contrive to meet—"

"No! You will not." Davenport smacked his palm upon the table, surprising even himself with the vehemence of his objection. "Stay well clear of Killingworth, Lady Olivia. He is not the sort of gentleman you should seek an acquaintance with."

"Is that an order, sir?" said Olivia softly.

The viscount's mouth compressed as the other man rolled his eyes heavenward. He didn't need the silent reproach to realize he had just made a serious blunder in strategy.

"Let me remind you that I am not subject to your authority," she went on. "Military or otherwise."

"I only meant—"

"Pax!" The resounding ring of a ladle striking the side of a pot punctuated Winslow's shout. Moderating his tone, he added, "Let us table further discussion of business until after the meal. Fine food is meant to be enjoyed in the spirit of good cheer rather than sharp words. Now Lady O, kindly take charge of passing the plates, and quickly, before my labor of love gets cold."

Grateful for the temporary truce, Davenport turned his attention to the brightly glazed earthenware bowl that was placed before him. "Er, what is it?"

"*Risotto alla Milanese.*" Winslow rushed around to sprinkle a liberal helping of the grated cheese over the dish. "*Buono appetito!*"

Whatever it was, the earthy aroma was heavenly. Seeing the others take up their spoons and dig in, he did the same. "Sublime," he murmured, accepting another glass of the Tuscan red.

"I am delighted to find you have an adventurous palate, sir, and are open to new tastes." Winslow added a pinch of ground pepper to his own helping, then passed it along. "I daresay a good many English gentleman would be unable to put aside their prejudices concerning what constitutes a proper meal, and turn up their noses at being served aught but a slab of beefsteak."

Davenport chewed thoughtfully, aware of the layered nuances in both the rice and Winslow's words.

After fetching the bread from the oven and another bottle of wine, Winslow went on. "Now tell me, sir, did you ever sample the delightful *vinho verde* of southern Portugal? It pairs extremely well with grilled fish. . . ."

The talk turned to foods and wines from abroad. Though the viscount's knowledge on either subject was limited at best, he found the commentary and descriptions highly entertaining. Part of the enjoyment, he acknowledged to himself, stemmed from seeing the smile slowly return to Olivia's face and hearing her add her own amusing observations on Indian cuisine. It was clear from her comments that unlike most high-born ladies, she had a good deal of practical experience in the kitchen. But that did not surprise him. Indeed, he was coming to expect—even anticipate—hearing the unusual from her lips.

Or perhaps the wine was merely addling his normally sound judgment. In any event, he realized he was chuckling along with the other man over her self-deprecating story concerning a recipe for curry powder.

". . . the color of the turmeric was so luscious that I got carried away and added a second jar to the blend. It looked absolutely lovely and the fragrance was divine, but the resulting lentils turned out hotter than Hades. Needless to say, we made some final adjustments before bringing the mixture to market."

"The blend has become quite popular in the Carolinas," added Winslow with a grin. "And quite profitable."

"You certainly make it sound . . . intriguing," said the viscount, his gaze watching the play of laughter in her eyes. "I should like to sample such a curry."

Lowering her lashes, Olivia slanted him an unreadable look. "I fear you might find curry a bit too hot for your palate, Lord Davenport." She shifted the angle of her spoon. "I was under the impression you did not care for the exotic."

"Why would you say that, Lady O? From what I have observed, the Valiant Viscount is not one to wilt under fire," exclaimed Winslow as he began to clear the table. "Why don't we all gather at your townhouse for a meal sometime soon—one that includes those divine red lentils, and a chutney of tropical fruit. Of course, I would be only too happy to serve as her humble slave in the kitchen."

"Ha! The day that you show any sign of servility is the day pigs will fly," she muttered under her breath. "I vow, Windy, if you don't watch your tongue, curry is not the only thing you are going to find a trifle hot in the coming days."

Winslow paused, plates in hand. "Er, speaking of hot topics, Lady O, I might as well break the other news now."

"What news?"

The insouciant grin faded from his face. "Since writing up the report on my investigation, a few new facts have come to light that I have yet to tell you." He pursed his lips. "Perhaps you ought to put down that knife."

Even in the soft light, Davenport saw that her eyes had taken on the gleam of polished steel. "Don't be melodramatic. By now you know there is not a great deal that can disturb me."

"I know," sighed her man of affairs. "But when you hear this, you are going to be out for blood, and I prefer it not be mine."

She lay down the blade. "Very well. I am prepared for the worst."

"No, you are not. But I suppose there is no getting

around it." He drew a deep breath. "Lady O, I—I have reason to believe that Fleming and Rundle is in the business of exporting a much more valuable cargo than Staffordshire china."

"Well, that's hardly a great surprise," she replied dryly. "Your notes made it clear that stolen goods were a large source of the firm's considerable revenue."

"Er, right. But my notes didn't spell out the full range of goods that the firm handles."

"You mentioned art. I assume that paintings, illuminated manuscripts—"

"Those things account for only a small part of the profits. I have just learned that the most lucrative of their dirty side businesses is the trade in . . . flesh."

She paled. "What—"

"People. Or, more specifically, young women. Whom they transport to the East, using the services of Grisham and Blake." Winslow's expression turned even grimmer. "The orders are specific. In the ledgers, gold-rimmed means a blonde has been requested, while ebony-colored decoration stands for black-haired beauty. You get the picture?"

Olivia was staring at him with unblinking eyes. "However did you get a clerk to disclose that?"

"You have your own ways of persuasion, Lady O. I have mine."

"What . . ." she began, then seemed to change her mind. "How—"

The point of his own paring knife was sunk into the chopping block. "I don't yet know all the particulars, but be assured I will keep at it."

The hairs on the back of Davenport's neck were standing on end. "Young women?" he repeated. "You are sure of this?"

Winslow nodded. "I don't have any hard evidence in my hands to prove it, but I have heard enough from a variety of sources to be convinced that it is true."

"Damn," he whispered. "But if we go to the authorities with your testimony—"

A short cough cut him off. "It would be best that my phiz not appear in the vicinity of the authorities, milord. I assure you, my word would hardly be taken as gospel, seeing as certain of my own activities have not exactly been . . . saintly."

Olivia had, in the short interlude, recovered her composure. "I expect a full report on the matter to be on my desk first thing in the morning."

Though his first reaction was to voice a vociferous protest, the viscount knew by now that such a tactic had no chance of success. Their previous skirmishes had shown that a frontal assault only stiffened her defenses. If he were to have any hope of keeping her out of the direct line of fire, he would have to come up with an alternate strategy.

An arctic lump suddenly formed in the pit of his stomach. Davenport leaned back in his chair, looking from Winslow to the array of iron implements hanging over his head.

Curse the damnable Ruby Lion and all the trouble it had spawned!

And yet, no curses or recriminations could dislodge the weight of guilt as the chilling realization set in.

He should have foreseen that his request might draw Olivia into danger.

But there was no use in hindsight. Now, more than ever, he had to find a way to counteract the evil eye of the red-orbed beast.

Chapter Eleven

A thick mist muffled the sound of the wheels as the carriage rolled through the darkened streets. Olivia stirred against the soft leather squabs, her own pensive silence mirrored by the viscount's. The evening had not gone exactly as planned, she admitted. While she had meant to observe the gentleman's reaction to the unexpected, she hadn't quite anticipated that the experience would bring her some surprises as well.

Like the fact that when Davenport peeled off a layer of his stiff reserve—along with his coat—he revealed an even more devastating smile than she had realized, not to speak of a wickedly seductive chuckle and sculpted set of muscular shoulders.

Even now, she could feel the tingling heat of their proximity through the thick folds of her cloak. Or perhaps it was merely the flush of the wine. She had imbibed a good deal more than was her wont, in hopes of dampening her growing desire for another taste of the viscount's lips.

No doubt he would be shocked beyond speech if he had an inkling of the highly improper fantasies that his presence was arousing in her. After savoring the delicious thought of what those shoulders would look like stripped of his shirt, Olivia let out a small sigh. On second thought, he probably would not be at all surprised by her lack of maidenly primness. From dress to deportment, he had made it abundantly clear—through looks as well as words—how much he disapproved of her.

But as she slanted a surreptitious look at his profile, its contours limned in the faint glow of the carriage lamp, she was surprised to see that his lips were curved ever so slightly upward.

Seeming to sense her scrutiny, the viscount cleared his throat and spoke for the first time since entering the carriage. "Might I inquire how you became acquainted with Mr. Winslow in India?"

"He came to my attention through his business connections around the harbor of Bombay." She knew it would probably be best to leave it at that, but she could not refrain from giving a brief summary of his career as a swindler. "However, a certain venture convinced him he ought to seek another line of work." She paused. "I think the exact words of his last client had something to do with slicing off his testicles and feeding them to the monkeys in Rajaipur Park."

"That might encourage a man to change occupations in a hurry," murmured Davenport. After a moment, he added a dry chuckle and a flare of amusement warmed his eyes to the color of liquid gold.

Olivia found herself slumping back against the leather, feeling as if her spine were molded of jellied aspic.

"Though if the client had caught Winslow with his porcinis and olive oil," he went on. "The monkeys would no doubt have been served up a feast to remember."

Had the reserved viscount actually cracked a joke? And a rather risque one at that? A lick of heat set her knees to tingling. "You enjoyed the meal then?" she asked. "I—I had wondered whether you might find it too odd for your palate."

"It was memorable, though I fear I consumed a few more glasses of that excellent wine than I am used to."

"I, too, probably had a trifle more than I should have."

"Are you feeling chilled, Lady Olivia?" He edged forward on the seat. "Here, allow me to draw the drapery across the window."

"Not at all. I am quite comfortable, sir," she replied. However, she could not repress another tiny shiver as his arm grazed hers.

"Are you sure? It seems to me—"

The vehicle gave a sudden lurch as it turned up one of the winding side streets leading away from the river. Davenport's hand ended up entangled in the folds of her cloak. "My apologies," he mumbled as the tips of his fingers brushed her bare shoulder. Quickly regaining his balance, he closed the drapes and sat back down.

"Think nothing of it," replied Olivia, wishing she could wrench her own thoughts away from the seductive slide of his thigh against hers.

But the heady Barolo and the viscount's continued closeness were having a deleterious effect on her reason. At the next jolt of the wheels, she allowed herself to be thrown sideways, twisting so that she ended up nearly on top of him, her breasts crushed against his chest, her cheek pressed hard against his starched collar.

"Do forgive my clumsiness, sir," she murmured, her breath stirring the folds of his cravat. "Anschul is still not used to navigating English streets."

Davenport had wrapped his arms around Olivia to keep her from slipping off the seat. "Er, quite," he replied gruffly, trying to steady both of them against the squabs.

Olivia felt him stiffen as another bounce threw her closer. "How terribly embarrassing." Lifting her chin, she tried to discern his expression, but the shadows kept his face as inscrutable as ever. "Especially as I am no doubt the last woman on earth you would wish to find on your hands." A sudden realization of the absurdity of the situation added a shade of stifled laughter to her voice. "Or in your lap."

His head lowered a fraction, the low light of the carriage lamp catching a strange glint of fire in his amber eyes. A sound seemed to stir from his lips—a whisper somewhere between a groan and a curse. She sighed softly, fully expecting a chilly rebuff to follow.

Davenport's response, however, was anything but chilly. Ever so gently, his mouth grazed hers. For an instant, she was aware of naught but a warm feathering of air against her cheek, then he kissed her again, the tentative touch quickly heating to a searing intensity that took her breath away. His lips were warm with the lingering spice of the wine. And with need.

Twining her fingers in his tawny locks, she pulled him closer and with a teasing nibble opened herself to a deeper embrace. He needed no urging to slide his tongue inside her. She moaned at the rush of liquid pleasure that surged through her at his probing intimacies—or perhaps it was the viscount who was making the sound. It was hard to tell anymore. Passions ignited, she was deaf to all but the thrumming pulse of heated blood reverberating in her ears.

As he sucked her lower lip between his teeth and gave another low growl, Olivia gave thanks to the heavens that, despite his stony reserve, the man was not impervious to desire. For some time, she had feared that the debacle of his broken engagement might have given him a distaste for women in general. However, the hard throb of his rising arousal against her thigh gave ample testimony that the viscount had not abandoned all interest in females, or foresworn the delights of the flesh. Indeed, his lush, lapping kisses were now roving down the line of her jaw and his hand, stripped bare of its glove, was tugging at the fastenings of her cloak.

That he found her attractive—at least physically—added a frisson of fire to her own heated response. Freeing her lips from his renewed embraces, she arched up to trail the tip of her tongue along the thin line of his scar.

"Olivia." She couldn't discern whether the hoarse rasp was said in exultation or accusation.

"Max." Her own mouthed whisper was nearly lost in the tangle of hair curling around his ear.

She sucked in her breath as his fingers splayed over her breast and squeezed into the sensitive flesh, pressing the palm of his hand into the point of her nipple.

Whether it was a surfeit of Italian wine bubbling up inside her or the heady essence of bay rum and earthy masculinity assaulting her senses, she felt a powerful intoxication flooding every fiber of her being.

How else to explain why she was moving her hips in a languid slide across the front of his breeches, taking a wicked pleasure in feeling his manhood shaft into an even more steely arousal? Wanton wench, she chided herself, though in truth she felt little guilt that any pretense to maidenly modesty was fast slipping away, along with the bodice of her gown.

It was, she assured herself, nothing more than a primal, animal attraction that had her mouth brazenly seeking to couple with Davenport's again, and her back arching under his touch, inviting his fingers to slip beneath the ruched silk.

With a ragged groan, the viscount bared her bosom. In the chill of the night air, she was acutely aware that the hardened little nubs were like two points of fire. Arching into his touch, Olivia reveled in the sensation of his stubbled jaw grazing over the ivory smoothness of her neck. Her zephyred sighs gave way to a unbridled cry as his palm pressed over one of the rosy aureoles.

"Ahhhh." Coherent speech seemed beyond reach. At the moment, the only clear thing her mind could grasp was the overwhelming need to thrust her hands beneath the pleats of the viscount's shirt and explore the muscled contours of his bare flesh.

A single stud popped free, the burnished gold disappearing with a lightning wink into the shadows of the floorboards.

"Sweet Jesus," he whispered against her skin, his voice smoky with heat as she began stroking caresses over the flat planes of his chest. "I fear in another instant that your touch will have me bursting into flame."

Olivia felt on fire herself. It had been an age since she had touched a man, and the feel of corded muscle and crisp curls was having a molten effect on her insides. Emboldened by his words, she tugged free the tails of his shirt and let her hand drift downward, skimming over the sculpted abdomen to tease at the intriguing line of hair that led down to his manhood. The taut stretch of his breeches outlined his heavy arousal, and after the barest of hesitations, Olivia slid her fingers under the waistband, moving tantalizingly close to—

A sudden jolt of the wheels rocked her back, forcing her hand to retreat.

"Bloody hell." Sounding as dazed as she felt, Davenport wrenched up at the grinding halt of the carriage.

"Albermarle Street, memsahib," called the Indian coachman.

Had they really arrived at the viscount's lodging so soon? Biting her lip in frustration, Olivia freed herself from the tangle of fabric and sat up abruptly. Usually the quiet efficiency of her servants was gratifying, but on this occasion she could not help wishing Anschul might have proved a tad less resourceful at finding his way through the unfamiliar maze of London streets.

"Damnation." The viscount muttered another oath as a creaking from above indicated that the man was already starting to climb down from his perch in order to lower the step. "We . . . that is, I . . . should not have been pawing over you like a randy beast, but . . ." His words trailed off in a fumbling search for his cravat, which had somehow come completely undone during their torrid embraces.

With a brusque tug, Olivia pulled up her gown. The last thing she wanted was an apology! Was he truly sorry he had kissed her and fondled her bare breasts? There was certainly no remorse on her part, but as to his feelings . . .

She kept her gaze averted. The viscount's physical attributes were wickedly obvious to the eye. But as for his real sentiments, he kept them well hidden behind a mask of flinty reserve. However, tonight she had glimpsed a slight fissure in the facade, and from what she had seen, it was clear Maxwell Bingham was not chiseled out of solid stone, no matter how much he wished to appear devoid of flesh-and-blood passions.

Passions.

If she had a choice in the matter, she would see to it that Lord Davenport's were aroused again in the near future.

His breath was coming in ragged rasps, as if he had covered several furlongs at a dead run, rather than the mere handful of yards from the carriage to the stone portico. Shirttails flapping and a length of limp neck linen trailing in the breeze, the viscount managed to reach his rooms without an embarrassing encounter with any of the other lodgers. And he gave harried thanks for his standing instruction that his valet not wait up for him. While his cravat may have wilted under the heat of recent events, the unmistakable bulge in his breeches gave clear testimony that a certain part of his anatomy had not.

What the devil had come over him?

Davenport leaned back against the closed door and sucked in a breath of air, seeking to marshall his skittering thoughts. Raking a hand through his hair, he slanted a baleful stare down at his disheveled coat, open waistcoat, and rumpled shirt, its starched collar now hanging woefully askew.

He must be thoroughly foxed, he decided. No—on second thought, he must be thoroughly insane, for not even a hogshead full of wine could account for him losing every last drop of soldierly discipline and gentlemanly scruples. Why, he had behaved no better than a damnable beast, pawing and slavering over the lady like a lion intent on devouring some morsel of flesh.

Grimacing, the viscount ran his tongue over his lower lip, still tasting the ambrosial sweetness of Olivia's kisses. The tingling warmth suffused the inside of his mouth, then sent a lick of lust spiraling down through his belly. Why, if the carriage had gone on any farther, he would never have been able to control his wild urges. He would have had her skirts tossed up around her shapely thighs, his breeches stripped down to his knees. . . .

A pulsing shudder warned him that such heated fantasies were dangerous to pursue.

Dangerous.

He, of all people, should know the dangers of allowing the flames of passion to flare in his breast. If one flirted with fire, there was always the chance of being badly burned.

And yet, perhaps her rare spark was part of the lady's exotic allure. There was no other way to explain why he felt inexorably drawn to her, like a moth mesmerized by an open flame. Olivia Marquand was quite unlike any female he had ever encountered. Supremely self-assured, she radiated a confidence that was completely opposite his own searing self-doubts.

Davenport was aware of his mouth quirking into a mocking twist. There must be a grain of truth to the scientific theory that opposites attract. Because for some unaccountable reason the lady had not been adverse to returning his kisses with a certain degree of warmth. Another frisson of heat coursed through him. Her hands stroking his naked flesh had been almost too much to bear, and in another instant she would have been touching . . .

His hands raked the damp locks away from his forehead. No doubt it was the potent combination of bubbling prosecco and heady Barolo that had her behaving so oddly. When she awoke in the morning, she would likely be appalled at the recollection of what had taken place within the confines of her carriage. Davenport could only pray that the spirits might also have the effect of fuzzing her memory come the morrow, just as it had fuzzed her reason this evening.

As he stumbled for his bed, he knew that he would have no such luck. Visions of her glorious body were certain to haunt his dreams for many a night to come.

* * *

Rules.

Pressing her forehead to the coach window, Olivia watched her breath fog the rain-spattered glass. She had long ago lost count of all the rules she had broken.

Even as a child, she had realized that hers was not a temperament suited to docile obedience. Possessing an inquisitive mind and stubborn streak of independence, she had sensed that meek acceptance of the strictures of Society would doom her to a life of servility and boredom. And that, she decided, was a prospect worse than any other fate she could imagine.

So she had defied convention and taken the risk of striking out on her own, ignoring every dratted rule governing the behavior of young ladies. It had not always been easy. She had made a good many mistakes along the way, some foolish, some funny, some painful. But she had few regrets about the life she had chosen. Her father had been a hard, unfeeling man, and the prospect of living the rest of her years under the thumb of another such tyrant had been unthinkable. The chances she had taken and the sacrifices she had made had earned her the sort of unfettered freedom of which few females could ever dream. She had a vast fortune, a satisfying occupation, and was subject to no whims but her own.

If the cost had been an occasional indefinable melancholy and a sharp pang of loneliness, it was a trifling price to pay. And if at times she was achingly aware of having no one with whom to share the small victories and disappointments of everyday life, that, too, could be dealt with. . . .

The coach hit a hole, jarring her cheek against the leaded pane. Olivia leaned back, bringing her fingertips up to soothe the sudden sting. To be sure, she could take care of herself, yet there was no denying she missed another's touch.

Seeing that men of her acquaintance sought a sort of solace in temporary relationships, she had allowed herself the same discreet liberties while in India. Her liaison had been a civilized affair, based on mutual respect and regard. However, when it had ended—the American charge d'affaires in Madras had eventually returned home to Washington and a wife—she had felt a pang of regret, but her heart had not been in any danger of breaking.

And now?

Over the thud of hooves and the snap of wet leather, she was aware of the erratic thump deep in her chest. A far cry from its usual steady rhythm, the pulse seemed to echo her own uncertainties. Olivia bit at her lip, still tender from Davenport's kisses. Despite her dislike of strictures, she had made it a cardinal rule in both her business and personal life never to allow her heart to become engaged.

As the wheels rolled over the cobblestones, her thoughts slowly spun full circle, back to the notion of rules. And an old English adage. Like the iron rims ringing against the pavement, the words kept going around and around in her head.

Rules were meant to be broken.

Chapter Twelve

✦◈✦

"Interesting?" Sprague speared a third piece of burned toast, then aimed his knife at the jar of strawberry jam. "You are invited to dine with the alluring Lady Olivia and her mysterious informant at some undisclosed location, and that's all you have to say about the evening?"

Davenport kept his eyes on the front page of the newspaper as he took a sip of his coffee. "It was. I learned a number of interesting things."

"Such as?"

He watched his friend wolf down a bite of his landlady's unappetizing breakfast offering and made a face. "Such as, I like Italian food."

Sprague paused in his chewing to fix him with a quizzing stare. "What in the name of Hades does that have to do with our investigation?"

"A great deal, actually. The fellow who served as our chef is as skilled at extracting information from the stews as he is at whipping up a *risotto alla Milanese.*"

Sprague's expression scrunched in disbelief. "A what?"

"Oh, never mind."

"Hmmph. The question that comes to mind is not

what were you eating last night, but what were you drinking?"

"Wine," replied Davenport, deciding against any further elaboration.

"Quite a lot of it, judging by the fact that you aren't making any sense." After a more careful survey of the viscount's pinched countenance and shuttered gaze, Sprague put down the last of his bread. "Hell, you look bloody awful. Along with overindulging in spirits, you appear as if you were involved in a tussle with an alley cat." His friend's eyes narrowed. "There's a faint scratch on your jaw and a red scrape on your neck—"

"A dull razor." Davenport fumbled with the folds of his dressing gown, hoping the dull flush rising to his cheeks would go unnoticed. "Blake has yet to learn the fine points of serving as a gentleman's gentleman."

Sprague raised a brow but refrained from comment as he poured himself another cup of coffee.

"Look," growled the viscount. "My appearance—hellish or otherwise—is the least of our concerns. We have a great many more important things to discuss . . ."

He left off speaking as his valet limped into the small sitting room and handed over a letter from the morning post. "Thank you, Blake." Tearing open the seal, Davenport skimmed over the sheet of paper as the ex-soldier retreated into the hallway. "Bloody hell—when it rains, it pours."

Sprague darted a glance from the dappling of sunlight filtering in through the leaded glass to the viscount's stormy expression. "Bad news from Lady Cara?"

"Yes and no. My father's condition has taken a turn for the better." Davenport refolded the letter and dropped it onto the table. "So much so that she has left him in the care of our aunt Beatrice and is hastening here to London."

"Females," muttered his friend. "Er, can't you exercise some control over her?"

"What do you suggest—a whip and spurs? Or mayhap a leash and collar?" snapped the viscount, unable to keep the edge of sarcasm out of his voice. "In case you hadn't noticed, my sister is not likely to submit to such measures with the docility of a well-trained hunter or hound."

"You have a point," agreed Sprague with a rueful grimace. "Lady Cara is definitely not the usual biddable schoolroom chit." He rubbed at his jaw. "Indeed, I have a feeling we had better get to the bottom of all this before the ladies have a chance to get any further involved."

"Amen to that." Davenport cleared his throat. "I take it you had a chance to read over the notes sent by Lady Olivia. Well, after meeting with her informant, I am convinced that the information is accurate."

"He must be unusually talented, to have come up with that sort of detail."

"You don't know the half of it," said Davenport under his breath. In a louder tone he added, "His style may be a trifle unusual but he is highly effective. It is as if he has eyes and ears in every nook and cranny of the city." He shifted a bit uncomfortably in his seat at the notion. Winslow was awfully adept with his cleavers. If he thought his employer's honor had been assaulted . . .

Cutting off the unpleasant thought with a slight cough, the viscount set aside his cup. "Indeed, very little goes on in Town that escapes his notice."

Sprague's powers of observation were fairly sharp as well. Leaning back in his chair, he folded his arms across his chest. "Max, there seems to be a great deal I am missing here."

"Nothing of any real import," mumbled Davenport.

However, the mention of the word "missing" did jog his memory. He had been so preoccupied with thoughts of Olivia that he had not given much mind to the disquieting bit of news Winslow had announced concerning missing girls and the traffic in human flesh. Horrific as it was, it had naught to do with the terrible tragedy threatening his own family.

Which he was doing precious little to stave off, he reminded himself roughly.

"There was one other ugly fact that Lady Olivia's man dug up regarding Fleming and Rundle," he said slowly. "Though in truth it has little bearing on us, save to confirm we are dealing with thoroughly dirty dishes. It appears they may be involved in a particularly vile sort of white slavery. The selling of poor but pretty young country lasses to the East—"

The front legs of Sprague's chair came back down to the floor with a jarring thud.

Noting that the color had leached from the other man's face, the viscount felt a pinch of alarm. "What is it, Spencer?"

"I, too, learned some rather disturbing information last night. That is why I am here at such an ungodly hour." His friend drew in a deep breath and avoided meeting Davenport's gaze. "In light of what you have just told me, I fear it may be even grimmer news than I first imagined."

The viscount calmly set aside his cup "Go on."

"You recall that we sent Woodley to have a little chat with Mary Gooding's friend?"

He nodded.

"It turns out she was the first of the girls to disappear. And . . . well, Woodley also heard rumors that a number of people have noticed a certain fellow seeking to cozen up to pretty young females who have recently arrived from the hinterlands." Sprague grimaced. "A fellow who fits the description of your brother."

Davenport felt a sickening lurch of his insides. "No. Not Kip," he declared, though his words rang a bit hollow. "I cannot believe he would ever be involved in anything so sordid."

"Not even if he were desperate?"

The viscount opened his mouth to speak but found the denial was stuck in his throat.

"I am sorry to be the bearer of bad news, Max. Mind you, it's not proof of any perfidy, even if . . ."

"Even if the coincidences are growing more and more damning?" Davenport gave a bleak smile. "Hell, Spencer, things aren't looking awfully good."

"No, they are not," admitted his friend. With a shrug of sympathy, he looked away, allowing the viscount a moment of privacy. "What would you like to do?"

Drown the awful truth in a deluge of brandy and laudanum, thought the viscount, finding the idea of seeking solace in oblivion rather tempting. But only for an instant. If ever there was a time not to succumb to the cowardice of self-pity, it was now. He would not break the bond of faith between Cara and himself.

Or Kip.

"Keep digging," he answered, the nails of his clenched fingers pressing into his palm. "Until I find my brother. And uncover the truth, no matter what it may be."

Sprague let out his breath. "I rather expected you would say as much. Now that we know to keep looking more closely at Fleming and Rundle, let me make another round of the clubs and see what else of interest I can turn up."

"I will go ask Taft if he knows anything of its owners. Or whether he can think of anyone else who might merit closer scrutiny." He ran a hand over his unshaven jaw. "And if we are lucky, Lady Olivia's man may discover further evidence."

"We are going to need all the luck we can get," murmured his friend as he reached for his hat.

They were going to need a lot more than luck, thought the viscount grimly. They were going to need a bloody miracle.

Her tremoring hands betrayed the depth of Olivia's outrage. Years may have passed, but the memories had not. The wrenching feeling of utter helplessness could still cause her to wake at night, sweat sheening her brow, the bedsheets twisted like manacles around her limbs. Nor had she forgotten the raw indignity of having no more rights in Society than a hound or a horse, and no recourse against the arbitrary injustices that men could impose on a female.

And she had been one of the lucky ones—a lady born into a position of power and privilege, with access to education and money. The foolscap crackled in the clench of her fingers. She couldn't begin to imagine what terrors might torture a poor young girl with no resources at all. If there was a chance in hell she could do something to stop the horrific crimes that Winslow had hinted at, she would gladly square off against the Devil himself.

Setting aside the sheaf of notes, Olivia swore loudly, first in Hindi, then in English, hoping the release of emotion might help restore a more measured tempo to her breathing.

"Did you call, memsahib?" Save for his white turban, Vavek appeared as no more than a smudged shadow in the darkened hallway just outside her study.

"You damn well know I did not," she muttered.

"It is time for tea," he announced, paying no heed to her pronounced scowl.

"I do not want any tea today."

"I shall bring it anyway." With a soft slap of sandals, he entered the room, balancing a large brass tray in one hand and a stack of files in the other. "You work too hard, eat too little, and frown too much."

"All of which a proper servant would not dare remark on." Sighing, she leaned back from her desk. Despite her snappish words, she found she was looking forward to the ritual of their daily break. Perhaps the genial warmth of the beverage might help melt the cold lump in her stomach.

Vavek remained tactfully silent as he went through the ceremony of straining the fragrant leaves and spices, then adding the exact amount of sugar that she preferred. It was not until he had swirled in a splash of cream and placed the cup and saucer by her elbow that she caught the stirring of concern in his eyes.

"Forgive me," she apologized. "Perhaps one of Guphta's cinnamon twists will help sweeten my sour mood."

He brought over the plate. "You are unhappy, memsahib?"

"No. . . . Yes." She bit into the mixture of tart spice and buttery shortbread. "I am . . . unsettled, I suppose."

"Ah." He gave a sage nod. "You do not yet feel at home in England."

For an instant, Olivia did not quite trust her voice to answer. "Mmmm," she murmured through a mouthful of tea. Brushing a crumb from her cuff, she stared at the brightly colored painting of the Hindu god Shiva that hung over the mantel. "Do you think it was a mistake to leave Bombay?"

His reply, when it came, was rather oblique. "You were no longer comfortable in India."

It was true, she supposed. Though she had been invited to many of the social gatherings of the expatriate English community, she was never really accepted as part of their close-knit society. She was too different. While they had clung tightly to the clothing and customs of home, she had chosen to live in a different part of the city, adopting native dress, making Indian friends, exploring Eastern philosophies. For years she had been happy moving between the two worlds, but of late she had begun to feel adrift.

Neither here nor there.

"And yet," she sighed, "I wonder whether I shall always feel estranged from——" Realizing that her sentiments were in danger of taking a maudlin turn, Olivia dismissed them with a slight shrug. "But I am different from most people. And quite glad of it." The gold bangles on her wrist tinkled gently as she gestured at the fine furnishings and expensive artifacts that decorated the room. "Indeed, a moment or two of melancholy is a small price to pay for all that we have achieved." Lifting the cup to her lips, she added, "And don't tell me the material world is but an illusion, for no amount of lectures on the subject will convince me to simply sit back in a lotus position and accept my karma. I prefer trying to enjoy this current life rather than slogging through fifteen reincarnations to reach a state of bliss."

"Patience is a virtue, memsahib."

"Patience is a platitude," she shot back.

A glimmer of white flashed from within the depths of his oiled beard, followed by a rippling of air no louder than the lapping of tea against the smooth porcelain. "You have yet to achieve the rapturous state of spiritual enlightenment that brings with it inner contentment."

Olivia's lips curled up at the corners. However blasphemous, she found herself thinking that at the current moment, she would gladly settle for the rapturous state of physical passion, and the sort of contentment that brought. "I fear that not even the pyrotechnics display over Vauxhall could illuminate my path to the Truth."

His laugh became a shade louder. "You never know. Divine enlightenment comes in many forms, memsahib."

"Well, make mine about six feet two inches in height, with the divinely chiseled features of a Greek god and—" Seeing the pinched expression that had suddenly come to her servant's face, she swallowed the rest of her wry words along with a nibble of pastry. "I see that Mr. Derrington was able to locate the files I requested."

"Yes, memsahib." Bowing to the abrupt change in subject, Vavek gathered the slim Moroccan portfolios from the tea table and carried them to her desk. "The purse you provided was ample incentive for the head clerk to come up with a key to the locked cabinets. Everything should be there."

Olivia had already untied the ribbons and was perusing the lists of lading.

After clearing away the china, Vavek paused to stare meditatively at the dregs in the silver strainer. "Trouble is brewing, is it not?"

"Don't tell me you have taken up the art of reading the future in tea leaves? It is bad enough that I am subject to lectures on philosophy and religion." She turned to a new page. "What makes you ask?"

"The presence of a cat."

Her brow took on a quizzical arch. "A cat? I wasn't aware that we had acquired a household pet."

"Cats seem to be a harbinger of danger for you. The last time we were in London, there was the Black Cat and the Jade Tiger."

Her servant had clearly not forgotten the events of the previous year—the Earl of Branford's nickname was the Black Cat, and one of the talismans they had been searching for was known as the Jade Tiger. She quickly dropped her gaze back to the page in her hands. "Well, I managed to escape unclawed."

The scrape of the tray over the lacquered wood was more than adequate expression of his skepticism. "And now," he went on, "The One Who Growls Like a Lion has come back."

"Lord Davenport?" Her attempt at nonchalance was somewhat marred by the fact that the sheet of paper slipped from her fingers. "Don't be imagining shadows where there are none. His arrival in Town has nothing to do with me."

"Ha! And pork may grow wings," replied Vavek, in precise imitation of her scoffing tone, if not her English.

"If you are going to be sarcastic, I suggest you stick to Hindi—the effect loses something in the translation."

A bejeweled finger gave a warning wag. "Do not make light of my warning, memsahib. There is trouble afoot. I do not imagine the white shadows that creep through the alleyways under the cover of the English fog."

Olivia paled. "Y-you have seen such things? Here in London?"

He stroked at his beard. "Yes. They were following the Lion when he called here. And trailed after him when he left." A note of reproach crept into his voice. "It would be a help for me to know why."

"I don't know why," she said in all truthfulness. "I

meant it when I said his troubles are not ours. As a small favor to him—and his sister—I asked Windy to gather some information pertaining to a private family matter. Other than that, I assure you the viscount and I are hardly on speaking terms."

His bushy black brows rose so high as to nearly disappear in the folds of his turban.

"However," she went on quickly, "as you have guessed, there is trouble brewing, but it is going to be entirely of my own making."

Aware of his near omniscient powers of observation, Olivia decided there was no point in trying to keep her plans a secret. With clipped precision, she gave a summary of Winslow's inquiry, including the unsettling evidence he had uncovered concerning the selling of young women into bondage.

"It is a terrible tale, indeed." Vavek's hand stole unconsciously to the jeweled dagger he kept strapped beneath his tunic. "As you see, there are predators on the prowl everywhere, not just in the jungles of Jaipur." A soft curse in Hindi sounded, followed by a mournful sigh. "Though I don't suppose it would have any effect were I to beg you to leave it to the proper authorities to hunt them down."

"None whatsoever." Olivia slapped open the second portfolio and fanned out its contents. "We both know nothing will be done if I leave it to them. Those responsible are a cunning lot. Papers have no doubt been falsified, magistrates bribed, and their identities well hidden under a veneer of respectability. And seeing as the victims are mere females—and poor ones at that— no one will care enough to ferret out the truth."

The lowering of his dark lashes did not quite obscure the pooling of concern in his eyes. "I have served you long enough to know that argument is as futile as trying to climb through the heavens to the summit of Chomolungma."

"Another one of your ancient aphorisms, handed down by the gods?" she asked, essaying a touch of humor. "Well, you have the right of it—I am quite as stubborn and immovable as the highest of your towering Himalayan peaks."

He did not crack a smile. "Lofty idealism is admirable. But take care, memsahib, that the storm of emotion I see gathering force in your eyes does not cloud your usual pragmatism."

A small shiver coursed down her spine at the uncanny echo of her own silent fears. "When have you ever known me to allow emotion to affect business?"

"The English have their share of proverbs," he answered softly. "Including one that says there is always a first time for everything."

Chapter Thirteen

❦

The viscount surveyed the crowded ballroom, feeling decidedly out of tune with the lilting laughter and lively music. Making polite conversation or capering through the figures of a country dance was not how he wished to be spending his evening, but Taft had suggested that a discreet questioning might elicit some useful information on Fleming and Rundle from one of the expected guests.

Davenport certainly hoped that would be the case. His day had been spent traipsing in what had felt like aimless circles around the Wapping docks. Despite blistering his toes, he had stumbled on nothing, save for towering crates of pottery, endless bales of tobacco, and mountainous sacks of rice. Hardly incriminating evidence that Fleming and Rundle was engaged in aught but respectable trade, or that Grisham and Blake was transporting aught but legal goods.

The weak arrack punch did little to wash the taste of frustration from his mouth. It was likely that any interrogation of the gentleman from the East India Company was going to prove just as great a waste of time.

And time was not a commodity he could afford to waste.

Still, he was here. With a scuff of impatience he turned for the card room. Perhaps Mr. Warrington was engaged in a hand of whist, or . . .

"Lord Davenport!"

The viscount's head jerked up as the flounce of a hem grazed his foot.

"La, I thought that was you! How delightful to see you again, sir."

He vaguely recognized the lady as a passing acquaintance of his aunt, though it had been several years since they had been introduced in the Pump Room at Bath. Her name was . . . Norris . . . Nettles . . . Nellerton . . .

"You do remember me, sir, don't you?" she said coyly. "Lady Nerringer. And this, as I am sure you recall, is my daughter Adelaide." A wave of her hand indicated a petite blonde standing demurely by her side. "Your dear sister and Addy became bosom bows during our visit to York last summer."

"Yes, of course." Davenport forced a smile as he regarded the twists of artfully arranged curls framing a heart-shaped face. "Of Turnbridge Wells," he added, hoping he wasn't confusing the chit with someone else. On hearing a nervous titter in reply, he doubted Cara would consider the young lady a good friend, but there was no denying her mother's choice of adjectives was in some ways fitting. He couldn't help but notice that the pale-yellow gown, cut slightly lower than befitted her age, was designed to show the chit's frontal endowments to full advantage.

The mother looked immensely pleased at his recalling the tiny detail. "Oh, and I was so afraid you might think me encroaching." Her glove came to rest lightly on his sleeve. "But as we happened to bump into each other just now, it would have been quite ill-mannered of me not to come and offer a greeting."

He murmured some pleasantry in response, wondering how to shake off her attention without appearing overtly rude.

"Surely, you were not trying to sneak off to the card room with all the older gentlemen," she went on. "And deprive the young ladies of the pleasure of your partnership on the dance floor."

"I am not a very adept dancer, Lady Nerringer."

"Oh, don't be modest, sir!" She gave a playful tap on his arm. "I am sure your footwork leaves nothing to be desired."

Neither did hers, thought Davenport with a sardonic sigh. As the music was just striking up, he saw he had been neatly maneuvered into extending an offer. He cocked an arm. "Then if Lady Adelaide would care to risk a bruised toe, might I ask the favor of your company in forming this set?"

"Of course she would." Turning to her daughter, Lady Nerringer nudged her forward.

The young lady's lashes fluttered. "Of course I would."

Clearly elated at having stolen a march on the rest of the room, Lady Nerringer's smile of triumph stretched wide enough to include a knot of other chaperones and their charges standing nearby. "Do make an effort to keep his lordship amused, Addy," came her whisper of last-minute advice. "As he has been away from Town, I am sure he is anxious to hear all the interesting events that have occurred in his absence."

Privately rueing the unfortunate delay, Davenport escorted the young lady to a less-crowded corner of the floor, searching his mind for some suitable topic of conversation. He was, however, relieved of the need of leading the conversation, for as soon as they glided into the first figure of the dance, Lady Adelaide began such a lively chattering about the latest ondits in Town that no more than an occasional polite murmur was required in reply.

In the face of her girlish efforts to please, Davenport found his initial irritation turning to ironic bemusement. Having been absent for so long from the swirl of Society, he had forgotten how egregiously silly young ladies could be. It was not really their fault, he knew. They had been carefully schooled to hide any bit of individuality or opinion beneath a froth of pastel colors and innocuous prattle. Yet compared to the tart common sense of his sister or the incisive intelligence of Olivia Marquand, his partner seemed to possess so little substance, he might have been guiding a feather across the floor.

And surely, she couldn't have sounded more like a peagoose had she tried.

"The weather has been shockingly cool of late, do you not agree, sir?"

"Shockingly," he replied, a wry smile twitching on his lips.

"Yes, but Lady Uxbridge simply insisted on having her picnic by the Serpentine, as she had ordered a number of the most darling little boats . . ." The girl's light trilling became indistinguishable from the soft melody of the violins.

Listening to both with only half an ear, Davenport found himself thinking how Olivia, with her compassion, her convictions, and her courage, could never blend into the background. Unlike the young lady hanging on his arm—who would no doubt agree that the moon was made of green cheese if he voiced the conjecture—Olivia was a constant challenge. Uncomfortable though it might be at times, the viscount realized that such passion added a certain spice to life.

Passion.

His eyes fell on the frilled folds of silk spilling out from the pale-lemon sash. The contrast was glaring. And the odd thing was, that while up until lately he had been convinced of his preference for neutral shades, now he wasn't so sure. Having become a bit more familiar with a palette of vibrant tones and richly textured hues, he wasn't certain whether he would ever be satisfied with color so leached of life that it appeared hopelessly dull.

Not, he reminded himself with a touch of black humor, that he was planning on decorating his existence with either of the two ladies.

". . . I vow I was never so shocked in my entire life, but I did not fall into a swoon. Unlike Emma Hartsfield."

Recalled to duty by a dramatic sigh, he essayed to appear at least mildly interested. "You don't say. And the mastiff did what?"

Two spots of pink appeared on her cheeks. "Took

hold of Lord Uxbridge's pantaloons and pulled. Hard enough to cause a horribly embarrassing rip."

At that, he could not contain a chuckle. "How very stalwart of you not to fall in a fit of vapors. The sight of his lordship's bare legs must have been a terrifying sight indeed."

Lady Adelaide smiled uncertainly. "Y-you think me brave, sir?"

"Exceedingly."

Her dimples deepened at the assurance. "Oh, well, Mama and Cousin Freddie thought so too. You see, the nasty dog then attacked the roast capon. . . ."

As a series of steps turned them toward the center of the ballroom, Davenport was about to resign himself to another interval of droning boredom when a shimmer of iridescent indigo caught his attention.

"Er, forgive me." He recovered from the errant slip in time not to make a complete cake of himself. Another few awkward steps brought them back into rhythm, yet the viscount could not help but steal another sideways glance.

No, he had not been mistaken. It was indeed Olivia, moving with the fluid grace of running water as she carried on an animated conversation with her partner. Davenport was too far away to hear what was being said, but by every nuance of body language, she appeared to be hanging on the gentleman's every word.

He recognized the fellow as the same one who had been dancing with her on their previous encounter at a London soiree. Tall, trim, and elegantly attired in a dove-gray coat that seemed to bring out a silvery sparkle in Olivia's eyes, the gentleman possessed a perfectly pleasant countenance, accentuated by laughing hazel eyes and a long, patrician nose that Davenport suddenly found himself wanting to squash to a pulp.

That the reaction was irrational in the extreme did not stop his fingers from fisting around Lady Adelaide's hand.

A tiny flinch from the young lady shook loose the grip of anger that had momentarily taken hold of him. He had no call to feel the slightest twinge of jealousy. Olivia Marquand was free to bestow her favors on whomever she pleased, be it Devlin Winslow or some cursed fribble in fancy dress.

"Forgive me," he repeated with a grimace. "As you can see, Lady Adelaide, I was not exaggerating my lack of polish on the parquet."

She did not have the temerity to agree. However, in mirroring his own eagerness for the ordeal to be over, she looked vastly relieved when the music came to a merciful end a few stanzas later and the viscount led her back to her beaming mother.

Vowing to dodge any further efforts to drag him onto the dance floor, Davenport plucked a glass of champagne from the tray of a passing footman and ducked into the nearest alcove.

"Absolutely not! Max would have my guts for garters if I were to allow any such a thing."

"And I, Mr. Sprague, will have your liver for fish bait if you do not." Cara calmly stood her ground and met the former officer's daggered glare with one equally as sharp. "Now kindly step out of my way."

"Lady Cara, you cannot be in earnest." Seeing his frontal assault parried, the viscount's comrade-in-arms was quick to regroup and try another tactic. "Be reasonable. Surely you know that I cannot escort a gently bred lady to an, er, establishment like the Wolf's Lair."

"Why not?"

He looked rather flustered by the question. "Why, er, because it would be a shock to your, er, delicate sensibilities——"

"Ballocks." Seeing she had rendered him momentarily speechless, Cara launched her counteroffensive. "In case you hadn't noticed, sir, I don't have any to speak of."

"But——"

"Besides, I did not ask you to accompany me. I need to speak with Max as soon as possible, and since Blake mentioned this Wolf's Lair as a place to which he might have gone, I don't intend to waste any more time in silly argument."

The viscount's grizzled valet looked stricken. "S-s-sorry, sir. His lordship said te tell you he might stop by there, if he didn't have any success at the ball he was attending. So when Lady Cara asked, she being his sister an' all . . ." He swallowed hard. "I had no idea it was a . . ."

Cara patted his shoulder. "It wasn't your fault. I bullied it out of you."

"Whose ball?" asked Sprague quickly.

Blake's face turned a rather bilious shade of green. "I-I didn't catch that name."

"I did ask the same thing," she murmured. "So, if you don't mind . . ."

"For God's sake! You have no idea what you are doing!" Harried into a lapse of gentlemanly manners, Sprague swore and threw his hands up in exasperation as he moved to block her path. "Have you ever been inside a bawdy house or a gaming hell?"

"No." She didn't bat an eyelash. "Which, now that you mention it, is another reason to insist on going. For quite some time I have been curious to see for myself just what all the allure is for you gentlemen."

An odd choking sound emanated from Sprague's throat, along with several muffled words that she thought included "plaguey" and "shrew."

"And," she added dryly, "I am not referring to any of the purely physical activities that take place within its walls. Having managed the family estate for several years, I have spent a goodly amount of time overseeing the breeding of sheep, so I am fairly conversant with the mechanics of the act."

Sprague's face turned an even more mottled shade of red. "No," he announced, finally galvanized into coherent speech. "I won't allow it, and that's flat."

"I am not quite sure how you intend to stop me." Tucking her reticule more firmly under her arm, Cara flexed her fingers. "Max has taught me a very nasty right cross, in case you were contemplating the use of physical force."

For an instant, Sprague looked tempted by the idea, but then contented himself with a curl of his lip. "You may know the name, but now that I think on it, you won't have much luck knowing where in London to look."

"Oh, I am sure that my coachman will manage to

find the place easily enough." She stepped around him and headed for the door. "Seeing as Blake also mentioned that it is located in Seven Dials."

"Bloody hell." Recognizing himself neatly outmaneuvered, Sprague had no option but to admit defeat. "Then gentlemanly honor allows me no choice but to come along." Trailing at her heels, he couldn't keep from adding a peevish mutter. "A pox on managing females. Has anyone ever mentioned that you are a cursed nuisance, Lady Cara?"

"So many that I have stopped keeping count." Without slackening her stride, she descended the stairs two at a time and hurried to the street. "Don't worry—Max will be the first to acknowledge you had no choice in the matter."

His reply was a string of words that did not bear repeating.

"Oh, come, don't be such a prig, Mr. Sprague. Where is your sense of adventure?"

"It must have fallen out of my cockloft. Along with my sanity."

"And your sense of humor," she quipped.

"There is nothing remotely funny about having to escort my friend's sister to a house of ill-repute owned by one of London's wildest rakes," snapped Sprague as he waved off the Bingham barouche and flagged down a passing hackney. "At least defer to me on one thing. Allow me to take you in a public conveyance rather than your family carriage, on the off chance that this little escapade may be kept under wraps."

"Whatever you say, sir," she conceded with a sweet smile.

*   *   *

Did the dratted man have to look so devastatingly handsome when he laughed?

Repressing a twinge that tugged between regret and resentment, Olivia forced her gaze back to Lord Bentham's smiling countenance and feigned a flash of amusement.

He paused in mid-sentence, a quizzical tilt marring the symmetry of his silvery brows. "Go ahead and kick me if you wish, Lady Olivia. I do have a tendency to prattle on when the subject of botany comes up."

Olivia hastened to allay any fears that he was boring her. "Not at all, sir. I assure you, your observations are highly diverting."

And in truth they were. His colorful narrative on the efforts to unearth a certain species of orchid in the wilds of Jamaica revealed a keen eye and droll sense of humor. A very keen eye, she warned herself, and one not easily fooled by a show of superficial laughter. She found herself liking him more for it. Determined not to hurt his feelings, she quickly schooled her features into an expression of rapt attention.

"Well, if you are sure . . ."

Over the years in business, Olivia had become quite skilled at masking her true thoughts, so another murmured assurance was encouragement enough for him to continue his commentary.

Would that she could exercise such iron control over the inner workings of her head.

She stifled a sigh. What did it matter that the viscount was all but drooling over some sweet little confection of a young lady? Of course he would prefer a nice, biddable miss—with not a hair nor a thought out of place—over an unconventional female who was not wont to stifle her own independent opinions.

Still, in spite of the concerted effort to make logic overcome emotion, she had to admit that her feelings were rather bruised. It was only last night that he had been kissing her with devouring passion. Why? Did he think of her as fair game on account of her off-color past and unladylike profession?

Her heart gave a tiny lurch at the idea that he saw her as naught but a wanton woman. And yet, she reminded herself, she was. She had no cause to complain that his attraction was purely carnal. After all, her own mouth had been just as hungry, her own hands tearing at clothing to savor the sweet feel of naked flesh beneath her fingertips.

Her palms grew warm within their covering of kidskin, while a shivering of goose bumps appeared on her bare arms.

"Are you feeling chilled, Lady Olivia?" Bentham's solicitousness only added to her discomfort.

"A bit fatigued is all," she lied. Not even to herself did she wish to admit to a pang of disappointment. Or a stab of jealous anger.

His query, however, afforded her a plausible reason for excusing herself from his company as soon as the last notes of the music had died away.

"This is not at all what I expected."

"Lord have mercy. Next time I offer to do a good deed for a friend, may I be struck down by a thunderbolt from the heavens," muttered Sprague. "Don't tell me you have given the matter a great deal of thought."

"Not a great deal," replied Cara as she turned for a closer look at the engraving hung over the sideboard. "But seeing as you gentlemen are always so eager to discuss these types of establishments among yourselves, it is difficult not to be slightly curious."

Her brother's friend quickly stepped between her and the offending print. "And just how would you know we gentlemen discuss places, er, like this, Lady Cara?"

Her brow shot up in amusement. "I take it you don't have any sisters, Mr. Sprague. Otherwise you would not be asking such a naive question."

"No." He ran a hand through his hair. "Thank God."

"And just what, may I ask, did you expect?" came a deep growl from the dimly lit hallway.

Cara spun around. She and her companion had been unceremoniously escorted into a small parlor off the entrance foyer by the hulking man who had admitted them, the door slamming shut as he hurried off to deliver Sprague's message. It had now been reopened, and though shadow obscured the figure who was lounging up against the molding, a flicker from one of the wall sconces caught the glimmer of iron-gray highlights in his hair.

"Oh, something a bit less . . . subtle," she replied thoughtfully, running an eye over the muted colors and rather tasteful furnishings before pointedly moving around Sprague and returning her gaze to the art on the wall. "By the by, is this an Antonioni?"

"Yes." The man stepped into the room. "Do you like it?"

Cara leaned in for a closer study. "Interesting." After regarding the naked tangle of intertwined limbs, jutting phalluses, and ripe breasts for another few moments, she tilted her head. "I hadn't realized there were so many variations on the same theme."

A low bark of laughter sounded, but it quickly died away as he turned to Sprague. "What the devil do you mean by bringing a respectable young lady here?"

"I—"

"The name is Cara Bingham," she interrupted. "And you are?"

"This is not a damn drawing room, Lady Cara—we do not go through the niceties of formal introductions, seeing as most of our guests would rather it not be known they were here." The sardonic sneer grew more pronounced "If you wish a name, I am called the Irish Wolfhound."

"Ah." She didn't so much as flinch at his deliberate rudeness. "So I take it that this is your Lair?"

"I am the proprietor."

"Excellent. Then we needn't dance a jig around what I wish to know, for I imagine you can tell me straight off whether my brother is here under your roof."

"I can, indeed. But whether I will is another matter altogether." His lip curled up to bare a flash of teeth. "I should not remain in business very long were I to freely disperse such information to every wife or sister who happens to knock on the door."

"Is it profitable?"

Her abrupt question seemed to take him aback for an instant. "The business? Yes," he replied softly. "I manage to make ends meet. So to speak."

"Now see, here, Wolf—"

"How very clever of you," Cara went on, ignoring Sprague's halting effort to nip off the exchange before the thinly veiled innuendos from the Earl of Killingworth became even more risque. "I do hope it does not require too much effort on your part."

"I assure you, I am quite up to the task."

"Bloody hell." Unable to contain his concern any longer, Sprague let out a growl that was nearly as ominous as one from the Wolfhound. "Need I remind you that the lady is a gently bred female?"

The pale gray eyes fixed him with an unblinking stare. "Need I remind you that it was not I who brought her here?"

"I doubt I shall ever be able to forget it." Sprague grimaced. "Seeing as we are both anxious to be rid of her, why don't you tell us whether Max is here?"

"But you heard what the Wolfhound just said, Mr. Sprague. He is running a business and doesn't give away his precious information for free." Looking annoyed with both men for assuming she had no say in the matter, Cara was quick to intervene. "How much will it cost me? And be forewarned that I don't have much blunt, so don't bother with trying to claw an exorbitant sum out of me."

"I am willing to negotiate the price." Despite his drawl of disdain, the earl could not prevent her gibe from causing a slight spasm to disturb his look of jaded cynicism. "Kindly step outside, Sprague, so that the lady and I may have some privacy in which to strike a deal."

"I'm not sure, er, that is . . ."

"What do you think? That I intend to throw up her skirts and feast on her virginity?" Killingworth looked back at Cara with a sardonic smile. "You are, I presume, a virgin?"

"Presume whatever you wish," she replied evenly. "I don't give a damn what some flea-bitten cur chooses to think, as long as I get what I want."

Her brother's friend winced. "Good God, Lady Cara, bite your tongue. You are not dealing with some lapdog," he warned in a low whisper. "Even the most battle-hardened soldiers do not seek to goad the Irish Wolfhound into baring his fangs."

He sought her arm, but she slipped out of reach.

"I really must insist—"

"Out, Sprague," ordered Killingworth as he moved in a step closer to her.

She stood firm in the face of his approach. "You may do as he says, Mr. Sprague. I am quite capable of fending for myself."

Sprague hesitated, but then marched out past the earl. "I will be right outside, in case you need me, Lady Cara," he muttered. "You have five minutes. Then, come hell or high water, we are leaving."

"Do you always ignore sensible advice, Lady Cara?" asked the earl, once the door had fallen shut.

"I often ignore what males consider to be sensible advice. There is a big difference between the two, though someone as arrogant as you would undoubtedly fail to recognize it."

"That may be so," he retorted with a menacing grimace. "Let me, however, offer a bit of advice that only a complete idiot would fail to recognize as sensible, Lady Cara. When trying to strike a bargain with someone, it is not overly wise to start off by hurling insults at his head."

"Actually, I am well aware of that. Just as I am well aware that any attempt at negotiating with you is probably a waste of breath. It is obvious you have a low opinion of females and aren't going to consider my request seriously."

Despite his obvious irritation, he could not disguise a glimmer of curiosity. "Then why did you agree to see me alone?"

"To show you not everyone turns tail and runs whenever you so much as make a noise." Cara squared her shoulders. "By the by, why does everyone appear so afraid of your bark?"

"Because I am accorded to be a dangerous, unpredictable beast," he replied. "You see, I tend to bite when I get annoyed. And my teeth are accorded to be sharper than most."

"Do you chew up the unfortunate young women who work for you, then spit them out when they are no longer of any use?"

For an instant, it appeared she had gone a step too far in baiting him. A wild light suddenly leapt to life in his quicksilver eyes, and as he leaned forward, anger bristled from every pore of his long, lean face. But just as quickly, he seemed to get a leash on his emotions and replied with a quelling cynicism. "You know nothing of the grim realities of life or of London, so do not presume to think you understand what goes on under my roof," he snapped.

"Perhaps you would care to explain it to me."

The earl gave a harsh laugh. "Nosy little cat, aren't you? Max should take a birch and spank some sense into you."

"Let him try."

"You have spirit, I'll grant you that." He paused for a moment. "Still interested in making a deal?"

"What is the price?"

"A kiss."

Her face betrayed her surprise, eliciting a rakish smile from the gentleman. "Haven't you been kissed before?"

"Why, you impudent whelp—"

Her words were cut off by a ruthless press of his mouth. At the same time, his arms wrapped around her, and with several quick strides, he had her pinned against the wall in an intimate embrace.

She meant to make a vociferous protest, but as his lips moved hard against hers, outrage gave way to a feeling she could not quite define. Her struggling ceased, her hands threaded into the graying curls and her words came out as a whispered sigh.

It was some moments before he finally stepped back and freed her hands. "A gentleman could make a far worse choice on the Marriage Mart than you," he said softly. "For at least he will likely not be bored in bed. Indeed, I wouldn't mind swiving you myself."

Cara gasped for breath. Then, after touching her fingers to her swollen lips, she uttered an equally shocking expression and let fly with a blow aimed at his cheek. It connected with a resounding crack.

His head snapped back, the angry red imprint of her palm quickly darkening his flesh. "That was for such an unspeakably rude insult." She raised her hand again. "And this, you arrogant hellhound, is for—"

He caught her wrist. "Is for what? The fact that for the first—and likely only—time in your life, you have tasted a bit of real passion?"

She went very still. "Do you really take pleasure in causing pain?"

Killingworth allowed her hand to fall away, then turned from the light, his angular profile unreadable in the dim flicker of candles. "Most people think so," he said evenly, moving noiselessly to the sideboard. "In answer to your question, your brother is not holed up at the Wolf's Lair. Unlike me, the viscount is a virtuous as well as a valiant gentleman." Taking up one of the bottles, he poured himself a glass of brandy and tossed it back in one gulp. "Now get out of here. Before you are recognized and your reputation ends up any more savaged than it already is. Trust me, the tabbies of this Town possess claws even sharper than mine."

Seeking shelter behind a screen of leafy lemon trees, Olivia found the narrow alcove gave passage into a darkened hallway, where the cool quiet was a welcome respite from the crowded ballroom. She slipped through the doorway and leaned up against the patterned wallpaper, breathing deeply to regain some measure of her usual sangfroid.

It was high time to apply the ice of reason to her thrumming blood, and banish the strange frisson of fire racing through her veins. The reason for her presence was business, not personal. She, of all people, ought not to have difficulty in separating the two.

After another few minutes, Olivia felt composed enough to face the lights and laughter, but as she turned to retrace her steps, a dark form took shape from the surrounding shadows and stepped forward to block her way.

"I do hope I am not intruding on some private tryst," drawled a familiar voice.

She stopped short. "Given who was here first, Lord Davenport, perhaps it is you who is expecting another person. I, on the other hand, was simply looking for a breath of fresh air."

"Indeed? It appeared that the atmosphere in the other room was quite to your liking."

The nerve of the dratted man! She had not been the one ogling a pair of half-bared breasts. "I am surprised you took notice of aught but what was dangling before your nose."

"I—" An odd little rumbling made it sound as if Davenport had something caught in his throat.

A cough, she decided, for surely it could not be a laugh.

He quickly recovered his voice. "I couldn't help but take notice of your presence. I had thought you did not care for such frivolous entertainments as these."

"I don't," she snapped. "I came looking for you."

Olivia saw his shoulders square to attention. "Why?"

"Because I have just discovered . . ." Some perverse impulse caused her to pause. It would only take a few moments to tell him about what she had found hidden in the ledgers, and yet, the whisper of music from beyond the archway stirred a seductive recollection of the time they had waltzed together. "We really ought not discuss it here, sir. I think it prudent to avoid being spotted in clandestine conversation."

"You are right." His breath feathered against her ear. In the darkness, she had not realized he had drawn so near, but now she was acutely aware of his closeness. "I suppose we had better take up position for the next dance."

The scent of bay rum mingled with masculine exertion was suddenly having an unnerving effect on her senses, for Olivia felt a rather delicious warmth steal over her at the prospect of once again being taken up in his arms. Shaking it off, she reminded herself not to get carried away by girlish fantasies. His proposal was obviously unmoved by any sort of tender sentiment. There had been no acknowledgment of their recent intimacy, only a gruff desire for information.

She drew in a small gulp of air and replied with a businesslike brusqueness. "Very well. Let me go out first, then come around to the entrance of the card room."

They were soon part of the crush of couples twirling in time to a lilting Viennese melody.

"What have you found?" demanded Davenport as soon as a series of spins had afforded them some privacy.

She took a moment longer to savor the feel of his

hand pressed to the small of her back, and the sensuous sway of their thighs turning in tandem before replying, "Ledgers."

"God Almighty. Do they prove—"

"They prove a great deal, but . . ." She took care to keep a smile pasted on her face. "But I think you had better have a look for yourself. Along with the listings of profits and expenses, there are a number of letters that appear to be written in code."

He hesitated, moving through a turn before asking, "Given the urgency of the situation, might we overstep the bounds of propriety this evening? I should like to come around to your townhouse as soon as possible."

"I think you know by now that I am not afraid to break the rules when something important is at stake, sir. Be there in half an hour."

Chapter Fourteen

"Well? What do you think?" The papers in Olivia's lap crackled as she shifted in her chair.

Davenport did not lift his eyes from the seemingly random arrangement of letters he was studying. "Your surmise is correct. It is definitely a code of some sort." He turned to the next page. "More than one, in fact. This first grouping looks to be a straightforward version of a simple Caesar cipher. It shouldn't take me very long to figure out the key. But the second set is far more complex. At first glance, I would guess that it is a Vigenere cipher."

"A Vigenere cipher?" Olivia made a face. "I confess, it looks like complete gibberish to me."

The viscount allowed a small smile. "It's meant to. Blaise de Vigenere was one of the most devilishly clever men in the history of cryptography. During the late fifteen-hundreds, he devised a whole new concept of codemaking. The strength of his cipher lies in the fact that he uses twenty-six distinct cipher alphabets to encrypt a message." He picked up a pencil and sketched a diagram on a blank sheet of paper. "It's based on a square, with *A* through *Z* arranged across the top and along the side."

She looked intrigued. "You mean to say there is a system to giving order to such chaos?"

"Oh, yes. Cryptography is based on complex patterns of logic and reason."

"How intriguing. I should like to learn more about it."

"That does not surprise me." Seeing a slight flicker in her expression, he was quick to add, "And do not interpret that the wrong way, Lady Olivia. What I meant was, you have the intelligence and imagination to find such a task challenging. Indeed, I am sure you would be very good at it."

"You think so?" Olivia edged her chair closer. "I would certainly need a great deal of help to learn the basics." Intent on studying the diagram, she did not look up. "This appears impossibly difficult, sir."

"It will take time to figure out the keyword," he admitted. Turning back to the first notes, Davenport started to scribble out a new set of letters. "However, while most of the papers you found inside the ledgers are the result of such painstaking encryption, this one must have been written in a hurry. The Caesar shift has been used since Roman times, and while it may serve to disguise a message from the casual eye, it's fairly easy to break using frequency analysis."

"Really?" Olivia was engrossed in watching him work. "I still cannot fathom how you see any discernible pattern."

His gaze angled up from the page. "It all depends what you are used to, Lady Olivia. Bills of lading, shipping schedules, cost analyses—such things that come easily to you seem incomprehensible to me." The viscount started a new line of letters, but for a moment his eyes lingered on her profile.

Would that there were an equally easy key to deciphering her expression.

He thought he detected a hint of admiration in her voice, but perhaps he was reading something into her tone that was not there. In truth, he had no real clue as to her feelings. As for her thoughts on what had happened the previous evening in her carriage, she had taken care to dance around the subject during their waltz. . . . Reminding himself that this was no time to allow his mind to stray, Davenport reached for a fresh sheet.

"I have figured out several of the vowels," he announced a short while later. "It shouldn't take too much longer to make out the rest of the letters."

Olivia rose. "May I get you some tea?"

"Thank you," he replied absently. Elbows braced on the leather blotter of her desk, he had quickly fallen into a rhythm of work, the scratch of his pencil on the grained foolscap punctuated by the muted ticking of the mantel clock and the soft crackle of the fire. It was a comfortable room, he realized as he tested the alphabet shifts, and one conducive to concentration. For all the exotic artifacts and vibrant hues, he felt oddly at home.

The scent of jasmine and bergamot filled the air as Olivia returned with an ornate brass pot shaped like a dragon and a service of china. From its fanged spout came a splash of steaming gunpowder tea.

Without looking up, the viscount took a first sip. "Damn," he muttered, putting his cup down so abruptly that a slosh of liquid spilled over the corner of his notes.

"Is Formosa Oolang not to your taste?" she asked dryly. "It is one of my most expensive blends."

He finished writing out the message he had just deciphered, then turned the paper so that she could peruse it.

"A meeting?" As she read on, her own cup rattled against its saucer. "Why, it's set for tonight!"

Davenport was already on his feet. "There is just time enough to make it," he said, darting a look at the clock.

"I take it you know what the Gilded Swan refers to?"

Several seconds ticked off before he answered. "A brothel near Jermyn Street. One that caters to a very jaded sort of gentleman." He turned to leave, grateful that she did not ask how he had come by such information. Any feelings of relief, however, were quickly swept away by the brush of her skirts against his boot.

"Not so fast, sir." She beat him to the door. "I am coming with you."

"The devil you are! Stand aside, Lady Olivia."

Olivia didn't budge. "I don't see as you have much of a choice."

She had left him little room to maneuver. "Be reasonable," he appealed. "It could be dangerous."

"All the more reason for not going alone." She took down a small lacquered box from a decorative plinth. "As a veteran soldier, you should know that it is not a wise strategy to move against an unknown enemy alone." A small pistol appeared in her palm. "Or unarmed."

His jaw tightened.

"Have I not proven a dependable ally in the past?"

"It's not a question of that—"

"Then of what! For God's sake, whether you approve of my unladylike actions or not, remember it was you who came to me in the first place. I am now as involved as you are—we go together or not at all." Olivia fisted her fingers over the weapon. "Make up your mind, sir. We do not have time to bicker."

"You—you will abide by my orders?"

"Without question."

"Ha—Hell will freeze over before that day comes!" Nonetheless, he gave a brusque wave of surrender. "Put on a dark cloak. And stay behind me."

"Tread softly," Davenport warned, his own hurried movements slowing to a snail's pace as he rounded the corner of an apothecary shop and edged into the alleyway behind the Gilded Swan.

It was the first time he had spoken since leaving her townhouse.

Olivia fell in step at his heels, determined to give no cause for rebuke. They had cut through Green Park on foot, and though it had taken great effort to keep up with his loping strides, she had not fallen behind.

The uneven ground was littered with broken slates, shards of glass and a number of other things she did not care to identify. Lined in a drunken row along one of the brick walls were a number of empty brandy barrels, stacked two or three high. Just past the last of them was the rear entrance of the brothel, a roofed doorway guarded on either side by a spiked railing.

Davenport stopped halfway down the line. Nudging open a space between the hogsheads, he signaled for her to enter, then squeezed in beside her.

Olivia did not need his grip on her arm to remind her of the need for silence. Though she hardly dared breathe, the pounding of her heart still echoed like cannon fire in her ears. The other noises seemed ominously loud as well—the creak of a shutter sounded more like a gunshot, the rasp of a loosened shingle like the scrape of a hobnailed boot. . . .

The tightening of Davenport's hand told her she was not merely imagining the sound of footsteps.

After another moment, three short raps sounded. A latch clicked. A door swung open.

"We've come from the Black Bird. You sent word?"

"Yes—I have come into possession of something that might interest a connoisseur of the flesh."

Connoisseur.

Olivia felt Davenport press forward. She did the same. Through the small gap in the barrels, she could just make out three men standing on the stone landing. One of them held a lantern, but it was unlit, making it impossible to see more than a murky silhouette of their shapes.

"Indeed?" The man who spoke pulled the brim of his hat down a bit lower. "It had better be something good to have risked such an urgent summons."

"Oh, it is." Her eyes could now make out a figure framed in the doorway. "I understand that the gentleman is seeking a fair-haired beauty to round out a matched set of six. I have a bit of porcelain in perfect condition, but we will have to move fast. Certain questions are being asked. . . ." The voice dropped to an inaudible murmur.

"Don't move," whispered Davenport. Crouching down, he started to inch forward.

At the same instant, a cat shot out from behind a mound of rotting garbage. Claws scrabbled over his boots and as the viscount stumbled up against the outer stack, the top barrel teetered and toppled to the ground. He fell to his knees, the small pistol skittering out of reach.

Over the muffled curses, Olivia heard the distinct click of a hammer being cocked.

"Hold your fire. It's only a sodding cat."

"We'd better make damn sure of it. Send your porters out the front to block off the alley. We'll make a search from here. Use a knife if—"

Davenport didn't wait for the sentence to be finished. A hard shove sent several more barrels flying, then he grabbed Olivia's hand and they sprinted back the way they had come. A door slammed as they reached the side street, followed by the clatter of steps. From the rear came the thud of racing feet.

Olivia felt a frisson of fear run down her spine.

"This way!" The viscount tugged her to the right and ducked into another narrow passageway. "Once we get to the other end, we can lose them in the maze of alleys that lead off to Saint Albans Street." Dodging around a wedge of fallen timbers, he quickened his pace. "But we must hurry."

She gasped and he turned just in time. A gate of solid oak blocked their way, its massive iron padlock shutting off any chance of finding a way out.

"Damn." Davenport looked back, but already the sound of pursuit was growing louder. He drew in a breath, then pushed her up against the wall. "Sorry," he muttered just before his mouth crushed against hers. Tearing open her cloak, his hands sought her gown and rucked it up around her knees.

It was, realized Olivia, their only hope of escape. With a scattering of hairpins, she shook loose her tresses and threw her arms around his neck. Kicking off a shoe, she slid her toes up to the crook of his knee, aware that the move was exposing a great deal of leg.

"Harder, luv!" Feigning a heated moan, she grabbed a fistful of starched cravat and wrenched it free. It fluttered through the air, tangling in a frothing of petticoat as his fingers pulled at the knots of her garters. The ribbons came loose and the silk stockings slithered down around her ankles.

His hips rocked into hers.

Arching back, Olivia touched the tip of her tongue to his cheek. "Here they come," she breathed, before opening herself for another deep kiss. Out of the corner of her eye, she caught the glint of a gun barrel taking dead aim at Davenport's back.

The weapon hovered for a moment, then dropped as the man turned to the figure behind him with a leering snigger. "Nowt here but some swell swiving one of the lightskirts from Jermyn Street."

"Looks to be a new girl." His cohort cut a crude gesture through the air with his pistol and took a step forward. "And a hot-blooded wench to boot. Wouldn't mind taking a turn at dipping my iron in the fire."

"You might well find your cock roasting over hot

coals if we don't get moving," warned the first man. "Come on—the Black Bird ain't one to cross."

After raking Olivia with a last, lustful look, his cohort backed off and allowed himself to be drawn away.

She waited perhaps a touch longer than was necessary before drawing back from the viscount's kiss. "I— I think they are gone."

For an instant, Davenport's eyes had a strangely molten fire to them, but it disappeared so quickly Olivia decided she must have been imagining things.

"To be sure, let us wait a moment longer."

Cool and calm, his voice sounded a good deal steadier than she felt, for as she shifted her stance, Olivia suddenly realized that his palms were pressed in an intimate caress of her inner thighs. She rather expected him to jerk them away, but they lingered for a heartbeat or two before he knelt down to retrieve her garters from the rutted earth.

"Here, allow me to help," he said softly as her trembling fingers fumbled at forming the knots. Smoothing the silk stockings into place, he tied off the ribbons with a sure hand. He located her missing shoe and slid it gently over her foot.

"Do you feel up to walking?"

"Yes, of course," she replied, more sharply than she had intended. "It is not as if my slippers are made of glass."

His locks, tumbled in disarray over his forehead by her heated advances, obscured his expression, but she thought she detected a quirk of his lips as he reached for his crumpled cravat. The collar of his shirt had come undone, and rather than loop the linen back around his neck, Davenport stuffed it in his pocket.

"Then we ought to be off." He took hold of her arm and Olivia found herself grateful for his closeness. "Before the hackneys all turn into pumpkins at the stroke of midnight."

She nearly stumbled. "I—I am surprised that you can make a joke at a time like this."

"Experience has taught me that it is at just such a time like this that a sense of humor is most needed." Before she could respond, his grip tightened and he urged her forward. "We had better hurry, Lady Olivia. We were lucky the first time around, but there is no telling when they might return."

Davenport lost no time in guiding her through the warren of alleys and out into one of the quieter thoroughfares of Mayfair. "I think it safe enough to stop here and wait for a passing hackney."

"If you don't mind, sir, I find I would really rather walk." Olivia could not quite explain why, even to herself. She rather expected an argument, or perhaps a gruff order. Instead, he settled her hand in the crook of his arm and turned in the direction of Half Moon Street.

"There were times after a battle when I would walk for hours—it didn't matter where—before I felt ready to return to my quarters."

It was the first time he had ever lowered his guard with her. An odd sort of fluttering stirred in her chest at being allowed a glimpse of what lay behind the mask of stoic reserve and she found herself clutching at his sleeve, afraid the moment might slip through her fingers.

"Had you always wanted to be a soldier?"

"Praesto et persto." She sensed an imperceptible tightening of his muscles. "It is not a question of what I wanted. A Bingham is expected to do his duty—stand in front and stand firm."

"I have always assumed a male has more freedom to choose his lot in life," she mused.

His lips curved ever so slightly upward. "I am not sure any of us are truly free to make such decisions."

Olivia found herself smiling. "Vavek would enjoy such a discussion on karma and fate. I am afraid I am a sad disappointment to him for favoring pragmatism over philosophy." As they passed through the flickering spill of lamplight, her wryness faded as well. "Were you unhappy in the military?"

"Ah, that is yet another question for which there is no easy answer." He said it lightly, but in turning his cheek, the faint line of his scar grew more pronounced. "I believe there are principles worth fighting for, Lady Olivia. But having lived through the horrors of war . . ." Davenport let out a slow breath. "I think that joining the diplomatic corps, or working for reforms in Parliament, would have put my talents to far better use." He shrugged. "However, my commission in the army was purchased while I was still in leading strings, so I marched in line with Father's expectations. I cannot really say I regret it."

"Your father sounds nearly as tyrannical as mine." She thought for a moment. "Growing up, did you like him?"

A pause, though slight, was unmistakable. "I respected him."

"That is not at all the same, sir."

"No. It is not." He walked on in silence for several strides. "You told Alex and me very little about the reasons you ran away from home. Your own father must have been worse than a tyrant to make life so unbearable."

Like the viscount, Olivia was an intensely private person. There were things she had never revealed, even to Winslow and Vavek.

"Forgive me," he murmured, noting her hesitation. "I seem to be trespassing far beyond the boundaries of proprieties in all manner of ways tonight."

His gaze held hers, and in that flickering instant there seemed to pass between them an acknowledgment of a bond that transcended their verbal skirmishes.

"He was a monstrous man," she said, her whisper so slight that Davenport had to strain to catch more than a stirring of air. "I had grown used to the beatings and the beratings. But when I overheard him offering me to one of his cronies in trade for a new stallion . . ."A shiver ran through her at the memory. She could still recall the reek of the brandy, and how the candlelight had caught every furrow and fissure the years of dissipation had etched on the two faces. "It was bad enough that marriage was part of the bargain."

"It is no wonder you have a low opinion of men and matrimony."

"It's not that," she protested. "It is the abuse of authority—"

He pulled a face. "Most gentlemen feel the question of authority is resolved by marrying a lady."

Her toe caught on the edge of a cobblestone. "So a man's word is law, so to speak?" The words slipped out with more shrillness than she had intended. Sharpening her tone to a more cynical edge, she quickly added, "Is that how you view matrimony—a legalized way for a male to run roughshod over a female?"

"I was endeavoring to make a jest, Lady Olivia, though I realize it is no laughing matter," he said. "As for my views on marriage, I try to keep a blind eye on that particular subject."

Davenport's opinion on the topic should certainly be of no consequence to her. Still, Olivia felt an odd little twinge at hearing his sardonic response. Ducking her head, she kicked at a loose pebble, hoping to send the emotion skittering off into the darkness.

"And what of you, Lady Olivia? Has the past hardened your heart to the future?" he asked after a lengthy pause. "Have you no interest in forming a permanent partnership?"

"I learned long ago to leave my heart out of the equation. I consider myself to possess a fairly shrewd head for business, so I cannot help assessing such a binding contract as a bad bargain. I already possess the tangible assets that most ladies want from marriage, it seems to me I would have a great deal more to lose than to gain."

"Not all men are cruel despots."

"And not all females are heartless jades," she replied softly. "But is is difficult not to be influenced by past experience."

He allowed an ironic smile. "Touché."

They walked on for some steps before he spoke

again. "Perhaps there are gentlemen out there who would not seek to change you, or expect you to forfeit the things you find challenging in life."

"You think so?" She could not keep a pinch of longing from her voice. "I have yet to meet one."

"What of the fellow you were dancing—"

The rest of Davenport's words were lost in a flurrying slap of leather charging over the slick cobblestones.

Olivia felt her arm seized from behind and was spun around just in time to glimpse a flash of steel cut past her face. Where it was aimed she couldn't tell, for a darker shape, moving with the same lethal speed, rose up to parry the blow.

There was a sharp ripping sound as the blade rent through Davenport's coat. Horrified, she opened her mouth to scream, but her throat had gone so dry that only a hoarse croak came forth. At the same time, the viscount wrested her free of the assailant's grip and shoved her away.

"Stay clear," he ordered, shifting quickly for a better angle to meet the attack. There was no mistaking the note of command, though he had spoken in barely more than a whisper.

And as Davenport circled the spill of gaslight, Olivia caught a glint in his eyes that made her swallow in surprise. She recalled having seen shades of uncertainty in his gaze before, along with fleeting regret and a number of other emotions she could not put a name to. But until that moment, she had never seen such a confident, cool-edged facet of fire in its color. It put her in mind of a piece of Siberian amber she had once seen, hard and translucent as ice, with a fly caught frozen in its depth.

Or a lion on the stalk, all lithe muscle and focused gold.

Indeed, the assailant appeared to sense the lethal power he was facing and began edging uneasily around the aureole of light, seemingly uncertain as to whether he was still the predator or had just become the prey. For a moment or two there was an ominous silence as the viscount matched each shift of step, each series of lightning-quick feints. Suddenly, the other man reversed direction and lunged in for the kill.

At the sight of the arcing knife, Olivia recovered enough from her initial shock to cry out a warning, but Davenport had already moved with the same quickness as his assailant to meet the new attack. She watched as the side of his hand slashed out, catching the outstretched wrist with a vicious chop that echoed with a sickening crack of bone. Spinning around, the viscount followed up with a flurry of hard punches that staggered his assailant and sent him reeling back into the shadows.

There was a clattered ring as steel fell to stone. Olivia heard a rasped oath, venomous in its hiss. An instant later it trailed off into the scuff of running feet.

"Are you all right?"

"Y-yes." It was, she realized, the first coherent sound she had managed to utter since they had come under assault. Still feeling rather breathless from the fury of the fight, she wrenched her gaze away from the darkened street to Davenport's visage. "I—I . . ."

Their eyes met and the rest of what she was about to

say died on her tongue. This, imagined Olivia with a tiny shiver, was the look the French soldiers had faced off against at Corunna. It was one thing to have read the accounts of Davenport's heroics in battle, and quite another to witness it in the flesh. And while the fierceness of the golden fire had dimmed slightly, she had a feeling she would never regard him in quite the same light again.

Lud, but this night had illuminated a whole new side of the viscount. As if she needed further reason to be attracted to the man. Drawing a breath, she sought to rein in the wild galloping of her pulse.

Davenport slipped a steadying hand under her elbow. "Olivia—are you sure you were not in any way injured?"

Belatedly aware of how foolish she must appear, staring up at him with the sort of open-mouthed expression of admiration she so detested in other ladies, Olivia forced a brusque shrug. "J-just thrown a little off balance, sir. You were quick to thrust me out of harm's way." Taken aback by the wobble still evident in both her gait and her speech, she added an oath. "You should have let me help—"

"If you wish to cut up at me over the way I handled things, you are welcome to do so," he said tersely. "At length, in fact, but only once we are safely inside your door."

Did he think she meant to launch into an attack of his courage?

"You—" Her eyes fell on the torn sleeve and the peek of bloodied linen showing from beneath the raveling wool. "Good Lord, sir, you are hurt!"

"What?" His brow quirked, then, as he followed her gaze, the viscount noticed the wound for the first time. "It's naught but a scratch. My hide is a good deal tougher than one of Winslow's morels, so there's no reason to be alarmed."

"Scratch or not, it needs to be treated right away." Olivia grasped his uninjured arm before he could demur. "Come along. I have a ready supply of ointments in my stillroom."

"As always, prepared for every contingency, Lady Olivia," he quipped, allowing himself to be turned in the direction of her townhouse.

Every contingency save one, she admitted, but only to herself, and in an inner voice no louder than the whisper of raindrops rustling through the leaves of her prize tea plantation.

Nothing, but nothing, in her arduous, hard-fought climb to independence had prepared her for the dizzying sensation of falling head over heels in love with Maxwell Bingham.

Chapter Fifteen

❧❀❧

"Damnation, I should have been expecting something like this to happen."

"Do you mean to say you have concocted a new blend of tea that allows you to see into the future?"

To her surprise, Davenport still appeared in a strange frame of mind, voicing quips rather than his usual muttered criticism about her brash language and deportment. Wondering whether it was her own wits that were not functioning quite properly, Olivia lowered her lashes and reached for a strip of linen.

"Unfortunately not, for the profits would no doubt prove astronomical," she replied, trying to match his show of unconcern. However, the gash to his arm was an all-too-vivid reminder of just how dangerous a turn events had taken. The thought of how close he had come to having his throat slashed caused a catch in her voice. "What I meant was, Vavek had warned me about having seen strange shadows in the night. But I thought he was merely imagining the threat."

"Vavek does not strike me as a fanciful fellow. You should take care to heed his warnings."

"I usually do." Olivia added one last dollop of ointment and began to wrap the wound. "Just as I usually react with more efficiency in this type of incident, rather than stand around like a helpless peagoose."

Davenport appeared almost amused by her words. "I should like to think this type of incident, as you put it, does not occur with great frequency."

"Like it or not, sir, it does. My business activities routinely lead me into scrapes that no other female of your acquaintance would even dream of facing."

His mouth twitched into a fleeting smile. "You forget I have a sister. And though she may not yet have matched your formidable exploits, I am afraid it is only because she lacks the opportunity, not the imagination."

"For which you are no doubt extremely grateful," she replied, her voice taking on a more brittle edge than she had intended. "I am already aware that you wouldn't wish your sister to be anything like me, so you needn't be sarcastic. Not that it is surprising," she was quick to add. "Indeed, I have been wondering why it was taking you so long to ring your usual peal over my head."

"I thought to refrain from such clanging until you appear more like your usual self," he said softly. "And I was not being sarcastic, Lady Olivia. You look alarmingly pale, so I was simply trying to tease a bit of color back into your cheeks."

Sure that her face was now seared with a crimson burn, Olivia ducked down and busied herself with tying off the length of linen.

"As for my sister," he continued. "I know you think me a martinet, but I have no desire to mold Cara into someone she is not. She should find her own way in life—and she could do a great deal worse than seek to emulate your courage and strength of character."

Perhaps the shock of the attack had affected her more than she cared to admit, for all at once, her knees went a bit wobbly, causing her chin to graze against his shoulder.

"Olivia." His arms were suddenly around her. "That's enough heroics for the evening. You may have the spirit of an entire regiment of Hussars, but even the most seasoned soldier is not made of iron. Sit down and let me fetch you a glass of sherry."

"I . . . You . . ." She closed her eyes for an instant, savoring the warmth of his support. "You called me Olivia. Now and earlier tonight."

"Did I? Forgive me for omitting the formality of a title." And yet, the viscount made no move to loosen his hold.

"Don't apologize. I was not implying it was unwelcome. Merely . . . unexpected." Her cheek was nestled in the folds of his shirt, which no doubt accounted for the strangely muffled timbre of her voice. "Though given that we seem to be kissing each other with alarming frequency, I suppose that a certain verbal intimacy is not unnatural."

"Very well, then I won't apologize for the use of your given name." His hand came up to cup her chin, tilting it back so that their lips were mere inches apart. "Nor will I apologize for this."

Slowly, deliberately, he lowered his mouth. The kiss had none of the explosive urgency of their previous embraces, but somehow it was even more erotic in its lush and languid exploration.

As he pulled her tighter, she felt the crush of his chest against her breasts and the contours of his thighs through her skirts. The brush with danger had aroused more than the primal male instinct of aggression, for she was suddenly aware of the hardening of muscle and manhood.

Olivia's own response was a shivering sigh. This was a man who was capable of assuming command, and for once in her life, she found herself wishing to yield. Nay, yearning to yield. It was impossible to deny the thrumming of need singing through her every nerve, and on hearing the echo of passion in the viscount's wordless whispers, she could not refrain from giving voice to her innermost desires.

"Max, come with me—"

Before the suggestion could be completed, the door to her study flew open.

"Memsahib." As usual, Vavek's carefully controlled baritone expressed neither shock nor censure, but as he looked from her to the viscount, Olivia caught a strange stirring in his coffee-brown eyes.

She jerked free from Davenport's embrace.

"You have visitors who claim to have a great urgency to see you."

"So great an urgency that there is no time to knock?" she muttered while trying to restore her appearance into some semblance of respectability.

"As you see, yes," he murmured, stepping aside just in time to avoid a collision with the onrushing Cara Bingham.

"I pray you will forgive the sudden intrusion, Lady Olivia!" Cape flapping, bonnet askew, the young lady nearly tripped on the fringe of the Turkey carpet in her haste to enter the room. "I'm rather desperate to find Max and I thought you might have some idea——" She stopped short on seeing her brother, then quickly recovered from her surprise. "Oh! How extremely fortuitous to find you here!"

"Extremely fortuitous," repeated Sprague, his expression stoic, save for the tiniest tic at the corner of his mouth. "I've braved all manner of peril during the Peninsular campaigns, but I'm not sure I could have survived any further forays with Lady Cara."

Feeling that her thoughts were in as great a disarray as her dress, Olivia retreated a step and searched for some suitably innocuous reply. She was, however, spared the effort of speech by Davenport's cool command.

"Well, Cara, we are all waiting to hear the reason for bursting in on Lady Olivia like a thunderclap sweeping down from the moors. And I hope, for your sake, that it is a damn good one."

As Olivia invited the others to be seated, Davenport reached for the decanter of sherry, relieved to discover that neither his voice nor his hand betrayed the true state of his nerves. He supposed the experience of commanding troops under enemy fire had something to do with the outward show of steadiness. However, no amount of flying lead or slashing steel had prepared him for the type of conflict he had experienced this evening. In facing off against the French army, the rules of engagement had been clearly spelled out. With Lady Olivia it was as if they had been encrypted in a Vigenere square devised by Lucifer himself.

How else to explain reactions that simply defied all logic and reason. One moment they had been at daggers drawn, only to find themselves a short while later in each other's arms, their lips, and hands going far beyond what the charade called for. More than clothing had been stripped away. For a fleeting interlude, Olivia had allowed herself to be vulnerable. But now? A sidelong glance at her revealed nothing, save that the momentary weakness in her defenses had quickly been reinforced.

As for himself, it was becoming harder and harder to deny his true feelings.

". . . been the very devil to track down, Max."

His sister's voice recalled him to another tenet of battle. It was imperative to concentrate on the present. Time enough later to puzzle over the intricacies of the heart.

"Go on," he murmured, trying to catch the drift of her narrative.

"Luckily, I ran into Mr. Sprague when I called at your rooms, and he suggested a visit to the Wolf's Lair."

Both gentlemen spoke at once.

"Bloody hell, Spencer! What were—" began Davenport.

"I promise you, Max, that's not exactly the way it happened," assured his friend, once he had stopped choking on his sherry.

"Well, of course it wasn't. As is usually the case with hardheaded males, I had to employ a spot of blackmail," admitted Cara, though she looked none too contrite about it.

"Bloody hell," repeated Davenport, not knowing quite what else to say on hearing that his sister had set foot inside one of London's more notorious bawdy houses.

"There is no call for cursing, Max. It was really quite uneventful, especially as that odious man who goes by the name of the Irish Wolfhound kept us confined to one of the front parlors, rather than allowing us entrance into any of the more interesting parts of the establishment."

"Thank the Blessed Trinity that Connor possesses a modicum of common sense," breathed the viscount. "Unlike some other gentleman I shall leave nameless."

Olivia took advantage of the ensuing awkward silence to offer her own opinion on the subject. "How interesting. So you actually managed to meet the elusive Earl of Killingworth?"

It was Cara's turn to express shocked dismay. "An earl!" She turned an accusing glare on Sprague. "You never mentioned that particular tidbit of information."

"Well, er, no, I didn't—and for good reason," he muttered, the harried look on his face signaling a mute appeal for reinforcements from Davenport.

"Damnation, Cara," said the viscount. "Killingworth's business interests are a closely guarded secret, and one that we promised not to compromise."

Her hands set on her hips. "When, in all the countless escapades you and Kip have scraped through, have you ever known me to be guilty of spilling the soup?"

He gave a grudging growl, forced to concede that her loyalty could always be counted on. That fact, however, did nothing to mitigate his annoyance with

her having met the earl in the first place. "I acknowledge your ability to exercise discretion. But be that as
it may, under no circumstances are you to seek further
acquaintance with the Irish Wolfhound."

"Don't bark at me, Max! I have had enough of such
beastly behavior for one night." By the cant of her
chin, it was clear that Cara's normally even temper had
been goaded to the point of snapping. "Be advised that
while I do not consider myself subject to your orders,
in this case you will not hear any argument from me. I
have no wish for another meeting. He may possess a
title and a pedigree but he is undoubtedly the most arrogant, ungentlemanly cur I have ever encountered."

Davenport felt his hackles rise. "What, exactly, did
he do to incur your wrath?"

She looked away, but not before he noted the two
hot spots of color that had flamed to her cheeks.

"Spencer?" he demanded.

"His language was, er, a trifle rude. At least when I
was present—"

He couldn't quite believe his ears. "Are you implying you left my sister alone with the Wolfhound?"

"Damnation, Max! They allowed me little choice. It
was only for a few minutes."

"The son of a bitch! I shall—"

Before he could shout anything further, Olivia in-
tervened. "It seems all of us are a trifle overset at the
moment. Perhaps it would be wise to refrain from further comment until tempers have cooled and the matter can be discussed in a calm and rational manner."

"An excellent suggestion," agreed Cara, with a suspiciously bright smile.

The alacrity of her response raised the direst of forebodings, but Davenport realized it was probably best to drop the subject. "Very well. But don't think you have heard the last on this."

"And don't think you can intimidate me with a bellowing roar," she retorted. "Why are men under the delusion that the loudness of their voice adds any weight to their words?"

The sound emanating from Olivia's vicinity was a very soft, but very unmistakable laugh.

The viscount stalked to the sideboard. "No doubt for the same reason that females think the force of their diversionary tactics serves as aught but a temporary distraction from their original transgressions." Refilling his glass with brandy rather than sherry, he countered his sister's aggrieved sniff with a tone of exaggerated politeness. "Now, if it is not too much to ask, might I inquire as to what was so pressing that you had to barge in on Lady Olivia unannounced, and at an hour considered most inappropriate for visitors."

"But you are here," she observed. Her eyes suddenly narrowed as she finally focused on the fact that he had been alone with the lady in a closed room, and with his coat off. "Which, come to think of it, also seems to beg an explanation."

Davenport cleared his throat. "There was a small mishap." As he shifted slightly, the bandage on his forearm came into view. Cara's hand flew to her throat, the tart reply she was about to make turning into a horrified gasp. "Oh, Max! The curse of the Ruby Lion has struck again."

"Nonsense." Davenport started to tug down his

sleeve, then thought better of it, seeing as the rumpled linen was streaked with blood. "There is no need to wax melodramatic, as if this is some plot out of a horrid novel. Footpads abound in Town. It was mere . . ."

"Coincidence?" finished Olivia with a lift of her brow. "Now it is you, sir, who are sounding no more sensible than a storybook character. Robberies are rare in this part of town, and in any case our assailant was aiming to kill rather than relieve us of any valuables." Seeming to sense that the viscount wished to downplay the incident in front of his sister, she omitted mention of their earlier encounter. She did, however, see fit to add, "There is no denying that our poking around has stirred up a nest of vipers."

The comment prompted another sharp intake of breath from Cara, whose countenance had turned ghostly pale. "Attacked? You, too?"

Davenport spun around. "What do you mean?"

"Two nights ago, at the inn outside Welvington, my maid awoke to the sounds of an intruder in our chamber. She cried out, rousing me as well. I grabbed up the pistol I keep by the bedside and shot out of bed to investigate, but managed to catch only a flash of white disappearing out the window."

"Cara—"

"And don't tell me it was naught but a figment of my imagination," she exclaimed, before he could go on. "Both valises were slashed open and their contents strewn about the floor."

"Damnation." As his fingers tightened around his glass, the viscount was aware that no amount of spirits, however potent, could dull the sense of dread churning in the pit of his stomach. First Kipling, now Cara. Was he helpless to defend those he cared about from harm? He winced at the recollection of sharpened steel cutting an arc toward Olivia's head. He had thought to keep her well distanced from any danger, but it appeared his battlefield prowess had grown as rusty as his social skills. He had made the cardinal mistake of underestimating his enemy. Now, Olivia, as well as his family, had been drawn into a web of deadly intrigue.

Setting the drink aside, Davenport pressed his fingertips to his temples. "I was not going to question your reliability, Cara. Only your frightening tendency to abandon all caution and rush to confront trouble head-on."

"But Max! How can you expect me to simply slink away when Kip is in mortal danger?"

The question did nothing to assuage his feelings of guilt. He looked away, to the brightly colored painting hung over the mantel. If memory served him correctly, Olivia had told him it was a depiction of the Hindu deity Shiva. The Great Destroyer. As he stared at the bold strokes of whirling limbs, he wondered how he was going to keep the ones he loved from being cut to shreds.

Christ Almighty. Davenport feared he would need not only the divine intervention of Brahma and Vishnu, but the entire pantheon of gods, from Abraham to Zeus, to succeed.

His eyes squeezed shut for an instant, then he was surprised to hear Olivia's voice cut through the darkness.

"You have no reason to rake yourself over the coals,

sir. You have made more headway in this investigation than could be expected, especially considering the lack of clues to go on. And no one could have anticipated all the evil twists and turns the trail would take. Rather than dwell on regrets and recriminations, perhaps we should concentrate our efforts on figuring out a strategy for countering the next move of our adversary." She paused as she walked to her desk. "However, to do that effectively, we will have to agree to treat each other as equals and lay all of the facts on the table."

Davenport admitted that it was an eminently practical suggestion, but the "we" had an ominous ring to it.

"Quite right," chimed in Cara, which only confirmed his fears. "I have a feeling there are a good many things you are not telling us."

"With good reason." As his earlier shouting had done little, save for setting her back up, Davenport attempted an appeal to logic. "I promised you I would do everything within my power to find Kip and save him from ruin. And trust me, I am. But I am also trying to protect you from harm. The grim reality is that it is a very dangerous world that he has allowed himself to be drawn into, one that no female should be exposed to. My task is difficult enough without having to worry over your safety as well."

His gaze shifted to Olivia. "Or yours, Lady Olivia. In light of recent events, I think the best course of action would be for the two of you to quit London and return to Saybrook Manor without delay. Things are no doubt going to turn even uglier, and I would rest a good deal easier knowing you both were far from the fray."

The only effect of his words was to stir a swirl of indignation in Cara's eyes. "That is incredibly condescending, Max. Over the past few years, I have proven that I am capable as any man in handling a challenge. I have managed the estate, dealing with all manner of mundane problems, and you have never questioned my ability or performance. I think I have earned the right not to be treated like some witless widgeon, to be shooed away at the first sign of trouble." As she paused for breath, her eyes looked to Olivia and then back to him. "You and Alex did not keep the ladies from playing an important role in an equally dangerous situation."

"In all honesty," murmured Olivia. "Your brother did not exactly encourage us to participate."

"So you ignored his orders." The jut of her chin became more pronounced. "Which is exactly what I intend to do." Seeing Davenport's hesitation, Cara pressed on. "Ignorance is not bliss, Max. And there is no guarantee that Saybrook Manor will be any safer than London, for we have had ample proof that the enemy can strike anywhere. To be forewarned is to be forearmed. You really have no choice but to admit us into your confidences."

"Loath though I am to admit it, your sister's words have some merit." Sprague, who had been observing the exchange between siblings with the same sort of horrid fascination with which he might watch a mongoose square off against a cobra, finally roused himself to speech. "Unfortunately, the ladies are already involved." He unconsciously squared his shoulders. "And as I have just witnessed what trouble Lady Cara can get herself into when she charges off half-cocked, my opinion is that our only hope of averting disaster is to, er, join forces, as it were."

All eyes fixed on the viscount.

After another quick look at the painting hanging above the fire, Davenport heaved a sigh and nodded, though he couldn't help wondering if he were stepping closer to the razored edge. "I suppose you are right."

"Well then, seeing as we are all in agreement, there is no reason to delay a council of war," pointed out Cara.

Davenport nodded again. "Spencer, you had better pour us both another drink before we sit down—I have a feeling we are both going to need it."

It was well past midnight before Olivia slipped into her silk wrapper and sat down at the dressing table to brush out her hair.

Lud, what a tangle.

Not the thick braid of raven tresses, but the web of intrigue, which seemed to be spinning its thread in an ever-widening circle. She could hardly blame the viscount for his concern. He was, she knew, a gentleman who held himself to the highest code of honor. Indeed, there was no mistaking the flash of fierce protectiveness in his eyes when he looked at his sister. Olivia didn't doubt that he would march unflinchingly into the deepest corner of hell and back again to keep Cara from coming to harm.

But what of the smoldering heat she had seen when

his gaze turned her way? Though his exact sentiments toward her were difficult to discern, the warring of conflicting emotions was obvious. Animal lust versus gentlemanly honor. Olivia felt a tug of guilt as the bristles of her brush snagged in a knot. He was fighting enough battles. Was she wrong to tempt him, however obliquely, into abandoning lofty principle for fleeting pleasure?

She examined her reflection in the mirror, not allowing herself to shy away from the glaring truth. There had been nothing subtle in her suggestion, she admitted, as a faint flush of red stole across her flesh. Despite the abrupt interruption, Davenport had surely sensed that the next words out of her mouth would have been an invitation into her bed.

Would desire have won out over discipline and discretion?

Olivia wasn't sure she wished to hazard a guess.

On one hand, a closer acquaintance with the viscount had only fanned the flames of her need to a crackling intensity. She wanted him on top of her, inside her, unleashing the passion she sensed was caged by his unhappy past. And her own.

Yet on the other hand, a small part of her feared that in surrendering to the moment, she might very well lose any chance of winning his lasting esteem. A tentative bond had formed between them this evening. *Friendship?* Perhaps. Yet she wanted so much more.

Not that there was much hope for that, she scoffed at herself, leaning in for a closer look at the multitude of flaws she spied on her features. It wasn't that she regretted her past choices, but they had left their marks, and Davenport was not blind.

Still, a last vestige of girlish innocence had her longing to be swept up from the hard realities of the business world to the giddy heights of fairy-tale romance.

Dismissing the foolish notion with a sigh, she settled for the cold, down-to-earth comfort of her ornately carved teak bed.

❧❀❧

Chapter Sixteen

"Stop making those clucking sounds." Olivia slapped down the inventory of spices she had been attempting to organize and turned her attention to the ledger of monthly expenses.

"*Moi?*"

"Yes, *toi*," she replied irritably. "If I wished to be surrounded by mother hens, I would purchase a farm."

Winslow tilted back in his chair. "Perhaps you are in need of a bit of mothering. You are, if I may say so, looking a trifle peaked."

"You may not. It is bad enough that all through breakfast I had to swallow a lecture from Vavek regarding the state of my appearance. I don't intend to endure the same impertinent comments from you."

"Oh, dear," he clucked. "Did you have a distressing evening? Perhaps you should go home and curl up under the covers. I could fix you a pot of chicken soup."

Thumping the ledger down upon the leather blotter, Olivia rose from her desk and gathered up her reticule. It was not as if she were getting any work done, she thought sourly. Her mind refused to concentrate on any of the mundane tasks she had tried to finish, preferring instead to dwell on the report of Winslow's latest forays into the stews. And the mention of bed only served as a further distraction.

She rather doubted a bowl of steaming broth, however nourishing, would serve to cure the ill that was plaguing her.

"What was that you said, Lady O?"

"Windy, I am warning you. . . ." After a moment more of rummaging through the chest of drawers atop the console, she found what she was looking for and shoved it into her bag. An idea, inspired by the latest bit of information Winslow had laid on her desk, had slowly been taking shape throughout the morning. It was, admittedly, an outrageous one, even for her. But desperate circumstances sometimes called for desperate measures. Though she didn't yet know the exact contents of the codes, she had an uneasy feeling that time was growing short to prevent another shipment of young women from being sent to the East.

The man of affair's voice lost its teasing tone. "Where are you going? Your coach won't be arriving for another few hours."

"Out," she replied curtly.

He stood up and reached for his hat. "An excellent idea. A little fresh air would do us both good—"

"Alone."

"I don't think that is a wise idea."

This time the word she uttered came out a good deal louder than a whisper.

Winslow blinked. "Did something occur to upset you last night?"

"You might describe . . ."

She was about to add that coming within a hair's breath of having one's throat slashed was a trifle upsetting, but caught herself in the nick of time. Despite his seemingly insouciant air, Winslow would stick to her side like a cocklebur if he thought she was in any danger. Considering where she was going, she did not want any company.

"You might describe a visit from Lord Davenport as upsetting," she finished. "He can be a very irritating gentleman."

"Indeed?" Winslow assumed an expression of angelic innocence. "My impression was that the two of you rubbed together quite well."

Not wishing to be delayed by a lengthy exchange of banter, Olivia chose to ignore the innuendo. She did, however, allow a touch of sarcasm to creep into her voice. "You are usually quite observant. I am surprised you failed to note that there is a good deal of friction between us."

"Unless I am losing all my marbles, I seem to recall you saying it was you who went in search of the gentleman in the first place. I thought you were anxious to ask his advice on the documents you obtained from Fleming and Rundle. Was he not of any help?"

"He is working on them." Determined to dodge further questions regarding what had actually transpired, she took her bonnet from the peg on the wall and turned for the front door. "Now, if your employer might be so bold as to issue an order, put your derriere in your chair and get back to work on that quarterly summary of our Caribbean venture. I expect it to be completed by the end of the day."

"It will be." Undeterred by her tone, Winslow was quick to match her move. "You still have not mentioned where you are off to."

"Madame Celeste has several sketches for gowns, and she wishes my final approval." It was not a complete bouncer, she told herself, trying to repress a tiny twinge of guilt. Even when annoyed with her man of affairs, she did not like to resort to telling him outright lies. "I won't be overly long."

"I suppose there can be no harm in making a short visit to Mayfair. I shall just step outside with you and flag down a hackney."

"Oh, very well," she agreed, allowing herself to be escorted out to the street and helped into the first passing vehicle.

However, as soon as it lumbered around the corner, Olivia rapped on the trap and ordered a change in direction.

The truth was no longer hidden in fog and shadow. It was clearly spelled out, stark black on glaring white, in the two sets of papers he had placed side by side. Davenport looked away for a moment, knowing it was futile to think that a curse, or a prayer, or a thunderbolt from the heavens might, in the blink of an eye, somehow cause the letters and numbers to rearrange themselves.

The Curse of the Ruby Lion.

It would make an excellent title for a horrid novel, he thought with a touch of gallows humor. Save for the horrid reality that it was his brother's neck that was encircled by the hangman's noose.

And the rope was drawing tighter by the moment.

Swallowing hard, Davenport again looked down at the column of numbers, then slid his gaze to the text he had deciphered from the coded pages. It was all there. Dates, price, and enough of a description of the merchandise that the heinous truth could not be denied.

Supply and demand. He recalled Lady Olivia saying it was a basic tenet of commerce.

His fingers tightened on the edges of the papers, causing an audible crackle. There were clearly others who understood the business of profit and loss. Others who were making a fortune selling young English women into slavery in distant lands. The exact details were still cryptic, but four names were listed at the end of the text, beginning with the Connoisseur.

And ending with Kipling Bingham.

He did not recognize the other two names. Nor had he figured out the significance of the list. Yet it was difficult to imagine how it could be anything other than incriminating.

For an instant the viscount wavered, tempted to consign the damning evidence to the flames licking up from the hearth. Life was, after all, a brutal business. Girls with no money and no family to protect them fell victim to unscrupulous dealings all the time. Even in London, the heart of civilized England, there were places where they were treated as chattel. Stopping one enterprise would not put an end to all the injustices in the world. Indeed, in the grand scheme of things, what did it matter whether one more drop fell into the ocean of wrongdoing?

He shifted in his seat. He could lie to Olivia, telling her he had failed to crack the code.

And Cara?

If he could find Kip and convince him—by reason or by force—to give up his role in the diabolical business, perhaps his sister might never need know the full extent of their sibling's perfidy.

Davenport's hands slowly unclenched, letting the papers fall back to the leather blotter. Much as he tried to tell himself he had a choice, he knew he did not. Like the mythical Pandora, he had lifted the lid on evil and now could not snap it shut, pretending he had never looked inside.

Besides, a part of him still refused to believe in his brother's guilt. Until he looked in Kipling's eyes and saw for himself that the person he knew no longer existed, he would cling to the hope that an exonerating explanation could be brought to light.

As if echoing his own warring thoughts, the door flew open with a thud, and Sprague stomped into the small sitting room.

"Hell's teeth." His friend did not appear to be in any better frame of mind than he was. "I have survived a sniper's bullet at Corunna, a forced march through the highest pass of the Pyrenees and countless clashes with Soult's calvary, but I am not sure I can make it through another encounter with your sister, Max."

"Surely she cannot have caused any trouble this morning. All I asked was that you escort her on a ride through Hyde Park while I worked on these papers."

The litany of Cara's more outrageous suggestions took several minutes to complete. "Of course I refused to take her back into Seven Dials," snorted Sprague. "But it doesn't stop there. When she saw there was no hope of getting me to go in that direction, she tried convincing me to make a trip to Tattersall's."

"That, at least, was not such an unreasonable suggestion," replied Davenport. "Females are allowed to set foot inside—"

"The devil take it, Max! She wished to negotiate the purchase of a stallion for . . . breeding purposes. I consider myself a loyal subaltern, but I draw the line at escorting an unmarried female to Tat's and having to assist in a detailed discussion on the, er, stamina and anatomical merits of a prize stud . . ." Finally taking in the spread of papers on the desk and the haggard pinch of the viscount's features, he ceased his grumbling. "Bad news?"

"Not good." Davenport's fingers sought the single fob hanging from his watch chain. A crested gold shield carved out of burnished gold, it had been a parting gift from Kip the night the viscount had set off with his regiment for the Peninsula. For luck, his brother had smiled, with a laughing reminder that the family motto translated as "Luck favors the bold." The talisman had seen him through the horrors of war. Now, if only a bit of its luck might rub off on another of the Binghams.

"I feared as much." Sprague's expression was a mingling of sympathy and resignation. "I'm sorry, Max. I truly am. From the beginning, we both suspected the situation was a grim one."

"Not in my worst nightmare could I have imagined it being this grim." Seeing the furrowing of his friend's brow, he went on to explain the gist of what he had just read.

Sprague fixed him with a searching look. "What do you intend to do about it?"

"It would be rather hypocritical to have fought all those years against injustice and tyranny abroad, only turn my back and ignore it here in London."

"No one could expect you to be a hero in this particular battle," his friend quietly responded.

"What then? Be a craven coward instead?" The question was directed more at himself than at Sprague. Without a pause, he shook his head. "I cannot, in good conscience, simply turn away. Kip is not the only one whose life hangs in the balance. There are others to consider—Mary Gooding, her friend Lizzie Stokes, and those poor souls we cannot even put a name to."

"It would not be cowardly to let Tony handle the matter."

"He can't. Crimes such as these do not involve his department and would be shunted off to the local authorities. The earlier information he supplied was done off the record, but he made it clear that his resources are stretched too thin by his official responsibilities to be able to continue such personal favors." Davenport let out a harried sigh. "As it is, he has already put himself in a precarious position. He can't afford to climb any farther out on a limb."

Sprague swore under his breath. Kicking at the fringe of the Oriental carpet, he lapsed into a stymied silence. However, after a moment of staring at the intertwined patterns, his chin snapped up. "Well, can't he use his influence for you with the local authorities?"

"How can I ask him to do that without real proof?" replied the viscount, unable to keep the frustration from roughening his voice. "We have only the word of a slightly shady clerk with dubious connections to the underworld and a set of ledgers obtained by outright bribery. We may be convinced that the odd occurances actually piece together into a horrible truth, but I can't ask Tony to lay such a case before his superiors until we have firm evidence to illustrate such an outrageous claim."

"What about mention of the Ruby Lion?"

Davenport's mouth set in a sardonic smirk. "Given that my recent battles with the bottle are not a state secret, I imagine any tale of cursed relics and shadowy specters would be dismissed as the ravings of an unbalanced mind."

Sprague's silence was tacit acknowledgment of the grim reality. Rising, he took up the poker and stirred the embers into a last lick of flames. "In that case, what is the next move?" he said after some moments. "I take it you have some plan of attack mapped out."

"Only a rough one, seeing as there is still so much we don't know. We can hazard an educated guess at what is going on, but we need to learn exactly who is behind these dastardly deeds and how they are managed if we wish to bring the miscreants to justice." His fist smacked softly into his palm. "There are three names listed along with Kip's. And I know just who to ask regarding their particulars."

"Wot!" Caught by surprise, the hackney driver nearly allowed the stump of cheroot to slip from his yellowed teeth. "Ye can't be meaning te go there!"

"On the contrary. And the sooner the better." Seeing he was on the verge of balking, she added, "There's an extra guinea in it for you if we make it within a quarter hour."

Greed quickly overcame any scruples he might have had about taking a lone female to the location she had requested. "It's yer own neck," he muttered over the creak of the wheels. "Or, more likely, some udder part o' yer body."

A curse and a flick of the whip urged the horse into a shambling trot. Avoiding the more traveled thoroughfares, he pulled up to the front of the address with several minutes to spare.

Squaring her shoulders, Olivia stepped up to the entrance and rapped on the door.

It swung inward for an instant before slamming shut in her face. Undeterred, she knocked again.

And again, this time with even greater force.

After a lengthy interval, another small opening appeared. Wedging her foot into the crack, she forced her way a step closer and sought a peek into the darkened foyer. As her eyes adjusted to the light, she found that only a few inches separated her from perhaps the ugliest face she had ever beheld. Hair the color of dirt and the texture of straw stuck out at odd angles from a head that looked flattened by too many blows from a fist. The nose resembled a mashed turnip, its misshapen mass only accentuating the thick spread of scarred lips.

Unblinking, Olivia held up her card. "I wish to speak with the proprietor."

His lips moved, but she was unable to tell whether the guttural sound that emerged was actual speech.

"It is a matter of great urgency," she added, hoping to move him to action. Given his height and girth, it was doubtful she could force her way in.

"The master be busy," came the burred reply.

Her half boot slid forward another inch. "Very well, I'll wait." Shifting her reticule from one hand to the other, she made a show of settling her shoulder against the door. "Indeed, I am prepared to stand here as long as it takes for him to see me."

A look of alarm flooded the man's slitted eyes. He hesitated, clearly caught in the conundrum of whether to admit her inside or to remove her bodily from the railed landing.

"What the devil is going on here, Loggins?" Irritation echoed off the walls of the hallway. "I count on you to keep disturbances to a minimum and yet Meechum has just come haring into my office, nattering on about some troublesome wench making a fuss outside."

Muttering a mile a minute, the man fell back and thrust Olivia's card toward the approaching figure. It was just as well she couldn't understand half of what he was saying, she thought, for the little she could make out contained some highly unflattering comments about females in general.

"Bloody hell." The door flung open with such force that it nearly ricocheted off the wainscoting back into her face. Unlike the previous doorkeeper, the gentleman now before her possessed a lean ranginess and striking features, not the least of which was a shock of raven hair liberally threaded with an unusual shade of iron gray. He was not precisely handsome, but there was a certain magnetism about the angular hardness of his face.

"This is not some damn Society drawing room, and I am not in the habit of entertaining social calls," he went on, his anger taking on an offensive drawl as he crumpled her calling card and tossed it aside without a glance at the engraved script. "So unless you are here to request employment, pick up your skirts and run along."

Olivia didn't flinch in the face of the deliberate insult. "You may stubble your snarls, sir, I am not easily intimidated," she replied in the same snappish tone. "I am looking for the Irish Wolfhound—is that you?"

"What do you want?"

"Just a few bits of information."

The silvery-gray color of his eyes shaded to the cast of tempered steel. "Why is it of late that certain people seem to think I am a walking encyclopedia? If you are in search of information, I suggest you take out a subscription to a lending library."

"Ah, yes. Lady Cara mentioned that you, like the girls you employ, expect payment for services rendered." The sudden darkening of his cheeks indicated that her cutting comment had drawn blood. Pressing on, she reached into her reticule and retrieved a heavy purse. "I can well afford whatever price you care to name."

"Rich, are you?" A mocking contempt was clear in his tone. "Did you sell your charms to some lecherous Croesus who lets you spend his blunt as you please as long as you let him into your bed?"

"No. Like you, Lord Killingworth, I am obliged to work for a living."

His hand clamped none too gently around her arm and propelled her into the small sitting room by the entranceway. "I, too, have a few questions to ask," he growled after kicking the door shut. "Beginning with, who the devil are you?"

"I was hardly attempting to keep it a secret," she pointed out, unable to refrain from a faint smile. "Perhaps you would care for another card?"

His angular features betrayed a twitch of consternation before hardening into a frown. "I'm in no mood for playing games."

"Neither am I. My name is Olivia Marquand."

"Marquand," he repeated softly. "Now, where . . ." His eyes fell upon the crimson brocade of the settee and he drew in a breath. "The scandalous Lady in Red?"

Olivia smoothed her sea-green skirts. "Yes, but as you see, I have faded into a life of quiet respectability."

A short bark of laughter came from Killingworth. "Barging into a bawdy house in broad daylight is hardly the sort of behavior to indulge in if you wish to maintain a spotless reputation with the *ton*."

"True. Assuming I was observed by anyone likely to gossip. But seeing as this is also a gaming hell, let us just say I considered the odds and decided the risk in coming here was worth the possible reward."

Despite the earl's poker face, she sensed her words had piqued his curiosity. After a moment of studying his well-manicured nails, he looked up. "What do you hope to gain from me, Lady Olivia? And what has it to do with Lady Cara?"

She decided to forego any lengthy bluffing and lay

her cards on the table. "I'm looking for information on some of the other places of pleasure in the area. As for Lady Cara, I am . . . a friend of the family."

Killingworth did not miss the tiny hesitation. "Has this to do with Max?"

She nodded. "I am in a position to offer him some assistance in hunting down a certain group of criminals he is after."

A wolfish grin—somewhat exaggerated to her eye—replaced the look of feigned indifference. "I trust that the Valiant Viscount has not allowed his sword to become rusty from disuse." His gaze slowly raked her from head to foot. "It looks as though he may have use of it."

"As I said before, you are not the only one who prefers not to waste time in games, Lord Killingworth," said Olivia as she turned and calmly regarded the lewd engraving on the wall. "By the by, I trust you did not pay too much for this. It is not one of Antonioni's better works."

"I got a very good deal on an entire group of them when Lord McKeever unexpectedly expired during a flurry of strenuous activity and his estate came up for sale. The best ones are in my private office. Would you care to offer your expert opinion?"

Ignoring the suggestion, she removed another item from her reticule. "I have made up a list—"

"Bloody hell—you too?" Snatching the paper from her fingers, the earl gave it a quick perusal. "How do you expect me to know these kinds of details?" he demanded.

"Only a very bad businessman would fail to know

the particulars of his clientele, or keep a close watch on what the competition is up to."

"Not another plaguey female who thinks that managing her pin money from quarter to quarter has given her an expertise in the field," he growled. "What would you know about running a business, Lady Olivia?"

"Quite a lot, actually. In fact, I'll strike a bargain with you. In exchange for the information I want, I will provide you with a comprehensive market analysis, along with a plan for reducing your costs and raising your profits by at least twenty percent."

He gave a dismissive snort. "As if you have the slightest notion of what sort of revenues the Wolf's Lair produces each month."

The series of amounts she rattled off wiped the smugness from his face. "What the devil! Are you some modern-day witch or wizard—"

"Just a lady with a head for numbers." Olivia smiled. "Now, do we have a deal?"

Chapter Seventeen

"What an unexpected pleasure to see you again so soon, Lord Davenport." Taking a seat on the rough bench opposite the viscount and Sprague, Winslow removed his hat with a deft little flourish. Although the sober colors and nondescript cut of his garments were a far cry from the sartorial splendor he had displayed at their previous encounter, they didn't disguise a certain raffish air. "A very great pleasure. Though I dare not imagine it is on account of my sparkling beaux yeux that you requested this meeting." Shifting his gaze, he fixed Sprague with a bold stare. "Who's your friend?"

"A fellow quite as skilled with a blade as you are," replied Davenport dryly. "So if I were you, I'd watch my tongue."

A pearly smile gleamed in the dim light of the chophouse. "Oooh, but I do so like a man who knows how to wield a sword."

The viscount couldn't help but allow a twitch of his lips. He was still not at all sure what to make of the enigmatic character facing him, but the man of affair's cutting sense of humor could not be denied. "Much as I appreciate your rapier wit, do you mind sheathing it so we might get right to the point? Your note did say you couldn't spare us more than a quarter of an hour."

"Very well." Winslow sighed. "Though the notion of thrusting and parrying with you for a bit longer is so . . . uplifting."

Davenport nearly laughed aloud, as much in response to Sprague's look of nonplussed confusion as to the man of affair's outrageously provocative banter. "As to our reason for seeking you out, it is exactly on account of your eyes. And your ears. Several new facts have come to light, and I am hoping you, with your unique, er, talents, might be of assistance." He began with Cara's odd encounter. "First of all, what do you know of any recently arrived strangers in Town—men dressed in exotic garb, probably topped off with flowing white robes."

"An interest in fashion? Sounds like the sort of fellows I might enjoy meeting."

"I doubt it. It is likely they also carry knives. Large, curved ones, with razor-sharp blades. And they seem to have no compunction about applying them to tasks outside of the kitchen—such as slashing the luggage of travelers. I imagine they would also have no aversion to slicing out the lungs and liver of an Englishman."

"On second thought, they sound quite vulgar." Winslow's face sobered as he sipped his ale. "I'm surprised I haven't heard any whispers. Such fellows would not go unnoticed. But then, my attention has been on other things of late." He broke off a small piece from the wedge of cheddar on his plate and took a bite. "Let me ask around in certain quarters this evening."

"I would appreciate it." Davenport watched the other man's dextrous movements. "But, er, be sure to exercise a great deal of caution. As I said, it may be they are not opposed to spilling blood."

Winslow exaggerated a shudder. "My dear fellow, I always proceed with the greatest of care when life and limb may be at stake. Believe me, I have no desire to have my testicles cut up and sauteed in a sauce of butter and white wine."

Sprague's knee gave a small jerk.

"I trust you are also using the utmost discretion in looking deeper into the dealing of Fleming and Rundle, especially in light of what happened last night." Seeing the blank look on the other man's face, he quickly added, "Didn't Lady Olivia mention the attack, and how close she came to having her throat slit?"

For the first time in their acquaintance, Davenport saw the man of affairs lose his saucy composure. His face paled, and the mask of nonchalance slipped, along with the bit of cheese that was hovering by his lips. "No!"

The word was no more that a hoarse whisper, but its vehemence caused the viscount to wonder anew at the exact nature of his relationship to the lady.

It took only an instant for Winslow to regain control of himself. "She did not see fit to mention that little detail," he continued in his usual drawl. His expression, however, had lost all trace of good humor. "Otherwise I should never have allowed her to go off by herself just now—"

"Damn—where?"

"To her modiste, but she did not expect to be gone for long."

Davenport relaxed slightly. "It is not likely she will run into any trouble at a dressmaker's shop."

"She should be back in the office shortly." Winslow's mouth compressed to a grim line. "At which time I shall nail her skirts to the floor until her own carriage comes to collect her."

"It is on account of the documents she obtained that we are here," Davenport continued, after the other man finished tacking on a string of muttered oaths to his avowal. "I have deciphered a number of important facts from the coded contents, including three names that may make reference to the leader." He could not bring himself to mention Kipling in that context. "Two are gentlemen of the *ton*—Lord St. Claire and Lord Bentham. The other is referred to only as the Connoisseur. It is hard to tell whether that is just a moniker for one of them, or a third gentleman."

Winslow's eyes had narrowed during the short narrative. "That certainly gibes with my latest discovery. As I told Lady O in my morning report, I managed to learn that Fleming and Rundle is controlled by a gentleman who, despite his depravity, belongs to the highest circle of Society. My sources, however, could not come up with his exact identity, only the fact that he is said to be a collector of fine objets d'art."

"I suggest you hone your efforts on the names I just mentioned."

"I agree." Finishing his ale, Winslow placed the glass down. "But at the moment, I do have an important business meeting scheduled." A glimmer of his usual humor lightened the somber mood. "And as my employer runs a tight ship, I wouldn't want to run the risk of losing my position over an unexcused absence."

"Just one other thing before you go." Davenport found himself hesitating. "I should like to get a copy of your report to Lady Olivia. And I . . . I should prefer it if she does not get wind of it. Or of this meeting, or any new information the three of us uncover."

"Might I ask why?"

His features pinched in a grimace. "Because if at all possible, I should like to cut off the heads of these vipers before she steps too close to their fangs. I am all too aware of the fact that the lady has a deucedly disturbing penchant for embarking on bold initiatives of her own, regardless of the risks."

"I have, on occasion, had reason to note the same thing myself," Winslow dryly observed.

"It's no joking matter," he growled.

"No," agreed the other man, his voice losing its light tone. "But much as I commend your gentlemanly concern, I cannot lie to Lady O. Aside from the, er, moral considerations, it is not a very practical, or very wise, strategy. She always seems to winkle out what is going on anyway. And trust me, trying to shield her from the sordid realities of life only makes her more determined to charge off and fight for what she thinks is right."

Uncomfortably aware of the truth of Winslow's words, Davenport was momentarily at a loss for a reply.

"The viscount isn't asking you to lie," explained Sprague. "But if the lady does not ask you a point-blank question, he is merely suggesting there is no need to bring up certain subjects yourself."

"Your friend has the face of Adonis and the mind of Machiavelli," murmured Winslow, before giving a martyred sigh. "Very well. I will do as you ask. But if I may be so bold as to offer strategic advice to seasoned soldiers, I would suggest you also begin mapping out an alternate plan—one that might help ensure this one does not blow up in your face."

Davenport could almost feel sparks licking along the length of his scar. As if Olivia had not already left him rather singed around the edges. However, when he spoke, his voice maintained a measure of cool composure. "If need be, I will handle Lady Olivia."

Winslow slanted him a probing look. "I have yet to meet the gentleman who can, though a goodly number have thought themselves up for the challenge," he said after a moment's pause. "However, I am willing to concede the possibility that in you, she may have met her match."

The viscount shifted just a fraction under the lengthy scrutiny, uncomfortably aware that Winslow's eyes were as sharp as daggers.

Looking away, he fell to making a search of his coat pockets. "Let us try not to put such speculation to the test, shall we?" Finding the small square of folded paper, he slapped it down on the table. "In making your inquiries about the three gentlemen, keep your ears open for any mention of these three young women." There was a fraction of a pause. "And for the name of Kipling Bingham."

Winslow's gaze honed to a finer edge. "Lady O has

not spelled out to me the exact nature of your interests in Fleming and Rundle, sir. Nor have I asked. However, might I inquire if the matter you are investigating also has to do with trafficking in human flesh?"

"I fear so," admitted Davenport. "When I first approached Lady Olivia, I had thought it was a matter of simple theft, otherwise I should never have involved her. But now . . . Damn, it's rather a long and complicated story."

Pursing his lips, Winslow discreetly palmed the pocket watch from his waistcoat and took a quick glance. "Unfortunately, one of our suppliers of sail canvas is due to arrive shortly, but let me think for a moment whether there is any way to push the meeting back to a later hour."

As the man of affairs took a moment to consider his options, the viscount could not help but notice the unusual timepiece. It was the one item of Winslow's otherwise drab dress that gave hint of his discerning taste. Wrought from an exotic shade of reddish gold, the elongated oval was decorated with an intaglio engraving of a fanciful dragon, the eyes glittering with two polished pink tourmalines—

"Bloody hell." Snatching it from Winslow's fingers, Davenport took a closer look. "Where did you come by this?"

"A friend," Winslow replied, smoothing over his initial surprise with a faint smile. "But if it truly catches your fancy, I could let you have it for a very reasonable price."

Without comment, Davenport handed the watch to Sprague.

"Bloody hell," echoed his friend. "The third item on Kip's list?"

A curt nod confirmed the guess. "It's not my fancy you need be concerned about," he said, handing the watch back to Winslow. "Seeing as the Yorkshire authorities and several of Bow Street's best Runners are currently chasing after it, you would do well to keep the damned thing tucked out of sight. Lord Blakely says it's a prize piece of Mandarin craftsmanship from the middle of the last century, and one of his most treasured heirlooms."

Winslow gave a dismissive sniff. "He's off by about fifty years and five hundred miles." He paused to run an appreciative finger over the polished gold before sliding it back into his waistcoat pocket. "And as for those oafs from Bow Street, every last one of them would have trouble detecting a Louis XIV armoire if it were wedged up his arse."

"Has anyone ever warned you that your cockiness may get you into trouble one of these days?"

"More than once. But while I am first to admit that my cock has an unfortunate penchant for wanting to lead me to places I should not stray, most of the time I am able to douse such tendencies with a splash of cold reason."

There was another coughing sputter from Sprague.

"Do," cautioned Davenport. "I'm serious, Winslow. Lady Olivia already finds enough fault with me without her waking up one morning to discover that I have also cost her the services of a trusted adviser."

"I am touched by your concern."

Ignoring the nonchalant drawl, the viscount drew

on his overcoat. "You had better go back and attend to business, in order to avoid arousing her suspicions. In the meantime, I should like to have a word with your . . . friend. I need to know how he came by that watch."

"It is not her suspicions I suspect are aroused," murmured the man of affairs. In a considerably louder voice he added, "Along with the other inquiries, I had better go around and question Newcombe myself about the ticker. With strangers he tends to clam up tight as a Belon oyster." Setting his hat at a jaunty angle, he rose. "Let me be off. I'll send word to you as soon as I have any further news."

Bentham?

Olivia's brows angled in dismay as she came to the last name on Killingworth's scrawled list. Witty, erudite, and charming, the gentleman had appeared a most unlikely customer for the prurient pleasures provided by the Wolf's Lair. She would never have guessed him to have such a voracious appetite for games of chance. Or for what lay between a woman's thighs.

But then, most people had secrets they took care to keep well hidden.

According to the Irish Wolfhound, Bentham had exotic tastes when it came to sex, and was willing to pay handsomely if the girls—sometimes two at a time—were willing to indulge his fantasies.

Her eyes fell back to the scrap of paper. After his initial reluctance, the earl had given her request careful consideration and come up with only three other patrons of the Wolf's Lair who met the criteria she had spelled out. It was, she knew, by no means a certainty that one of the four gentleman on the list also went by another, more mysterious, moniker. Yet logic had led her to conclude that the best place to begin searching out the identity of the Connoisseur was among those who were frequent visitors to places of vice.

She already knew the person they sought was both extremely smart and extremely clever. That Winslow had come up with the clues indicating he was also a gentleman of title and a collector of fine objets d'art narrowed the field of possible suspects considerably.

And now, with Killingworth's contribution, it had grown even narrower.

Leaning back against the squabs, Olivia began making mental notes, organizing and analyzing the information with the same precision and attention to detail that she brought to her business concerns.

Slowly but surely, an idea began to take shape.

Sprague watched as Davenport straightened the sheaf of papers and put them away. "You mean to say, Lady Olivia actually employs that odd fellow as a clerk?"

"Her right hand man, so to speak."

A slow smile came to his friend's face. "Think the lucky dog has that hand up her skirts?"

Davenport shoved home the desk drawer with enough force to rattle every one of the brass pulls. "Actually, I am not sure Mr. Winslow is particularly interested in the petticoat line," he said through gritted teeth.

"You mean to say . . ." Sprague blinked.

He felt a bit ashamed of himself. The remark had been deliberately malicious, for while Winslow exhibited a number of odd quirks of behavior, Davenport didn't know him well enough to comment on his personal life. And that, he admitted, had a great deal to do with his testy mood. The question as to the exact nature of Winslow's relationship to Olivia was like a stone lodged in his boot, rubbing raw against a sensitive nerve.

Trying to put his irritation aside, he quickly replied, "I did not mean to imply any such thing. He's clever enough to use outrageous behavior to deflect scrutiny from his real self. But in all truth, I have no idea what sort of attractions the fellow favors."

"Well, I, for one, certainly would not mind wrapping my fingers around the lady's luscious breasts or running a caress up those shapely thighs—"

The glass that had been sitting on the viscount's blotter suddenly shattered against the hearth in a splash of amber, sending up a shower of shards. An instant later, Sprague's back hit up against the wainscoting, the rest of his words choked off by a hand fisted in his cravat. "Unless you wish to have your teeth rammed down your throat, you will not speak of Lady Olivia in aught but a respectful manner."

"What the devil has got into you?" Shaking off the viscount's grip, Sprague reacted with injured indignation. "I meant no offense. You may wish to keep a monk's hood pulled over your eyes, but don't ring a peal over my head if I wish to go ahead and admire the view."

Davenport slowly unclenched his hands. "Sorry," he

muttered. "I suppose I am feeling damnably frustrated . . . over the lack of progress in our investigation. On the surface, Saint Claire and Bentham appear perfectly respectable gentlemen. But then, of course, they would. And mention of the Connoisseur left even Tony looking mystified."

"It's understandable that your nerves are coiled tight as a watchspring." Sounding somewhat mollified, his friend pulled a face. "You know, it might not be a bad idea to have a closer look at the Wolfhound's establishment." He gave a tug to the tails of his waistcoat. "An ancillary benefit could be that come morning, we might both be in a more relaxed frame of mind."

"You go ahead." Tempting though the offer was, Davenport doubted the tension gripping his innards would be eased by any morsel, however tasty, that the Wolfhound could toss his way. "In my current frame of mind, I doubt I would be good company for anyone." He grimaced. "Including myself."

Sprague took a moment to pour a fresh brandy and placed it on the edge of the desk. "You know," he said slowly, "there is a saying about all work and no play making Jack a dull boy."

"I'm afraid it's rather too late for that. If I get any duller, my edge won't cut through melted butter."

"Your edge must be dull as dishwater if it hasn't yet occurred to you that pleasure is not the only reason I am suggesting a visit to the Wolf's Lair."

Davenport frowned, feeling that his brain must indeed be submerged in sludge.

"Think on it carefully, Max . . ."

The swirling of brandy in Sprague's glass cast a jumble of crazy patterns upon the wall. Staring at the slippery shapes, their hide-and-seek play a mocking taunt to all his efforts, he was beginning to see naught but doubts. . . .

"We have learned that Fleming and Rundle is engaged in the trade of human flesh, right?" pointed out Sprague.

He nodded.

"And now, Winslow has discovered that it is a gentleman of rank who secretly controls the company. So we have a titled villain who traffics in women."

The picture Sprague was sketching suddenly snapped into focus with a frightful clarity. "Connor?"

"Let's face it, he certainly is familiar with the seamier side of London life, and has the experience and connections to put such an operation together. Not only that, he has a pressing need for blunt. Lots of it."

"Even so, it's hard to believe the Wolfhound could be that vicious."

Sprague's jaw hardened. "He has always had a reputation for wildness."

"But not cruelty. And aren't you forgetting that it was Connor who directed us to Fleming and Rundle in the first place?"

"One doesn't survive in the stews without possessing a great deal of cunning. Seeing we were on the trail of Grisham and Blake, it would be diabolically clever to appear to be helping us. A pawn in place at the firm could be readily sacrificed, and the operation moved to the cover of another business."

"Winslow was right—you have a deucedly Machiavellian turn of mind. Do you really think him the shadowy collector of fine art reputed to be at the head of all this?"

Sprague gave a low snort. "I have never known Connor to collect aught but enemies. However—"

"Despite all the rumors, I am not convinced he is capable of such evil," insisted Davenport, not quite sure why he was being so doggedly stubborn in defending the earl.

"You don't like to think the worst of people, Max." His friend's sigh expressed equal parts admiration and exasperation. "It is both your strength and your weakness. But in this case I fear your loyalty is misplaced." Carefully sidestepping the shards of broken glass, he began a measured pacing before the hearth. "Mr. Winslow was not the only one out asking questions last night. After leaving you and the ladies, I stopped in at a few of the other gaming hells frequented by the *ton*. Word there was that several of the Wolfhound's demoiselles have not been seen at work for over a month. Poof!" The snap of his fingers echoed off the stone mantel. "Disappeared without a trace. Rather a curious coincidence, don't you say?"

Any last argument was swallowed in a low oath. "Damn his hide."

"Aye." Sprague reversed direction, the firelight tinting his countenance with a deep reddish glow. "There may be an innocent explanation, but if there is not, the hunter is about to become the hunted."

The thought of the helpless girls who had fallen prey to the earl's perfidy caused a clench of cold fury in Davenport's chest. "If it takes going to the ends of the earth, we shall track him down and bring him to justice."

After a moment, however, anger was joined by an even more chilling sensation. Cara. He suddenly recalled that she had not hesitated to march straight into the Wolf's Lair. Nor had she been the least bit intimidated by a confrontation with its proprietor.

His sister was far too fearless for her own good. In any battle—especially one that concerned the welfare of others—she would charge into the fray, unflinching as a seasoned Hussar, heedless of facing superior strength or numbers.

And Olivia? She was even worse.

Still, they would not . . . they could not . . .

Raking a hand through his hair, Davenport assured himself that they were safe from Killingworth's claws. Cara was attending a soiree with their aunt, and after the incident of the previous evening, Olivia's bearded servant was sure to be keeping a close watch on her. But somehow, the words rang hollow inside his head

"Even if it is true, the ladies cannot be in imminent danger," he muttered, hoping that voicing the words might give them more force.

"No, of course not." But Sprague did not look overly convinced either. "Though with those two," he added under his breath, "I dare not allow my imagination to take rein."

They exchanged uneasy glances.

"I suppose it would not hurt to check on them," said Davenport.

"That might be a wise strategy," his friend quickly agreed. "On second thought, it might be best not to risk stirring up suspicion by having both of us make an appearance at the Wolf's Lair." The grimness of his expression was momentarily broken by a wry quirk of humor. "Quite frankly, I'd rather have my assignment than yours."

But before either of them could take up their coats, the viscount's valet gave a tentative knock and announced that a caller was demanding entrance.

"Sorry fer disturbing ye, sir, but he says it's right—"

"Urgent," finished Winslow, elbowing his way past Davenport's valet. "I've brought a copy of the report." He waited until Blake had closed the door before adding, "As well as the news that Lady O is still missing."

"Let us hope she is merely engaged in some routine errands." Davenport turned his attention to the pages he had been handed, trying to ignore the stab of apprehension he felt at hearing Olivia had not yet returned to her office. "In any case, it would be a waste of time to try combing the stews when we have not the slightest idea of where to start. Instead, I suggest we concentrate on unmasking the Connoisseur."

"I couldn't agree more," said Sprague, his walking stick tapping impatiently against the knife concealed in his boot.

Winslow perched a hip upon the viscount's desk and took a small gold snuffbox from his pocket. "We would have a much greater chance of doing that if you would consent to take me into your full confidences, sir. Unless I know all the facts, I can't be as effective in using my talents to their best advantage." He paused to inhale a pinch of the pungent tobacco. "At the very least, it might prevent any further missteps in regard to Lady O."

"I had every intention of filling you in—" Davenport stopped abruptly as the lid of the box flipped shut. "Here, let me see that!"

"Dear me." With an exaggerated sigh, the man of affairs handed it over. "I suppose you are going to tell me that you recognize another one of my recent acquisitions."

The low oath from Davenport as he examined the enameled detailing confirmed the assumption.

"Your friend should guard his prized possessions a bit more carefully if he does not want them to end up in places where fellows with a discerning eye may purchase them for a mere song."

"The tune I wish to hear from your lips is, exactly where did you find this?" snapped the viscount. "Was it from Newcombe?"

Noting the drawn expression on Davenport's face, Winslow dropped the display of sardonic teasing and turned just as serious. "No, one of my other sources. Why—"

"You had best hear it all from the beginning." The viscount drew a deep breath. "Which all started with a series of thefts in Yorkshire. . . ."

He went on to give a summary, taking care to include all the salient facts, including the disappearance of the Ruby Lion and the painful personal revelation of his own brother's apparent involvement in the misdeeds.

"Satan's prick," swore Winslow.

"Kip was not always evil—"

"No, no, that's not what I meant." Now fully alert and poised on both feet, the man of affairs plucked the snuffbox back from Davenport. "Look, give me an hour."

"But where—"

The question was brushed off. "I'll explain later, sir."

By the time the report had been reviewed several times, and a list of notes and questions prepared, an hour had long since passed. After darting yet another uneasy glance at the mantel clock, Davenport could no longer sit still. First Olivia, and now Winslow appeared to be missing action. He could only pray that Cara had not also taken it into her head to go off.

Damn. He would give the blasted fellow five more minutes before following up on the urgent note he had sent to Olivia's townhouse . . .

"Sorry for the delay." The knock was still reverberating on the door as Winslow pushed his way in.

"I trust you were engaged in something more pressing than a stop for prosecco or porcinis," responded Davenport rather sourly. "Time is of the essence—"

"Nevertheless, I think you might find this little tidbit worth the wait, sir." The man of affairs dropped a small bundle onto the desk. "At least I hope you do. I had to pick several locks to get at it."

It took a moment for the viscount to untie the thin silken cord and let the covering of felt slip away, taking his breath with it. There in his fingers lay a familiar sight, one he had seen countless times since his youth.

"Where . . . how . . . who . . ." he whispered hoarsely, staring down at the Ruby Lion.

"I told you, I have an eye for interesting items. If I had known earlier that this is what you were looking for . . ." Winslow let the sentence trail off as he took a small jeweler's loupe from his waistcoat pocket and held it out. "There is one thing I wish to point out. I took the liberty of making an inspection and, well, I think you ought to take a closer look at the mane."

Davenport examined the sculpted gold. "There appears to be a dark substance caught in the carving." The lens dropped a fraction. "Dried blood, if I am not mistaken."

He knew he was not—he had seen way too much of it to harbor any doubts.

"So it seemed to me."

The viscount felt a sudden chill steal through his veins. Was it Kip who had left the telltale traces of violence upon the small statue? The ruby eyes, their glittering red a mocking contrast to the dull rust-colored smudges, stared back at him with an unblinking opaqueness that made him want to dash it to bits against the wall.

Curse the damn thing! To think that such a small, inanimate object could have stirred up such a maelstrom of pain and suffering. . .

His fingers closed in a fist. He had better find a way to tame the beast. And quickly.

Chapter Eighteen

❧❦❧

That the lady had arrived back at her townhouse, unscathed and at her usual hour, should prove their fears unfounded, Davenport told himself. It was hardly a matter of concern that Olivia was not presently at home. Not when the daily post routinely delivered a host of invitations to elegant soirees.

Still, he felt irrationally irked. Halfway down the marble stairs, he stopped, then turned abruptly and retraced his steps.

"On second thought, I would like to leave a message for Lady Olivia," he announced as the door swung open again.

The servant, a tall, solemn man with skin the color of grated nutmeg, pressed his palms together and cocked his head expectantly.

"In writing."

Looking unsure how to handle the unexpected request, the man continued to fix him with a mute stare.

The viscount sketched a line of script in the air. "Pen and paper. A note. It won't take long."

There was another prolonged silence before the soft slide of sandals brushed over the checkered marble and the wave of a hand indicated that he should enter.

Without a word, the servant led the way past the curved staircase, but rather than usher Davenport into Olivia's study, he continued on to the end of the hallway and drew open a door.

The small room was dark, save for a pooling of light cast by two scented oil lamps across a cluttered desk. Seated behind a stack of open books and an array of dried leaves and finely ground powders, Vavek looked up from dipping a paintbrush into a bowl of ochre-colored liquid.

Though Davenport was becoming accustomed to the eccentricities of the lady's household, his brows shot up in surprise as he caught sight of the intricate patterns of pigment now covering a good portion of the servant's exposed forearms. A second glance showed the delicate swirls to be a whimsical intertwining of flora and fauna, which seemed quite out of character. The inscrutable Indian did not strike him as a very fanciful sort of fellow.

Seeing that Vavek did not appear inclined to speak, the viscount cleared his throat. "I understand that Lady Olivia is out for the evening . . ."

His pause for confirmation was met by a curt nod.

"Might I leave her a note? It's rather important."

Another nod, accompanied by a sleight of hand that produced a sheet of foolscap and a quill pen from beneath the folds of his rolled-up sleeve.

"Ahem." Davenport moved closer to the desk. "I don't suppose you know where she is. Or when she will return?"

The brief shrug may or may not have been an affirmative.

"Chatty bugger, aren't you?" he muttered, reaching for the inkwell with a stab of impatience.

The oiled beard gave a hair of a twitch before the servant's face once again schooled itself into an expressionless mask. "One can learn much by merely observing, memsahib."

"I don't doubt that a trained eye spots all manner of things." Davenport forced himself to match the other man's unblinking gaze. "Such as the existence of shadows that stalk the night."

"I watch for any danger that might threaten my lady." As he spoke, the sinuous strokes of his brush outlined a crouched feline, its tail turning into the looping twist of a hooded serpent. "I have been with her for many years and would not see her hurt in any way."

Momentarily distracted by the display of artistry, Davenport watched in fascination as the curlicues of the cobra became a parrot. "You are quite skilled with your hands. Do the designs have a special meaning?"

"Sometimes." Turning his palm inward, Vavek dashed off a quick sketch, then held it up for Davenport's inspection.

The room was quite warm, and the perfume of mulled spices combined with the flicker of the flames and the deft movements of the servant's fingers was having a hypnotic effect on his senses. It took an instant or two for the viscount to register that the image was neither bird nor beast, but a man. A man with flowing locks swept back from his brow and a large phallus jutting out from his thighs.

Before he could react, the Indian set aside his brush

in favor of a small, curved dagger and scraped away a portion of the still-wet pigment.

"Ah," said Davenport softly. "I think I get the message." The quill lay untouched upon the sheet of paper. Finding that the words he had intended to pen had lost a touch of their urgency, he made no move to take them up. "What makes you think I present any threat to the lady?"

The murky light and ghosting tendrils of smoke rendered the man's expression even more unreadable. "Cats," came the cryptic reply.

"Cats?" repeated the viscount, trying hard to make the connection between cats and a severed cock.

"Cats appear a harbinger of danger for memsahib. First, the Black Cat crosses her path, then the Jade Tiger. Now there is mention of a Ruby Lion." Three fingers jabbed the air, jeweled rings flashing from each knuckle as they pointed at the viscount's tawny mane. "And you. A flesh and blood lion who is perhaps the most dangerous of them all."

"Me?" Davenport let out his breath. "I am naught but a scarred beast. I present no threat to Lady Olivia. Indeed, I am doing everything in my feeble power to see that she comes to no grief."

Intoning a lengthy muttering in Hindi, Vavek sat back and contemplated the squiggles of henna on his bared forearms, looking for all the world as if he discerned a preordained pattern. "I think," he added in English, "that you underestimate your power."

Davenport was unsure of how to answer. Mimicking the overlapping tracings of earthy orange, the other man's meaning seemed layered with a confusing complexity. And he had not proven overly adept at unraveling conundrums of late.

"Like the currents that swirl in the sacred Ganges, you have some elemental pull on memsahib."

No more than she had on him! he admitted to himself. Yet aloud, he attempted to appear unmoved. "And what do your drawings tell you—that it is a bad thing?"

For the first time, the viscount detected a ripple of doubt in the depths of the other man's eyes.

"I am not certain. I sense rather than see danger. As of yet, it remains too indistinct to define."

"Well, let us try to keep it that way," snapped Davenport. His head was beginning to spin with the effort of trying to follow the vague hints and innuendos. "It would be a damn sight more helpful if you would leave off the mystical meanderings long enough to tell me where Lady Olivia is at this moment." His eyes narrowed in a critical squint. "I take it as you are here, she is unaccompanied."

Vavek had no such trouble interpreting the viscount's meaning. Bristling at the suggestion that he had been derelict in his duties, he pulled at the point of his beard. "A gentleman came by for her in his carriage. It is, she assured me, the way it is done here in England."

Davenport could not argue with that. Still, he could not refrain from asking, "Tall, silver-haired? With a beaky nose?" The appendage was rather prominent, he thought, and he had the urge to find fault with something about Olivia's admirer. The cursed jackanapes's dress and deportment were above reproach. . . .

"Yes. Lord Bentham—"

"What!" Petty irritation gave way to a roar of real alarm.

Vavek was up in a flash, the billowing sleeves of his tunic tumbling down to hide the temporary tattoos and the knife that was now gripped in his hand.

The viscount forced a firmer hold on his emotions. Up to that moment, he had been unaware of the gentleman's identity. But simply because Bentham's name appeared on a list was no proof of guilt. Like Kip, he might be no more than an innocent pawn.

"Actually, you may tuck your blade away. There is no need for rushing out and slicing off anyone's pego quite yet," he said. "I don't believe Lady Olivia is in any imminent peril."

The other man slowly sheathed his weapon, yet a look of cold-blooded resolve lingered. Davenport had seen similar expressions on the faces of soldiers willing to fight to the death to defend their comrades. He did not doubt for an instant that Vavek would hack off an army of limbs to keep Olivia safe.

It made him wonder at what terrible ordeals the two of them had faced together, for in his experience, a bond such as theirs could only have been forged by shared adversity. Though he had been given a rough sketch of her early life, the viscount realized there was still so much he did not know about Olivia, her years abroad, and the sacrifices and sufferings she had endured to survive.

The air of cool confidence she wore fitted as flawlessly as her stylish gowns. The effect was so seamless he only recently had come to realize that beneath the artful disguise—a well-acted charade of silk and skin—lay a figure far more vulnerable than he ever imagined.

The closing of the brass paint-box lid, sounding eerily akin to the snap of a predator's jaws, punctured the strained silence. "A lion does not roar without reason," said Vavek, carefully wiping his brush clean and setting it down.

"I was voicing displeasure," growled Davenport in reply. "I do not especially care for the gentleman."

"Why?"

The viscount shrugged, aware of the sublime irony in their sudden reversal of roles.

Then, in asking himself the same question, he could not help but wonder if he were more like a lion than he cared to admit. Was he snarling because he saw the other gentleman as a rival? Had some primal instinct, long caged behind a veneer of civility, broken through and overpowered the carefully cultivated manners of a gentleman? Nothing else could explain why he wanted nothing so much as to rake his nails over Bentham's patrician face.

Vavek's response to the wordless gesture, though for the most part muffled in his thick beard, nearly caused Davenport to chuckle. In keeping with the switch of character, the servant's curses, as well as his queries, were coming in English.

That is, unless the Hindi vocabulary had suddenly expanded to include the words "bloody" and "arse."

"Oh, very well." The viscount relented. Vavek's show of anger, however brief, had made him appear human, rather than some statue whittled from a log of rock-hard mahogany. "I don't like to be kept in the dark either."

Inscrutable as ever, the other man's face leaned in closer to one of the lamps, the wavering aureole of light casting his features in harsh relief.

"The truth is, Bentham's name appeared on a rather incriminating document. I don't yet know why, but in and of itself, it is not proof of any perfidy on his part. To be fair, he may be only another victim caught in a web of intrigue."

Davenport was not sure how much Vavek knew of their investigation, but he suspected it was a great deal. Sure enough, the servant evinced no surprise at the announcement. He merely asked, "Does memsahib know this man is under suspicion?"

"Good Lord, I devoutly hope not."

"You pray to your deity, and I shall pray to mine."

"Better yet, tell me which of the myriad entertainments in Town they are attending, and I will stop in myself, to check that nothing is amiss."

For several moments, the only sounds were the brush of bare feet over the parquet and the faint hiss of the lamps as Vavek circled a small prayer rug by the hearth. Davenport knew that while the question was a simple one, the implications were complex. He was asking the Indian to make a leap of faith—a step, once taken, from which there was no turning back. It would acknowledge that the viscount had crossed the line between friend and foe.

"Kensington."

If the viscount had not been alert for an answer, he might have mistaken the zephryed word for a sigh.

As luck would have it, he knew the lady—an aging dowager whose penchant for serving costly champagne always attracted a crowd—and the exact location. Two birds with one stone. His mouth quirked in grim satisfaction. Cara, in the company of their aunt, was making an appearance at the very same ball, which saved him the trouble of dancing all over Town, trying to keep one step ahead of whatever machinations the ladies had in mind.

With a nudge, Davenport pushed the pen and blank paper away. "I won't have need of these. I'll deliver my message in person."

"Might I ask your advice on something, sir, seeing as you seem so knowledgeable on the subject of art and antiques?" Olivia had waited until the figures of the dance had brought them to a more secluded part of the ballroom.

"Why yes, of course." Bentham looked pleased by her request and the throaty, confidential note in which it was voiced.

"I have a collection of special books I am thinking of having rebound. However, I am loath to entrust them to just anyone."

"What sort of books?"

"Rather . . . naughty books, I'm afraid." A coy smile teased her lips into a playful pout. "Does that shock you?"

Was she mistaken, or did the glint of good humor in his eyes sharpen to a more speculative edge?

"Not at all," he assured her. "A worldly lady like you, who has lived in the exotic environs of the Orient, can only be expected to have sophisticated tastes."

"Ah, how nice to discover a gentleman who understands such things." Olivia moved her hips just enough to cause the silk of her skirts to brush against his leg. "Perhaps you would care to have a look at them?" Her lashes lowered demurely. "To offer your expert opinion on who might be the best person to handle them."

"I should be more than delighted. With all due modesty, I am considered somewhat of an authority in the field of valuable collectibles, so I am sure I shall be able to help you find what you are looking for, Lady Olivia."

"Thank you. I had hoped that would prove to be the case." She paused, exaggerating her hesitation. "A— and please call me just Olivia. I feel we have become good enough friends to dispense with formalities."

"Olivia, then." The thrum of his rising anticipation was palatable in any number of tiny ways—the press of his fingers at the small of her back, the angling of his head to bring his lips a hair's breadth closer to her cheek, the shortening of his stride as the muscles in his thighs grew taut. "And you must, of course, call me Robert."

"It would be my pleasure . . ." Though his intimacy sent a tiny shiver through her, Olivia forced herself to concentrate on business. Purring a breath of air that tickled his ear, she added, "Robert."

She could not recall ever having flirted so shamelessly with a gentleman before. And yet Bentham, whose wits were obviously not wanting, did not seem to find anything suspect about her forward manner. Perhaps, she noted wryly, because the greater part of his attention was riveted on the front of her gown.

That men—even the most intelligent of them—could be easily distracted was something she had discovered early on in business. In this case, the ploy consisted of whisper-thin silk cut low and snug to enhance the curves of flesh, the color a lush peach she had learned was his particular favorite. The fact that Bentham was attracted to large breasts was another bit of intimate information passed on by the Irish Wolfhound, and while she was not overly endowed with such charms, a few judicious tucks and bits of padding accentuated her bosom.

The result was apparently acceptable, for the gentleman could not seem to tear his eyes from her plunging neckline.

"Would you care to set a date and time?" he asked. "If I read you correctly, these are not the sort of valuables you wish to leave lying around . . ." His gaze took another dip downward. ". . . collecting dust, so to speak."

"I am very careful when it comes to my prized possessions," agreed Olivia.

And, she warned herself, she ought to take care to apply the same caution to her neck as well as her books. If Bentham was indeed the Connoisseur, he was a man of consummate cunning and intelligence. Her sex provided her with a distinct advantage, but she would have used her brains to come out on top.

At the moment, as the dance called for them to separate in a series of artfully orchestrated spins, instinct was telling her that it would be a mistake to give in too quickly. The best course of action lay in drawing out the chase, whetting his appetite with more teasing talk, and perhaps a titillating taste of the pleasures he could expect to savor, so that lust might lead him to make a fatal slip.

"Perhaps we might discuss the arrangements in greater privacy," she suggested, once the steps had brought them back together.

Bentham watched as a gust of breeze from the open French doors stirred the curls at the nape of her neck. "A stroll in the garden would no doubt afford the opportunity for a more intimate discussion. Why don't I fetch us some champagne when the set is over and escort you outside."

"Oh, what an excellent notion," she murmured, as if it had not been the one foremost in her mind.

The gentleman's absence gave Olivia a chance to collect her thoughts. Choosing a sheltered spot among the shadows of the decorative greenery, she reviewed her strategy for the coming interlude, then took a moment to survey the room, curious as to whether any of the other gentlemen on Lord Killingworth's list were in attendance. Light glittered off the crystal chandeliers and a myriad of candelabrum were ablaze, yet the flutter of colored gowns and wink of jewels made it difficult to pick out an individual in the crush of guests. Abandoning the effort, she turned away, only to notice a tall figure move out from one of the recessed archways and take up position on the outer perimeter of the dance floor.

It had been the distinctive shading of his hair that

had caught her eye. *How interesting.* She watched the Irish Wolfhound step rather stiffly into the first figures of a waltz. Discreet inquiry on her part had confirmed the gentleman's own emphatic assertion that he avoided Society soirees like the plague. And yet, here he was, in the thick of things.

Even more interesting was the fact that he was dancing with Cara Bingham. What, she wondered, could have brought such an unlikely couple together? By all accounts, their first meeting had not exactly taken place under the most civilized of circumstances. Indeed, Cara's cheeks had become suspiciously pink the other night at the mention of the roguish earl. It was intriguing to speculate on what could have occurred during the brief encounter to cause her embarrassment. Given the sardonic bite of the Wolfhound's sense of humor and the young lady's feisty spirit, Olivia could well imagine that the fur had flown.

However, in spite of his bark, Killingworth did not strike her as quite the vicious brute he wished to appear. She doubted he would have trespassed too far past the bounds of propriety with an innocent, especially one who was the sister of an erstwhile comrade.

Yet in watching the hardening angles of the earl's profile and the growing tilt of the young lady's chin, Olivia had to presume they were not discussing the state of the weather or the latest pattern plates in *Le Belle Assemblee.* Such topics would hardly be bringing such a menacing scowl to the Wolfhound's face, or . . .

Her speculation was cut off by yet another brusque movement close by.

Like the unusual iron-gray shade of the Wolfhound's locks, the tawny gold mane of the viscount was hard to miss, even in a crowd. Edging sideways past a portly member of Parliament and a lady who resembled a Bond Street confection in her layers of sugary lemon and white tulle, Davenport halted by one of the massive urns flanking the main entrance. He, too, appeared to be scanning the guests.

Olivia quickly drew back. Her plans for the evening had definitely not included an encounter with the viscount. The slightest misstep with Bentham could trip up her carefully choreographed strategy.

To her relief, Davenport spotted his sister and began squeezing his way through the couples milling by the punch bowl. At the same time, Bentham reappeared from the refreshment room, two crystal coupes of champagne in hand.

Accepting her glass with a grateful smile, Olivia needed no encouragement to quicken her steps toward the terrace.

"What the devil did you mean by dancing with that dog?" It was only through a concerted effort that Davenport managed to keep his voice low enough to avoid attracting attention. He had arrived too late to catch the earl, so his sister was left to take the full brunt of his ire. "Didn't I tell you to steer well clear of Killingworth?"

"And didn't I tell you that I have no intention of being ordered about as if I had no more sense than a flea?" Cara glared back at him with a mutinous expression. "Besides, I could hardly refuse his offer in front of

Lady Keppel and Mrs. Rushton without causing an unpleasant scene."

Somewhat mollified by the explanation, he allowed his jaw to relax. "Still, I don't know why the Wolfhound would want to be prowling around you. It makes no sense."

Two faint spots of color formed on his sister's face. "No, indeed. What gentleman would seek out a bossy beanpole when he can choose among a bevy of dainty young lovelies."

"For God's sake, Cara, you know I did not mean to imply—"

"Unless, of course, he had an urgent message to deliver to the beanpole's brother," she went on, ignoring the halting apology. With a deft flick of her fingers, she removed a square of paper from her glove and pressed it into his palm. "Here, he asked me to pass this on to you as soon as possible."

Davenport frowned. "Why you?"

"Because you were not at your rooms when he stopped by, Max," she replied in some exasperation. "Well, aren't you going to read it?"

He wasn't at all sure he wanted to do so in front of her, but sensing that her feelings were already somewhat bruised, he didn't have the heart to refuse.

A stealthy peek at the message revealed a single scrawled sentence.

"Well?" repeated Cara, adding a little kick to his ankle to nudge out a reply.

The viscount had hesitated, more out of puzzlement than any attempt to keep the contents a secret. "He wishes to meet with me."

"What for?" Though the music had started up again, she took care to keep her voice a whisper. "Has he learned something of . . . Kip?"

"He doesn't say." His fingers slowly closed around the note. "He has simply spelled out a time and a place for later tonight." That the time was just before dawn and the place a corner of Hyde Park more favored by footpads than fancy toffs were details he chose to leave unsaid. Still, Cara's face betrayed a spasm of concern.

"Why the melodrama of a Minerva Press novel?" she wondered, her question giving voice to his own misgivings. "What sort of meeting demands such clandestine caution?"

What sort of meeting, indeed?

Given the earlier speculations regarding the Wolfhound and his motives, Davenport was inclined to think the worst. However, hoping to allay his sister's alarm, he answered with a nonchalant shrug. "We shall see in short order." He tucked the paper away with a show of unconcern. "Killingworth tends to do his prowling at night, so there is nothing unusual about the request."

She was about to reply when he added, "You, on the other hand, would be granting me a huge favor by promising to make an early evening of it. Find Aunt Honoria and ask her to take you home. And stay there."

Her expression turned from one of alarm to one of outrage. "It is not as if I am still in the schoolroom, Max. You never thought to question my competence these past few years, when I was handling the responsibility of running the estate. Yet now, you think to trundle me off like a child, with a pat on the head and the promise of hot milk and a warm apple tart?" A note of bitterness had crept into her voice as she leaned in closer and placed a hand on his arm. "Olivia is not so very much older than I am, and yet you do not seek to send her to her room."

"I damn well would if I could find her," he growled.

"Then you ought to head out to the gardens," Cara shot back. "For she passed through the French doors not five minutes ago."

The idea of Olivia wandering outside by herself sent a sudden frisson of alarm snaking down his spine. Had Killingworth also spotted her going off? The darkened paths and lush foliage afforded plenty of cover for any predator.

"Please Cara, just do as I ask. I—I will explain later." Trusting that her good sense would prevail over pique, he turned abruptly, looking for the quickest route to the terrace. In his haste, he failed to hear his sister add that the lady was not alone.

Nor did he note that as her glove was dislodged from his sleeve, it brushed against his pocket and came away with the folded paper.

Davenport paused at a fork in the path, straining to hear any faint crunching of gravel above the splash of the fountain. The light from the torches did not penetrate past the first twist of the boxwood hedge, leaving the sprawling maze of sheltered bowers and narrow walkways illuminated by naught but the occasional glimmer of moonlight.

"Damn," he muttered, not knowing which way to

turn. Then, urged on by a low burble of laughter from the bushes to his right, he veered off in the opposite direction.

After another hurried traverse brought him hard up against a marble faun, the viscount swore again. Could Cara have been mistaken? He had no desire to stumble upon illicit lovers, and in all truth, he could not imagine what would lead Olivia to venture this far from the main festivities. Deciding to circle back, he edged around another statue.

Only to stop short, as if he had run into a wall of solid stone.

A sculpted satyr, its lascivious leer limned in the pale light, was staring him in the face. It was, noted Davenport, a look mirrored by the flushed countenance of the gentleman leaning heavily into its ivy-twined thighs, a lady pressed between the twin expressions of male lust.

She, however did not seem to be voicing much of an objection to the scandalous liberties being taken. Head tilted back against the carved chest of the beast, she had allowed her companion's groping hand to slide down to the ruffle of her bodice.

"Sweet Heaven, you are a veritable Venus." A groan sounded. "God, how I want you."

The viscount went whiter than the smooth Carrara marble. The gentleman, as well as the object of his desire, were all too recognizable.

"Mmmm." Olivia's murmur was smoky, seductive. "But much as I hate to say it, we had best exercise restraint here. Someone might see us. And while I care naught for the strictures of Society, it would be unwise for me to allow my reputation to be ruined."

Bentham's panting was audible above the ambient noises of the night. "Yes. Of course." The words were slightly distorted as he pressed another hungry kiss to the curve of her neck. "Forgive me, my dear," he went on thickly, his lips lingering for one last taste, "for finding it nigh on impossible to tear myself away from your ambrosial charms."

Though he had the burning urge to grab Bentham by the throat, Davenport kept a grip on himself. Something in her voice made him decide to hold off.

A sigh sounded in answer to the apology. "It is a shame that there are not some other, more . . . interesting gatherings to attend here in Town, where one would be free to partake in something more stimulating than staid quadrilles and weak ratafia punch."

"Oh, but there are, Olivia!" Bentham eagerly replied, his hips pressing into the folds of her skirts. "I am privy to a private party that takes place regularly. A very exclusive gathering I am sure you would enjoy. The next one is soon, on . . ."

Olivia turned her head at that instant, and her sharp intake of breath cut off any further details. "It appears we have company."

Averting her eyes, she shook out the silk bunched around her knees. Her companion stumbled back a step.

"Ah, Davenport." Bentham recovered his equilibrium on seeing it was not some high stickler who had caught them. A conspiratorial wink followed, which only increased the viscount's urge to punch out the other man's deadlights.

"I regret you had to witness our, er, indiscretion.

But seeing as we are all experienced adults, I trust you will agree there is no harm done." Bentham didn't bother trying to straighten his cravat or tug the tails of his coat to cover his obvious arousal, but contented himself with flicking a stray leaf from his sleeve. "Just as I trust we may count on your honor as a gentleman to keep mum for the sake of the lady."

Davenport made no effort to blunt the razored sarcasm of his words. "The lady need have no doubts concerning my honor as a gentleman."

"How very kind of you, sir." Olivia placed a hand on the other man's arm. Her expression appeared as unemotional as chiseled stone, but his eyes detected two faint spots of color on her cheeks. "Robert, if you don't mind, I would like to return to the ballroom. I find it has grown decidedly chilly out here."

Bentham assumed a smile, but in the instant their gazes met, the viscount saw the show of good humor did not extend past his thinned lips. "Of course."

Davenport did not budge, forcing the other man to go around him. "Don't think you will escape so easily," he said softly as Olivia made to pass by. "I will be calling on you later—and I suggest you be alone."

Chapter Nineteen

"It was . . . business, not pleasure."

Davenport's jaw unclenched enough for him to speak. "Be damned with that! What you are doing is much too dangerous. You are dealing with the devil, and have seen what he and his legions are capable of."

With methodical precision, Olivia straightened the pleats of her gown. "My plan is perfectly reasonable."

"It is perfectly insane." He had experienced an initial wave of relief on learning that her interest in Bentham had not been personal. But it was fast evaporating.

"Unorthodox and unusual, perhaps. But hardly irrational. Indeed, the very unexpectedness of it only makes it more likely to succeed."

He could not help but note that her hand was resting atop a book bound in crimson kidskin. As he stared at the graceful fingers, trying not to recall their caresses of Bentham—or their tingling touch on his own flesh—they began to drum on the grained leather ever so lightly.

"You and Mr. Sprague have yet to come up with a specific strategy," she went on. "We have to stop the next shipment from sailing, and to do that we cannot be afraid of risking a bold strike at the heart of their organization."

Davenport wrenched his gaze up to meet hers. "Olivia, I beg you to step back and leave it to me. We may not appear to be accomplishing much, yet you yourself know that most of the time victory is achieved through methodical plodding, rather than any risky move. I know how strongly you feel about the girls, and I promise, come hell or high water, I shall find a way to unmask the Connoisseur and save them from being transported to the East."

She seemed surprised by his use of her name, the martial light in her eye briefly flickering to a softer glow before regaining its fiery glint. "I cannot step away," she whispered. "I simply cannot."

A heavy silence hung between them, punctuated by the quickening tempo of her tapping.

Davenport's fingers began to drum an answering tattoo. "Then might you spell out your plan in more detail?" He was not at all anxious to hear what she had in mind. However, aware that a direct order to retreat from the action would only fan the fires of her resolve, he hoped to spot a weakness in her scheme. Maybe then he could convince her to back off. "Just how do you intend to coax Bentham into making any incriminating revelations?" Despite his attempt to remain calm, he could not help but demand, "By making love to him?"

"I . . . do not think it will come to that," she answered slowly. "It seems to me a more effective strategy is to make a business proposition the Connoisseur will find impossible to pass up. After all, this is all about money, and if a better offer for the shipment is made, I have no doubt he will snap at it."

Trying to mask his growing fear and frustration, the viscount took several measured breaths before responding. "You cannot even be sure that Bentham is the man we seek." He decided to leave off mention of the Wolfhound's name. The fewer suspects she was pursuing, the better. "But whoever he is, the Connoisseur is not likely to take that sort of business offering from a lone female seriously."

"You are right." Her eyes did not quite meet his. "But a couple would be convincing. One whose jaded sensibilities hunger for something really exotic. And whose purse can well afford to pay for the privilege of satiating such tastes."

"A couple . . ." Even on repetition, the words defied comprehension.

"Yes. Like you, I have come to the conclusion that alone I would have difficulty in convincing the Connoisseur of my depravity. The presence of a man is required to give full credence to the charade. And Bentham was agreeable to the suggestion that I bring someone else along to the party."

"You appear to have given the matter great thought," replied Davenport with a softness that belied the true state of his emotions. "Have you chosen a partner?"

There was a flicker of hesitation. "I thought you might agree to help."

"Did you?" His hand tightened to a fist and its impact on the table caused the book to jump several inches in the air. "Well, let me put that particular notion to rest."

"Very well." She paused again. "Then I shall just have to ask someone else."

Another smack sent the book skittering across the polished wood. "I swear, I shall boil Winslow in a vat of his olive oil if he so much as considers agreeing to such a masquerade."

Olivia's lashes dropped, the thick fringing of ebony accentuating a face so white and rigid that it might have been carved out of marble. Her voice was equally cool and devoid of emotion "Windy is not the only man in London from whom I may request a favor."

Of that there was little doubt, the viscount realized, his heart sinking. He could well imagine there was no lack of males willing to jump at the chance to offer their services. Drawing a breath suddenly became difficult, as though a slab of stone had fallen atop his chest.

"No." Somehow he managed to squeeze out a coherent sound.

The angle of her brows grew more defiant. "I am sorry—but there is nothing you can do to stop me, sir."

He could think of one thing, but the fear that she would manage to escape from even so formidable a guard as Vavek made him abandon the idea in a hurry. "No one else," he rasped. "It was I who drew you into this sordid mess in the first place. So if you are intent on exposing yourself to such insane risk, I have no choice but to come along."

Her hand slowly nudged the crimson book in his direction. "Then you had better study this. Bentham was anxious that I also bring a sample from my collection of Indian manuscripts. If we are to put on a convincing performance, you are going to have to know what you are getting into."

Handling the covers as if they were red-hot coals, Davenport ventured a peek inside. And was struck mute. It was just as well he had temporarily lost the power of speech, he decided, for he would no doubt have regretted uttering the string of profanities that came to mind.

Though, clearly, the lady before him was not easy to shock.

Bloody hell. His gaze remained glued to the contents as he thumbed back several pages. There were mostly pictures, and only a smattering of text. Pictures of men with impossibly large cocks, in impossibly contorted positions, doing impossibly erotic things to females. Who all seemed to be wearing impossibly blissful expressions.

Davenport didn't dare think of what his own face must look like. Ducking to hide the furious flush that had risen to his cheeks, he thrust the book into his pocket and rose.

"Still willing?" she asked.

"I—I will give you my final answer in the morning."

Olivia nodded. "I shall understand if you wish to withdraw the offer. But with or without you, I am going to attend Bentham's party."

Though woven of gossamer silk, the paisley dressing gown felt like a sack of stones as she slid it over her bare shoulders. It was, of course, not the only thing weighing heavily on her. Twisting the sash around her fingers, Olivia stood knotted in indecision. Was she making a grave mistake? It wasn't often that she questioned her intellect or her instincts, but in this case, she felt strangely unsure of herself.

To calm the odd sense of uncertainty, she reached for the rosewood box on her dressing table. Inside were several vials of colored oils and a small brass brazier. Choosing the jade green, she pooled a bit of the liquid in the center of the metal bowl and lit the candle beneath it. The scent of juniper quickly perfumed the air, its fresh fragrance mixing with the more primitive undertones of an Asian jungle.

In the dim light of the bedside candles, she opened a second vial, which contained the essence of roses. Breathing with a rhythmic depth, as Vavek had taught her, she dabbed a few drops on her forehead, her temples, and lastly, her lips. The result was almost immediate—she could feel a slight ebbing of the tension from her spine and a relaxing of the tautness in every muscle as she inhaled the subtle sweetness.

With a swooshing sigh, Olivia then seated herself cross-legged on the carpet, the lush silk of her wrapper spilling over her folded knees and bared calves. Indian gurus used meditation to clear the mind, but try as she might to empty her consciousness, she was all too aware that her thoughts continued to spin like whirling dervishes inside her head.

A weeping girl, manacles around her wrists. A sneering assassin, a small gold lion, cursed with ungodly evil.

Such images brought a chill back to her bones. And

yet, it collided with a lick of heat that seemed to curl up from her very core. Hot and cold. No wonder she was feeling off balance.

It was impossible to shake the vision of Davenport, his piercing, amber eyes lit by some inner fire. At times he looked tortured, as if it had been kindled by demons, while at other moments she could have sworn it was some other emotion that had him ablaze with an all-too-human intensity. She tried to put a name to the spark, but it seemed to elude simple definition. "Seductive" was the only word that came close. Sinfully seductive . . .

Without a knock of warning, the door to her bedchamber swung open.

"Hell and damnation!"

Olivia did not have to open her eyes to know it was not Vavek's sandaled step that had crossed into the room.

"I demand that—" The viscount stopped short, his anger taking on a bite of concern. "Olivia! Have you fallen ill?"

She looked up, trying to maintain her calm in the face of his sudden reappearance. "No, I am exercising an age-old Indian discipline designed to induce a sense of inner peace. And eternal enlightenment."

"God be merciful—I would be eternally grateful if it granted you a temporary flash of common sense."

Catching the drift of his eyes, Olivia was aware that her lotus posture, while meant to encourage inner revelations, was also exposing a great deal of her outer person. The dressing gown had gathered up at the waist, allowing a peek at bare thighs, while the sash had loosened enough that her breasts were hardly covered.

"If you have come merely to ignite another quarrel, you may as well put your flint and steel away." Smoothing the silk back over her naked skin, Olivia unfolded her limbs and rose. "I have no intention of engaging in any more fireworks. No arguments, no matter how booming, are going to dissuade me from doing everything in my power to save those unfortunate girls."

To her surprise, the deliberately belligerent announcement elicited naught but a silent little quirk of the viscount's lips. His gaze remained shuttered as well. She thought the amber color looked slightly more molten than usual, but it might have been a mere play of light. Indeed, the quixotic flickering of the candles was casting all manner of strange shadows across his features.

Intent on studying his face, Olivia didn't realize how close she had pressed in until his palms touched the ridges of her shoulders. Yet still, he did not speak.

"Why have you come?" she asked, her voice mirroring the slight unsteadiness of the tiny flames. His continued reticence was growing unnerving. "If not to ring a peal over my head."

His answer, when it came, was barely more than a whisper. "Damnation, Olivia. If I thought roaring to the Heavens would do a lick of good, I should rattle the stars in their firmament."

"Max," she said, only dimly aware that she had spoken his name. "Do you mean you have made up your mind about taking part in the charade?"

His hands slid upward to frame her face. "Charade? What charade?"

Olivia hesitated, feeling her mouth go unaccountably dry. "P-pretending to feel passionate sexual desire."

"Is that what you think we have been doing?" Without waiting for an answer, he wrenched away. Like a flash of fire, the crimson book appeared from the depth of his pocket and rocketed toward the hearth. "Are you truly determined to go on with this, no matter the consequences?"

"Yes."

Once again, she was aware of his touch, lighter than a tropical rain, tracing a path along her lower lip. "Then God help me, I have no choice but to come along."

"Of course you have a choice."

"No, Olivia." Davenport's roughened voice cut her off. "Indeed I do not."

It was no longer the tip of his thumb she felt but the sudden, searing heat of his mouth covering hers. The taste of him—need, desire, vulnerability—was infinitely more potent than any spirits she had ever consumed. Her lips parted, not for any attempt at speech, but in a silent plea for him to flood her with a deeper draught of fire.

Locked together, the force of his embrace made her stagger back a step, the hem of her dressing gown catching in the tangle of legs, pulling it from her shoulders. Only the loosely knotted sash at her waist kept her from being stripped completely naked. The bunched silk was quickly crushed against her by the press of his thighs and the growing ridge of his manhood. His fingers, no longer gentle, tangled in her hair, tugging loose the thick braid, so that the tresses tumbled in disarray over her back. Their wild urgency was matched by the thrust of his tongue.

Head tilted, she touched its tip with hers, and felt a shudder course him, as if she had set a match to a volatile fuse.

"The devil and all his legions take me, Olivia," he rasped, the faint stubbling of his cheek scraping against her flesh as he slid his mouth down the arch of her neck. "I fear I have lost all control and am about to explode into flames."

She eased her hands inside his coat and peeled it away from his unresisting arms. Next she unknotted his cravat, and let it slither away to join the other garment on the floor. Her fingers then found the fastenings of his shirt.

Davenport stiffened, the air catching in his lungs.

"No, keep breathing, Max."

The crisp linen quickly yielded to her efforts. A flutter of white set the light and shadows to swaying, and upon the far wall a pirouette of patterns danced across the surface.

Olivia felt a sigh of sheer pleasure escape her lips as she pressed her palms against his chest and reveled in the texture of the whisper-light hair curled against the sinewed stretch of flesh. Drawing slow, ever-widening circles across his torso, her touch dropped lower, until her probing fingers found the jagged white line that cut across one of his ribs.

"Yet another ugly scar," he whispered hoarsely. "I

have so many I have lost count. There is one here . . ." Davenport grasped her hand and drew it to a spot just below his hipbone. "And here."

"There is nothing ugly or shameful about them. Rather they are marks of honor, Max. It takes courage to stand and fight, no matter what form the enemy takes." Arching on tiptoes, the hardening points of her breasts grazing taut muscle, she kissed the trace of the old wound by his eye.

A groan sounded in response to her touch. Though he spoke no words, Olivia heard the desire in his voice. Her own need licking hot within her, she teased her tongue along the length of the faint white line, all that was left of the vicious saber cut he had suffered in Portugal. "My brave, stalwart lion," she murmured, with a light nip to the corner of his mouth before sliding her lips to cover his.

Davenport wrenched her off her feet. His arms tight around her waist, he held her hard, the earlier rhythm of his breathing abandoned to the urgency of the deepening embrace. As their passion became more frenzied, he began sliding her up and down against his arousal.

"Max! Oh, yes, Max." She broke away from the kiss to cry out his name. The sensation was more wildly exciting than anything she had ever experienced. Her nails raked down his back and as her legs spread to wrap around his surging hips, the tangle of silk finally fell free.

"Olivia!" The look in his eyes was that of raw hunger. "You taste of cloves, of cinnamon, of . . . of things I can't begin to describe. Even the very air around you is spiced with some mysterious essence that puts reason to rout."

"It is a special blend of oils," she managed to reply. "Made up for me by a friend of Vavek's—a Hindu holy man from Lahore who claims they possess a healing power."

"It would take a miracle of the gods for that, sweeting," he groaned. "But all I want now is your touch, and the ecstasy that it brings."

"Then come." Taking hold of his wrists, she felt for a footing on the carpet and led him to the ornately carved teak bed. "Lie back," she urged, nudging him down into the tumble of tasseled pillows. A tug sent one boot arcing through the air. Following on its heels was the other.

Davenport twisted as her fingers skimmed over the front of his breeches and hooked inside the waistband. As she hurriedly worked the garment from his thighs, a muted cry echoed through the room, urging her to greater haste. Deliciously aware of the throbbing anticipation, both between his legs and her own, she tugged harder. The fabric quickly yielded to her efforts, sliding down over his knees.

Stripped to naught but a pair of thin cotton drawers, the viscount lay in tawny splendor against the deep mulberry of the coverlet. Candlelight licked over the contours of flesh that looked as though they had been chiseled out of gold. Though she had viewed a great many gilded treasures in her travels, the sight of him sucked the air from her lungs.

He seemed to be having some difficulty breathing as well.

"Let yourself relax. Surrender to the moment," she whispered, aware that her own steely discipline had melted to liquid desire. Reaching for one of the glass vials, Olivia tipped out a drizzle of its honey-colored contents on his bare chest. Drawing herself up over the edge of the bed, she straddled his hips and began to massage the scented oil into his flesh.

"Almond and jasmine to soothe the body." A touch of the tension was eased from his corded muscles. "And the spirit."

As her stroking dipped lower, he caught her hand. "I have not the saintly discipline of an Eastern monk." Tipping her back, he tore free the knot of his drawers. They slithered down his hips and his erection sprung free, the thick shaft shaded in dark silhouette against the flat planes of his belly.

Olivia felt a clenching of her insides. She found him inexpressibly magnificent. Inexpressibly masculine. Inexpressibly mysterious. "Max," she panted, rimming the hooded head with her still slick thumb. "Oh, Max, please, I can't bear it another moment." Her hand glided down his shaft, leaving a sheen of oil. "Make love to me."

She was suddenly aware of being lifted into the air, then lowered so that the tip of his shaft was just caressing the folds of her feminine flesh.

"Tell me you want me, Olivia." It was as much a plea as a demand.

"I want you, Max. More than I ever imagined was possible."

"God help me, I want you as well, Olivia. I had sworn to keep you at a distance, but now . . ." His words gave way to arching desire.

As she rocked in tandem with his surging hips, savoring the exquisite intimacy of Davenport inside her, Olivia looked up and found her gaze locked with his. In the amber depths, she saw raw passion and aching need.

Any lingering vestige of self-control went up in smoke. She had once thought that making love with him might bank the fire of attraction, but instead, the flames were shooting up higher, threatening to consume every last bit of her person.

She rose and fell, faster and faster, until there was nowhere else for the heat to go but to ignite in an explosion that rocked her to the core. A cry burst from her lips, and was followed by a series of sizzling jolts.

An instant later, his voice joined hers, convulsing together in a tangle of sweat-sheened limbs upon the sheets. For an interval, the only sound in the room was the rasp of breath and rumple of linen. Then Davenport slowly rolled to one side and propped himself up on one elbow.

Olivia felt strangely bereft as his warmth withdrew from her body.

It was a moment or two before he spoke. "You deserve more than a coward for a companion."

She reached out to take his hand. Their fingers entwined. "What are you afraid of, Max?"

"You," came his ragged reply. "Me." He closed his eyes. "Ghosts. Demons. The knifing void I feel when you leave the room. Need I go on?"

"You think you are the only one who has fears?"

Davenport's mouth crooked in a mocking twist. "You don't flee from them. You have always had the strength to stand up to your doubts. I, on the other hand—"

"You see only your own flaws instead of your admirable qualities. It takes true courage and character to conquer despair. As for me . . ." She found herself mirroring his ironic smile. "I sailed halfway around the earth in hope of fleeing the past. Only to find the future far more frightening."

His grip curled around her wrists, holding her tight. "What are the things you fear most, Olivia?"

She had never dared admit to such intimate pain, not even to Winslow or Vavek. But for some reason, saying it aloud was itself a relief. "Like you, I hardly know where to begin. Maybe with an aching loneliness. One that seems to stretch out before my eyes in an endless path with no horizon."

Drawing her close so that the dull thudding of their hearts echoed in tandem against their still-heated flesh, Davenport stilled the tremble of her lowered lids with his lips. "Perhaps we may draw courage from each other. Even if it is only temporary." His gentle kiss moved down to draw the sting of salt from her cheeks.

They both lay still for some moments, before Olivia reached once again for her vials and dipped into the rose-colored oil. "In the Orient, red is thought to confer a certain power, an inner strength, to its wearer."

"Ah. That explains the mystery behind the Lady in Red."

"I suppose that has something to do with it." She gave a wry smile. "In any case, it seemed fitting, given my scarlet past."

Rather than reply, the viscount watched her movements in the guttering light. "You seem to possess a world of experience."

Olivia paused in feathering her fingertips through the burnished curls of hair. "I have had a man inside me before, if that is what you mean." She hardly dared look up, for fear she would see a flicker of disgust, but a furtive peek showed that the swirl in his gaze seemed to be a different sort of emotion.

"Winslow?" he demanded in a barely audible whisper.

"Good heavens, no. Our relationship is not at all of that sort."

Looking oddly relieved, Davenport hesitated before asking, "Does he . . . not care for females?"

"I have never thought to ask."

"Well, whoever the cursed fellow is, I should like to borrow Winslow's cleaver and carve his damn liver into tidbits for the monkeys of Bombay."

"The cursed fellow's liver is innocent of any misdoing," she murmured. "I fear the blame lies somewhat lower."

A husky chuckle rasped in Davenport's throat. "I intended to work my way down piece by piece. Though I might consider leaving his toenails intact."

"No need to be roused to violence. It is not . . . important."

"It is to me." His palms were suddenly on her waist, the firm grip, warm and possessive, sending a quiver through her core. But even more touching was his expression as the quirk of humor faded into a sweet uncertainty. "Did you love him?"

"No. We were friends, but nothing more."

"Good." There was a savage intensity to his voice she had not heard before. Tightening his hold, he eased her forward until she was pressed against the rekindling heat of his maleness. "What of us, Olivia? Are we merely friends?"

"I—I hardly know how to describe in words the strange attraction that seems to draw us together," she gasped.

"I, too, am finding speech is inadequate." Davenport parted her thighs and slid his hand through the damp curls and slick flesh, still warm with the passion of their lovemaking.

She cried out as his finger dipped into her passage. He smiled at the sound of her pleasure, his lips curving to cover the throbbing point of pulse at her throat. He was no practiced libertine, but the thought of the erotic pictures had aroused a wicked fire in him. His gaze blurred in a haze of crimson, Davenport teased his touch back over her pearled nub.

"Max!"

A powerful thrill rippled through him. "Tell me what you want, Olivia," he commanded.

"I want you." Her nails raked down his back, tracing lines of red along the planes of corded muscle. "In me, over me, around me."

What had become of the disciplined soldier and proper gentleman? It was the last coherent thought he had.

With a hard thrust, he sheathed himself to the hilt in her exquisite warmth. He heard her breath catch, then a soft whisper—eager, urging. Needing no encouragement, he rocked back, only to enter her again. And again.

Olivia writhed beneath him, impatient to match his quickening tempo. As she arched to meet him, his grip found one of the pillows and wedged it beneath her hips, opening her more fully to the rhythmic rise and fall of his body.

She moaned and nipped at his shoulder as his shaft glided through the folds of her honeyed flesh. Her legs slid up his, wrapping around his waist. "Kiss me here, Max." She guided his mouth to the tip of her breast. "And here."

Her lips were roving as well, trailing tongues of fire over his fevered face. The bedposts shuddered and groaned. Another lick and surely the tangle of sheets would ignite into flame.

Their eyes met and held. She smiled, with a tenderness so fragile he hardly dared breathe for fear of shattering the moment.

"Don't stop."

He was going more slowly this time, drawing out the pleasure. But her soft whisper stripped away every last vestige of self-control. Engulfed in a wave of desire, he surged forward, joining them more deeply as one.

A breeze from the window fanned one of the tapers, the flare of light a vivid reminder that their first meeting had taken place during the full force of a storm. Thunder. Lightning. Davenport was suddenly deafened by a rumbling in his ears. Blinded by jagged bursts of fire. A white-hot flash exploded, sending out a gushing of sparks. A hoarse cry sounded. It took him an instant to realize it was not just his own voice, but hers as well, echoing together off the bedchamber walls.

The wild flickering of the candles slowly died down to a soft glow. Drained, both of them lay in a state of languid repose. Davenport lay on his back, gazing through half-closed eyes at the darkened ceiling. Her head was resting on his chest. "What say you now, Olivia?" he asked after some minutes. In the stillness of the room, his whisper sounded very loud. "Just friends?"

"Yes . . . No . . . What I feel is beyond words."

"Beyond reason. Beyond fighting any longer." His voice was muffled in a tangle of raven curls. "Olivia, we can no longer deny that things have changed between us."

A sliver of space appeared between their spent limbs as she curled into herself. "I—I don't see why. I told you I was not a virgin, so you need not feel compelled to be . . . noble."

"But we must—"

She covered his mouth with a trembling hand. "Please, Max. Let us not speak of that now. Neither of us—"

"Lady O!" The door of the bedchamber gave way to Winslow's shouldered impatience.

"Oh," he repeated, the syllable taking on a considerably different tone. But after pausing for no more than the blink of an eye, the man of affairs continued his hurried march into the room.

Olivia had just enough presence of mind to tug up

the sheet, trying to cover the awkwardness of the moment—as well as the curve of her bare derriere. "This had better be rather urgent."

"Indeed it is," replied Winslow. Holding a brace of candles aloft, he stepped around the viscount's crumpled coat. "I told Vavek to bring up a pot of chai. Or," he added with an air of innocence, "does his lordship prefer coffee this early in the morning?"

"What the devil—" began Davenport, finally finding his voice.

"I am about to get to that, sir, but first I thought you might wish for something hot and bracing to serve as a proper wake-up." He batted his lashes at Olivia. "I trust you slept well?"

"Windy," she warned. "Another flippant comment from those lips and you are liable to be retrieving your precious teeth from somewhere in the vicinity of your boot heels."

The man of affairs flashed a pearly grin, then his face turned serious. "I trust any impertinence will quickly be forgiven when you hear the latest news."

"What news?" asked Olivia quickly.

"Mary Gooding has been found."

"What! How?" Davenport bolted upright, unmindful that he was wearing naught but a sheet. "Where—"

Winslow waved off the questions. "I am not privy to all the particulars, but apparently your sister met with the Wolfhound—"

"God Almighty, I forgot all about the note! My shirt . . ."

Winslow retrieved it from the carpet, tactfully

omitting any comment on the jumble of other cast-off clothing around it.

He yanked on a sleeve before asking gruffly, "And what of my brother?"

"I think you had best hear the whole story from Mary," replied Winslow. "She is with Lady Cara at your aunt's residence. Mr. Sprague is standing guard." All trace of teasing gone from his demeanor, he stood up. "I took the liberty of ordering your carriage to be brought around without delay, Lady O. I shall tell Vavek to stubble the tea and await you downstairs."

Chapter Twenty

❧❦❧

"I—I hardly know how to begin, milord." Mary Gooding had not looked up from where her hands lay fisted in her lap. A heavy shawl—one of Cara's, by the look of its quality—was draped around her hunched shoulders and a lace cap obscured most of her face. Still, several rents in the muslin of her sleeve and the pale hollowness of her face were very much in evidence. "It's all my fault."

"Let us leave regrets and recriminations for later." Folding his arms across his chest, Davenport leaned into the fluted molding, trusting that he had managed to cover up the sorry state of his own clothing. "All that matters at this moment is preventing any further harm from being done. And in order to do that, you are going to have to explain to us what you and Kip are involved in."

Mary's stammer grew more pronounced. "I—I . . . that is . . ."

"For heaven's sake, Max, can't you see that you are frightening her with that gruff tone and intimidating stance." Cara rose and placed a reassuring hand on the girl's arm. "Take your time. Despite his growls, my brother doesn't bite."

"I am not afraid, Lady Cara. Not for myself. I am just so very sorry for all the trouble I have caused," she said softly.

"I am sure that you are," he said, trying to modulate his rising anxiety. "And Kip as well." Though there were quite a few questions he wished to ask, he could not help jumping to the one that was foremost on his mind. "Where is he?"

"I don't know!" Her voice was once again close to cracking. "Things went wrong from the start . . . I didn't want him to . . . but the Ruby Lion . . . he told me to run . . . and now . . ."

Cara interrupted the girl's disjointed stammerings with a squeeze to her shoulder. "We know you are terribly upset, Mary, but the only way we can help is if you tell us the whole story."

"I shall do my best." After a sniff and swipe of her sleeve across her cheek, Mary began.

"It started with the letter from my friend Lizzie, who had found work here in London. It seemed that one night, on a visit to a tavern with some of the other servants, she had somehow lost her way in a warren of back rooms and overheard a conversation between two men—one that made her blood run cold. She tried to slip away unnoticed, but feared they had caught a glimpse of her. For the next few days, she had the feeling someone was watching where she worked. It frightened her. Enough so that she wrote and said she was thinking of coming home, even though a position like hers was a coveted one."

"I know Lizzie Stokes," interjected Cara. "She's a sensible girl, and not one to make up stories just to get herself noticed."

Mary nodded. "That's right. So it upset me enough to send word to Kip, asking if he would stop around and make sure she was all right. Except it was too late. When he did, he discovered she had disappeared." She drew in a ragged breath. "I—I would have never dragged him into this had I imagined anything like this would ha-happen."

"We know that." Cara put an arm around the girl's heaving shoulders and handed her a handkerchief. "No one could have imagined such evil."

Davenport rubbed his cheek, unconsciously tracing the length of the scar. "What did he do? Did he report it to the authorities?"

"They dismissed it as just another lass run off with a man. So Kip decided to do some looking around himself."

"Foolish pup, what the devil was he thinking . . ." muttered the viscount under his breath, but a warning look from Cara caused him to bite off the rest of his comment.

Mary gave another watery sniff. "It didn't take him long to uncover a few rumors. Men tend to talk a bit freely with other men, and Kip has a way with putting people at ease. The more he heard, the more he realized what a horrible thing he had stumbled onto. Kidnappings. Whispers of girls sold into slavery." She wiped at her eyes. "I—I did try to tell him to stop, that it was too dangerous to pursue on his own. But by then, he was determined to save Lizzie. And . . . the others."

"Why didn't he come to me?" demanded Davenport.

The girl's eyes avoided meeting his. "Your father had been awfully hard on Kip of late. I—I think he wanted to prove he could be just as brave as the Valiant Viscount, just as deserving of the Bingham name."

Davenport silently cursed the old earl's rigid notion of honor. And his own self-absorption for leaving him blind to the needs of his family. "I see. So what then?"

"He managed to make contact with someone high up in the ring. He didn't tell me all the particulars, just that he had been able to make a deal. The leader was apparently a collector of art, and was willing to trade Lizzie in return for a number of valuables."

"How did Kip know what sort of things?" It was Sprague who asked the question.

"He was given a list. A very specific list." Mary bit at her lip. "Whoever he is, the gent is familiar with the estates in Yorkshire and knew exactly what he wanted."

"So that is why Kip came home so suddenly," murmured Cara.

"Aye. I kept telling him it was far too dangerous, but he said a life was worth far more than a few trinkets. And that, in the end, we would get them back to their rightful owners. I was scared, but I couldn't very well let him do it alone."

"That was quite brave of you—but you could have come to me," said Cara.

Mary hung her head. "I should have. If only . . ."

Davenport feared that to dwell on "what-ifs" might cause the girl to lose what little composure she had left. "How was the exchange to be made, once you had the items?" he asked quickly.

"Kip had it all arranged. There was to be a meeting

in London. We made our way south, without any pursuit from the authorities—though Kip was on edge enough to think we were being followed by some sort of . . . ghost." Her expression mirrored his own disbelief, but Davenport signaled her to go on.

"In any case, we made it safely to his quarters in Town. But instead of bringing Lizzie, two men came, armed to the teeth. Luckily Kip had thought to keep watch. We barely escaped through a back window."

"He set his own rooms as the rendezvous?" The viscount's lips thinned. "That was a mistake."

The girl hung her head. "Yes, it was. By that time, even Kip admitted we were in over our heads. I did convince him to seek your counsel, rather than attempt any further contact with the criminals, but we learned you had just left Town."

Once again, Davenport found himself cursing coincidence. "You should have sent word—"

"Oh, we would have, sir!" exclaimed Mary. "If there had been a chance. It was on the way back from your rooms that they attacked again. I was waiting for him at the corner of Upper Brook Street and saw two men spring out from the alley way. They had him down in a trice, and were hitting him. And then a knife flashed." Tears began to streak her cheeks, but she managed to keeping going. "I screamed, but there was no one else near. And then . . . and then . . ." A sob finally drowned out her whisper.

"And then?" prompted Cara gently, after allowing an interval of tears.

"Another figure appeared from nowhere. The one in white—"

"What?" Davenport could not refrain from voicing his surprise.

"I swear, I saw him! Then everything became a blur. There was more scuffling, but it didn't last long. All I know was that in a blink of an eye, the villains were gone. And so were Kip and the figure in white." Mary looked on the verge of breaking down again, but a hug from Cara seemed to steady her nerves. "I didn't dare return to Kip's rooms, so I just began wandering blindly, having no idea where I was going or what I was to do. I had no money, and the valuables had been in Kip's pocket. Luckily for me, I ran into a girl who heard me crying and offered me a place to stay."

Davenport arched a brow. "The Wolf's Lair?"

"Y-yes, I think that is what it is called. Sally said I was welcome to stay in her room—her private chamber, not the place she, er, worked—until I could figure out what to do. I was too confused to think clearly for a bit, but then I asked her if she could help me send word to you, sir."

His expression turned even more questioning.

Catching his look, she explained, "It seems Sally mentioned it to her . . . employer and he came to meet with me. The Wolfhound is a rather intimidating man, but as he said he was a comrade of yours in the army, I decided I should trust him with my tale." She gave a small lift of her shoulders. "He told me he would see to everything, so . . . here I am."

"Hmmph." That explained a good deal, thought Davenport, but there was much still shrouded in mystery. "You have no idea who the strange figure in white could be?"

Mary shook her head. "Nor do I know the name of the place where Kip first made contact with the criminals, or that of the man he met." Her mouth took on a pained twist as she blinked back tears. "Indeed, it seems I know very little that will be of use in saving him or Lizzie."

Seeing the bleakness of her expression, the viscount couldn't help but hold out a ray of hope. "Things aren't quite as desperate as they seem. We have managed to learn a great deal about their organization. And as to the man in charge, we have a plan for flushing him out."

Sprague, who had looked ill at ease throughout most of the discussion, leaned forward in his chair, clearly relieved that some action other than guarding a strong-willed female seemed imminent. "What's the plan, Max?"

"I would rather not say."

Olivia, who had looked on the verge of speaking, remained silent, though her brow did curve in a questioning arch.

Davenport gave a tiny shake of his head. He had no intention of baring the details of what they meant to do. Not when he fully intended to have an alternate strategy worked out by then.

"That's damn—er—deucedly unfair, Max." Sprague looked miffed. And rightly so, conceded Davenport, as his friend continued to grumble about the dangers involved. "You can't be meaning to confront the enemy on your own."

"I am not going alone."

The announcement only served to aggravate Sprague's

pique. "I see," he replied stiffly. "So you prefer to go into battle with fresh troops?" His eyes narrowed as they shifted to Winslow. "Didn't figure you to be the sort of fellow to shift your allegiance."

Damnation. Feeling caught between a rock and a hard place, Davenport could only mutter, "It is not what you think."

His friend did not look at all convinced.

Aware of the tension in the air, Cara quickly spoke up. "How can we help?"

"By staying out of further trouble," he snapped, his control perilously close to the point of breaking. "I have enough to think about without having to worry what you are going to do next. Your reputation will end up blacker than India ink if word leaks out that you have been visiting places like the Wolf's Lair. Or meeting with rogues like Killingworth."

"To hell with my reputation," Cara shot back, her face shaded with a viscous scowl.

"Hell is exactly where it is going, if you persist on taking such foolhardy risks."

"Well, I would gladly sit down to tea with Lucifer himself if I thought it would help Kip." Her tone turned even more defiant. "And as for Killingworth, it's a good thing I wasn't afraid to confront a notorious rake." She gave a small sniff. "His manners are most ungentlemanly, but despite the show of teeth, he does seem to possess a modicum of decency."

"I still don't quite understand about Connor and the clues we uncovered," muttered Davenport, deciding to leave the subject of the earl's behavior with his sister to a later time. "There are still a number of unanswered questions concerning money and his missing . . . employees."

"Sally says he is a very decent employer," offered Mary in a small voice.

"My discussion with the gentleman was extremely brief," said Cara.

And, judging by the flush suffusing her face, extremely belligerent, noted Davenport.

"Lord Killingworth did not deign to elaborate on his motives," she continued. "That he was expecting someone else to show up for the meeting might have had something to do with his churlish demeanor. And the fact that he was forced to escort two females out of the park, when clearly he wished to distance himself from us as quickly as possible."

"It was a lucky thing I had been tracking his movements, and came upon them just outside the upper gates," said Sprague. "As your sister says, Connor was more than happy to turn the matter over to me."

"As to the Wolfhound's personal affairs, I am pursuing a few leads on the matter." Winslow, who for most of the discussion had busied himself with the preparing and pouring of tea, finally spoke up. "In another day or two, I think I may have tracked down enough facts to offer an explanation."

"That can wait for now," said Olivia. "As I think we are all in agreement that Killingworth is no longer a suspect." She turned a critical eye on the viscount. "Which I might have been able to point out earlier, had I been aware of your suspicions." Anticipating the question he was about to ask, she added, "It was the Wolfhound who gave me Bentham's name and three others, along with information on their personal preferences."

Curiosity won out over anger. "How in the name of Hades did you get him to do all that?"

"I'm not sure we care to know the details," murmured Winslow.

After shooting her man of affairs a quelling look, Olivia answered. "By offering him a business proposition that was mutually beneficial."

Davenport started to speak, then thought better of it. At the moment, the less he knew of the meeting, the better.

"Killingworth supplied us with certain facts as well," pointed out Sprague. "But it may have been naught but a clever ploy. And turning Mary over to us may only be another tactic designed to throw us off the scent."

"Well, the only way to know for sure is to run the real vermin to earth as quickly as possible." It was Cara who cut to the chase. "Max, how long before you can put your plan into action?"

He hesitated, then looked to Olivia.

"Tomorrow evening," she answered.

Chapter Twenty-one

❧❧❦❧❧

"Sublime," pronounced Bentham, the carriage lamps catching the gleam in his eye.

Olivia wasn't sure whether he was referring to the sheerness of her silk sari or the illustrated pages he had just finished thumbing through. "So you think it an interesting collection?" she asked softly. "One worth treating with special care?"

His gaze darted to her breasts. "Most interesting, Olivia."

She forced a sultry smile. After allowing him a moment longer to admire the show of cleavage, she shifted just enough to cause her cloak to obscure the view.

Bentham edged a touch closer.

Had she made the right decision in slipping off on her own? Mary Gooding had made it clear that Kipling Bingham was innocent of any involvement with the Connoisseur. In light of such revelations, a more measured approach to trapping their adversary was the logical move. A few more days to gather the proof of the man's perfidy . . .

But a few days might be too late.

Despite the closeness of the carriage, Olivia felt a

sudden chill. She could remember all too vividly what it was like to be a female alone in the world and without protectors. No matter the risk, she could not abandon her plan of ensuring the shipment of "porcelain" never set sail. But she meant to do it without involving . . . Max.

After last night, she could not think of him as Lord Davenport, or the Lion—only as Max. A man so very different from the others who had dominated her life. He was caring, compassionate, and supremely unselfish, while her father and her competitors in the world of commerce were manipulative, greedy, and focused on aught but their own well-being. She could not bear to think of him facing new threats on account of her, and a plan he had quite rightly called foolhardy in the extreme.

He had taken enough risks, suffered enough wounds. She loved him too much to ask him to compromise his integrity. That he had been willing to march into danger with her, despite his misgivings, had made her even more determined to go it alone. This was her battle, best fought with her weapons. Over the hard-fought years of building her business, she had come to accept that sometimes it was necessary to sacrifice principle for pragmatism. She had done things she was not proud of. But, for the sake of Davenport, and the young women who had no other hope, she was willing to do what was needed. Even if it meant she must dance with the devil.

Would that she could be adroit enough in the coming *pas de deux* to keep from tripping up.

The viscount would be furious, of course, on learning the party was really for this evening rather than the following night. As would Vavek and Windy, once they discovered her deception. But by then, it would be too late for any of them to stop her.

After it was over, she prayed she would find some way to make her peace with Max.

Forcing her lungs to keep working with some degree of normalcy, Olivia turned her attention back to her companion. "You must tell me more about your own collections, Robert," she murmured, settling her hand in the crook of his arm. "Have you a specialty— something in particular that attracts you?"

"Oh, yes," he replied without hesitation. "Salt-cellars from the Italian Renaissance. Many of them are made of the finest gold and precious stones. The craftsmanship is exquisite as well, for a number of the leading sculptors of the day were commissioned to design such objects. Verrocchio, Michelangelo . . ." His tone took on a harder edge. "I possessed a magnificent assortment. But not any longer."

"And why is that?" She felt a strange prickling traverse the length of her spine. "It does not sound like the sort of collection one would give up, not without receiving something equally valuable in return."

"I would not have parted with it for the world," sighed Bentham. "Unfortunately, my townhouse was broken into recently, when I was out for the evening. The thief seemed to know that my servants had been given the night off, and the exact location of where the items were kept."

"How terrible." Olivia had no difficulty in appearing surprised. "Are the authorities making any progress in solving the crime?"

He cleared his throat before answering. "I chose not to report it. You see, it occurred while I was at the same gathering to which we are now traveling. And as a number of . . . uncomfortable questions would no doubt arise as to where I was, and why I routinely request that my servants absent themselves from the house, I considered it more prudent to keep quiet about the whole affair."

"I see." She dropped her gaze, recognizing that, in the blink of an eye, things had suddenly taken on a whole new perspective. Her intuition, a sixth sense honed by years of dealing with knaves and thieves who masqueraded as gentlemen, told her Bentham was not her real quarry.

"But enough of such unpleasant matters," he breathed, sidling across the soft leather seat so that his thigh pressed up against hers. "This is supposed to be an evening devoted to the pursuit of pleasure."

"I am counting on it." Olivia fluttered her lashes, hoping a show of flirtation would mask the small shiver of revulsion stealing over her. What was wrong with her? In the past, it had never been difficult to impose a detached sense of pragmatism over emotion. She had simply steeled her will and done whatever was necessary to achieve her goals, no matter how harrowing or unpleasant.

But now? She had not realized it until that moment just how dramatically her feelings had changed over the last few weeks.

"Do tell me more about what to expect this evening." Catching the slide of his palm up her leg, she stalled for time by making a coy show of stroking the tips of each finger. After the night spent with Max, the idea of another man touching her intimately made her nauseous. She wanted nothing so much as to wrench open the carriage door and flee, seeking shelter in the comforting strength of her lover's arms.

Had she lost her nerve, as well as her heart?

With her erratic pulse echoing an urgent warning in her ears, Olivia forced herself to still such fears. She couldn't afford a flinch of emotion. Not now, when all hope of success hinged on her ability to improvise under pressure.

"And the other guests—are you intimately acquainted with most of them?" Shutting out the last, lingering bit of doubt, her mind set to work at forming an alternate to her original strategy. It wouldn't require any real change in tactics. Bentham no longer loomed large as the likely villain, but the man she sought was sure to be there. All she needed was a hint of where to turn.

"Yes, we know each other well, and are very particular about whom we invite to join our group."

"How flattering, but please tell me more." Toying with his cuff, she allowed her touch to graze the inside of his wrist. "I find knowing what to expect makes it easier to perform at my best."

"My dear Lady Olivia, I imagine any performance of yours would be worth the price of admission."

Despite the dim light and her own distracted state of mind, she had been aware of a certain nervousness creeping into Bentham's demeanor over the past few minutes. His next words explained why.

"Er, and speaking of admission, there is a small matter I should mention now. You see, there is a ritual that takes place for each new member admitted into our little group. An initiation, if you will."

He paused, as if waiting for encouragement to go on.

"Ah. A proof of commitment."

"Precisely. I knew a lady of your discerning intellect would understand." His face appeared to relax slightly, though at the same time, his fingers were tightening on the spine of the erotic book. "Our host is a connoisseur of the arts, too."

Connoisseur.

The whispered word caused the tiny hairs on the back of her neck to stand on end.

"He has an eye for the rare and unusual. And, of course, for things that possess great beauty. So it is customary that a first-time guest present him with a token of appreciation at being included in such an exclusive group."

"A paltry price to pay for such an honor," she murmured. "You think the book is enough?"

"Oh, quite enough," he replied, his lips seeking hers.

She deflected his advances with another question. "Do I perchance know him?"

"We wear masks, so as not to reveal our faces. Anonymity allows for a freer intercourse of ideas." Bentham leaned back and withdrew a bunching of black silk from his pocket. "I suppose we ought to don them now, seeing as we are getting close to our destination."

As Olivia knotted the black silk over her eyes, its resemblance to a hangman's hood did not escape her. A noose was going to tighten around someone's neck tonight. She would have to do a very careful balancing act to ensure it was not hers.

"Shiva be skewered!" Davenport's roar rattled several of the jade figurines on the sidetable. "What happened to that mystical second sight of yours?"

"I don't have eyes in the back of my head, memsahib."

At another time, the viscount would have found it diverting to discover that Vavek actually possessed a sense of humor. Now, however, he was not in the least amused. "You should have bloody well known better than to turn your back on her."

The servant's beard drooped. "She asked for jasmine tea. A special blend that she only requests when one of her terrible headaches is coming on. I did not think she would stoop to such a trick with me."

"How long has she been gone?" demanded Davenport.

"I sent Anschul to you as soon as I returned to an empty chair."

"I don't suppose there is any hope that she left a clue as to where she was heading?"

The other man's brown eyes darkened to an opaque black, confirming the surmise.

"Damn."

A rumbling of Hindi sounded suspiciously like an even more vehement oath.

He thought for a moment. One did not have to be a skilled intelligence officer to figure out there was only one option for learning her direction. "Lend me your blade."

Vavek's fingers curled around the hilt of the jeweled dagger. "I am coming with you."

Davenport eyed the turban and brightly colored tunic. "Your presence is hardly likely to go unnoticed." He held out his hand. "Leave it to me."

The tall case clock ticked off several seconds, and then the curved steel slapped down on his palm. "May the lion slay the venomous snake."

A swoosh rent the air as the viscount tested the weapon's heft. Satisfied, he concealed it beneath his coat. "The viper will find he is not the only one with fangs."

It took precious little time to flag down a passing hackney, but every moment felt like an eternity. Silently cursing his way through the twists of the London streets, Davenport arrived at his destination in no mood to be trifled with.

"I don't care if he is bedding the Prince Regent— take me to him this instant." Shoving his way past the doorman, Davenport started down the hallway. "Or I'll find him myself."

"No need to get your drawers in a twist, Max." One of the scarlet doors cracked open, revealing the shadowed presence of the Irish Wolfhound. His coat was off and his cravat loosened, a tumbler of whiskey balanced in one hand. "As you see, I am right here, and have no objection to acceding to your request. But do stop shouting. It's bad for business."

The glass was knocked to the floor as Davenport grabbed the earl by the throat and forced him back inside the small office. "Where is she?"

"Which lady have you lost now?" came the baiting reply. "You aren't very good at keeping a hold on females, are you?"

Before he realized what he was doing, the viscount had the other man hard up against the wall and the blade pressed to the base of his jaw. "Perhaps not, Connor," he snarled, blinking away the haze of red that had momentarily obscured his vision. "But I can handle this little beauty well enough to slice you from ear to ear if you don't tell me everything."

The only reaction from Killingworth was a slight curl of his lip. "Well, well, so the Valiant Viscount still has some blood in his veins. I feared that there might be naught but tepid dishwater left in its place." The glimmer of teeth became a tad more pronounced. "But even the dullest of dishwater might be brought to a boil by the sizzling charms of Lady Olivia."

A tiny beading of blood suddenly welled up from a prick to the earl's neck.

"Damn your hide." Davenport caught himself before the knife did more than scrape the skin. Still, fear and frustration pushed his voice to the brink of cracking. "I swear, if you have laid a finger on Olivia, I'll rip out your liver with my bare hands." His grip, already fisted in the folds of the Wolfhound's cravat, tightened. "And the same goes for my sister. I may lack your formidable skills at seducing females, but I have plenty of experience in defending my troops from enemy attack."

The earl maintained his unflinching demeanor. "An honorable speech, Max, but quite wasted on me. I should have thought it would be clear enough by now that Lady Olivia is in no danger from me. . . ." His pause was nearly imperceptible. "Nor, for that matter, is Lady Cara. Even if they were, my impression is that both females can look out for themselves."

"Give me one solid reason to believe you, rather than sly riddles and innuendos."

With a crooked finger, Killingworth calmly raised the weapon an inch or two. "Put that away. You are much too noble to murder someone for no good reason."

"Sending Olivia into a deadly trap would be more than enough reason." The blade remained poised at a lethal angle. "You supplied her with names and number of tantalizing leads."

The implied accusation finally goaded a show of the much-feared Wolfhound temper. "You think I set her up? Why, you bloody, ungrateful pisspot! I should slice through your own damn windpipe—and cut off your balls to boot." Ignoring the danger to his now throbbing artery, he leaned forward, his lean features made even harsher by a cast of righteous anger. "For your information, she assured me she was gathering the information to pass on to you. Are you telling me she—"

"Has disappeared. Yes, that's exactly what I'm saying. She has gone off with Bentham." He brought the knife a fraction closer. "The question is, where?"

In the light of the lamps, the earl's eyes flickered in hue from a silvery lightness to hard pewter to gun-metal grey. "The first place I would look is Lord Ravenwood's retreat. In addition to his residence in Mayfair, he keeps a more secluded place on the northern edge of Regent's Park that he uses to conduct his more private affairs. Bentham is part of a select crowd that attends a regular gathering there."

Davenport wanted very much to believe his old comrade, but he couldn't afford the luxury of sentiment. Allowing himself to be mislead might cost Olivia her life. "I need proof you are telling the truth."

"Sod off." Killingworth's infuriating arrogance was back, but after a moment he grudgingly added, "My character is by no means lily white, but I am not in league with the vermin you seek."

"Then tell me why you are not turning a profit here!" demanded the viscount. "And what has become of the girls who have gone missing from your Lair?"

"Those matters are my own private business and have nothing to do with you or your lady."

He drew in a breath, then let both hands fall away. "I won't appeal to your conscience, as you claim to have none, Connor. But I'm desperate—time is of the essence, and a misstep on my part may prove fatal to Olivia."

"Then what are you waiting for?" growled the earl. "The place you seek is of red brick, faced with an arched limestone entrance and surrounded by a hedge of hawthorne. The quickest route is to take the New Road and pass by St. Stephen's church." Seeing there was still a flicker of doubt in Davenport's eyes, he added a low curse. "If you must know, the girls who have gone missing from my Lair are not the victims of foul play but have . . . retired. One to a snug little cottage in Devonshire and the other to a tavern in Essex. A portion of the profits from this place help make it possible."

Not even in the wildest flight of fancy could the viscount have imagined such an explanation. "Why the devil—"

"I have my reasons," he replied tersely. "Which are none of your bloody business. And I swear, if you ever breathe a word of it to anyone, your mangled carcass will be feeding the alley rats."

Without waiting for a reaction, the Wolfhound elbowed his way past Davenport and stalked to his desk, where an unstoppered decanter sat upon the blotter. "Now go rescue your damsel in distress and make sure the bloody bastard never harms another woman. After all, you have plenty of experience in being a hero, Max."

Thrusting the knife back into hiding, Davenport turned for the door, but not before voicing a halting acknowledgment. "I—I am much in your debt."

"More than you think." Killingworth tossed back a swallow of the amber spirits. "Damn it, that was expensive Islay malt you spilled, and being intimately acquainted with my finances, you are aware I can ill afford to waste a drop."

"I understand you are quite the connoisseur, sir." Watching closely, Olivia was quite sure her deliberate choice of words had piqued a reaction from within the slitted eye holes. "I trust what I have to offer will meet with your approval."

The gentleman's gaze, though partially obscured by silk and the subdued lighting, was clearly focused on the outline of her figure through the sheerness of the sari. "Have you brought me something special?"

"I hope so." Olivia did not recognize the voice as yet, but was quick to observe a number of other details. He was taller than Bentham, and broader in the chest, though not nearly a match for Max. . . .

Max. No—she must not allow herself to be distracted by thoughts of him.

"If you find the subject of interest," she went on softly, "we might discuss it in more depth."

The gentleman moved a step closer. "What is this gift?"

"A book of hand-illuminated wood engravings from India. Depicting the many variations of pleasure to be had with a female."

"It sounds as if it is worth a closer look."

Bentham was quick to hold out the volume. "Yes, yes, I have it right here."

Their host brushed off the offer with a slight flick of his wrist. "I would rather the lady show it to me herself."

"B-but . . ." Alarmed that he was about to forfeit his own treasure, Olivia's escort attempted to come up with a compelling excuse. "I was about to show the lady around the crimson boudoir. I know she would appreciate—"

"I shall see that our newest member is given a proper tour of the premises."

There was no denying the note of curt dismissal. Though he looked for a moment as if he wished to object to the arrangement, Bentham thought better of argument. Handing the book over to Olivia, he retreated to where refreshments had been set out and fell to drowning his disappointment in a bottle of champagne.

Wetting the tip of a finger with her tongue, she paged to one of the more provocative pictures. "The artist appears quite knowledgeable about female flesh, don't you agree?"

He studied it briefly before lifting his eyes to meet hers. "Indeed. And I consider myself an expert in the field."

"Really?" On the pretext of showing him another of the intricate poses, Olivia sidled close and leaned over his arm, so that the silk stretched over her breasts. "As it happens, I, too, have a keen interest in the subject."

Taking the volume from her grasp, he closed the covers with a soft snap and slipped it into his pocket. "I look forward to a more leisurely perusal of your gift. But at the moment, I would rather take advantage of the opportunity to explore the subject with a fellow collector."

"I am rather new at it." Teasing her voice to a provocative purr, she added, "No doubt I can learn a great deal from a real connoisseur."

As she spoke, Olivia made a surreptitious survey of the surroundings. Aside from indicating a taste for the sumptuous style of Louis XIV, the furniture and art gave no hint as to the identity of the host. Not that she expected a portrait of the miscreant to be hung over the ornate marble mantel of the drawing room.

But perhaps if she could maneuver him into a more private setting, she might spot a telling clue.

Her companion had turned to converse with another couple, who were already nude to the waist, and the diversion gave her further chance to observe the other guests. Bentham had lost no time in finding a new companion, a Rubenesque blonde whose bare legs were spread wide upon the brocade sofa to receive his humping attentions. A number of other people, in various stages of undress, were drifting off to adjoining rooms while a foursome by the hearth was engaged in some form of group play that was eliciting a chorus of heated moans.

"Forgive me, but the duties of a host are hard to avoid," he murmured, his hand pressing the small of her back. "Perhaps we should retire to somewhere we will be less likely to be interrupted, Lady . . . what shall I call you?" He guided her past an enormous crystal punch bowl with a carved ice phallus jutting from its center, the tip of which was spouting a potent mixture of pink champagne and brandy. "As you might have guessed, along with our masks, we all assume a moniker that obscures our real identity. It makes what goes on here that much more intriguing."

"I am very attracted to intrigue," she murmured. "As for monikers, you may call me Lady O." Her thumb rimmed one of the cloisoinné buttons of his waistcoat. "And you, sir—have you a special name?"

"It seems you are comfortable with the Connoisseur."

"Very comfortable."

They had moved through a set of double doors and halfway down a hallway leading to the rear of the house before her companion paused before a painting of Lysistrata being ravaged by a swan. After a moment of silent contemplation of the scene, he turned. "How very fortuitous that the two of us, who have so much in common, have found each other."

His tone was soft and velvety, but Olivia was all too aware that beneath it lay an edge of steel. She took only an instant to improvise. "I have a confession to make, sir." Her head dropped demurely. "Our meeting was no coincidence."

As his hand casually brushed a mote of dust from his sleeve, she caught a glimpse of the gold signet ring. A type of bird crowned the quartered shield, but more than that was impossible to make out.

"Go on."

"I thought, given certain of your enterprises, you might be interested in a proposition. A very lucrative proposition."

He went very still. "Any enterprises I might have are hardly a matter of public record, Lady O. Indeed, I would dare to say that sensitive information of that nature is a very closely guarded secret. How have you come to hear of such things?"

Olivia drew in a breath, telling herself that this was no different than business. The early stages of negotiations were often the most critical as the parties involved made their first feints, looking for any sign of weakness. She also knew that the slightest slip of the tongue would put at risk more valuable cargo than spiced tea.

"My partner and I make it our business to be informed about a certain area of commerce. To do so, we employ a network of sources that are highly reliable and highly discreet. It is expensive, of course, but I am sure that a gentleman of your discernment can appreciate the advantages of such an arrangement."

"Money is no object, then?"

"None whatsoever. When an opportunity attracts our eye, we are quite prepared to pay what it takes to outbid any competitor."

His posture gave away nothing, but Olivia was confident she had hooked his interest. "Is your partner present here as well?" he asked.

A twitch of the gossamer sari bared her shoulder. "No. We decided that in this case, I might be better equipped to handle the initial negotiations."

A bark of laughter sounded. "Very clever of you. Good—I only deal with those who display brains and bold initiative. You, Lady O, appear to have both."

She repressed a shudder as his arm coiled around her waist. The slither of melton wool against her sari reminded her of a cobra moving through mango leaves.

"Let us proceed to somewhere more comfortable and discuss this proposal of yours at greater length."

He indicated the far door, which gave entrance to a large study with glass doors leading out to a walled garden. At one end of the room was a massive desk of blackened oak that looked to date from Elizabethan times. To its left were a set of gilt console tables in an intricate Egyptian style, while to its right a set of bookcases extended from the floor to the carved acanthus-leaf molding.

The Connoisseur brought her to the sofa facing the hearth and invited her to take a seat. "May I pour you something to drink?" he asked, moving to the inlaid sideboard and taking up one of the decanters arrayed on a silver tray.

"A small sherry," she murmured, noting that he had chosen a rich ruby port for himself.

There was a faint clinking of crystal, then he settled in next to her. "Shall we toast to the good fortune that has brought us together?"

Things were going quite smoothly. Olivia smiled as their glasses touched. And yet, at the taste of the rich wine warming her throat, a small voice in the back of her head could not refrain from whispering a warning.

Perhaps too smoothly.

She shook it off as overwrought nerves. "To fortune," she agreed. "Both of us stand to make a goodly one if we can agree on a deal."

"Which is?" Smiling, he crossed a leg and took another sip of his spirits.

"You are selling a shipment of . . . fine porcelain to a dealer in Damascus."

His expression didn't change. "Ah, yes, the porcelain. An extremely rare and valuable shipment. It took much searching to assemble the matched set requested."

"Undoubtedly." Olivia, too, paused for some sherry. Though its viscous sweetness was a bit cloying for her taste, she thought it prudent to match his show of nonchalance. "Therefore, we are prepared to pay a premium for it. Say, fifty percent more than our competitors."

"A most generous offer." As if caught up in consideration, the Connoisseur held his glass up to the banked fire and began to spin it slowly within his fingers.

"We have a very interested—and very wealthy—client in New York. We would, of course, need to inspect the merchandise," she continued, finding it unaccountably arduous to move her lips. Despite the sheerness of her garment, the room seemed terribly warm, and the refractions of red were proving an eerie distraction. She could not help noting their unpleasant resemblance to bloodstains.

"That might present a logistical problem," he replied after setting his port aside.

"Not really," she replied. "I assume they are being kept safe in a warehouse. You have only to tell us where we might meet you. That way, there would be no need to move the merchandise." Uncomfortably aware of his arm casually draped over the cushions, Olivia shifted on the sofa, fighting the feeling that the room itself was taking on an odd tilt. "It would not take long—I am sure I can convince my partner that we need only see a representative sampling before closing the deal."

"You appear to have thought of everything."

"I believe in being very thorough. It is the best way to eliminate the possibility of m-making m-mistakes."

"A wise approach. However, you have made a rather large one . . ." Striking out with the speed of a deadly snake, the Connoisseur knocked the glass from her hand and ripped the mask from her face.

"You failed to realize you are not dealing with a fool, Lady Olivia."

Unable to react with aught but a mumble, Olivia fell back against the damask pillows. "Th-the w-wine . . ."

"Yes, it was drugged," he sneered, removing his own mask. "Did you and your partner really think I would allow you to disrupt such an ingenious operation?"

She did not recognize his face, but his eyes, reptilian in their flat, remorseless stare, were even more frightening than the poisonous malice of his taunting.

"Not that you could—my arrangements are far too cunning and clever for an interfering female and a scarred soldier to affect. But I find your meddlesome activities have become a bit of a nuisance. It's time to be rid of them. And you." A smile stretched his lips. "How very accommodating of you to have saved me the trouble of sending another minion after you."

"My partner knows everything. He will come after you."

That he would be too late sent a stab of regret knifing through her. Not for the loss of her own paltry life, but for the loss of the future. A chance for sharing more of herself with Max.

"Davenport?" The harshness of the Connoisseur's laugh rasped across her consciousness. "It's well known he spends most of his time holed up licking old wounds, so don't count on the Valiant Viscount to have much fight left in him. Let him try to stop me. It will only show he is as hopelessly naive as his brother. And just as easy to dispose of."

Olivia felt the haze in her eyes grow darker as fingers began to tighten around her throat.

The gloating now sounded as if it were coming from very far away.

Chapter Twenty-two

❦

The house was just as Killingworth had described.

During the bone-rattling ride to the place, the pieces of the puzzle had all jarred into place. The thugs that he and Olivia had overheard behind the brothel had referred to the Black Bird as their leader. Now, after the confrontation with Killingworth, he was quite sure the villain was Ravenwood.

Stealing past a grouping of large rhododendrons, Davenport used the leafy cover to camouflage his approach to a set of narrow mullioned windows near the scullery door. A quick glance showed the small storeroom to be deserted, and the blade of his knife made quick work of opening the latch. Once inside, he followed the sounds of drunken laughter to the main drawing room, where amid overturned glasses, guttering candles, and discarded clothing, a number of guests lay locked in the throes of sexual passion.

Just enough light limned the thrashing limbs and contorted faces for him to make out that Olivia was not among them.

Davenport stepped back from the doorway in disgust, his boot grazing the bare buttocks of a man who had passed out facedown down on the parquet. Seeing as his presence was unlikely to draw any notice, he abandoned stealth for speed and began a hurried search of the nearby rooms.

The devil take it. He tried to tamp down a spark of panic at the notion of Olivia somewhere in this hell with a man who made Lucifer appear a shining angel. He had spotted Bentham among the debauched revelers, so he was even more certain the real fiend was Ravenwood.

But where was he?

Working his way down a darkened hallway, Davenport came to a paneled oak door with twin keyholes guarding the latched handle. A touch of his shoulder revealed it to be unlocked. As he eased it open, he caught the shift of two shadows and the echo of the boastful taunt.

Seeing he had no chance of reaching the sofa in time to stop the knife aimed at Olivia's throat, Davenport seized the nearest object at hand and hurled it at the shape looming over her. Catching the other man by surprise, the blow of the silver candlestick jarred the weapon from his grasp and sent it skittering across the carpet.

"Well, here I am, Ravenwood—at your disposal."

A hiss of breath was audible above the crackling of the coals.

"I, too, have chosen to make things easy for you." Angling his own blade to catch the light, the viscount advanced another step into the room, intent on keeping Olivia's assailant distracted from his original target. "No need to employ another skulking minion to do the dirty work, is there? Not when you can finish the job yourself."

The Connoisseur—whose unmasked face was indeed that of the Marquess of Ravenwood—had already slithered away from Olivia and was hurriedly searching for his knife in the pooling of the velvet drapes.

"Or does your bravado trickle away, like warm piss down your leg, when you aren't facing a female or a green lad?" he challenged, using the barbed words as a further edge to keep him off balance.

The goading drew a snarled reply. "It appears both Binghams are too blind to see when they are overmatched. I'll slice out your other eye before putting a period to your miserable existence."

"You are welcome to try." Davenport kicked aside a small lacquered table, smashing its delicate legs.

As he had hoped, the deliberate destruction drew a gnashing of rage from his adversary. "That was a priceless piece of Sung Dynasty—"

"Sod the Sung Dynasty." His foot connected with a marble pedestal, sending an intricate vase of spun Venetian glass crashing to the floor.

A stirring on the sofa, accompanied by a groggy murmur, had assured him that Olivia was still alive, but he dared not pause, even for an instant, from his attack. Pressing forward, the viscount found another target. A moment later, a curio cabinet filled with Sevres snuffboxes shattered against the marble hearth.

"Damn you!" Ravenwood lunged forward, seeking to catch the viscount off guard with a vicious slash. He had recovered his weapon, and from the way he picked his opening and wielded the blade, it was clear that he was experienced in its use.

The bite of steel, however, caught nothing but a

thread of sleeve. Spinning to one side, Davenport dodged the thrust and retaliated with a kicking blow that buckled the other man's knee.

Cursing, Ravenwood fell heavily against the French doors. Amid a shower of broken glass, the latches sprung open, sending him sprawling onto a narrow stone terrace. He was on his feet again in a trice, retreating to the verge of grass.

Ignoring the stone ornament that caught him with a glancing hit, the viscount came after him.

"Give yourself up now." Much as he itched to bury his dagger in the other man's ribs, Davenport fought to control his baser instincts. "And I promise you'll be turned over to the authorities for a fair trial." A flash of pointed jabs drove Ravenwood back another few steps. "Instead of me gutting you like a pig, which is what you deserve."

The answer was a spitting obscenity.

The two of them circled warily, feinting, parrying, probing for an opening. Ravenwood possessed a certain prowess in back-alley fighting, but it quickly became evident that his moves were no match for the expertise of a seasoned soldier. Relentless in attack, the viscount used his superior skills to maneuver his adversary closer and closer to the line of privet hedges, cutting off any path of escape.

A slide sideways revealed a small opening in the greenery. Seeing a chance of slipping away, Ravenwood chanced a wild slash that forced Davenport back, then darted through the opening. For a moment, the viscount feared he might lose his quarry in the depths of the gardens, but after several sharp bends, the path proved a dead end, leading only to a small space devoted to specimen plantings.

Boxed in by a wall of high holly and thick yew, Ravenwood skidded to a stop.

Slowing to a measured stride, Davenport approached.

As the other man whirled for what looked to be a tiny gap in the tangle of branches, his foot slipped on the loose gravel and he fell to his knees. Fury spasmed across his face, then suddenly smoothed into a mocking smile. "Very well—I surrender." With a nonchalant shrug, he held out his arms and dropped his knife. "Not that it matters. The only thing you will ever pin on me is a penchant for perverted pleasure." The cynical spread of his lips grew wider. "And even that will be hushed up by the higher authorities, seeing as several influential gentlemen have had a taste of what lies behind my doors."

The truth cut to the quick, and for a fleeting moment Davenport was tempted to take justice into his own hands. His weapon gave a murderous twitch, but he stilled the sharpened point inches from the unarmed Ravenwood's throat.

"Get up," he growled. "I'll not stoop to your level of depravity. But we shall see who has the last laugh. I, too, am not without friends in the highest circles."

"My ankle . . ." grunted the other man, gingerly feeling at his bent leg. "I'm going to need a hand."

The viscount leaned over.

He should have known the miscreant would have one last dirty trick up his sleeve. He flinched back, an instant too late to avoid the rip of the hidden dagger cutting across his wrist.

His own weapon slipped from his bloodied grip. Off balance, Davenport managed to ward off the first stab aimed at his heart, but before he could recover his footing, a second strike lashed out.

He felt the prick of steel against his flesh. . . .

But instead of plunging into his chest, the weapon gave a faltering twitch, then slid harmlessly toward the ground, followed an instant later by Ravenwood himself. With a shuddering thud, the marquess fell facedown on the stones, the hilt of a jambiyya protruding from his back.

A figure stepped out from the bushes. Every bit of exposed skin was slathered in indigo, accentuating the spectral whiteness of his flowing robes. A heavy silver bracelet, incised with an intricate pattern of interlocking lines, gleamed from his right wrist.

As if, thought the viscount wryly, such exotic decoration was needed to draw attention to the matching curved weapon clasped in the darkened fingers. Sensing that any defensive move would be not only fruitless but foolish, he stood calmly, awaiting the stranger's approach.

"Lord Davenport." The soft sound was like the stirring of sand in the wind.

"So, you are not merely a figment of the imagination," he murmured, as much to himself as the other man.

"I am quite real," came the reply. There was a moment of silence. "As is the dilemma I now face."

"You are wondering whether to slice my throat or cut out my spleen?"

The midnight shading made it difficult to tell if the

stranger's lips quirked up. "If my intention was to murder you, or any of your family, I have had ample opportunity."

Davenport inclined his head in acknowledgment. "True enough. Then what is it you seek from us?" he asked, though the sight of two large rubies winking out from the rhinoceros-horn hilt gave him an inkling of the answer.

"Only what is rightful property of my family. A talisman was taken from us long ago. One that possesses a powerful—"

"Curse," completed the viscount.

The stranger nodded. "That it has fallen into the wrong hands has brought troubles to all of us. But in its proper place, the Ruby Lion can also be a healing force. Or so my father believes." He drew a deep breath. "Indeed, he is desperate to believe it, for his youngest son, my half brother—a boy of only six—has been suffering from a wasting disease for nearly a year, and the healers offer no hope. The pain of it is killing my father as well."

"I am sorry." Having experienced his own share of heartache of late, the viscount found it impossible not to sympathize with the poignancy of the man's plight. "There is nothing so precious to us as the ones we love."

The stranger fixed him with an oddly searching look. "As a last resort, I promised I would find the Ruby Lion and see it returned to its place of honor. It had proved a most elusive beast. But now . . ." He stepped closer. "I have reason to believe you know where it is."

"Yes."

"What say you to a barter—brother for brother?"

Davenport felt a sharp lurching in his chest. Having lived through the loss of too many comrades on the field of battle, he had assumed the worst concerning his missing sibling, especially in light of Ravenwood's taunting words. "Kip?" He hardly dared breathe the word for fear of extinguishing hope. "He is . . . alive?"

"He was badly injured in an attack by this lowly hyena." The stranger gestured at the lifeless corpse of Ravenwood. "But yes, he survived, though I admit to being a bit disappointed that the Ruby Lion had slipped from his pocket during the fight. At first he was too weak to be moved from the place of refuge I had found here in London. And then . . . You English have an expression." He grimaced, as if struggling to find the precise language. "When you hold something of value that may be used to your advantage."

"A bargaining chip," supplied the viscount.

"Ah, yes. Something like the markers you use in your games of chance." The stranger gave a twist to the silver bracelet circling his wrist. "So, will you agree to trade gold and rubies for flesh and blood?"

"In a heartbeat."

A crescent sliver of white, pale and fleeting as the scudding moon, flashed on the other man's face. "I am pleased to see you are as honorable a man as I had hoped you would be. I trust you are as anxious as I am to make the exchange. Does an hour afford you enough time to fetch the Ruby Lion and meet where your sister is staying?"

A bit overwhelmed by the incredible turn of fortune, Davenport managed naught but a wordless nod.

In a ghostly flutter of white, the stranger disappeared as stealthily as he had appeared.

Now if only his luck would hold. Picking up Vavek's knife, Davenport rushed to retrace his steps, eager to gather up Olivia and put an end to the curse of the Ruby Lion.

He had not gone very far, however, when the uneven crunch of gravel warned him that someone else was moving about in the maze of hedges. Wiping the bloodied blade on his torn sleeve, he raised an arm, ready to fend off a new attack.

"M-max!" Though still a trifle unsteady on her feet, Olivia was feeling her way along the narrow path, a small pistol clasped in her shaky fingers. Seeing it was him, she dropped her aim. "Lud, I feared you might . . ."

The rest of her words were squeezed off in a sweeping hug. "No need for reinforcements," he murmured, the words a trifle slurred as his lips sought assurance that the curve of her cheek was no mere apparition. Recovering a measure of self-control, he set her back on her feet.

"That monster—"

"Is dead. The battle is over, Olivia. The girls are saved—and so is Kip."

She reached up to feather a fingertip over the bruise at the corner of his mouth. "Then against all odds, we won?"

The magnitude of their victory was beyond measure, he realized. Devils and demons—both real and imagined—had been driven back into the hell from which they had sprung. And all because her indomitable courage and compassion had challenged him to stand firm in the face of all enemies.

"Yes, we won," he replied. "I will see to it that Sprague and the authorities begin a search through the Rundle and Fleming warehouses before the night is over. The girls will soon be found." His blood suddenly ran ice cold as she smiled, the brave tilt of her chin and the luminous light in her eyes reminding him of what casualties his side had nearly suffered in order to win the day. Had he lost her, he might as well have allowed Ravenwood to cut his heart into a thousand little pieces, for it would have given up the ghost on its own accord.

Her breath sounding a rush of relief, Olivia swayed slightly. "How did you know where—"

"You are not the only one who can add. With the Wolfhound's help, I put two and two together."

She flinched, her lips quivering in the face of his gentle teasing. "Oh, Max, I never meant . . . I wish to explain—"

He brushed a fleeting kiss to her cheek. "There is much we need to talk about, but I fear it will have to wait a bit longer. There is one last foray to make." Lifting her into the circling shelter of his arms, he set out in a loping stride for the side gate.

Olivia watched with a rather wistful smile as Davenport and his siblings enfolded each other in an emotional reunion. It was a touching sight, though one that was a bittersweet reminder of her own awkward position on the periphery. Feeling very much the outsider, she retreated into a corner of the library, to accord the family a moment of privacy.

The Curse of the Ruby Lion.

As she stared at the gilded spines, her lips gave a rueful quirk. Max had not been exaggerating when he had scoffed that it had the ring of a lurid novel. Yet in this case, truth had proved even stranger than fiction.

During the carriage ride back to Mayfair, he had managed to recount the gist of what had happened. And while at first she wondered whether her senses were still suffering the effects of the drugged sherry, a stop at his quarters to collect the precious talisman and the subsequent appearance of the spectral foreigner had convinced her that the story was not merely a twist of her addled imagination.

It was very real. And so, too, was the pale young man who had materialized from out of the gloom, his frail form supported in an indigo grip.

The exchange had taken naught but a few moments. A wink of gold had marked Davenport's movement as he handed over the small statue and received Kipling Bingham in return. The viscount had added a muted thanks, and his hope that all ills would be healed, now that the Ruby Lion had been restored to its rightful owner—sentiments echoed by the other man before he bowed and melted back into the night mists.

No sooner had the foreigner disappeared, than the door to the townhouse burst open and Cara, alerted by an earlier warning from Sprague that something was amiss, had hurtled down the steps to assist the viscount in bringing their brother inside.

Amid all the shuffle and tears of joy, Olivia had not minded bringing up the rear, a solitary figure set off from the others. It was just as well, she assured herself. She was so used to being on her own that it would be too difficult to change. Too frightening.

Steadying herself against the shelves, Olivia drew back deeper into the shadows.

Davenport had not let go his hold on Kipling.

"Enough questions, Max!" scolded Cara. "And leave off shaking him like a terrier who has just been handed a bone. He needs to be tucked into bed this instant."

"Just trying to rattle some sense into his bonebox," murmured the viscount. In truth, he was still trying to assure himself that the figure in his grip was real and not a figment of some cruel dream.

"And well you should," croaked Kip. "I deserve to be thrashed to within an inch of my life for all the trouble I have caused."

"Aye."

Cara gasped as Davenport raised a hand. It hovered in midair for an instant, then pulled Kipling close. "However, as someone else has already done so, I'll refrain from meting out further blows," he added, wrapping his brother in a heartfelt hug. "Damn it, you scamp. I love you."

It was, he realized, a word he was no longer afraid of saying.

For a moment, Kipling went limp with surprise at the unexpected display of emotion, before embracing the viscount with a convulsive sigh. "Love," he repeated in a ragged whisper. "It is a word Tarek used in describing the power of the Ruby Lion, but I—I never imagined I would hear it from you, Max, or any male of the family." A catch in his voice forced a hard swallow. "In truth, I expected you to be angry with me. And disappointed. I have made a real muck-up of being a true Bingham."

"To hell with old expectations, Kip. Father and his generation had their own rigid notions of honor, but I have no intention of being bound any longer by the past." Davenport's arms tightened. "God knows, I have made enough mistakes of my own to have learned there is no simple definition of the word. The three of us should be allowed to interpret its nuances for ourselves. Somehow, I trust we shall get it right."

"Oh, Max," After dabbing the drops from her lashes, Cara reached up to trace the line of his scar. "I knew in my heart you could defeat all the devils."

His lips crooked in a faint smile. "You had more faith in me than I did."

"I am not the only one," she replied rather cryptically. Her touch lingered for an instant before dropping to Kipling. "But enough of words. The important ones have been spoken—the rest can wait until morning. Kip is near dead on his feet and I insist on seeing him up to his room."

Too weak to put up an argument, her younger brother allowed himself to be tucked under her wing and led off.

Davenport, however, was not quite done with what he had come to say.

Olivia looked back toward the books, fully expecting the viscount to follow his family upstairs. At least she wasn't likely to be abandoned for too long. Cara had mentioned earlier that Winslow was on his way. No doubt Vavek, with his uncanny ability to sense trouble, would not be far behind.

A loyal friend. A devoted servant. Added to a vast fortune and an unfettered independence, most people would count her richly rewarded for any disappointment she might be feeling.

She sighed, trying not to let her spirits turn as blue-deviled as the foreigner's indigo flesh. There was no reason for Davenport to cast a backward glance in her direction. Now that he had found the core piece of his life that had been missing, his searching was over. He could move on.

And what of her?

Along the way, she, too, had lost some integral part of herself, but a hollowness in her chest warned that a heart, once allowed to stray, might prove irretrievable. . . .

The thick weave of the Oriental carpet must have muffled the viscount's steps, for she wasn't aware of his approach until his breath, barely more than a zephyr, stirred against the nape of her neck.

"*The Travels of Marco Polo.*" As he read aloud the title, the inflection in his voice was impossible to interpret. "Are you contemplating a journey?"

Unsure of just where she stood with him, Olivia retreated a step.

"I—I have been thinking about returning to Bombay." It was suddenly too painful to remain where she was, so close, and yet so far. . . . She turned for the door. "But right now, I really should be leaving. You have your family to think of, and I ought to be returning to my own home."

"You think I am going to allow you to sail out of my life again?" The breadth of his shoulders, suddenly just inches away, blocked off view of all but corded muscle and stubbled jaw. "I don't intend to repeat the mistakes of the past."

Olivia felt herself go very still.

"Before you go anywhere, I have an offer to make."

"An offer?" she repeated, afraid to look up and reveal the longing in her eyes.

"Yes, an offer. Or perhaps I should call it a proposal." Ever so gently, Davenport lifted her chin. "Marry me, Olivia."

"You cannot mean that."

He stood firm. "Why not?"

"Because when you write up all the assets and liabilities on paper, you will see you are getting a bad bargain. I am too unconventional, too opinionated, too—"

The touch of his lips, warm and pliant in tracing the curve of her cheek, caused the rest of the protest to dissolve in a whispered cry.

"We are not talking of ink and parchment, Olivia." His fingers twined in the twists of her tresses, scattering hairpins as they went. "We are talking of flesh and blood. Of frailty and passion. Of fire and laughter. Of feelings that cannot be defined by the columns in a ledger."

Her mouth began to quiver.

"I love you."

"And I . . ." Turning away from the last, lingering shadows of the past, Olivia opened herself to his embrace. "I never dared dream I could love a man as much as I love you, Max. I shall try not to make life too piquant for you."

"Oh, I find I have acquired a taste for spice." After a long and lush kiss, he drew a breath. "You know, of course, that you could command a much loftier match than marriage to a battleworn soldier with minor title and a near empty purse."

"Yes, I could trade myself for power and position. Things that are utterly worthless compared to your courage and honor." She felt her mouth tug into a crooked smile. "I think I started falling in love with you the moment you limped into my drawing room with Lord Branford, so steadfast in spite of your wounds."

"I have no such reservations—even with only one eye functioning, I recognized in that first flash of crimson that the Lady in Red had won my heart." He pressed his cheek to hers. "To be sure, it has taken us long enough to set aside our doubts and fears. But our spectral friend did tell me the Ruby Lion could be a source of healing as well as pain, for its power comes from love."

As he looked up, Olivia saw his expression was one of touching tenderness.

"In the end, its curse has turned into a blessing."

It took her a moment to realize that the pearling of moisture on her lashes was tears.

"Now, any other objections to marrying me?" murmured Davenport as he kissed them away.

"None that I can think of." She melted into his arms. "But my brain is not functioning all that clearly."

His hands slid up to cup her breasts. "Everything else seems to be in perfect working order." He gave a soft laugh, but as it died away, the humor faded from his face, replaced by a much more serious mien. "There is just one other thing we need to make clear." He kissed the tip of her chin. "Don't fight any more battles alone, Olivia."

"Is that an order?"

"No, a request. A wise soldier quickly learns that one of the cardinal rules for earning respect is not to issue orders that have not a snowball's chance in hell of being obeyed." He gave a wry smile. "To put it in military terms, I look at a marriage between us as a strategic alliance—a joining of equal forces."

"We join rather well," she murmured, an inner light turning her eyes silvery with amusement. "In business, it is called a merger of assets."

"Mergers, eh? I find myself growing immensely curious to learn more about the nuances of business, my love."

Olivia gave a throaty laugh, intimately aware of his heat through the sheer silk of her sari.

"I have a feeling that with the right guidance, I might be very good at handling that part of your business empire."

"Mmm. I think you already have a natural aptitude for the subject." She shivered as his hand slipped inside the folds. "And a very good grasp of the essentials."

Their low laughter muffled the sound of the door swinging open.

Winslow, leaning nonchalantly against the molding, grinned on catching his employer in the clasp of a scandalous embrace. "A joining of forces? A merger of assets? In terms of cooking, I would describe it as the art of combining contrasting ingredients, then exposing them to just the right amount of fire in order to create a felicitous union of flavors."

Vavek, who had padded up behind the man of affairs, stroked his beard. "The Buddha would call it karma. A spiritual union on a higher level of—"

"My dear chap, I daresay that contemplation of a spiritual union is not the foremost thought on the minds of Lady O and her lover."

"Neither is a long-winded discussion with friends," interrupted Davenport. "Not when I am in the middle of trying to convince the lady to accept my proposal of marriage."

"Well, you seem to be going at it from the right direction."

"Windy . . ." warned Olivia, though her attempt at sternness did not quite hit the mark.

Her man of affairs flashed a saucy wink. "Yes, yes, I can see our presence is superfluous. Especially as the Valiant Viscount has everything so well in hand."

Crack!

Winslow pulled the door shut just in time for the book to bounce off the paneled wood rather than his head.

"Now, where were we?" Olivia dusted her fingers on Davenport's lapel before sliding them to the placket of his shirt.

"I believe we were just getting down to working out the details of a formal contract."

"I am accorded to drive a hard bargain, Max." A button worked free, then another. "This could turn into a rather lengthy negotiation."

"Oh, I think I am up to the challenge, my love."

THE PASSION DOESN'T NEED TO END...

LOOK FOR THESE BREATHTAKING PERIOD ROMANCES FROM POCKET BOOKS

JULIA LONDON | **HIGHLANDER UNBOUND**

On a mission to save his legacy he lost his heart.

LIZ CARLYLE | **A DEAL WITH THE DEVIL**

She is a liar and possibly a murderess, but he's drawn to her with a passion he's never known.

CONNIE BROCKWAY | **MY SEDUCTION**

In the company of a Highlander, no woman is ever entirely out of danger.

ANA LEIGH | **THE FRASERS: CLAY**

They tamed the Wild West—but couldn't tame their love.

KRESLEY COLE | **THE PRICE OF PLEASURE**

He came to her rescue—but does she want to be saved?

SABRINA JEFFRIES | **IN THE PRINCE'S BED**

His legacy is the crown, but his destiny is her love.

Not sure what to read next?

Visit Pocket Books online at
www.SimonSays.com

Reading suggestions for
you and your reading group
New release news
Author appearances
Online chats with your favorite writers
Special offers
And much, much more!

POCKET BOOKS
A Division of Simon & Schuster
A VIACOM COMPANY

POCKET STAR BOOKS
A Division of Simon & Schuster
A VIACOM COMPANY

10421